Hope Alone by Ruth Meyer is an amazing read. It features easily relatable characters that have been through difficult and tumultuous moments but whose faith serves as an anchor even in the worst of times. Faith's family has been through it all - from abandonment by a spouse to dealing with teen pregnancy and a devastating accident. Their lives are far from perfect and sometimes they make mistakes. Still, their story offers a strong lesson on the liberating power of forgiveness and the unwavering presence of God even in the darkest of moments. The novel also contains themes of restoration and growth through overcoming trials by the power of God. It also speaks to Christians to shine God's love on other people. Adeptly written, Hope Alone by Ruth Meyer is an encouraging and eye-opening read.

Reader's Favorite

I'm still hooked! I fell in love with the Neunabers immediately in Grace Alone. I happily followed their faith journey through Faith Alone, and eagerly devoured the third installment, Hope Alone. Ruth has developed rich characters and a compelling plot line that keeps readers turning pages. Every time I think I know what's going to happen next, I am surprised. These novels are an authentic glimpse into the life of a modern Christian family. The dialogue is real and laugh-out-loud funny. The Christian faith shines through in a very honest and natural way. Moms, teachers, youth workers, deaconesses, and pastors can display these books proudly in their libraries and share them with anyone who is looking for a Christian option for young adult readers, wholesome entertainment, or just a straight-up fantastic read.

Kathleen Mills
Deaconess, Goulburn - Murray Lutheran Parish
Shepparton, Victoria, Australia

In loving memory of Jaclyn, who has realized the hope we have in Christ as she now beholds her Savior face to face

Copyright © 2019, Ruth E. Meyer
www.truthnotespress.com

TruthNotes Press

All rights reserved. Unless specifically noted, no part of this publication may be reproduced, stored in a retrieval system, or transmitted, in any form or by any means, electronic, mechanical, photocopying, recording, or otherwise, without the prior written permission of TruthNotes Press.

ISBN: 978-1-7338075-1-7

Unless otherwise indicated, scripture quotations are from The ESV® Bible (The Holy Bible, English Standard Version®), copyright © 2001 by Crossway, a publishing ministry of Good News Publishers. Used by permission. All rights reserved.

Scripture on pp 330-331 are taken from the HOLY BIBLE, NEW INTERNATIONAL VERSION®. NIV®. Copyright © 1973, 1978, 1984 by International Bible Society. Used by permission of Zondervan. All rights reserved.

The study note quoted on p 277 is from The Lutheran Study Bible © 2009 Concordia Publishing House. Used with permission.

This is a work of fiction. Names, characters, businesses, places, and events are either products of the author's imagination or are used in a fictitious manner. Any resemblance to actual persons, living or dead, or actual events or places is coincidental.

Stock images © Adobe Stock
Cover design by Sunset Rose Books

Interior formatting, print and ebook, by Reveries Co.
www.reveriescompany.com

HOPE ALONE

A NOVEL BY RUTH E. MEYER

THE SOLA SERIES

TruthNotes Press

Here we have a firm foundation,
Here the refuge of the lost:
Christ, the Rock of our salvation,
Is the name of which we boast;
Lamb of God, for sinners wounded,
Sacrifice to cancel guilt!
None shall ever be confounded
Who on Him their hope have built.
—Thomas Kelly, 1769-1855

CHAPTER 1

An ear-piercing shriek woke Grace Neunaber out of a dead sleep, and she groaned as she checked the time. Four seventeen. Next to her, David stirred and mumbled into his pillow, "Evelyn this time?"

Grace sighed wearily. "Yes. When will their antibiotics kick in? Charlotte was just up an hour ago. They're going to wake up Katie too." She didn't make a move to get out of bed, secretly hoping David would offer this time, but her husband didn't move a muscle. Rolling her eyes, she asked, "Would it kill you to get up with them *once*?" It had been eight months since the household had grown to include an additional three infants and a puppy, and it was taking its toll.

"You're better at it than I am," he replied sleepily. "Besides, I have a job to get to in the morning."

Her anger flared. "While I sit in the lap of luxury at home, sipping wine and eating bonbons? No, David, I am busy all day long taking care of *your* children, so don't you dare insinuate that I don't have a job! I am drowning in the work involved in the upkeep of this house, and it's still a mess! Most days I don't even get out of my PJ's or comb my hair until the girls are down for a nap. And my perpetual lack of sleep is not helping. I'm turning into a crazy woman!"

By now, Charlotte was wailing along with her sister, and Katie in the next room over was starting to whimper in her sleep as well.

"Fine! I'm up!" David shot back. "Who do you want me to get?"

"Forget it," Grace said coldly, throwing the covers off. "I've got it."

"No, I'll come," he sulked. "I'm awake anyhow."

Both sullenly padded across the hall to their twin daughters' room. Grace walked over to Evelyn and let David deal with Charlotte, who was a fussier baby anyhow. *Serves him right*, she thought resentfully. *This is what I deal with all the time.*

They calmed the babies in silence, their shushing the only sound as the girls' fussing died down. Grace rocked Evelyn and rested her head against the cushion as she did so, closing her eyes for a brief respite. *Ah, parenthood,* she thought caustically. *It'll be the death of me yet.*

A mere hour and a half later, Grace dragged herself out of bed to wake the rest of the household and help the kids get ready for school while David showered and got dressed.

Jackson came in like a whirlwind, as always. He tossed his backpack on the floor and rummaged frantically through it, papers flying everywhere. The boy certainly had a flair for the dramatic.

"Mom, you have to fill out this form! It's due today!" he said urgently as he located the wadded-up sheet he was seeking. "I can't go on the AR reward trip if you don't sign it!"

Grace was in her bathrobe, sitting between two high chairs

as she took turns spooning baby food into the mouths of Evelyn and Charlotte.

"Jackson!" she admonished, looking at the form. "This is dated a week ago, and you're just *now* giving it to me?"

"I forgot!" he protested as he poured cereal. "It'll take you two minutes! Just do it, please?"

Gritting her teeth, she set aside the baby food and hastily scribbled the required information as Katie entered with a hairbrush and ponytail holder.

"Mommy, can you fix my hair?" she asked sweetly.

Grace looked at her first grader and sighed. The poor child had inherited her own thick, curly hair, and it was every bit as unmanageable. This morning her hair looked like a rat's nest, which meant that she'd been tossing and turning during the night as usual.

"Get the detangling spray first," she said, turning back to spoon a few bites of rice cereal into the mouths of Charlotte and Evelyn, who were smacking their hands on their trays in protest at not being fed.

Katie ran to do her mother's bidding as Grace heard Freddie yell, "Watch out!"

Before anyone could react, their Labrador puppy came running in, her nails scuffling across the tile floor, getting muddy footprints all over. She jumped up and placed her front paws on the table, sniffing for anything she could find.

"Freddie!" Grace shrieked. "Get the dog out of here!"

"Sorry, Mom!" he called as he ran in after his puppy. Not for the first time, Grace wondered why they'd gotten the dog for Freddie's birthday in the first place. After a few weeks of insanity, she had banned the dog to the fenced-in yard. It was Freddie's job to feed her every morning, but sometimes he forgot to shut the door all the way, allowing the dog free access to the house.

"Pluto, come!" Since Pluto was nowhere near trained, she ignored Freddie's command and continued to sniff for scraps of food. Jackson caught her by the collar and dragged her over to Freddie, who obediently led her out of the house again. Katie returned with the detangling spray, and Grace set to work on the laborious task of brushing her daughter's hair as David entered the kitchen.

"Just cereal this morning?" he asked. It was his usual question, but this morning it irked Grace, who was still smarting from their tiff a few hours before.

"Yes, David, *just* cereal today," she said. "I'm sorry I didn't have time for eggs Benedict. I'm a bit busy. *My* shift already started!"

"I'm just asking!" he returned. "For Pete's sake, you don't have to bite my head off."

Katie looked up fearfully. She hated conflict of any kind, and the tension in the air was palpable.

Freddie rejoined them and asked, "Uh, guys?"

"That's what married people do," Jackson informed his younger siblings knowingly. "They fight."

Grace winced at her fourteen-year-old's comment. This was not the way she wanted to send everyone off to school. But at the same time, she was still ticked at David. So rather than making a snide comeback, she chose to do the grownup thing. She gave everyone the silent treatment.

"Mom?" Faith entered the scene a few moments later, holding ten-month-old Griffin and sounding slightly panicked. "Can I have some wipes? I thought I had another box, but I can't find them anywhere. I need to put them in the diaper bag for Mrs. Sullivan. I've gotta leave. Aaron needs to be at school early today."

Grace stifled another sigh. While she was thankful that Aaron was such a supportive boyfriend for not being Griffin's father, it was difficult to work around yet one more schedule.

"Sure, sweetie," she responded. "There should be a few extra boxes on the shelf of the changing table."

"Thanks," called Faith over her shoulder as she hurried upstairs.

"Did you eat anything?" Grace shouted after her.

"No," she yelled back. "I didn't have time. I'll grab something at Aaron's house."

"Be sure you do! You shouldn't skip breakfast!"

An uneasy silence now fell over the rest of them as David and Grace continued to ignore each other. Faith bustled out the door, calling goodbyes to everyone, and then Jackson rushed to get his backpack so he could make it out in time for the bus.

After Jackson left, David attempted to be cheery as he said, "Okay, Freddie and Katie, we've gotta go too. I need to get to the office. In the car on the double." David hustled the two out the door, pausing to give Grace an obligatory kiss, which she reluctantly accepted.

In the relative silence of the house, Grace shook her head. She was about to go crazy, no question about it.

When her phone rang that afternoon at two thirty, Grace rolled her eyes. It was David's ringtone. *He'd better be calling to apologize,* she thought, miffed that he hadn't called sooner. This was the only time of day she had to herself, when the girls were down for their naps. Although she supposed she should make better use of this time by cleaning or folding laundry, all she could usually accomplish was taking a shower, clearing the table from breakfast and lunch dishes, and loading the dishwasher. The house was a complete disaster, and she knew she could make more of an effort while the girls napped, but she just didn't have the energy to do it.

"What?" she answered.

"Well, hi to you too," David replied on the other end, his voice tight.

She took a deep breath. Already this was starting off badly. "I'm sorry," she said. "That was rude. How are you?"

"Not great. I don't have time to explain right now, but could you pick up Katie and Freddie in the car line today? Something came up, and I'll be delayed."

"David! I'm not even remotely ready to leave the house!"

"You have half an hour. That's plenty of time."

"The girls are still sleeping! They need this! They missed their naps completely yesterday because we were at the doctor for their ear infections. The medicine is finally kicking in, and they're having good naps now. I don't want to wake them up if I don't have to."

"I know it's inconvenient, but I take Katie and Freddie home the vast majority of the time. Please, Grace. Just for today."

"Why can't they just do after-school care like they usually do when you have to stay for a few minutes?" She hated how whiny her voice sounded even to her own ears.

"Grace, I can't explain right now! I don't know how late I'll be!"

"David—"

"Yes or no?" he interrupted.

"Oh, *fine*," she groused. "I'll do it. But I'm not happy about it."

"Noted. See you later."

With that, he hung up, leaving Grace to pout on the couch.

Now she'd have to get herself ready, wake the twins, strap both the girls into their car seats, and drive the two miles to school to wait in the infernal car line. Neither Evelyn nor Charlotte was particularly patient in the car, so they'd likely whine the entire time. *What's so important for him, anyhow?* she thought resentfully. *Does he even care what an inconvenience this is for me?*

Groaning, she rose from the couch and stepped over the baby toys on the floor to go to her room and yank a pick through her tight black curls. Evelyn was waking up on her own, but sure enough, she had to wake Charlotte up and drag them both to school in bad moods. She stewed about how inconsiderate David was the rest of the afternoon until he walked in the door at four fifty.

"How kind of you to grace us with your presence," she remarked snidely. "Mind telling me what's going on?"

She saw the muscles work in his jaw, a sign that he was trying not to lose his patience. "Later," he said shortly, then walked upstairs to their room.

Grace could tell her husband's mind was a million miles away the rest of the evening, though she wasn't sure if it was because of the tension between them or something else. She hated that they were acting this way to one another, and she hated even more that the kids were witnessing it. But she was too stubborn to make the first move toward reconciliation, so she told herself she'd wait to speak with him in private rather than trying to patch things up in front of the kids.

But she couldn't avoid him forever, and she *was* curious about what had "come up" with him that afternoon, so she seized the opportunity when they put the twins to bed and the other kids were occupied. As she and David slipped out of the girls' room, she grabbed his hand and led him across the hallway to their own room. Shutting the door behind them, she fixed him with a hard stare and demanded, "Okay, David, *what is going on?*"

He motioned for her to take a seat on their bed as he ran his hand over his short hair, a gesture Grace recognized as his nervous habit. This only served to make her more apprehensive. She perched gingerly on the bed as he stretched himself out on his own side. He took off his glasses and put them on the nightstand deliberately.

"David! Just tell me already, would you? What's wrong?"

He looked straight up at the ceiling and said in a monotone voice, "I have a call."

Sucking in a sharp breath, Grace searched his face for any hint of emotion, but there was none. It was his perfect poker face, but it irritated Grace. She wanted to know what he was thinking.

"You mean, a job offer at a new school?" she asked timidly, although she already knew the answer.

"Yes."

"As principal?"

"Yes."

Grace shut her eyes. She had no idea how the call process worked in the Lutheran school system. David had already taken the call to St. John when she'd met him four years ago, so she hadn't been privy to any of the decision making that accompanied a call.

"Where?"

"St. Louis."

The blood drained from her face, and she asked, "Missouri or Michigan?" It was a ridiculous question. Few people outside the state even knew there *was* a St. Louis in Michigan.

"What do you think?" he snorted. "Missouri, of course."

Heat rose to her cheeks. "You don't need to be snippy with

me. I'm just clarifying."

He inhaled deeply and held his breath for a second before releasing it slowly. "I'm sorry. It's been a long day. Yes, St. Louis, Missouri."

"So what does this mean?" Grace could hear her voice rising in pitch. "Do they just assign you there or can you say no? You don't have to take it, do you?"

David pushed himself to a sitting position. "No, I don't *have* to take the call."

Grace breathed a little easier. He could turn down the offer. *Relax, Grace. There's no way David would uproot our entire family. Maybe he's already told them—*

"I told them I'd give it prayerful consideration and get back to them." David's voice interrupted her thoughts.

"So we're moving to St. Louis?" The tightness in her chest returned.

"I didn't say that!" David sounded exasperated now. "I told them I'd take a few weeks to pray about it before deciding anything. It looks like a great opportunity from my initial impression. I had a conference call with a few members of their school board and their senior pastor today, and it went really well."

"Senior pastor," Grace said dully, the knot in her stomach growing tighter by the minute. "That sounds like a bigger congregation, then."

"It is. It's about twice the size of St. John. Pretty big school in Lutheran terms. Two classrooms per grade. I'd have my own secretary and an assistant principal."

"*What?*" Grace was fighting genuine panic now. There was no way David could resist a call that tempting. "David, I am *not* moving to St. Louis!"

"That's really not your decision to make."

"Well, thank you very much, *dear*," she spat back. "I'd like to think I have a *little* say in where we live! I don't want to drag this family across the country so you can have a staff!"

David's patience had worn thin as well. "It's seven hours away, Grace, hardly across the country. We could make that trip in a day. And besides, this is not about you! This is *my* career we're talking about!"

"Listen to yourself, David! You also have a family to consider, remember? Someone here has to be the voice of reason! We haven't even been in this house a whole year yet! We have twins who are eight months old. We have two mortgages already. And now you're suggesting we pack up and move again? Seven hours away? I'm barely hanging onto my sanity as it is, and that's *with* the help of my family! What do you expect me to do down there when I need help with child care?"

Tears sprang to her eyes as another thought occurred to her. "And what about Faith? She's going to be staying with Liv and Andy while she goes to college. We'd never see her or Griffin at all if we moved. Don't you care to see your own grandson?"

"Oh, my *word*! Grace, I haven't accepted the call! You make it sound like I'm the bad guy here, trying to whisk you away from your family. Don't you think I haven't already thought of all the things you just mentioned? I *know* this is a shock. One of my college classmates is a teacher down there, and he submitted my name. They called to interview me about it two weeks ago, and—"

"Whoa, wait! What? So you've known about this for *two weeks* and you're just now telling me this? David!" She was both dismayed and angry. "Since when do we keep secrets from each other? Especially if they involve, oh, I don't know, *moving our family halfway across the country*?"

David spoke through clenched teeth. "*This* is why I didn't tell you sooner, Grace. This conversation right here. I *knew* you wouldn't be happy about it. An interview is one thing. They interview half a dozen people for the job. Maybe more. So just because I had an interview doesn't mean I'll get the call. I didn't want to tell you anything and make you fret unless they ended up extending the call to me. Well, they did, so here we are."

"At least I would have had time to get used to the idea. *This*, on the other hand, is like getting hit with a ton of bricks. I'm completely blindsided by it. I do *not* want to move. Especially not to St. Louis."

"You know what? This is a great opportunity for me. Honestly, I don't even know what to think yet. Yes, it would be a challenge for sure. But can't you at least be slightly encouraging? They must have a lot of confidence in me and my abilities to handle this big of a school. *You*, on the other hand, apparently do not have that same confidence."

He launched himself off the bed and strode quickly from the room in a huff, leaving Grace in tears. She was fuming at David, but she was also terrified. The absolute last thing she wanted to do was move now. Yes, she knew when she'd married David that he wasn't guaranteed to stay in Mapleport forever. But honestly, was it too much to ask that he at least stay a few more years? She was barely making it through the twins' infancy as it was. Suddenly she found herself wishing that David wasn't such a good principal after all.

CHAPTER 2

Grace and David didn't say a word to each other the following morning. The kids all felt the tension and got ready for school in subdued moods themselves. From the furtive glances between Faith and Jackson to the worried frowns both Katie and Freddie wore, Grace could tell they weren't used to the unsettling silence between their parents. When David left with Freddie and Katie, he didn't even give Grace their obligatory kiss.

Grace held her head high until she heard the car back out, and then she buried her face in her hands and sobbed. Evelyn and Charlotte were scared at the pitiful sounds emanating from their mother and started to whine themselves. Soon they were howling right along with Grace.

"What on *earth* is going on here?"

It was Olivia. Grace straightened up quickly and grabbed a semi-clean burp cloth to wipe her face. Despite the eight-year difference in age, Grace and her older sister were best friends. What would she ever do without Olivia? The thought made her break down again as fresh tears flowed.

"Gracie! Are you ill?" Olivia sounded almost frantic. Grace rarely caved in to such a display of emotion. Olivia rushed to the table and knelt down beside Grace, pulling her into a hug. She accepted the embrace and cried on her sister's shoulder, tuning out the noise of the babies.

"Da-David has a… c-call!" she hiccuped, barely able to get the words out.

Olivia inhaled sharply. "To…?"

"St. Louis!" wailed Grace.

Olivia's eyes widened and her mouth formed a perfect "O," but she said nothing. Instead, she did what Olivia did best. She went into action. Briskly, she stood and grabbed the washcloth from the table to wipe the girls' faces. Then she calmed each of them in turn and put Evelyn in the exersaucer and Charlotte in the jump seat.

Once they were happily situated, Olivia cleared the breakfast dishes from the table, wiped down the counter, and poured a fresh cup of coffee for Grace, complete with a generous dollop of half and half, just the way she liked it. Then she marched back to the table and handed Grace the mug.

"Take a drink," she commanded. "You need some strong coffee." She waited until Grace had taken a few sips before prompting, "So, the call…?"

With a deep sigh, Grace told her sister about the previous evening's conversation and concluded, "I'm so mad at David right now. *So* mad. He never even told me about that interview! I don't like it that my husband is keeping secrets from me."

"Frankly, I'm pretty mad at him myself," Olivia said. "It was downright rotten of him to just throw this at you. Want me to have Andy beat him up?"

Grace breathed out a mixture between a sob and a laugh. "Tempting," she admitted.

"Consider it and get back to me. The offer stands. But he can't go back and redo anything, so you have to move on and make the best of it."

Tears clouded Grace's vision. "But I don't *want* to move on!"

"Sorry," Olivia grimaced. "Bad choice of words. I meant you have to deal with it from here. Gracie, you know I don't want you to move anywhere, especially not that far away. You're my best friend. I'd be lost without you. But," Olivia conceded after a shuddering breath, "you have to do what's best for your family. And if that means moving to St. Louis…"

"Liv, how can we move anywhere now? The twins aren't even a year old. And Faith and Griffin…" She bit her lip and looked away, hating how much she sounded like a spoiled child.

"Deep breath, sis. Don't get worked up again," Olivia instructed. "I get that you're upset, but let's try to be as neutral as possible. Let's look at this from David's standpoint." She pursed her lips and looked thoughtfully into the distance for a moment before clasping her hands and leaning closer to Grace.

"Okay, he didn't tell you about the interview because he didn't want to worry you. I don't totally agree with that, but I guess I can see where he's coming from. If he hadn't gotten the call, no harm done. He didn't want to stress you out over nothing. In a way, I guess that shows he was trying to… I don't know… shield you."

"Maybe," Grace said reluctantly.

"But when he got the call, he *knew* you'd be upset. So he's in a no-win situation. And whether you're happy about it or not, you have to realize this is a really big deal to him. So much of a man's worth is tied into his career. It's a huge honor for him to get this call, Grace."

"That's what scares me."

Olivia went on. "And as much as I hate to say it, your first priority lies with *him* now. Remember, the Bible says that a man should leave his father and mother and be united to his wife. The leaving and cleaving thing."

"I didn't think he'd take the leaving part quite so literally," Grace mumbled.

Her sister laughed. "It just means your closest earthly relationship is with David now. That needs to take precedence. Your loyalty has to be to him. And he has to know that too."

"You make it sound so easy, Liv!" Grace threw up her hands. "Seriously, what would you say if Andy decided to open a pharmacy in San Francisco or something?"

"I'd react exactly the way you're reacting," Olivia confessed. Both chuckled at her admission before she continued. "But I'd also hope someone would remind me of the things I'm telling you. I know it's not what you want to hear, but it's what you need to hear."

Her eyes on the floor, Grace nodded, but her sister wasn't finished. "You two need to discuss this alone. Tell you what—you guys go out tonight. Andy and I will watch the kids for you. Be sure to communicate your feelings and concerns to David, but try not to get mad or accusatory. Tell him you're proud of him for getting the call. If he doesn't feel like you're on his side, Gracie, it doesn't matter what anyone else says. You're the only one whose opinion matters to him."

"I know," Grace said, rolling her eyes. She was getting tired of the advice to be a supportive wife. But she knew Olivia was trying to be helpful. Grace breathed in deeply and stretched her neck on both sides, trying to release some tension. "Do you and Andy ever fight? I mean, like, *real* fighting? Over more than who gets to tell a story?"

"Heavens, yes! We fight all the time! We're both opinionated and strong-willed. It's a perfect formula for disaster."

"Then how come you never come to *me* for advice when you fight? Why am I always the one to go to you?"

"Because I'm the older one. I'm supposed to have all the answers, remember?" she teased. "One of our worst fights was back when the boys started first grade." To Grace, that seemed like an awfully long time ago now that Olivia and Andy's kids were all in college. "Andy wanted me to go back to work to help pay the bills, and I had absolutely no intention of doing so."

"You obviously won that argument."

"It was ugly. We barely spoke for a week. We made all these passive-aggressive barbs at each other. I didn't tell you about it because I was embarrassed to say anything. That was back when you and Bob were actually happy together, and I didn't dare admit that I thought I'd made a mistake marrying Andy."

"Liv! Are you serious?" Evelyn let out a perfectly-timed squeal just then, as if she were protesting the very thought herself.

Olivia waved her hand dismissively. "That's hardly news. I rather suspect most husbands and wives have the same regret at some point. Andy and I have had dozens of fights that left me wondering what I ever saw in him. But thankfully we stuck it out, and I'd like to think we're stronger for it. Now when we fight, we don't let it drag on for an entire week. Usually just a few days." She winked at Grace, who chuckled half-heartedly.

"I'm glad to know it's not just us, then," she said. "Bob and I fought constantly by the end. But I was hoping since David and I are both Christians that we wouldn't do that."

"Oh, trust me, hon, Christian couples fight too. Matter of

fact, I'm convinced the devil works *harder* to split up Christian marriages. He doesn't want them united in their witness for the Lord, and he doesn't want them passing on the faith to the next generation. Christian marriages and families are on the front line of attack."

"Thanks for the encouragement. So my marriage to David will be *harder* than my marriage to Bob?" Given the way they'd been acting the past two days, Grace found the statement easier to believe than it should have been.

"I didn't say that," Olivia objected. "David and Bob are very different. And you're different now too."

"At least with Bob I didn't have to worry about moving across the country." Her voice held a trace of bitterness in it.

"Careful, Gracie," warned Olivia. "Don't go there. It's dangerous to compare one relationship to another. Remember what you just said—you and Bob fought constantly by the end. You know you guys didn't have a fairy-tale marriage by any stretch."

"It hasn't exactly been a fairy tale here lately, either," Grace confessed.

"But how much of that is just stress from the girls being sick?" Grace glanced at her daughters inadvertently as Olivia went on. "You haven't had a good night's sleep for a number of days, and that takes a toll on a person. Overall, your relationship isn't defined by arguing. And David isn't about to leave you the way Bob did."

Grace raised her eyebrows to concede her sister's point. "Besides," Olivia added, "Christians have a powerful tool non-believers don't: prayer. We have God on our side, strengthening us when we're weak and forgiving us when we fail."

"True."

The two lapsed into silence until Olivia spoke again. "Hey, why don't you go clear your mind? Go hop on the elliptical," she suggested. "I've got the girls. Maybe I'll pop them in the double stroller and take them for a walk. It's a gorgeous day."

"That sounds wonderful," said Grace. "Thanks, Liv. For everything. I still feel rotten about all this, but not *quite* as rotten as I felt before you got here. You're the best." She leaned over to give her sister a fierce hug before escaping to her room to exercise. The physical activity usually put her in a better frame of mind. At this point, she needed all the help she could get.

CHAPTER

3

David was surprised to find Olivia in the kitchen when he brought Freddie and Katie home from school that day. He knew she came at least once a week to spend time with Grace, but she usually left before the rest of the family came home.

"Date night!" she said in a perky voice, answering his unspoken question. "You and Grace need some time alone. Andy will be over in an hour or two when he gets off work. We'll be fine here with the kids. Take Grace to Olive Garden. And be sure to get wine. You could use some."

Having no idea how to respond, David simply turned and walked upstairs to the master bedroom. He knocked twice to let Grace know he was there, then walked in. She was already getting dressed to go out, which made him mad. He felt like she and Olivia were sneaking around behind his back, talking about him and plotting their own schemes. He was still stewing about the debacle the day before, so this only heightened his irritation.

"What is this?" he demanded.

"What is what?" she replied frostily.

"This so-called date! What are you guys up to? Trying to set the mood at a nice dinner alone so you can attack me about all the reasons this is a stupid call and why I should refuse?"

"Oh, please! Is that what you think? For your information, this was Liv's idea. I don't really want to go. But she's right—you and I need to discuss this, and maybe if we do so in a public place, we won't end up yelling at each other. We might actually be civil to one another this time."

"I never said you could tell Olivia about the call."

"So now I need your permission to speak to my sister? You never said I couldn't."

"This isn't public knowledge yet, Grace! The only person who knows is Pastor. I told him today privately. The teachers don't even know. Our *kids* don't even know yet!"

"David! What do you expect? I am *freaking out* here! I had to tell someone, and why wouldn't I tell Liv? She knows me well enough to realize when something is wrong. And trust me, it was painfully obvious this morning that I wasn't my usual self. I was sobbing at the table, and the girls were screaming right along with me. We made for quite the symphonic trio."

David paused at this information. He knew how emotional Grace had been since the twins were born, but he hadn't realized how hard she would take the news of his call.

"Let's just go get this over with," she continued. "Liv means well, and we really ought to discuss this like adults. I need to go nurse the girls before we go, but I'll be ready in about half an hour. That'll put us at the restaurant a little after five."

She left the room, and David clenched his jaw. They *did* need to talk about the call, but he was leery of the discussion. He knew Grace was dead set against the idea, and he didn't want dinner to end up being a guilt trip from her. Childishly, he pouted for a few minutes on the bed. He was starting to regret ever getting the call in the first place.

The two drove to Olive Garden in stony silence. Grace sat with her arms crossed as she stared out the passenger window, silently seething at her sister for forcing this date anyhow.

When they got to the restaurant, they continued to ignore one another as they were seated. They busied themselves with poring over the menu, both taking much longer than necessary to examine the entrée selections, but once their waiter had taken their orders, they could no longer avoid each other. The problem was, Grace didn't want to start the conversation, and she rather suspected David didn't either.

Finally David spoke, though not about the topic they'd come to discuss. "Remember when you gave me dinner here as a Christmas gift that first year?" he asked.

Grace softened ever so slightly. That was a good memory. "We went to the art museum first."

"And you wore your black dress." He smiled at her. "It's still my favorite."

She returned his smile tentatively. "I wore it to Le Poisson first, you know," she reminded him.

"Yes, but I'd kind of rather forget our first date," he admitted with a grimace.

"What, you don't like being reminded of how you broke up with me?" she teased.

"It got your attention, didn't it?" he returned smugly. "You weren't serious about Christianity until then. I simply softened your heart toward God."

She gasped in mock horror. "David! If Pastor could hear you now! You sound like a heretic, claiming responsibility for the Holy Spirit's job!"

He grinned broadly. "You've come a long way since then,

my dear. You sound more and more like a bone fide Lutheran every day."

They laughed together, and she decided they'd broken the ice enough to get on with what needed to be discussed. "I'm sorry about yesterday, David," she began. "We got off to a bad start and never really recovered. I was mad at you all day, so our discussion last night was bound to go poorly. I'm sorry for acting in such a childish way."

"I'm sorry too," he answered. "It was a pretty rotten day all around."

"It really was. But, David, what's happening to us? We never used to be like this, but lately we've both been on edge and snippy toward each other. This isn't how I want our marriage to be."

"Me neither."

"I just want to feel like I'm more than the maid and nanny," she continued, relieved to finally be voicing her feelings. Perhaps David's call was a more pressing issue to discuss, but Grace needed to vent first. "Our house looks like a daycare with high chairs, Bumbos, an exersaucer, jump seats, and toys in abundance. Not to mention three cribs and two changing tables in the rooms, plus a double and single stroller in the garage and closets stuffed with boxes of diapers."

Grace knew she was complaining, but she couldn't help herself. Part of her recent frustration was that she didn't think David could possibly comprehend how hard it was for her to be home with the girls all day. She needed him to understand at least a bit of her difficulties so she didn't grow to resent him as she had Bob.

"I can't keep up with the housework at all. I'm doing at least three loads of laundry a day, but none of it ever gets folded. I haven't dusted or mopped or vacuumed in ages. The only time

I get to myself is when the girls are napping, and all I accomplish after showering is the dishes. By the time I get *that* done, the last thing I want to do is more housework."

Shifting focus slightly, she went on. "I want to wear something that doesn't have baby food, baby drool, snot, or spit up on it. I want to wear my black dress again, if it even fits me anymore. I want to wear makeup again. I want to be able to fix my hair for once. Not that it makes a difference." Her tightly curled black hair was unruly at best, a constant source of grief for her. "I feel like all I'm good for anymore is taking care of babies. I spend half my day nursing or otherwise feeding the girls. I want to be more than a mother. I want to feel attractive again," she ended, her voice low as she stared intently at the ice in her water glass.

"But, sweetheart, you *are*," David assured her gently, taking her hand in his own across the table and prompting her to look at him. "Seeing you in the role of new mother has made me view you in a completely new light, and watching you care for our babies makes you even *more* attractive to me, baby food and spit up and everything. I still think you're the prettiest woman in the whole world."

A lone tear escaped down her cheek, and she pulled her hand away to wipe it off as he continued.

"I know it's hard, honey. I never anticipated how time-consuming little babies could be. They say that adjusting to a new baby is a huge strain on any marriage, and we have *three* of them in our house, not to mention four other kids whose schedules we need to work around! All things considered, I'd say we're doing pretty well."

"It depends on the day," she said pointedly.

"Granted. But overall, it hasn't been a *terrible* adjustment. The twins have ear infections now which makes them fussier, and whiny babies grate on a person's nerves. Part of our current state of mind is just frustration and exhaustion from their current temperaments."

"True," Grace reluctantly conceded.

"But if I'm understanding you correctly, I think you're frustrated by the amount of housework that comes along with such a large household, yes?"

"Oh, yes."

"Then what can we do to change that?"

"Hire a maid?" she suggested hopefully.

David chuckled. "Unless you can find one who will work for nothing, I doubt we can manage that." Then his face brightened as an idea struck. "Actually, that's a great idea!"

"Getting a maid?" She raised an eyebrow at him doubtfully. Her husband was way too frugal to go for that.

"After a fashion. Let's ask your mom and Olivia if they'd be willing to help out once a week. They both helped after the twins were born. I'm sure they'd be happy to do so again." Although both had come regularly through the fall and early winter, after Christmas break everyone seemed to think Grace would be able to handle the twins on her own. However, she *wasn't* managing very well without help.

"That's not a bad idea," Grace mused. *But what if you take the call?* a little voice in her head wondered. *Mom and Liv won't be around then.* Wisely, though, she decided not to voice that concern. She and David were finally having a decent discussion, and he was trying his best to be helpful. She didn't want to ruin the moment.

"They can help with the stuff you mentioned—folding laundry, mopping, vacuuming... But why stop there?" David seemed excited as he continued. Grace could tell he was proud of himself for coming up with such a brilliant plan. "We're missing out on a gold mine of child labor in Freddie and Jackson. Faith is more than pulling her weight with Griffin, and she's really matured a lot over the past year. Now it's time to make the boys step up to the plate. They can do their own laundry, and they're plenty old enough to do more than the dishes and sweeping. I'm sure there are all sorts of responsibilities they can handle."

They paused as the waiter delivered breadsticks and salad, then returned to their discussion. "If Mom and Liv are willing to help out again, that would really be wonderful," Grace admitted as she munched on a breadstick. "I'm far more motivated to clean if someone else is there to help. And maybe while they're around, I can actually use the elliptical again. I've been on it a whopping three times since the girls were born. I still have twenty pounds or more to lose."

"You look great to me," said David. "But if exercising makes you feel better and gives you more energy, go for it. Shut yourself in our bedroom and let Liv or your mom deal with everything else. And I promise I won't walk in on you while you're on the elliptical." He smirked as she laughed at the memory of one of their first encounters, when she'd answered the door hot and sweaty after he interrupted her exercising.

"It's amazing I didn't scare you off for good," she murmured, reaching for his hand again.

"On the contrary, my dear. Each time I caught you unaware, it only made me fall for you that much harder." He squeezed her hand and then, apparently finding that to be inadequate, stood slightly and leaned across the table to kiss her.

It was their first real kiss in two days. It felt good to kiss her husband again, even in the middle of a crowded restaurant. When he sat down, Grace knew it was time to address the real reason they'd come. "David, I need you to know something. Before we talk about any logistical stuff, I want to tell you that I'm really proud of you for getting this call. Last night was a knee-jerk reaction, and like I said earlier, I was still mad at you from our fight in the morning. But I'm clear-minded enough to realize that this is an honor for you. You're a wonderful principal, and if you took this call, I know you'd do great there."

David looked pleased by her words. "Thanks, honey," he said softly. "You don't know how much that means to me, especially knowing how strongly opposed you are to the notion of moving." He paused to take a sip of water. "But don't worry. I've already decided not to take it anyhow."

"What? David!"

"It's terrible timing, as we both know. We have two mortgages, it's too far away, and we have too many young kids to uproot. It's a whole new ball game considering a call when you have a family."

"No, listen. I admit I'm secretly hoping you'll refuse the call in the end, but you can't do it now without really considering it first. I don't want this to be some passive-aggressive tactic to make it out like you're the martyr sacrificing your career advancement for the sake of your needy family." She held up her hand as he started to protest. "Maybe you aren't trying to do that now, but in the future it may come back to haunt you, and you might get resentful, thinking we're the ones holding you back, wondering what could have happened if you'd gone. I don't want that hanging over us. You need to be serious about considering the call. You only got it yesterday. We can't make a decision like this in a day."

"Grace, you were right last night. All the objections you raised are serious considerations. With two mortgages already, there's no way we can tack on a third. And we're still adjusting to having twins. I can't take you away from your support system now when you need it most. It's not fair to you."

"But, David, this is *your* call. It's not fair to you to say no because of me. True, I don't want you to take it, but I want it to be because *you* don't want it rather than you not wanting it because you know I don't want you to want it!"

They looked at each other a moment after her last statement, then burst out laughing together.

"That was rather a cumbersome sentence, wasn't it?" she admitted.

"Yeah, but I get what you're trying to say."

"Let's not either of us make any rash decisions yet, okay? Give the idea time to sink in after the initial shock. And in the meantime, why don't you tell me about the school and church?" Grace suggested. "I didn't even give you the chance last night."

He seemed happy she'd asked and spent the next ten minutes or so filling her in on the details and showing her their website on his phone. She couldn't deny that it looked like a great school, and there was much more to do in the St. Louis area than there was in Mapleport. Grace's stomach tightened. From David's standpoint, the call was certain to be tempting. Maybe *too* tempting.

When their food was delivered, they fell into contemplative silence until Grace spoke again. "Do they want you to go down for a visit?"

"I really ought to. It's sort of expected. They may even cover part of the travel costs."

Grace was not pleased at this bit of news. "Should I go too?"

David cocked his head, considering. "Maybe? I can see it either way. I'd like to have you there so I get your input, but I know it would be tough to get away from the kids."

That was Grace's concern as well. Since she was still nursing the girls, that complicated matters. She could only imagine how disastrous dragging them along to St. Louis would be. "I'll think about it," she said. "We can decide later."

"That's true. We'll decide *together*." His underlying meaning was not lost on Grace. He wasn't just referring to the visit. He meant they would make a decision about the call together.

When they finished their meal, David paid the bill and they walked out together holding hands. Grace felt much better about the situation, or at least about the status of their relationship. As they reached the car, David opened the passenger door for her, but she turned to him before climbing in.

"Sweetheart, you know I'm apprehensive about this, but I want you to know that I trust you. If you decide that moving to Missouri is the right choice, I'll stand behind you. I just want to be with you, no matter where we live. You're my husband, and I'll love and support you anywhere."

David pulled her into a hug. "That's all I wanted to hear you say," he whispered. "Thank you."

He gave her a lingering kiss right there in the parking lot, which she gladly accepted, not caring who else could see them. Then David helped her into the car, and as they drove back home, she reached over to take his free hand. She meant what she'd said, but at the same time, it would be a whole lot easier to keep her word if they kept their current address just a smidge longer.

CHAPTER 4

"Okay, everyone, let's settle down. We have some important news to share." Grace clapped twice and spoke loudly over the chaos of regular dinner conversation, trying to stifle her apprehension. She and David had decided to tell the kids about the potential call before he shared it with the teachers and school board. But Grace had a suspicion the kids would react in much the same way she had. It wasn't going to be pretty.

The older kids quieted down, though all three babies kept slapping their high chair trays and babbling. Still, it was relatively calm, so David spoke up. "Guys, you need to know something that isn't public knowledge yet. It will be soon enough, but for now, let's not tell anyone, okay?"

"Oh, no," moaned Jackson. "Mom's pregnant again, isn't she?"

"No, no, nothing like that," David assured quickly.

"Then someone *else* is?" Jackson asked, giving Faith a pointed look.

Faith glared at him as David spoke. "No one is pregnant," he promised firmly. "This has to do with me. I have a job offer to be principal at a school in St. Louis."

The announcement was met with dead silence all around. Even the babies seemed to sense something and momentarily ceased their babbling. Then suddenly everyone spoke at once.

"I don't want to move!"

"Where *is* St. Louis?

"There's no way I'm packing again!"

"I don't want to switch schools!"

"We just moved into *this* house a year ago!"

"What about me? I'm already enrolled in college here!"

"Whoa!" shouted David, holding up his hands. "Everyone calm down. I'll answer your questions one at a time, but first you need to know that we haven't decided anything yet. I have a call—a job offer, that is—but I haven't accepted it or declined it. Your mom and I want you to know about it because it's *possible* that we will move over the summer."

Chaos erupted once again, and David whistled through his fingers to get everyone's attention. "I know this is a surprise. Your mom and I are sort of in shock ourselves. Katie, St. Louis is in Missouri, about seven hours from here. Freddie, I don't relish the thought of packing and moving again so soon either. Faith, I know you're already enrolled in college here. If we were to take this call, I see no reason why you would have to change your plans. You'll be living with the McNeals anyhow. And Jackson, I know you don't want to switch schools. Frankly, no one does. It would require a lot of changes all around, and some would be challenging, to be sure. Your mother and I are considering all these things as we pray about it and make a decision."

From the looks on the kids' faces, it was obvious none of them were happy about the prospect, but Jackson was the first to react. "Well, great!" he erupted, glaring at David. "Here we go again! I *knew* you guys shouldn't have gotten married! We never would have *thought* of moving if it hadn't been for you. You know what? Go ahead and take the stupid call! I'm not going. I'll stay with Grandma and Grandpa, but I am *not* moving to Missouri!" He slammed his fist down on the table, causing Griffin and Charlotte to startle and begin crying. Abruptly, he stood and ran upstairs, slamming his door behind him.

Faith swooped Griffin into her arms and took him downstairs to the little apartment they shared, tears streaming down her own face.

Without a word, Grace unstrapped Charlotte and rocked her back and forth to calm her. Katie was crying now as well, and she crawled into David's lap and burrowed her face into his chest. He hugged her in return and turned to Freddie.

"That didn't go very well, did it, bud?" he asked sadly.

"Not really," Freddie replied. "But Jackson always overreacts. He'll calm down. I'm not sure I really want to move either, but if we do, I guess it's sort of exciting. It would be neat to see a new state. We could do it."

Grace's breath caught in her throat as she looked at David. Of everyone in the house, Freddie's reaction had been the most grown up. At that moment, Grace was extremely proud of the maturity of her fourth grader.

Grace slid into bed next to David and snuggled up to him, resting her head against his chest. She knew he was discouraged about the evening. Jackson hadn't emerged from his room at all, except to use the bathroom once. Katie cried three more times after dinner, and Freddie seemed like he was in a daze. Faith slipped out of the house after putting Griffin down, and Grace had no doubt she'd gone over to tell Aaron.

It seemed like it was David versus the rest of the family.

"I'm sorry," she finally said.

He seemed to understand her comment. "Hey, we knew the kids wouldn't be happy about the call, right?"

"We were certainly right about that one, huh?" He chuckled wryly and she continued. "Let me ask you something. If you were still single and got this call, what would you be thinking right now? Would you be excited about the possibility?"

David considered a moment before responding. "You know, I think I would be pretty excited. Bigger school, bigger paycheck, more of a challenge…"

"And now? With all of us harping on you not to take it?"

"Honestly, I wish I'd never gotten it at all. I never intended this to cause a family feud. I don't want to turn everyone against me. If I could go back, I would have told them at the interview that we had no intention of moving at this time, and that would have been the end of it."

"Fair enough. But that doesn't answer the question. The fact is, you *did* get it, so what are your thoughts now? Do you secretly wish you could take it but feel guilty about it because of us?"

He blew out a short breath. "I don't know… Sort of, I guess. It's a really tempting call, Grace. But at the same time, I need to consider the needs of our family too. If I'm just looking at it from a selfish standpoint, that's not fair to any of you. It's a lot more complicated than I thought it would be."

"Are you happy here?"

David seemed surprised by the question. "Of course!" he assured. "Why wouldn't I be?"

"I mean at St. John. Are you happy in your vocation there? Or do you feel restless?"

"No, I don't feel restless. We have a great bunch of teachers, and there's relatively little drama going on, and I work really well with Pastor, so… yes, I'm happy here."

"Would you be equally happy there?"

"Well, I… I don't know," he faltered. "That's a good point. I haven't spoken to either pastor enough to know if we see eye to eye on things the way Pastor Lixon and I do. And with a larger faculty comes a greater possibility for tensions and such. It's always a risk when you accept a call. There's never a guarantee that everything will work out wonderfully."

"True."

"You think I shouldn't take the risk," he stated flatly after a few moments.

"I didn't say that!"

"Your silence said it."

"What's that supposed to mean?"

"You were inferring that since it's never a guarantee, it's not worth the risk of moving our family five hundred miles away when I'm already happy here."

"*You* said it, David, not me." She was only too happy to point that out.

He sighed. "At this point, I'm leaning that way. It's not worth uprooting us all and making everyone in this family mad at me. I *am* happy here. We have a great church and a great school, and our kids are all happy and doing well. Why mess with that? Besides, the mortgage situation is prohibitive at best."

Grace smiled in the dark. She knew the mortgage dilemma would get to her husband. He was very concerned about keeping a budget and making the best use of their money. It was eating away at him that their other house hadn't sold yet, despite having been on the market for a year. The housing market in Mapleport was really down, and people just weren't moving into the area. So to put a second house up for sale in Mapleport was not a wise financial decision by any stretch.

"Sweetie, if you decide to stay, you know I won't argue. But again, I want you to be at peace with the decision. I don't want you to decline out of guilt or pressure from us. Even Jackson will come around in time if we move."

David chuckled. "I wouldn't count on that."

"Then we leave him here with my parents," she teased back. "Faith and Griffin will be with Liv and Andy. We'd go from nine people in the house to six! Hey, maybe that's not such a bad idea after all. Let's go!"

They laughed together, and both settled into silence. But even after David's breathing had evened out, indicating he'd fallen asleep, Grace stayed awake. Despite her light words to David and her assurances of the previous evening, she had an uneasy feeling in her stomach and a sense of dread about what the next few months would bring.

CHAPTER 5

Faith smiled at Aaron as they finished their duet between the first and second readings. They had sung a two-part arrangement of "Come, Let us Fix Our Eyes on Jesus," based upon Hebrews 12:2, a fitting verse for Jackson and his fellow confirmands in front of the church wearing white robes and red carnations.

Glancing at the two pews where her family was sitting, Faith was glad Jackson had such a showing of support. Andy and Olivia McNeal were there along with their twins, Justin and Jason, who had just returned from college the day before. Both sets of grandparents were present, but Faith felt a twinge of sadness as she remembered her two great-grandparents who were not there. Both had entered their eternal rest within the past year.

Pastor Lixon's sermon that day focused upon Acts 4:12. "'Salvation is found in no one else,'" he quoted in conclusion, "'for there is no other name given under heaven by which we might be saved.'" He paused to look at the eighth-grade students in the front row. "Remember that verse as you continue along life's path. There will be people who tell you that there are many paths to heaven; that it doesn't matter what you believe so long as you're sincere. But I exhort you today, don't fall for those lies. Our Bible verse clearly states that Jesus is the *only* way to heaven. Only Jesus lived a perfect life in our stead and took the punishment we deserved. And it is only through Him that we stand blameless before our Father in heaven. My prayer for you is that you keep the vows you will make today, being willing to suffer all—yes, even death—rather than fall away from that beautiful truth. Salvation is found only in Jesus Christ. Amen."

When it was time for the rite of Confirmation, the eighth graders filed up to the front in alphabetical order. Pastor Lixon led them through the questions to affirm what they believed and proclaim their intentions to keep the faith and continue going to church. Then it was time for the individuals to kneel and receive their Confirmation blessings.

"Jackson Robert Williams," Pastor spoke as he placed his hand on Jackson's head, "the almighty God and Father of our Lord Jesus Christ, who has given you the new birth of water and of the Spirit and has forgiven you all your sins, strengthen you with His grace to life everlasting. Amen."

Faith felt downright proud of her younger brother, an emotion she rarely felt toward him. Jackson was the first in their family to have this kind of Confirmation service. Faith had already been in high school when they'd become Christians, so she and her mom had attended an adult information class and had been received into membership by adult Confirmation. Faith felt a bit envious of Jackson going through a service like this.

"Jackson, your Confirmation verse is Ephesians 6:13," Pastor continued. "'Therefore take up the whole armor of God, that you may be able to withstand in the evil day, and having done all, to stand firm.'"

Biting her lip to hold back a small smile, Faith wondered if her mom and David had suggested the verse because of Jackson's contentious nature. Putting on the armor of God and fighting against the devil was a far better type of combat.

When the service was over, the newly-confirmed students filed out behind Pastor and stood in the narthex, awkwardly accepting congratulations from other members. Jackson was clearly embarrassed when his family came out of the sanctuary and hugged him one after the other.

Following pictures in the front of church, the family exited into the parking lot. The warm May sunshine was welcome, and everyone was in high spirits from the lovely service. Faith and Aaron were stopped by an elderly member, who complimented them on their duet, while the rest of Faith's family wandered off in the opposite direction, talking and laughing together.

"Hey, you two sounded great up there," a voice spoke from behind them as they finished their conversation.

Faith froze as she stared at Aaron, seeing in his eyes the same incredulous reaction. She didn't need to turn around to know who was speaking. That deep, confident voice was one she'd recognize anywhere. With a sense of dread, she turned toward the speaker. She knew all too well those intense blue eyes, the smile displaying perfect teeth, the dark blond hair expertly styled with gel, that attractive face she'd fallen for so many months ago.

Spencer Young.

The three of them stared at each other for a long moment until Spencer spoke again. "So this is Griffin, huh? Mom was right. He's adorable. Hi, buddy," he addressed the baby in a sing-song voice. "How ya doing?" He looked at Faith. "He has your eyes. Is he rolling over yet?"

Aaron snorted in derision, and Faith laughed. "Spencer, he's almost eleven months old! He's been crawling for a few months. He's starting to pull himself up on furniture to stand. At this rate he could even be walking before he turns one." She felt a swell of motherly pride as she spoke of her son.

"Oh. I don't know much about babies."

"Obviously," Aaron mumbled with another snort.

Faith could feel the tension between Aaron and Spencer and quickly turned to Aaron. "Could you take Griffin over to my parents?" she asked, shifting Griffin to her other hip. "I'll be right there. Promise." She looked into his eyes, silently pleading with him to comply.

Reluctantly, he nodded, and Faith breathed a sigh of relief. "Time to go with Aaron, sweetie," she sang, handing Griffin to him. He took the baby with ease.

As Aaron and Griffin walked away, Faith grabbed Spencer's elbow and pulled him to a more discreet spot at the edge of the parking lot. "Spencer, what are you doing here?" she hissed, well aware that other members were casting curious glances their way as they made small talk around them.

"Going to church," he said innocently, his eyes wide.

"That doesn't answer my question. Why here? Why now? You've never been to church before. What little game are you playing?"

"Faith, listen. You have every right to be mad at me and to distrust me. But I'm a Christian now. Really," he insisted at her skeptical look. "Short version of the story is that I started going to church with my roommate last semester. I came back here because I want to talk to you about everything that happened between us. I owe you an apology. And I want to do what I can to support you and Griffin now."

Faith folded her arms over her chest, looked up into the sky, and bit her lip, trying desperately to control her emotions. "Spencer, don't! Don't do this to me right now! You have no idea what's involved in raising a baby. It's so much harder than I thought it would be. Since the *father* of the baby abandoned me—" she glared at him for good measure "—my family has stepped in to fill the void. Without their support, I would have either dropped out of high school or put Griffin up for adoption by now. I get up at five thirty to feed him and get him ready, and I take him either to Aunt Livy's, your mom, or Aaron's mom, depending on the day. I cut out all extracurricular activities. I didn't even get to play volleyball my senior year."

She paused for a moment to compose herself. Her voice was getting too loud. "I pick Griffin up on the way home from school, do homework, help Mom with the twins while she gets dinner ready, and fall into bed when I finally get Griffin down. I haven't slept through the night since he came home from the hospital, and I'm constantly exhausted. I couldn't do this alone, but thankfully I have lots of help. And *you* aren't one of those helpers! Besides, I'm with Aaron now. He's been there for me from the very beginning, before I even appreciated him."

The tears she'd been fighting were dangerously close to spilling over. Spencer's sudden reappearance had affected her much more than she'd thought possible. She was shaking and kept her arms tightly crossed to disguise that fact. Telling him how drastically her life had changed in the past year had drained her emotionally as well. Her life was nothing like that of a "normal" high schooler.

"I know it's hard on you," Spencer answered, looking down at the ground. "I'm sorry. And I'm glad you and Aaron are together now. He's a good guy. And he has a mean right hook," he added with a rueful smile.

Smooth, Spencer, she thought, narrowly avoiding an eye roll. Instead, she threw up her hands in exasperation. "What do you expect me to say or do? I haven't thought about you for months, and now here you are telling me you want to start supporting us? What does that even mean? Financially? Emotionally?"

He rubbed the back of his neck. "I want to get involved in Griffin's life somehow. I can help over the summer. Faith, he's my son too! Can't I at least get to know him?"

Her eyes were burning as she glared at him. "You didn't even *want* him!" she hissed, leaning closer to him so no one else would overhear. "You told me to get an abortion! And now you want to *help*? I don't think so!"

"I know, I know. Faith, I was wrong. I was so wrong—about everything. Will you just give me a chance to explain myself to you? To apologize properly? I owe you at least that much. Let me take you out for dinner tomorrow night. Please, Faith. Just dinner. I need to talk to you." His eyes were pleading, and Faith groaned. He was giving her the look, the one he used to make a girl's heart melt. She hated that look. But she hated herself even more because his look was working.

"Oh, *fine*," she groused. "Just dinner."

He grinned away like the Cheshire Cat. "Perfect. I'll pick you up at six."

"We moved since the last time you were at my house."

"I know exactly where you live," he replied with a saucy wink. Spencer's normal self-confidence had returned. "Wear something nice. I'm not taking you to McDonald's."

With that, he kissed her cheek and scooted away before she could protest.

***

Aaron sulked as he carried Griffin across the parking lot to Faith's family. He didn't like this at all. Why would Spencer pick now to show up again? What was he up to?

When he reached the Neunabers, David saw him and broke out into a big grin, reaching out to take his grandson from Aaron. "Hey, there's my little guy! How are you, G. David?"

David looked at Aaron. "You and Faith sounded wonderful, as always. Beautiful arrangement." Then he looked around. "Where is she, by the way?"

Reluctantly, Aaron motioned with his head to indicate the spot on the other side of the parking lot where Spencer and Faith were talking. David glanced over, and his face hardened. He led Aaron a few steps away from the rest of the group. "What is *he* doing here?" he asked in a low voice.

Aaron shrugged despondently. The question burned in his mind too.

"Hey, look at me, son," David commanded, his voice still low. Aaron raised his eyes, and Faith's stepfather continued. "I've been in your shoes. Before Mrs. Neunaber and I got married—before we were even engaged—we went to my cousin's wedding. As luck would have it, her ex-husband was there. A friend of the groom, as charming and suave as the day is long. I felt like he was taunting me all weekend, ushering her to her pew, asking her to dance, kissing her on the cheek. I was beside myself with jealousy. And I was terrified, because I knew they had a history together. An intimate one, at that. They had shared something she and I didn't yet share, and that made me very unsure of myself."

Shifting uncomfortably, Aaron wondered if Mr. Neunaber had read his thoughts. Faith and Spencer did have a son together, and while Aaron tried not to dwell on it, that fact was always in the back of his mind.

"Don't let Spencer get inside your head," continued David. "You've proven yourself to Faith by being a constant source of support and encouragement to her ever since she told you she was pregnant. Spencer, on the other hand, did exactly the opposite. It'll take a long time for him to earn back any trust at all. Faith trusts and respects you, and she knows you respect her in return. Believe me, that goes a long way with women."

Aaron nodded, knowing Mr. Neunaber was right, but still felt uneasy about Spencer's sudden reappearance. And just then, he saw Spencer kiss Faith's cheek and saunter away. His heart plunged, and he had the sinking feeling that he was about to lose her.

"Aaron, it's just dinner!" Faith protested. "It's not a big deal! He wants to explain things to me and apologize. I at least owe him that much, especially if it's true that he's a Christian now."

"*Just dinner* at a restaurant. A *nice* restaurant. With a guy who happens to be the father of your baby. Call it what you want. It's a date. And it *is* a big deal. At least, to me it is," Aaron groused. It irritated him that Faith wasn't taking this as seriously as he was.

Sighing in exasperation, she asked, "What did you expect me to tell him?"

A few choice expressions ran through Aaron's mind, but he deemed it best not to vocalize them. Instead he said, "At the very least, he could have talked to you at your place. Or his," he amended, knowing no one could ever have a private conversation in Faith's house with nine people around.

"Besides," he continued, "I don't like it that he's home for the summer now. Just watch—he's gonna want to help watch Griffin. Think about it, Faith! Spencer's mom watches Griffin once a week as it is. Mark my words—Spencer will exploit that this next month while we're still in school. You'll have to encounter him every time you drop Griffin off and pick him up. He'll probably answer the door with a sleeveless T-shirt to show off his biceps. Maybe even without a shirt at all to show you his pecs."

While Spencer was tall, lean, and muscular, Aaron was stocky and barely had two inches on Faith. Suddenly this difference seemed very important to him.

"Hey," she said softly, taking his hands in hers, "who's the one who encouraged me to keep the baby when Spencer told me not to? Who told David I was pregnant so I wouldn't get an abortion? Who took me to the hospital when my family was out of town? Who did I say was Griffin's father after he was born?"

Heat rose to Aaron's face as he recalled Faith telling the nurses he was the father so he would be allowed to see her after she gave birth.

She wasn't finished. "Who came with me to the hospital nearly every day for a month until Griffin was ready to come home? Who's been part of his life all along? *You*, Aaron. And now you're worried Spencer will come back and smooth talk his way into my good graces? He abandoned me. Frankly, I'm going to dinner with him because I *want* to hear him apologize to me. And if it costs him a bit of money to do so, all the better!"

Aaron breathed out a short laugh. Money was no object to the affluent Youngs. "I guess," he said reluctantly. "But I don't have to like it. Will you at least call me when you get back? You know I'll be on pins and needles the whole time, wondering what's going on."

"I promise," she said lightly, raising herself ever so slightly on her tiptoes to kiss him. "Now, let's go join the others before they start to wonder what we're doing down here…"

As they went outside to join the rest of her family for Jackson's open house, Aaron tried very hard to push Spencer out of his mind, but it wasn't easy. All he could think about was Spencer escorting *his* girlfriend to dinner the following evening, using all his charm. Maybe Faith believed Spencer's motives to be sincere, but Aaron had his doubts. He didn't trust Spencer Young one bit.

CHAPTER 6

When Spencer rang the doorbell the next evening, Faith was chagrined to see him dressed in khakis and a dark blue button-down shirt with the top button undone. He knew she loved that color on him. It complemented his sparkling blue eyes, making them look like deep oceans. The way his shirt fit accentuated his muscular arms and torso. Clearly he'd still been working out in college. Spencer Young was certainly easy on the eyes.

David was with her to meet him at the door with a stern warning, while Grace hovered nearby with Griffin in her arms, glowering at Spencer for good effect.

"I expect you to take good care of this young lady tonight," David said in his stern principal's voice. "Treat her with respect and dignity. You claim you've changed, but frankly, my last impression of you is unfavorable at best. I don't like the fact that you're taking Faith anywhere, but you're right about one thing—you *do* owe her an apology. I want her home by nine o'clock tonight. That's plenty of time to get to a restaurant, order, eat, and talk. Not one minute past nine. You are on a very short leash, young man."

To his credit, Spencer accepted the chastening without defending himself. He simply said, "I completely understand, sir. I hope in time to prove myself to you, but you have my word that I will be a perfect gentleman tonight with your stepdaughter."

Spencer held out his arm for Faith, and David reluctantly stepped aside, exchanging looks with her as she passed. Ignoring Spencer's arm, she marched past him and let him scurry to catch up. She could feel David's eyes on her as Spencer opened the passenger door of his Mustang. She felt incredibly self-conscious as he did so. Must he make this look like a real date? She could get in a car on her own, for heaven's sake.

After Spencer backed out of the driveway and started down the street, he glanced in her direction. "You look really pretty," he said. She was wearing a modest sundress with a short-sleeved white cardigan over it. She'd debated about what to wear, but figured that a sundress could be either casual or classy, depending on the situation.

Ignoring his comment, Faith asked, "Where are we going?"

"Le Poisson."

"Spencer!" She felt a surge of panic. "What are you trying to do? You have to make reservations at least a month in advance for that place! How long have you been planning this? No, this isn't right. I don't want to go there. It's too much like a real date." Her cheeks burned as she recalled the first and last time he'd taken her there. It had been the night of Homecoming, and after the dance they'd gone back to his house and… Faith closed her eyes. She didn't even want to think about that. Why, oh why, had he picked Le Poisson? It was a blatant reminder of that evening a year and a half ago.

"Relax," he assured her. "The reservations were originally for my parents, but they couldn't use them because my dad got called away on business last week. I figured we may as well go instead. They make a mean grilled bass. Besides, I told you I wasn't taking you to McDonald's didn't I?" He grinned at her sideways from the driver's seat.

Faith crossed her arms over her chest and wished she'd never agreed to dinner in the first place. How in the world was she going to explain this to Aaron? The very thought of telling him made her stomach churn. He was insanely jealous as it was. This was not going to help the cause. At all.

They drove silently for a few minutes, Faith staring out the passenger window, half-seriously contemplating whether or not she should jump. At length, she resigned herself and ventured into safe territory. "So how's college?" she asked.

He jumped at the chance to engage in conversation, and the rest of the way they talked about his classes and college life. By the time they reached Le Poisson, Faith was slightly more relaxed. Spencer jumped out and jogged to her side of the car to let her out, then escorted her into the restaurant on his arm.

Call it what you want. It's a date... Aaron's words floated through her mind, and Faith immediately let go of Spencer's arm, feeling rather like a child caught with her hand in the cookie jar. They were seated and she thoroughly inspected the menu, settling upon the Gingery Grilled Salmon Steak with Peaches because it was one of the most expensive things on the menu. As he'd indicated, Spencer opted for the Grilled Bass with Olives and Artichokes. Their waiter, Geoffrey, assured them that both were excellent choices.

Their orders placed, Faith sipped her water and took great pains to smooth her napkin over her lap. When she'd worked up her courage, she looked him in the face and asked, "Well?"

Spencer burst out laughing. "There's the Faith I remember," he said fondly. "No use beating around the bush. Just get right to the point. Okay. Fair enough."

Now it was his turn to sip his water nervously as he struggled with how to begin the conversation. After a deep breath, he clasped his hands on the table in front of him, looked her in the eye, and spoke.

"I need to ask you to forgive me. For a lot of things. I'm sorry for the way I behaved last year, how I acted when I found out you were expecting, and how I treated you while you were pregnant. I... I'm ashamed of myself looking back."

For once, his usual self-confident façade had fallen, and he was vulnerable. Faith had never seen him like this before. She felt like she was finally getting a glimpse of the real Spencer Young. As he continued, his voice caught. "First of all, I'm sorry... *really* sorry about Homecoming."

No, Spencer, don't go there, Faith begged silently. *I don't want to relive those memories.*

Unfortunately, Spencer didn't sense her reluctance and pressed on. "I was a senior, I was on the Homecoming Court, I was a star on the football team, and I had the prettiest girl in school as my date. I knew you didn't want to sleep with me, but I... I told you if you really loved me you would do it for me. That was very, very wrong of me. And I knew you were upset about it afterward, but I tried to laugh it off as first-time jitters and pressured you to try again. You knew half the girls at school would have jumped at the chance to be with me, but you were different, and I saw you as... as a challenge, I guess. I can hardly live with myself even saying so out loud. I was a complete jerk, and I'm so sorry that I treated you like that."

Hot tears spilled down her face, both from his admission and from the shame she felt as she recalled that sordid chapter of her life. Spencer looked truly remorseful, the raw emotion plainly showing in his eyes. She couldn't speak over the lump in her throat, and she looked away, not wanting him to see how much he'd affected her.

Geoffrey picked that moment to deliver the hot rolls and butter, pretending not to notice her tears as he gallantly set down their plates. Faith used the distraction to wipe her face, and when he left, she pushed the food aside. Now was not the time to eat. They had a conversation to finish.

"Then when you found out you were pregnant, I told you…" He shut his eyes as if the memory of it was too painful. "I wanted you to abort the baby," he whispered huskily. "Little Griffin wouldn't be here if I'd had my way."

Without thinking, Faith grabbed his hands across the table, both needing and offering support as she desperately tried to stop her tears. Spencer struggled to compose himself before going on. "And when you didn't get an abortion and people started to find out, I was mad, so I told people it wasn't even my baby. I spread lies about you to make myself look and feel better. I mean, who *does* that? But you held your head high and ignored the taunts of other students, and you never bothered to correct the gossip. You let people think less of you without slandering me in the process. You're a far better person than I can ever hope to be, Faith."

Her shoulders were shaking from her sobs, and she pulled her hands from his to cover her face. She was terribly shaken by the painful memories of the past year and a half. Spencer rose from his side of the booth and slipped in next to her, pulling her into a protective hug. For a few minutes, they sat there as she cried on his shoulder.

When she pulled back, her eyes felt swollen as she looked at him accusingly. "I was so hurt, Spencer. You told me you loved me, but then you dumped me because I wouldn't sleep with you anymore. And when you told me to get an abortion, I seriously considered it, because I figured my mom would kill me if she found out. I didn't want a baby to ruin everything for me, and with you telling me to get rid of it, I almost did."

Drawing a shuddering breath, she soldiered on. "Aaron was the one who stopped me. I told him I was pregnant when we were practicing music at church. I had to tell someone, and he was in the right place at the right time. Even though I made him swear not to tell anyone, he told David the very next day. I was furious with him, but David and Mom were both really supportive of me, and convinced me to keep the baby. If Aaron hadn't told him, I don't know if I would have made the same choice."

Now it was her turn to look ashamed, and she lowered her eyes and continued in a whisper. "Aaron was there for me when you weren't. He wasn't embarrassed to be seen with me, and he was a friend when I most needed one." She paused to blow her nose before continuing.

"Griffin was born six weeks early. No one in my family was in town when my water broke, and it was Aaron and his mom who came to get me and take me to the hospital. He came with me almost every day when Griffin was in the NICU." She looked Spencer in the eye. "He was there a *month*, Spencer. A whole month, and you never came *once*. The nurses all thought Aaron was the father, and I let them think that. He may as well have been. He's been so good with Griffin, and I don't know what I would have done without him. I… I love him," she finished, her voice cracking as she looked away.

"I'm glad you guys are together," Spencer said. "You deserve a decent guy. Remember that fight we had in the lunchroom last year?" She grimaced. It was hardly something she could forget. "It was my fault," he admitted. "I made spiteful comments about you, knowing he would defend you. I didn't expect him to punch me, but I was at least hoping he'd make a fool of himself in front of everyone. Because I was…" He swallowed hard. "Because I was jealous of him. Here I was, the pretty-boy-football-star-hotshot-senior, jealous of a junior I looked down on as a nerd and a dork. But he had something I didn't have: you. He had earned your trust and your friendship, while I had completely squandered both of those things. And it made me mad. But deep down, I wasn't truly mad at him. I was mad at myself."

Again, they paused as the waiter delivered their main dishes. Geoffrey appeared offended that they hadn't touched the rolls and didn't need refills on their water. He gave them a tight smile and backed away.

Spencer took the opportunity to go back to his side of the booth, and Faith wiped her eyes on her napkin again. Both ignored the food as Spencer spoke. "But you're wrong, Faith. I *did* come to the hospital."

"You… you did?" Faith looked into his eyes to determine whether he was being serious or not.

"Your mom called my mom to tell her when Griffin was born." This surprised Faith. She didn't know her mom had informed the Youngs, and *she* certainly hadn't told them. With a twinge of guilt, she realized she ought to have given them that courtesy herself.

"We were visiting my brother out in California when Griffin was born," Spencer said, "but when we got back, he was still in the hospital. I did a stake out one day. I mean, he's my son, right? I at least wanted to see what he looked like." Spencer paused and cleared his throat, staring at the basket of still-untouched rolls. "But I didn't want to go in alone and ask for him. I didn't know if they'd even let me see a preemie. So I sat in the parking lot and waited for you in my car. I figured you probably went most days, and I planned to ask if I could visit him with you. But when you got there an hour later, you were with Aaron. I realized I wasn't part of your world—Griffin's world—anymore."

He was still gazing at the rolls, and despite herself, Faith felt a swell of pity. "I didn't know that, Spencer," she said gently, covering his hand with her own. "I would have let you meet him." Even as she said it, she wondered. *Would* she have welcomed his presence when Aaron was with her? Probably not.

Spencer pulled his hand away and barked out a harsh laugh. "Sure. Considering we weren't even on speaking terms, and you were with your new boyfriend, I'm sure you would have been thrilled if I just showed up out of the blue."

A surge of anger coursed through her. "What, like you *just did*? Don't you realize that's *exactly* what you did to me on Sunday? We haven't spoken since school ended, I'm dating someone else, and voila! Here you are, showing up out of the blue!"

"What did you expect me to do?"

"You *do* have my phone number."

"You wouldn't have answered a call or text from me!"

"How do you know?"

Spencer opened his mouth to respond, then closed it again. "This isn't getting us anywhere, Faith. I know we need to clear the air, but arguing in the middle of this restaurant isn't solving anything. This isn't why I wanted to take you out." Faith winced at his choice of words. He may as well have come right out and said "date."

"What I really wanted to do tonight was make things better,

not worse," he went on. "The fact is, I messed up so many times that I can hardly expect you to forgive me, but I have to at least try. Yes, I've made a mess of things. I was a jerk pretty much my entire senior year. But I'm trying to change now. I'm trying to be a better person, and I want you to know that."

"Um, okay…?" How was she to respond to such a statement?

"After I saw you and Aaron at the hospital, holding hands as you went inside, I figured that was, like, some sort of sign for me to stay away. Maybe it was just an excuse, but I convinced myself it was for the best. I went off to college a month later and threw myself into the party scene, which, trust me, wasn't hard." Faith could just imagine.

"But one day my roommate asked me why I was wasting my time partying so much, and what I really wanted to do with my life. I was kind of mad at him, like he was trying to get all preachy. He knew I wanted to be a doctor, and I seemed to have things together, but he could tell I was… I don't know, aimless, maybe. So he asked me to come to church with him just for kicks. Trust me, that was the last thing I wanted to do, but he kept pestering me about it, telling me I'd like it, so finally I went with him just to get him off my back. I'm telling you, it was nothing like I expected. There was a band up front, and the pastor was wearing jeans, and it was totally laid back. Almost like a concert. Great music, good message… It was awesome. So I went with him a few times and then they had this altar call thing, and I… I finally realized that was what I was missing all these years, so I went up to the front with a bunch of other people and invited God into my heart. Best decision I ever made."

Faith was having trouble processing everything. This wasn't at all what she'd expected. "So you're not a Lutheran?" was all she could manage, realizing she sounded exactly like the character from *Catch Me if You Can*, inflection of her voice and all.

"Oh, gosh, no. I mean, no offense, but your services are too stuffy for me. I need some kind of emotion in church."

Faith thought back to the many times she'd choked up while singing a hymn or hearing Pastor Lixon proclaim the beautiful news of forgiveness through Jesus. How could one *not* get choked up when realizing that the God of the universe had taken on human flesh to die for the sins of the world?

"Then what do you believe about Jesus?" she asked, frowning slightly.

"Same thing as you! I believe that God loves me and takes me for who I am. Now I'm trying to live my life to glorify Him. And part of my journey in getting right with God is asking you to forgive me."

Faith noticed he hadn't even used the name "Jesus" in his answer. Nor had he expressed any confidence that he was, in fact, forgiven.

"But Spencer," she argued, "there's no 'journey' in getting right with God. I mean, sure, there's a path you take leading up to that point, but either you're right with Him or you aren't."

She realized that had come out badly, and she shook her head to try again. "I didn't grow up Christian, either. But when Mom made me go to the adult instruction classes with her, I was blown away at how incredible Christianity really is. Jesus died for me and rose three days later. Because I believe in Him, I know I'll go to heaven when I die. Either you believe in Jesus as your Savior, or you don't. There's no in between. My forgiving you has nothing to do with your standing in God's eyes. Sure, part of living a Christian life is making peace with others and being reconciled when possible, but that has no impact on whether or not you're right with God."

She couldn't quite read the expression in Spencer's eyes. "So does that mean you *won't* forgive me?" he asked in confusion.

"Not at all!" Then, realizing her answer could be taken either way, she hastened on to clarify. "I mean, *yes*, Spencer, I forgive you. It means a lot to me that you apologized. Everything that happened between us has sort of been a big dark cloud over me. I'm happy with my life—most days, anyhow—but sometimes when I think back to that whole time last year, I can't help but cry. It was so hard, so painful. But at the same time, had none of that ever happened I wouldn't have had Griffin. Or Aaron. So good has definitely come out of it, but it's still hard looking back."

"Can I make it up at least a little bit now? Can I help with Griffin? I'm back from college. I can watch him for you this last month while you're in school. I'd love to get to know him."

Faith squeezed the lemon wedge into her water and took a sip, stalling for time. *Aaron sure called this one*, she thought wryly. "I... I just don't know, Spencer. Don't put me on the spot like this and ask me to make an immediate decision. Let me think about it. I don't know if I want you to come in and upset the delicate balance we have. It's just too much for me to process now."

"That's fair," he conceded. "But I'm serious, Faith. I want to help if I can. Just say the word, and I'll do whatever you ask."

"I'll keep that in mind," she said, suddenly needing to get fresh air. "Look, can we just take this stuff to go? I'm sorry, but I'm not hungry right now, and I don't want to pick at my food with the waiter hovering around asking how it tastes. Let's just go, please?"

He nodded and signalled Geoffrey to ask for to-go boxes and the bill. After paying, Spencer grabbed both boxes, and they walked out together. Faith was relieved the conversation was behind them, but she knew another one awaited her at home, not to mention a phone call to Aaron.

Aaron. She had the sudden need to see him in person, to feel his arms around her and know that somehow they'd work through this. So as Spencer put their take-out boxes in the backseat, she snuck her phone out of her purse and sent a quick text to Aaron, her thumbs flying over the small keyboard.

Meet me at my place? 20 min?

She slid the phone back in her purse as Spencer climbed into the driver's seat, allowing herself to relax a bit. Aaron would come. Of that she was certain. No matter what happened in the past, she was with Aaron now. And that's how it was going to stay.

CHAPTER 7

The ride home was mostly silent. Faith didn't know what to say after a draining conversation like the one they'd just had. When they pulled up to her house, she saw with relief that Aaron's car was already there, a fact that did not escape Spencer.

"Looks like you have your bodyguard ready," he joked wryly.

Faith started out of the car, but he grabbed her hand. "Please think about what I said. Anything I can do to help you now, I will. I was too immature and self-centered to man up before, but I'm ready."

He pulled her closer for a kiss on the cheek before he released her hand and stepped out to accompany her to the door, pausing to grab her to-go box for her. Faith fervently hoped that David or Aaron hadn't been peering through the blinds to see his kiss. She'd never hear the end of it.

At the porch, Spencer waited a respectful distance away to make sure she got in before he headed back to his car. Faith was relieved he didn't walk her in. No one inside wanted to see him anyhow.

Aaron was waiting for her in the entryway and engulfed her in a hug as soon as she shut the door behind her. "Are you okay?" he whispered.

That did it. Faith's tears spilled over as she accepted his embrace. She felt so *right* in Aaron's arms. Why did Spencer have to come now and make everything so confusing? She would have been content had she never seen him again. This was too much for her to handle emotionally. It was already challenging enough to juggle single motherhood and schoolwork.

Aaron held her for a few moments until she pulled away and gave him a shaky smile. He led her into the living room where Grace and David waited. David was already standing and walked over to give her a hug as well. *David makes a good dad*, she thought. *Just like Aaron does for Griffin.* He'd stepped in when Spencer walked away. But now Spencer had walked back in. What a mess.

When David released her from the hug, Faith tossed her dinner box onto the coffee table. Grace and David both froze as they recognized the signature blue cursive letters of "their" restaurant. Aaron tensed as well.

"It's not what you think," she rushed to assure them. "His parents had to cancel reservations, so we took them instead. I didn't even touch my food. The conversation was too emotional. It took a lot out of me."

She sank down on the couch with a deep sigh. Aaron sat next to her and put his arm around her, and she leaned against his shoulder, closing her eyes. After collecting her thoughts, she related the gist of the conversation, though not the nitty gritty of Spencer's apology. That was still too raw, too personal. That part was meant for her alone.

After she finished speaking, everyone was silent for a few

moments. At length, David spoke up. "I don't like it," he stated flatly.

"Neither do I," Aaron said.

Grace sat silently, carefully observing her daughter.

"He hasn't had any contact with you for over a year, and now he wants to get involved? Why? What is his ulterior motive here?" asked David.

"I told you he'd try this," Aaron reminded her. "He's trying to get on your good side by using Griffin. Maybe even use him as leverage later. I don't trust him."

"But what if he really *has* changed?" Faith asked mournfully. "I mean, his confession of faith was weak at best, but what if he's a struggling new Christian who doesn't understand it yet? What if he needs a bit of guidance and encouragement? I do know a thing or two about new beginnings."

"Same here," Grace murmured.

"Then again, maybe he's playing you. He knows how much your faith means to you, and maybe he's trying to impress you by pretending," Aaron insisted. "I'm sorry, but I'm just not convinced."

"Only time will tell, I guess," said David. "If his actions match his words, then we'll know he's sincere. In the meantime, though, be very careful, Faith. You're a trusting person, and that's a good thing in general, but Aaron's right. Spencer could well be pretending to be someone he's not to get something he wants. I'm even uneasy letting his mom watch Griffin this month, because Spencer specifically asked if he could help watch him. I don't know that I want him around my grandson."

Inexplicably, Faith was irritated by their reaction. While she herself wasn't convinced that Spencer's motives were entirely pure, David and Aaron hadn't spoken to him themselves. What did they know about him? She knew him better than they did. How could they judge his motives and sincerity?

Faith moaned and put her head in her hands. "I can't think about this anymore," she said. "I'll sleep on it and see what the morning brings. Tomorrow is Aunt Livy's day to watch Griffin anyhow. Mrs. Young doesn't get him until Wednesday. I don't have to make a decision about it right this second."

"You're right," agreed Aaron, apparently perceiving that she needed space. He stood and said, "A good night's sleep is exactly what you need. I'd better get back home myself."

"Let me walk you to the door, son," David offered. The two walked outside together, speaking in hushed tones.

Grace walked over to sit in the spot Aaron had occupied next to Faith. She put her arms around her daughter and asked quietly, "Why don't you tell me how *you* feel?"

Tears sprang to her eyes at her mother's concern. "Oh, Mom, I'm so mixed up! I don't know what to think. On the one hand, I can't blame David and Aaron. I don't know that I trust Spencer yet, either. But, Mom, you didn't see the look in his eyes when he was apologizing to me. He was so… vulnerable. I've never seen him like that before. He meant it, Mom. He didn't just give me a general 'Sorry for everything' sort of apology. He was specific… almost uncomfortably so. It was like I was reliving everything that happened between us from the very beginning. And trust me, I wouldn't want to live through that again. It was painful on so many levels. But when he apologized tonight, it was like talking to an entirely different person."

Taking a shuddering breath, she continued. "When I fell for him last year, it was shallow from the start. Not at all like my relationship with Aaron. Spencer was charming, and I felt like a princess on his arm. But he used his charm for the wrong things. You know… like… physical things." She felt a blush spread to the roots of her hair, knowing all too well where that had landed her. "But, Mom, seriously. Tonight he was sincere," she insisted, looking into her mother's face. "He's the Spencer I wish he had been last year. I could have fallen in love with that Spencer for real."

Grace stroked her hair as she spoke, allowing Faith to speak without interruption. David reentered the house after his chat with Aaron and started to come back into the living room, but Grace shook her head, and he took the cue and went upstairs to their bedroom instead. Faith was grateful. She needed this to be a mother-daughter moment.

"Mom, what should I do?" she whispered. "He *is* Griffin's father. How can I deny him the chance to see his own son? I can't very well tell his mom that I don't want her to watch Griffin anymore just because Spencer's home now. And I really want him to be sincere about being a Christian. I don't think he quite understands it yet, but he's on the right track. In a way, I want him to get a second chance because I know how it feels to be given a second chance myself. To have my sins forgiven and to know that those sins don't define who I am. I want him to experience God's forgiveness like I have."

"I know, sweetie. Both you and I have experienced that in a way a lot of Christians never have. Remember the one Bible verse—'He who has been forgiven much loves much, but he who has been forgiven little loves little?' You and I both have 'major' sins in our past, taboo sins that many lifelong Christians haven't committed, so we know how powerful God's forgiveness is. I think partly you might want to see the same change in Spencer's life to be reminded that it's true for you as well."

"Exactly! If I can be forgiven for getting pregnant in high

school, can't *he* be forgiven for getting me pregnant? For wanting me to get an abortion? Jesus died for his sins too!"

"Yes, He did," agreed Grace.

Faith pulled away from her mother and did a neck roll, trying to relieve some tension. "I don't know what I'm going to do about Spencer's offer. But I can tell Aaron doesn't want him around Griffin at all. He's mad at Spencer for the way he treated me, and now he's totally jealous. He thinks Spencer is coming back here to try to steal me away. How in the world am I ever supposed to handle both of them?"

"I wish I had an easy answer, honey. You're in a hard place for sure."

Both sat quietly for a few more moments longer until Faith spoke. "Thanks, Mom, for understanding. And for taking the time to see how I feel about all this. I just want to do the right thing for everyone involved. Right now I feel like no matter what I do, I'm going to let someone down."

"I know the feeling," Grace said. "But don't let other people tell you what you should do or how you should feel. Pray about this. Let God's Word influence you, rather than what others are pushing you to do."

"I just wish God would tell me in person, the way He talked to Moses."

Grace laughed. "I've wished the same thing many a time myself."

Faith suddenly realized she was famished, and turned to her mom. "Wanna split a salmon steak with me? Get those Omega-3's?"

"I was hoping you'd ask! It smells heavenly."

Mother and daughter shared the dinner, though Faith barely tasted the expensive entree. She could think of little else than Spencer Young.

CHAPTER 8

"He's with *Spencer* today?" Aaron exploded, then lowered his voice as other students in the hall looked at him curiously. "Faith! What are you trying to do? We didn't talk about this!"

"Mom and David and I discussed it last night," she answered him. Aaron bristled at her tone. It was the soothing voice she used when trying to calm Griffin. It irked him to think she was doing the same for him.

"It's only a month until we're out of school anyhow," she said, "and Mrs. Young always watches Griffin on Wednesdays. It would look bad to change the routine now. It's kind of like… supervised visitation."

Aaron scowled. "I don't like it. Didn't I call this one? Bet he was the one to answer the door this morning too. Did he have a shirt on? Or was he working out in their state-of-the-art personal gym?" He couldn't help the edge of sarcasm that crept into his voice. For crying out loud, who had a personal gym, anyhow? From the reports he'd heard, the Youngs' entire third story was dedicated to a workout area, and Spencer's build was proof he made regular use of it. Aaron could never compete with that.

"Oh, Aaron, really now," Faith sighed. "Of course he had a shirt on. And his mom was right there, just like she always is. It'll be fine. Once the summer gets here, I don't have to worry about child care anyhow. I'm throwing him a bone now, that's all. Show him I'm willing to give him a shot, even if it's a small one. After all, how can we tell if he can be trusted if we don't give him the chance to prove it one way or the other?"

The one-minute warning bell rang, and Aaron had to bite back his reply. They were outside Faith's classroom, but his was five doors down. He needed to hurry. Grudgingly, he said, "Maybe. We'll talk at lunch."

She leaned over to kiss him lightly. "I can't wait." Her eyes sparkled as she made eye contact with him, and despite himself, Aaron softened. Her eyes were the most amazing thing about her, and she could make him melt whenever she looked at him like that. As Aaron hustled off to his classroom, he wondered if Spencer had noticed the same thing.

Faith rang the doorbell and waited until Spencer opened the huge oak door and ushered her into the Youngs' spacious foyer. A curving staircase graced the left side of the entry hall, leading to their open second-story family area. An elegant chandelier hung from the cathedral ceiling.

"He's sleeping," whispered Spencer unnecessarily. The room where Mrs. Young set up the Pack 'n Play was on the far end of the hallway on the second floor. There was no way Griffin could hear them from here.

"Still?" Faith was surprised.

"I took him for a walk after lunch, and we got back later than he usually goes down, Mom said. He didn't fall asleep until one fifteen."

"Oh. Then it should be okay to wake him up. I don't want him to be up all night."

"Sure, but can I get you anything first? Bottled water? Kale chips?"

They laughed together. Mrs. Young was a health nut, and her idea of junk food did not match Faith's in the least.

"I'm fine, thanks. Where is your mom, anyhow?"

"She had to run out for a few minutes."

Faith shifted uneasily. What was Spencer trying to do? Other than a sleeping baby, that meant the two of them were alone. The last time they'd been by themselves in this house, Faith ended up pregnant. She flushed at the memory and ran her fingers through her hair, a subconscious nervous habit.

Spencer seemed to follow her train of thought. "Relax," he assured her. "She had to mail a package for my dad before the post office closed. She should be back any minute. Dad called at three, adamant that this package be sent today, and she raced out to do it before Griffin woke up. I don't think she trusts me with him when he's awake."

Faith laughed shakily, still on edge. "How'd it go today?" she asked.

"It was great. I've never been around a baby all day like that. He's a cutie. How could he not be? He takes after his mommy."

"Spencer, stop," she protested. She didn't need him trying to sweet talk her.

Just then the door that led toward the garage opened, and Vivian Young's footsteps clicked on the tile floor. She was wearing her customary high heels. The woman always looked like she had stepped from a fashion magazine, her highlighted hair perfectly coiffed, makeup expertly applied, nails manicured, and jewelry to coordinate with her stylish outfit.

Faith wondered how Mrs. Young managed to keep up with Griffin wearing such impractical outfits for babysitting, but she wasn't entirely sure she wanted to know the answer. Griffin grabbed everything to put into his mouth, and she couldn't understand how Mrs. Young could wear necklaces and dangling earrings if she ever held Griffin at all. It wouldn't surprise Faith to learn that she hired someone to come watch the baby for her on Wednesdays. Come to think of it, she couldn't imagine how she'd managed to raise three children of her own. Vivian Young was very different from Faith's own mother.

"Ah, there you are, darling," she breathed when she saw Faith. "He was a dear today, as always. We had a delightful time. Spencer was marvelous with him. Griffin took to him right away. I'm so glad it worked out."

"I'm glad it went well too," Faith assured her, "but I really do need to wake him. He'll be up too late otherwise and that would throw off the morning for Mrs. Sullivan."

The conversation stalled abruptly at the mention of Aaron's mother, so Faith stepped around Spencer and walked up the elegant staircase. He followed.

They reached Griffin's room, and Spencer grabbed her hand on the doorknob to stop her before she entered. "I know my mom is a little weird, but she does a good job with him," he insisted. "She knew exactly what he needed when he cried, and she's more affectionate with him than you might think. She sat with him on the couch and played patty cake and peek-a-boo and sang songs and everything. I've never seen her like that before. She's usually so… put together, I guess. But she's good with Griffin. You should know that."

Faith thought it was sweet of him to stand up for his mother. "Thanks for letting me know," she said. "I have to admit, I sometimes wonder what she does with Griffin. She doesn't seem the type to get down on the floor with him and crawl around."

They both chuckled, and she opened the door to sneak in. Griffin lay on his stomach with his legs tucked underneath him, his bottom sticking up in the air.

"Look at him, Spencer. That's his favorite position," Faith whispered. "You're supposed to put babies on their backs to sleep, but he always rolls over and curls up like this." She gazed at Griffin lovingly.

"He's absolutely adorable," agreed Spencer.

He was standing close behind her. Too close. Faith quickly crossed the room and reached down into the Pack 'n Play to waken the baby. Griffin began to cry but calmed down as she snuggled him in her arms and shushed him. He rubbed his face into her chest, as if wiping the sleep from his eyes, then sat there blinking, his brow furrowed in a slight pout.

"Time to go home, sweetie," Faith crooned, swaying him slightly from side to side. "Mommy has lots of homework today. You'll be a good boy now that you've had a good nap, right?"

She looked up to see Spencer watching her with a look of awe on his face. "Wow. You're so… I mean, you're like… You're a real mother."

"What's that supposed to mean?" she asked with a laugh.

Spencer looked embarrassed. "It's just that this is the first time I've seen you really interact with him. It's neat to see how you've stepped into the role of Mommy. You're good at it."

"Thanks, Spencer." Faith was surprised how much his compliment meant to her.

"So did I pass the first test?" He grinned. "Do you trust me enough to bring him next Wednesday too?"

"I'll have to confer with my discussion panel back home," she replied, only half-joking. He laughed and grabbed the diaper bag off the floor before escorting her back down to the foyer.

"Goodbye, darling," Vivian called from the other room. "See you next week!"

Faith said her goodbyes and walked out to the car. She leaned down to strap Griffin into his car seat, and when she straightened and turned around, she was startled to find Spencer right there.

"Oh!" she exclaimed. They were barely six inches away from each other.

"I'm really glad I got the chance to spend time with him today," Spencer said without backing up. "He's a great kid. And I do want to be there for you now. For both of you. I'll do anything I can to earn back your trust."

Faith slid sideways against the car so she could back away from him. He was standing way too close for comfort. "Thanks," she mumbled, averting her eyes. "I'll be in touch."

Without giving him a chance to kiss her cheek the way he seemed to like to do, she scooted around the back of the car and slid into the driver's seat, leaving him to close Griffin's door. Good grief, was *this* what she had to look forward to every Wednesday? Thank heavens it was only three more weeks until school was out. Then maybe she could avoid Spencer for the summer.

But as quickly as she had the thought, it was replaced with a sobering realization. Spencer wasn't going to let her go that easily.

CHAPTER 9

When Wednesday rolled around again, Aaron tried unsuccessfully to hide his pleasure that Faith had asked him to accompany her to pick up Griffin from Spencer's house. He'd warily accepted the fact that Spencer would have access to Griffin once a week, but it didn't sit well with him that Faith had to spend time with Spencer as a result. He could just see Spencer inviting her to stay for dinner. *But he wouldn't dare pull such a stunt if I'm with Faith,* Aaron thought, feeling a swell of pride as if he was her protector.

He was feeling pretty good about himself until they pulled up to the Youngs' mini mansion. Suddenly, Aaron's self-confidence deflated. He was dismayed at the copious property. He knew the Youngs were rich, but this house was incredible. Aaron's own house suddenly seemed rather mediocre in comparison.

When they rang the doorbell, Spencer answered excitedly. His expression faltered slightly when he saw Aaron with Faith, but he quickly recovered.

"Hey, guys, come on in! You'll never guess what Griffin did

today!" As he spoke, he led them to the carpeted den beyond the formal living room, much more suitable for babies.

"He took three steps!" Spencer announced triumphantly as they walked into the den to see Griffin holding onto the edge of the couch, Mrs. Young perched nearby as his spotter. Spencer dropped down on the floor on his knees close to Griffin and encouraged him to try again, opening his arms in invitation.

"Come on, buddy! Come here! You can do it! Show Mommy what you can do!"

Aaron could see by the look on Faith's face that she was crushed. She felt guilty enough that she had to farm her child off every day during school. She'd missed a number of milestones already—his first smile, the first time he crawled, and now, his first steps as well.

Griffin bounced up and down happily before plopping down on his bottom, pitching himself forward into crawling position, and making a beeline for his mother on his hands and knees.

Faith scooped him up when he reached her and gave him a hug. "Did you walk today, G? What a big boy you are! Mommy's so proud of you!"

"Seriously, he did. Check this out," Spencer said. He yanked his phone out of his pocket and pulled up a video he had taken. Sure enough, Griffin was standing by himself, swaying a bit unsteadily before taking one halting step, followed by two more quick ones that made him lose his balance. "Good job, buddy!" came Spencer's encouraging voice on the video.

"Ohh!" exclaimed Faith, her voice a mixture of affection and dismay. Aaron felt certain Spencer didn't know her well enough to pick up on this fact.

"I know, right?" he gushed. "I was so proud of him!"

You're *proud of him?* Aaron thought resentfully. *You didn't even know the kid until a week ago!*

Masking his irritation, Aaron said cheerfully to Griffin, "Way to go, little man! There's no stopping you now!" Griffin lunged toward Aaron, who took him from Faith as he cast a smug glance at Spencer.

Spencer tapped a few buttons on his phone and said, "There! I sent the video to you."

"Thanks," replied Faith. Then abruptly she said, "We need to get going. Aaron and I have an economics quiz to study for."

Aaron could tell she needed to get out of there, so he grabbed the diaper bag before Spencer could make the offer. With a few last-minute pleasantries, they were off, strapping Griffin into his seat before buckling in themselves. Aaron drove in silence until they turned out of the neighborhood, then said quietly. "It's not your fault, you know."

She seemed to know exactly what he meant, because she burst into tears. "*I* should have been the one to see him take his first steps!"

He reached over to rub the back of her neck. "We both knew it was gonna happen any day. It was just a matter of time. And odds were, it was going to happen while we were in school."

"But of all people to see him walk first, why Spencer? Why not your mom or Aunt Livy?"

Aaron didn't answer. He wondered the very same thing. Matter of fact, he wished more and more that Spencer had stayed in Ann Arbor where he belonged.

CHAPTER 10

"Mr. Neunaber, do you have a minute?"

David glanced up from his desk in surprise. It was ten thirty in the morning, which was normally a quiet time in the office. Parents who needed to talk to him came first thing in the morning or at the end of the day before picking up their children. Catching sight of his visitor, he was even more shocked. It was Clay Henderson, president of the school board.

"Of course, Clay! Come in. What's on your mind?"

His stomach tightened with apprehension. Last year when Faith had gotten pregnant, Clay was the one to make an issue out of it at their meeting. Since then, the two had been cordial, but generally distrustful of the other. David was wary of Clay showing up in his office unannounced.

Clay's eyes darted around the room, looking at everything except David. He sat in a chair opposite the desk and stared at a picture on the wall before speaking. "Did you have a good trip to St. Louis last week?"

"It was very nice, thank you," David replied noncommittally. He certainly wasn't going to tell Clay

Henderson about the trip he'd taken to visit the school that had issued him the call, nor how impressed he'd been with St. Louis itself. It was a family-friendly city with many affordable activities. He could easily picture their family in such a setting.

"So you think you'll be taking that call, then?" asked Clay.

"I'm not at all sure at this point, Clay." David wondered why his visitor was here. The timing of his visit was ironic, given the fact that he'd received a phone call from their realtor just an hour ago. Someone had made an offer on their old house that he was willing to accept. Provided Grace would agree, they could be free of the financial burden of a second mortgage. That did change the situation considerably.

Clay breathed in deeply and dared to look at David at last. "I know we don't have the best rapport between us," he admitted. "And you know how I feel about your daughter having a baby as a teenager and all." He held up his hand as David started to object. "Let me finish. But I've come to respect you and your family for standing by each other and for deciding to keep the baby and bring it up in the faith. You're making the best of an undesirable situation, and I can respect that."

David nodded in acknowledgement, and Clay continued. "Besides that, you're a good fit for our school. After Mr. Kaiser left, the general opinion was that the next person in here would fall short in comparison. He did a lot of good for our school and church. And I had my qualms about you when you arrived. But you've exceeded my expectations and a lot of other people's besides. You're the right man for the job, and I'd hate to see you go so soon."

He stood suddenly, as though he'd said too much. "Well, there. I've said my piece. I'll leave you to your day."

He started to leave, but David stopped him. "Clay!" He

stood to address his visitor. "Thank you for your honesty. I'm sorry things have been so strained between us this past year. My pride was still smarting from that awful meeting last February, and I've been distant toward you at best. If we can, let's put that behind us, shall we?"

"I'd like that," said Clay. "I'm sorry too. I had no right to confront you like that in front of everyone. I was out of line. But if you're willing to put it behind us, so am I."

David extended his hand, and Clay shook it firmly, the two men looking each other in the eye. Then Clay turned and left the office. Amazed, David sank back down into his chair. He was continually humbled at the people the Lord chose to place in his path. Never in a million years would he have picked Clay Henderson for the job.

That afternoon, David returned home in an ebullient mood. He waltzed in the door and picked Grace up, circling her around twice before setting her down to kiss her soundly.

"Well!" she exclaimed with a laugh. "I guess you had a good day?" It was rare to see her husband in such a mood. She liked the spontaneity every once in a while.

"Come with me," he invited in response. "Let's go upstairs."

Her eyes widened, wondering what exactly he was suggesting. He laughed when he saw her expression. "I just need to talk to you, that's all. Freddie, keep an eye on the girls, will you?" Without giving Freddie a chance to respond, David led the way upstairs. Grace was dying of curiosity. Whatever his news, he was obviously excited about it.

As soon as David shut the door to their room, he grabbed Grace's hands and told her, "We're staying here."

"What?! David, are you serious?" She was hopeful but incredulous. He'd come back last week from his visit to St.

Louis so excited she was certain he would take the call. All week he'd been talking about how much there was to do in St. Louis, how nice the school was, and how well he got along with the faculty there. Grace regretted not going along on the trip, but she just couldn't be away from the twins for three days while they were still nursing. But since David's return, Grace had braced herself for the inevitable news that they'd be moving again in the next few months.

"I'm absolutely serious," he replied, bringing her back to the present. "And you'll never guess who helped me make up my mind."

"Pastor?"

"Clay Henderson."

"What?!"

"Suffice it to say we had the first decent discussion we've had since that meeting, and after he left, I really started thinking about things. I've been largely looking at the call from a pragmatic standpoint. You know—what makes the most sense financially and in terms of career. But Clay made me think about it differently. I prayed about this a lot today—more than I've been doing," he confessed with an apologetic grimace. "I should have been praying about it regularly from the start. But I feel like I'm not done here yet. Like God has something more He wants me to do. I'm completely at peace with the decision. We're staying."

"Oh, David!" Grace leaped into his arms, not even trying to contain her excitement. "I'm so glad. And not just that we're staying, but that you're the one who made the decision. It would be so hard to pack up and move again, especially so soon after our other move. I guess you didn't want to worry about three house payments at once, huh?" she teased as she released him from the hug.

"Wow, I didn't even tell you about that," David said. "Mary called to tell me our other house has an offer."

"What?!" Grace was starting to feel like a broken record.

David quickly filled her in on the details of the sale, and Grace could only nod her approval. The offer was less than their asking price, but they'd expected as much. And given the fact that they'd already lowered the price once, she'd been starting to despair that it may never sell.

Her husband went on. "Mary called before Clay came in. God sent him at exactly the right time. I was already starting to check available housing in St. Louis and crunch numbers to see how feasible it would be if I took the call."

Grace's head was spinning from all the information. "So even after all that, you still decided not to take the call?" She had to be certain she was understanding him correctly.

"Yes." David's voice held no doubt. "*This* is where we're supposed to be for now."

She saw the look in his eyes. He really was at peace with the decision. "That's wonderful," she said. "I was so hoping you'd decide to stay here. Can we tell the kids tonight?"

"You bet! It'll be a relief to have Jackson on my good side for once!" He and Jackson had achieved only a wary truce.

She laughed and wrapped her arms around his neck. "David, you've made me a very happy woman, I'll tell you that."

He gave a mock pout. "I thought being married to me made you a happy woman!"

"That too, of course," she teased, giving him a long kiss. Grace felt the tension of the last few weeks melt away as he responded in kind. That kiss alone was worth it all.

CHAPTER 11

The last Wednesday of May was a welcome relief to Faith, knowing it was the last time Spencer would have to watch Griffin for her. When Spencer answered the door, he ushered her into the den where Griffin was toddling about clumsily. He was getting better with his walking but still had the awkward gait of a baby not completely stable on his feet. When he saw his mother, Griffin clapped his hands and wobbled over to Faith, who swung him up into the air.

"Hey, buddy! How are you? Mommy missed you today!"

"He was great," Spencer answered in lieu of the child. "Mom even got him to try tofu at lunch."

Faith wrinkled her nose. "I have no idea how you grew up eating that way."

He laughed. "Actually, I didn't. Mom didn't get all into health food until a few years ago when her sister was diagnosed with breast cancer. They made this mutual pact to totally revamp their eating habits and fight off disease with good nutrition and stuff. But I wasn't in on the pact. I still go for a juicy burger with a side of greasy, salty fries."

"I'm with you," Faith agreed. It suddenly dawned on her that she knew nothing about Spencer's family health history. For Griffin's sake, she really ought to find out if there was anything hereditary of which to be aware.

"So you ready for exams next week?" asked Spencer, changing the subject and breaking into her reverie. "I'm warning you, trig was brutal last year."

"Thanks for the encouragement," she moaned. "I'm barely hanging on in that class as it is. I really need a B on the exam so I can get a B in the class."

"You'll be okay," he assured her. "Just be careful when you take the exam. Double check your answers."

"Speaking of exams, I don't need you to watch Griffin next Wednesday. We have half days all week. Aunt Livy is coming to our house each morning to help Mom watch Griffin and the twins there. It's only a few hours each day. And then, of course, it's summer, so I guess this is it. You're off the hook now."

"Yeah, so, about that…" Spencer began, absently scratching his head. Faith's heart plunged. She had a feeling she knew what he was about to say.

"Um, I wondered if… I thought… Maybe I can still take him one day a week, seeing as how we're just starting to get to know each other. I'm doing a summer internship with my dad again, but it's flexible. I can work around your schedule. Can we arrange something?"

Faith didn't like the sound of it at all. "Well…" she waffled, stalling for time. "I'm not sure what to say. I hadn't even thought of it until you mentioned it." That was a blatant lie. She'd been fearing as much, but didn't want to admit it to Spencer. "I mean, I don't *need* you to watch him since I don't have a summer job. He sort of *is* my summer job. So, I guess… I don't know…"

"At the very least, you could use a break, right? It's gotta be tough being a single parent. Let me take him one day a week for you. Please?" He gave her his most charming look, and Faith could hardly say no.

"Well… I suppose," she said, still not comfortable with it.

"Great! Which day?"

She blew out an irritated breath. Spencer was persistent, that was certain. "I don't care. Fridays, maybe?"

"That's perfect. Want me to take him next Friday? It'll give your mom and aunt a break, and then after exams you and Aaron can go out and celebrate. Griffin and I will be fine here. With Mom hovering around just in case, of course."

Faith laughed. That actually sounded really nice. "Okay, sure."

Spencer grinned widely, looking immensely pleased with himself. He helped her get Griffin's things together and walked the two of them out to the car. As Faith backed out and waved a goodbye, she had a feeling she'd just been duped, but she couldn't quite figure out how.

CHAPTER 12

Grace's eyes clouded with tears as the band started the cheesy music for "Pomp and Circumstance." How was it possible that her baby was graduating from high school already?

The students filed in alphabetically, wearing their caps and gowns and smiling proudly as parents and other relatives competed to snap pictures and take videos on their phones. At last, they reached the W's, and Faith started marching down the aisle. David squeezed Grace's hand when they caught sight of her, and Katie squealed and waved.

The ceremony was stereotypical of most graduations, the speeches longer than they needed to be, and the exhortations to the graduates far more poignant to the parents than to the students. After the diplomas were handed out, the students moved their tassels from one side of their mortarboards to the other. Then they broke out into cheers as they tossed their caps into the air.

It was pure chaos afterward as giddy teenagers accepted hugs and posted for pictures while families tried to push through the mass of people to find their new graduates. When

Grace and her family finally made it to Faith and Aaron, they exchanged hugs, and everyone fussed over their diplomas. In the midst of the excitement, Faith glanced up and gave a little squeal.

"He came!" she gasped.

Grace turned to follow her daughter's gaze and froze. Standing a mere thirty feet away was her ex-husband, Bob Coleman. David saw him as well and tensed next to her.

"You... you *invited* him?" Grace asked in disbelief.

"Well, yeah," answered Faith, biting her bottom lip. "I mean, he *is* my dad. I know he walked out on us, but I was eleven when he left. I remember him more than the other kids. And some of those memories are actually good ones."

Grace's throat tightened. Faith was right. She'd been devastated when her father left, and until a couple years ago had assumed he'd left because of the kids. It probably meant a lot to Faith to have him there, a step in her healing process.

"Let me go say hi to him real quick," pleaded Faith. "I want him to at least meet Griffin."

Grace exchanged a glance with her husband and nodded at him. David reluctantly handed Griffin to Faith. Grace knew he didn't trust Bob one bit.

"Aaron, want to come?" offered Faith.

Aaron was clearly torn and looked to Grace and David as if gauging their reaction.

"Go ahead." David spoke into the void, surprising Grace. "Maybe we'll introduce the twins to him afterward."

Faith, Aaron, and Griffin walked away as Grace looked at her husband in astonishment. "What was *that* all about?" she hissed. "He hasn't even met his own daughter yet! Why would I want him to meet our girls?" A familiar stab of pain accompanied the memory of Bob leaving her for a younger woman when she was pregnant with Katie.

"I don't want to see him at all," Jackson seethed darkly. "I've got nothing to say to him."

Katie looked confused. "Who are we talking about?"

"Your father, sweetie," Grace said gently.

"I already have a daddy," said Katie, her brow creasing in bewilderment.

"That's right. We do," Jackson said adamantly.

Grace's eyes widened. For him to side with Katie about David being their father now was unfathomable.

"I didn't even remember what he looked like," Freddie said. "You look a lot like him, Jackson."

"Who cares?!" Jackson exploded, causing the people near them to jump and look at him in alarm. "I'm *not* him, so just shut up!" He wheeled around and shoved his way roughly through the crowd, seemingly on the verge of tears.

An uneasy silence settled over the rest of the family as Jackson stormed away. Grace had been been watching the interaction between Bob and Faith with one eye. The two had exchanged a tentative hug, and Bob shook Aaron's hand and tousled Griffin's hair. They were laughing together at something, and then Faith gave him one last hug before she and Aaron turned around in search of Aaron's parents.

Helplessly, Grace looked to David, her eyes asking for advice. This was the worst possible time for Bob to show up in their lives again, and she didn't know what to do. No, check that. It could definitely be worse. He could have showed up at the graduation party at their house. That would have been far more awkward. At least here they were "safe" with the presence of so many other people around, and they could always make an excuse to leave.

David shrugged and took her hand possessively. "Katie,

Freddie, do you want to meet him or not?" he asked softly. "Mom and I are going over to talk to him. You can always go over to Grandma and Grandpa if you'd rather."

Katie and Freddie looked at each other until Katie spoke. "We'll go with you," she decided as Freddie nodded. Together they made their way to Bob, who grinned as they approached.

"Well, well, if it isn't the happily-married Neunabers," he greeted them jovially. "Mr. Principal, good to see you again!" He held out his hand, and Grace noted that David made eye contact as he returned the handshake firmly, apparently not wanting to give any hint of weakness.

Next Bob turned to Grace. "Hey, sweetie, how ya doing?" he asked. Grace stiffened as he leaned over to give her a hug. "Still as beautiful as ever." Grace felt heat rise to her cheeks while Freddie and Katie stared wide-eyed at the exchange, and David bristled beside her.

"I didn't realize Faith had invited you," she answered, ignoring his comments entirely. "But since you're here, would you like to meet Katie?" Her voice held a trace of scorn.

"You're just as pretty as I imagined you would be," Bob addressed the seven-year-old daughter he was meeting for the first time. He squatted down to be at eye level with her. "You look just like your mommy."

Katie looked dubiously at Grace, who pulled her into a protective hug from the side. "She certainly has my hair at least, don't you, honey?" Katie nodded at her mother, still unsure of what to say to this stranger.

"And you're Freddie," Bob continued, standing up and extending his hand to the ten-year-old. Freddie clumsily shook his father's hand. "Man, I haven't seen you since you were, what, two? Time flies, huh?"

Grace opened her mouth to make a sharp retort, but David

spoke first. "I guess you've heard we have twins now," he said in a slightly triumphant voice. "Charlotte and Evelyn. They're over there with Andy and Olivia." He gestured to the other side of the crowd where they could see Olivia throw her head back, apparently laughing at something Andy said.

"Ah, yes. I was wondering how long it would be before you had kids of your own. And twins at that, huh? Well played, Mr. Principal. Well played." He grinned at David, his expression a mixture of amusement and mocking. "I see Jackson's with them too."

"Yes. He chose not to join us over here with you," Grace said pointedly.

Bob's cocky expression faltered momentarily, but he recovered quickly. "Same old Jackson, huh? Will of iron. But hey, I did get to meet Griffin and Aaron. But Aaron's not—"

"That's right!" she interrupted hastily, not wanting to open the paternity can of worms in front of Katie and Freddie. She was certain Spencer was lurking around the premises somewhere, but she wasn't about to point him out to Bob. The less he knew, the better. "She and Aaron started dating after Griffin was born. We couldn't be happier that they're together."

"That's great, sweetie. It really is. I'm glad to see our girl happy."

David was practically turning blue next to her, and Grace knew it was taking all his self-control not to make a sharp comeback. Bob was particularly good at goading him.

"Yes. Well! Always interesting to see you again, Bob! Katie, Freddie, let's go get some pictures with Faith, shall we?" She hustled them away before turning back. "And, Bob, seriously, don't call me sweetie."

Bob just smirked as they walked away. "You got it, sweetheart," he called after her.

Despite the increased decibel level with everyone home from school for the summer, something was wrong with Jackson. He wasn't acting like himself. He was… Well, he was *behaving*. Jackson was usually the one to rile up his siblings and draw attention to himself and shout to be heard. But now he barely said anything to anyone. He sat quietly at meals, eating politely, and he even did his chores without objecting. Something was going on.

As soon as the girls were down for their naps, Grace knocked on the door to Freddie and Jackson's room. Freddie was outside, trying in vain to teach Pluto to roll over, so Jackson was alone in the room. When he summoned his mother in, she found him lying on the bed, staring dully at the ceiling.

"Hey, hon, you have a few minutes?" she asked.

"What'd I do wrong this time?" responded Jackson in a flat voice.

Grace's heart broke a little at the question. "Nothing at all, sweetie! I just want to see what's on your mind. You've been really distant lately. I can tell something is bothering you." She tentatively sat down next to him on the bed, not wanting to upset him.

Jackson didn't answer, but he squeezed his eyes shut and appeared to be trying not to cry. "Jackson, please. Tell me what's wrong," she begged, taking his hand in her own.

He did start crying then, a fact that truly alarmed Grace. Her fourteen-year-old was tough as nails. The last time Grace had seen him cry was… She honestly couldn't recall.

"Come here, Jackson," she invited, pulling him into a

protective embrace, fighting tears herself. She held his head to her chest and stroked his light brown hair the way she used to when he was younger. With a guilty twinge, she realized she couldn't remember the last time she'd truly hugged him. Her arms tightened around her son.

At length he spoke what was on his mind. "I don't want to be like him," he whispered fiercely.

Grace knew he was referring to Bob. "Be like him, how?" she asked.

"I don't even want to *look* like him! I don't want anything to do with him! He *left* us. He broke your heart and practically ruined our lives. You always tell me I'm strong-willed like Dad, but I just want everyone to stop comparing me to him!"

Grace's conscience was pricked. She *had* told Jackson a number of times that his personality was similar to Bob's. And his middle name was Robert, an obvious nod to his father. But it had never occurred to her that Jackson perceived these things as insults.

"Honey, I'm so sorry," she murmured. "You're absolutely right. I shouldn't compare you two. You are your own person, and you are *not* him. Jackson, look at me." She waited until he lifted his head to meet her eyes. "Never be ashamed of who you are. God made you exactly the way He intended. There's no one like you anywhere else on this earth, no matter how much you look like your father." She smoothed his hair back and tried not to dwell on her last statement. The older Jackson got, the more he resembled Bob when she'd first met him.

"In terms of personality, yes, you're strong-willed," she continued. "So are Aunt Livy and Uncle Andy! And yes, your father happens to have that trait as well. But that's just one small component of who you are. You have your own talents and interests that make you completely unique. You are *not* a clone of your father. You are you. And I love you exactly the way you are."

Jackson sniffled and wiped the back of his hand across his cheeks impatiently. Some of his spunk was returning. The real Jackson wouldn't be caught dead crying. "Thanks, Mom," he mumbled, clearly embarrassed by his vulnerability.

"You're welcome," she said, kissing him on the top of his head. "So you wanna go out and try to help Freddie with Pluto?" she asked, knowing he needed to move on to lighter topics. "Maybe if we can get that dog trained I'll actually let her in the house on occasion!"

Jackson snorted. "No way," he vowed. "I'm not wasting my time on that mutt. I have to start practicing for football. I want to be a starter on JV as a freshman. *Someone's* gotta help out their offense. It was terrible last year."

Grace smiled broadly. His boasting was further proof that he was feeling better. "Then you'd better get out there, mister," she teased. "The summer's wasting away!"

He chuckled and gave her a quick hug before he hopped off the bed and grabbed his football. "Thanks again, Mom. I love you." He reddened at the mushy sentiment and started to leave the room.

"Jackson!" He turned back. "I love you too."

"I know," he grinned, and left the room whistling cheerfully. Grace shook her head as he left. She never thought she'd say it, but she'd missed the old Jackson. The house was far too dull without him.

CHAPTER

13

Faith smiled across the lawn at Aaron, who was talking to some church members. They had decided to throw a joint graduation party at her house, and the backyard was crowded already. Faith's extended family had shown up in full force, and she had just introduced her cousins, Amber and Victoria, to her best friend, Chelsea.

Suddenly, Victoria's eyes widened as she looked beyond Faith and Chelsea. "Who is *that*?" she asked in a stage whisper.

Faith and Chelsea turned to see the latest arrival and froze as they saw Spencer sauntering through the gate. "Why is *he* here?" Chelsea asked, her eyes narrowing. "Did you invite him? I'm sure Aaron didn't."

Faith sighed heavily. She should have known he would come. "No, I didn't invite him, but I invited his mom out of obligation."

"So, who is it?" Victoria prompted. "Whoever he is, he's *gorgeous*."

Chelsea lowered her voice. "That's Griffin's father."

Victoria turned a deep shade of red as she realized the

connection. "Oh, gosh, I… I didn't know. I'm sorry, Faith… I just…"

"It's totally fine," Faith assured her. "He *is* cute. Why do you think I fell for him in the first place?"

The girls chuckled uneasily as Chelsea muttered, "Heads up, ladies. He spotted us."

Victoria looked terribly uncomfortable as Spencer approached with a confident smile. "Good day, ladies," he said grandly as he reached their group. He nodded civilly to Chelsea. "Congrats on your graduation, Miss Graves." Then he turned to Faith and kissed her cheek before handing her an envelope, which undoubtedly contained at least a few crisp one hundred dollar bills. "Congrats, kiddo. Mom couldn't make it, so I offered to bring her card. Which of course means she didn't dare venture to a backyard party. Her high heels might sink into the mud." Despite her flaming cheeks, Faith giggled at his astute description of his mother's real reason for not coming.

Amber and Victoria were staring unabashedly, and Chelsea glanced nervously in Aaron's direction, probably to see if he had witnessed the kiss.

"So who are these fair maidens?" Spencer continued, oblivious to the discomfort he was causing. "Church friends? Maybe I *should* check out your church after all…" He flashed a dazzling smile at Victoria, whose face was turning redder by the second.

"These are my cousins," Faith said. "Amber and Victoria Barlowe. Their mom is David's sister. They live in Wisconsin," she added pointedly.

"Too bad," Spencer sighed forlornly, still looking at Victoria. Chelsea faked a gag, but the girls were saved from having to respond by the appearance of Aaron and Justin.

"Spencer, what a surprise!" Justin exclaimed. "Didn't expect to see you here."

"Nor I," Aaron seconded with a *look* at Faith.

"Hey, man, what's up?" Spencer addressed Justin, shaking hands with him. "How's Tech? You playing football for them?" The McNeal twins had been on the Mapleport High football team with Spencer.

"Nah, no time for sports. I don't know how I'd manage with all the class work I have," Justin answered. "What about you? You aren't playing for U of M?"

Spencer snorted. "Yeah, right. I'm nowhere near their caliber." Then, as if noticing Aaron for the first time, he said, "Ah, Aaron! Congrats to you too. Off to Concordia come fall?"

"That's right," said Aaron shortly.

"And I'm going to CMU, thanks for asking," Chelsea inserted sarcastically.

"Central Michigan, huh? Mount Pleasant. Which is neither on a mountain, nor is it pleasant. But hey, good for you! Got your major picked out yet?"

"Not a clue."

"Don't feel bad. I don't know what I want to go into, either," Victoria said. "I'm going to the University of Wisconsin come fall. I just signed up for core classes for the first semester."

Spencer grinned at her. "Then congratulations are in order for you as well, Miss Barlowe. My, my, we do have a lot of recent graduates here, don't we? Well, I don't want to intrude. Just came by to drop off Mom's card. Have fun this afternoon. See you on Friday, Faith." With that, he gave a cheery wave and sidled away, whistling a tuneless melody.

Chelsea cringed at his comment, and four pairs of eyes turned questioningly to Faith, who felt the blood drain from her face. "So! That was Spencer!" she said brightly. "Let me just go put this card inside and see if Griffin's still napping. Excuse me, please."

"I'll join you," said Aaron dryly, matching her quick gait as she hurried to the house. When they got inside, he turned to her with narrowed eyes. "Care to explain what *that* was all about?"

Faith moaned. Leave it to Spencer to bring up the Friday visit thing in front of everyone. She hadn't even told Aaron about it yet, a fact which did not bode well for her at this moment.

"So, I… he…um, he asked if he could watch Griffin one day a week during the summer, so…"

"Faith! Are you serious? That was the reason you didn't take a summer job—so you wouldn't have to worry about what to do with Griffin! And now you're farming him off to Spencer once a week? I knew it! I *knew* something like this was gonna happen. And you're just letting him do it!"

"Aaron! He is Griffin's *father*! I can't very well tell him he can't see his son!"

"Yes, you can! He shirked his responsibilities from the beginning! He gave up any so-called rights he ever had!"

"But he's different now!" Faith insisted. "Besides, I don't want him to feel like he has to stoop to legal means to get his way."

Aaron gave a mirthless chuckle and shook his head. "Does your stepfather know about this?"

"Oh, please! I don't need to get *Daddy's* permission for every little thing I do! I'm a big girl!"

"I just wonder what he and your mom think about it. Personally, I don't like it at all."

"Neither do I."

"Then tell him you changed your mind. He's doing this to get close to *you*, you know. Griffin is secondary."

Faith bit her lip to hold back her defensive response. "Please, Aaron, let's not get into a fight," she pleaded. "Not today. Not here. This is supposed to be a happy time. Let's not give Spencer the satisfaction of ruining our graduation open house. I don't know what he's really up to, but I'm not interested in him at all. I love *you*. You don't have to worry about Spencer. Let's just forget he was even here today and go out there and enjoy the rest of the day. Please?"

He blew out a slow breath. "You're right," he agreed. "No more fighting."

"Good." She gave him a long kiss, and when she pulled back, she gave him the most dazzling smile she could. "*That's* what I want to remember about today." After peeking in on Griffin to ensure he was still sleeping, she took Aaron's hand to go back outside.

The rest of the afternoon was less eventful, and by the last half hour, things were starting to wind down. Since it was getting toward dinner time, David suggested ordering pizza to go along with the leftovers from the party. There were twenty-five people between all the family members, even if three of them were babies who wouldn't eat the pizza. David and Andy were about to leave to pick up the order when Pastor and Ann Lixon walked in.

"I'm so sorry," Pastor apologized. "We planned to be here two hours ago, but as we were getting ready to leave, I got a call that Edgar Miller was taken to the hospital. We spent the afternoon there."

"Oh, no!" exclaimed Grace. "Is he okay?"

"Thankfully, yes. He collapsed, and Betty feared he'd had a heart attack or a stroke. She was frantic when she called me.

From the sounds of it, I thought he was in critical condition. Turns out he was dehydrated and got a bit of heat stroke while working in his garden. That's the good kind of hospital visit, though. I wish all of them were that easy."

"We're glad you could make it. And I'm glad Edgar is okay," David said. "Help yourselves to whatever food is left, and stick around until we get back with the pizza."

"We don't need to stay," Pastor protested. "It's family time now. We just wanted to drop off our card and assure you we hadn't forgotten."

"What's two more people?" joked Grace. "Come on, I'll introduce you to David's family." She led them to his parents before they could protest.

Half an hour later, everyone did their part to polish off the eight large pizzas David had ordered, settling around the folding tables and chairs set up in the backyard.

"So you're off to my alma mater, huh, Aaron?" Pastor Lixon addressed him.

"Oh, really? You went to Concordia, Ann Arbor, too? I didn't realize that," replied Aaron.

Nodding, Pastor said, "It was a junior college when I was there. I went to Ann Arbor for two years, then on to Fort Wayne senior college for two years before moving on to seminary. I have good memories of Ann Arbor."

"Such as…?" prompted Mark Sullivan, Aaron's dad.

Pastor laughed. "There was one time some of us decided to rewrite the signs for the dorms. They're all named after people from the Bible—Miriam, Sarah, Jonathan, Timothy, and so on. I was in Ruth dorm myself. We made new signs in Hebrew for the Old Testament names and Greek for the New Testament ones, then hung them over the door to each dorm. Then instead of referring to the 'east' and 'west' sides of campus, we called them the 'Greek side' and the 'Hebrew side.'"

"That's such a nerdy pastoral thing to do," Ann teased her husband.

Her comment elicited laughs from the assembly, and Carol asked, "So is that where you two met?" Faith was surprised her grandmother had spoken up around so many other people.

"Actually, no. We didn't meet until he was at the seminary," Ann said.

"A friend of mine was the field worker at her church," Pastor explained. "He set us up on a blind date. Only after we were on the date did I realize the term had a double meaning. She was a special education teacher and taught a classroom of students who were blind."

"Didn't see that one coming," quipped Walt. Faith rolled her eyes at her grandpa's humor. He was a hopeless punster.

Amidst the chuckles and groans, Pastor continued. "The other guys at the sem teased me that I was dating a blind lady, and I was scared she would be offended, but instead she rose to the occasion. She came to visit me on campus and drove up wearing sunglasses, then got out of the car with a cane as if she really was blind. She had me from then on."

Ann smiled. "We were married within a year so I could go with him on vicarage."

"I don't think her father quite knew what to make of that," Pastor said. "Fathers can be very protective of their daughters."

Trevor guffawed, and Greg shot his son-in-law a warning glance. "Don't go there," he cautioned.

Sally giggled. "Oh, Dad, it's not *so* terrible."

Greg sighed wearily. "Go ahead. I'll never live this one down."

"When Sally and I got engaged, we called her parents to tell them the news," Trevor began. "We were both on the line, and when Sally told them about our engagement, Greg asked me, 'What's your last name again?'"

Everyone burst out laughing, and Mary Anne spoke up to defend her husband. "Mind you, they were both in Wisconsin, and we were in Michigan. We'd only met him once when we went to visit."

"Still, Grandpa, that's embarrassing," Victoria giggled. "You could at least have asked Grandma after you hung up!"

"She didn't know either!"

More laughter followed his remark, and Jason spoke up as he reached for another piece of pizza. "At least Aaron doesn't have to worry about that," he said with a wink at Faith. "But getting back to college, let me give you recent high school grads a bit of advice. Never park in the staff lot."

Justin chuckled knowingly as his twin brother continued. "So I was running late to class one day—"

"You're *always* running late to class," Justin interrupted.

"Hardly the point! Anyway, the student lot was packed. I couldn't find anywhere to park. So I figured, what the heck? I'll park in the staff lot. Only an hour, right? No one will even notice. But when I came back out at the end of class, sure enough, I had a parking ticket on my windshield."

"It gets better. Wait for it..." inserted Justin with a mischievous grin.

"So then I was running late again the next day," Jason continued, "and the same thing happened! Student lot was full again! So I thought, hey, I'll park in the staff lot and just leave that ticket on my windshield so it looks like I've already gotten a ticket. Genius, right? But when I came back out, there was a second ticket on top of the other one, and a note on the back said, 'Old tickets don't work.'"

Laughter again rang through the backyard, and Andy boasted, "That's my boy. Sounds just like something I would try."

"Unfortunately, it does," Olivia agreed. "The apple doesn't fall far from the tree. Let's not even get into the stuff *you* pulled in college."

"My junior year, my fraternity decided to get a Christmas tree—" Andy began, but his wife cut him off.

"Oh my gosh, that was *disgusting*! Don't tell them about that!"

"How can a Christmas tree be disgusting?" asked Sally, grinning.

"They decorated it with *underwear*! Everyone donated a pair. How nasty is that?"

"Awesome!" Jackson breathed in admiration, as everyone else either shuddered or laughed.

"Do *not* suggest that to your dorm mates, young man!" Amy warned Aaron.

"It's not Aaron I'm worried about," moaned Grace. "I know that look on Jackson's face. He's filing that away for future reference. Thanks, Uncle Andy."

"I do what I can," Andy said humbly, then lowered his voice to an exaggerated whisper. "See me later, Jackson. I'll give you all sorts of great ideas." Grace did a face palm as Jackson gave his uncle a thumbs up.

Everyone laughed, and Pastor grinned at David. "This is one of the things I most love about being a pastor," he said. "Spending time with families and getting to know them. We aren't related to a single soul here, but no one questions our presence. We're accepted into your midst almost as part of the family."

"You may as well be," Grace insisted. "You know practically our entire life stories!"

"Hey, anyone up for bocce ball?" Jason asked the assembly at large. "C'mon, Jackson, I know you'll play. Faith? Aaron? Pastor?"

Pastor chuckled and rose from the table. "I suppose that's our cue to leave, Ann," he joked. "We may be practically family, but I must draw the line at lawn games."

His comment drew laughter once again, and everyone started to disperse. Faith smiled in satisfaction as she helped clean up. It had been a wonderful party, and even Spencer hadn't managed to ruin the day.

CHAPTER 14

Summer was a rude awakening for Faith. While the rest of her newly-graduated classmates were off earning money with summer jobs and hanging out together on weekends, she helped her mom take care of the babies and wondered how on earth her mother ever got anything done around the house at all. Caring for three babies was exhausting, physically and mentally. It had been difficult to work around Griffin's schedule while she was in school, but this was challenging in a completely different way. She'd never realized how taxing it was to be around such young children all the time, and she found she wasn't nearly as patient as she'd once thought. Now she was grateful for her arrangement with Spencer so she could get a day to herself once a week.

One Friday in July, Faith decided it was high time to broach two subjects that had been weighing upon her mind. As Spencer ushered her into his house to pick up Griffin, she asked, "Do you have a few minutes?"

"For you, anything," he said with a wide grin. "Make yourself comfortable. What's on your mind?"

Faith pulled out a form and handed it to him as she perched on the couch. "I need you to fill out a family health history," she said. "I don't know anything about your family at all, and Griffin should know if there are any health concerns on your side."

"That's a good point," Spencer agreed. "Men in my family tend to have heart problems. My dad had a heart attack about ten years ago, and my grandpa died of one. Plus one of my uncles had a leaky valve that required surgery. Maybe that's partly why I want to go into cardiology." He fell into silence as he worked through the form.

When he handed it back to Faith, he said, "Hopefully the only thing he inherited from me is dashingly good looks." Spencer wiggled his eyebrows at her with a mischievous smile on his face, and she laughed.

"I'm glad to see your old ego is still alive and well," she teased, then leaned forward and turned serious again. "Listen, Spencer, there's something else I want to talk to you about. I feel like we didn't completely finish the conversation that night at Le Poisson. I have more I need to say to you."

"Go ahead," he invited, leaning back into the armchair as he crossed one ankle over the opposite knee.

"I'm not sure I really communicated what I meant when we were talking about religion. I don't know what exactly you believe about God, but I want you to at least know what I believe."

He looked surprised by her comment. Frowning slightly, he answered, "Go on."

"You mentioned that you wanted to ask my forgiveness as part of your journey in getting right with God." She paused as he nodded in affirmation. "But the way you said that made it seem like there was something *you* need to do to earn heaven.

That's not how it works. Jesus did it all, Spencer. You don't have to do anything else. The work is done."

"Sure, *His* work is done. But now I have to do mine. I need to live a life that glorifies Him and follows His example."

"So who is responsible for your salvation? Jesus? Or you?"

"Jesus, of course. But I also have to live a life pleasing to Him."

"Or what? You won't go to heaven?" Spencer looked slightly confused as he considered how to answer her question, so she continued. "See, here's the thing. If Jesus isn't one hundred percent responsible for my salvation, I'll never get to heaven. There's no way I can ever glorify Him enough or live a good enough life to please Him. It's all His work. None of mine."

"But that seems to be an excuse to just live any old way," argued Spencer. "Like saying, 'Oh, I can't be good enough, so I won't even try. I'll just keep on sinning because God will forgive me anyhow.' It's sort of an easy way out. No offense."

"But that's not what I'm saying at all," she insisted. "Yes, Christians are called to live a godly life, but that's not what saves us. And there's no way anyone on this earth can ever get to a point where they stop sinning. It's impossible. No matter how hard I try, I will never be perfect. Every day I sin. I'll always need God's forgiveness."

"Why is this such a big deal to you? I don't have to believe exactly what you believe, do I?"

"No, but I'd like to know that you at least believe in Jesus."

"I do."

"Okay. Well... good." It wasn't the strongest confession of faith she'd ever heard, but then again, she never would have been able to have this kind of conversation with Spencer a year ago. He *had* changed for the better, and if it was his newfound faith that made the difference, then obviously it was impacting his life positively. Faith was glad his roommate had kept after him about going to church.

"You know," he said with a sly grin, "I've been to your church already. Why not come with me once and give it a try? You might like it more than you think you will."

"Nice try, Spencer. Very suave," Faith returned with an eye roll. "Aaron would never let me live it down if I went out with you, even to church. Nor would you."

He laughed good-naturedly. "Got that right," he admitted.

She checked the time on her phone and stood. "I'd better get going. Griffin and I have an invitation to eat with the Sullivans tonight."

"Enjoy," Spencer said, standing as well. "And hey, maybe you two could stay and eat dinner here next week? My dad will actually be home, and he hasn't seen Griffin in ages. I know he'd like to see him again."

Faith squirmed. She didn't want to accept the invitation, but she could hardly refuse. Leonard Young didn't seem the doting grandfather type, yet it was only fair for him to see his grandson. She stifled a grimace, knowing he'd trapped her.

"Alright, we'll come," she answered, hoping she wouldn't live to regret the decision.

"Excellent!" exclaimed Spencer, a happy smile lighting up his face. "See you next Friday, then!"

"Next Friday," she confirmed, then picked up Griffin and carried him outside before Spencer could trick her into anything else. She hadn't the faintest clue how she would explain this one to Aaron.

CHAPTER 15

The ringing of the doorbell interrupted Sunday's family movie night, and David exchanged a frown with Grace. The babies were down, and everyone else had settled in to watch *Shrek* together. Even Aaron was there, lying next to Faith on the floor, a bowl of popcorn between them. They weren't expecting any visitors.

David slipped off the couch and walked to the front door to find his neighbor standing there, looking slightly uncomfortable.

"Ken! What can I do for you?" he asked in surprise. They regularly exchanged pleasantries outside, but weren't in the habit of making house calls on one another, especially not in the evening.

"Hi, David. Sorry to bother you like this." He shifted his weight from one foot to the other. "I wonder if I could show you something?"

David was taken aback, but followed Ken across the Neunabers' yard and up to the Morellos' garage, where the side window was broken. His stomach tensed. He knew exactly what had happened.

"I'm really sorry to have to bring this up, David, and I don't want to get anyone in trouble, but I'm pretty sure your boy did this. Jackson was out here earlier this afternoon, throwing the ball. I think he was trying to hit that tree." He indicated a large elm in the Neunabers' front yard. "Like target practice or something. But when I came out later to get a beer from the fridge in the garage, I noticed the window. And this was on the floor."

He held out a white baseball that David immediately recognized as Jackson's. He sighed wearily and took the ball from his neighbor's hand.

"Go easy on him," pleaded Ken. "He's just a kid. I broke a window or two myself in my day. It's a boy thing. But I do ask that we work something out to replace the window…" He trailed off.

"We will cover the cost of a new window," David assured him. "It's only fair. Our homeowner's insurance will probably take care of it, but we'll still have Jackson work it off with chores. He has to take responsibility for his actions. What bothers me most is that he didn't tell anyone about it."

"Aw, he was probably just scared," Ken insisted. "Like I said, I don't want to get anyone in trouble."

"Well, I'll talk to him and check on our homeowner's policy. We'll be in touch."

"Sure thing, David. Thanks."

David left to go back to his own house, silently seething at Jackson for neglecting to tell them about the window. By the time he walked in the front door, he was fuming. He stormed into the living room, and when everyone looked up in alarm, he pointed at Jackson and said, "Come with me. Now."

He led the way to Jackson and Freddie's room upstairs.

When the door was shut, Jackson demanded, "What gives? Why are you mad at me?"

Rather than respond, David held out the baseball. Jackson looked at it and shrugged. "So what? It's a baseball. Big deal."

"Yes, it *is* a big deal, Jackson! You threw this ball through the Morellos' garage window and didn't tell anyone about it! Did you think no one would notice? You think they weren't going to figure out what happened?"

"Why would you think I did something so stupid?"

"Jackson! He *saw* you in the front yard this afternoon, tossing the ball at the tree! I get that you want to practice your pitching, but seriously? Could you pick a worse place?"

"Exactly! I'm not that dumb! If I want to pitch, I do it against the fence in the backyard so I don't have to chase it all over the place. I don't aim at a tree!"

The kid had a point, but David shook his head. "Mr. Morello saw you practicing, Jackson. And then he found this in the garage near the broken window. How else would you explain it?"

"I don't know! But it wasn't me!"

"Okay, Jackson. Stop. Just stop. I know you don't want to get into trouble, but you're digging yourself deeper. If you would have confessed from the very start, I wouldn't be nearly as upset. But the fact that you didn't tell anyone, and now you're *still* trying to deny it—that's inexcusable. I find lying very detestable, Jackson."

"I'm not lying!"

Jackson glared at him, and David glared right back. His stepson was impossible sometimes. "Until you're ready to tell the truth, you are not allowed out of this house. You will apologize to Mr. Morello, and you will work off the cost of that window by doing extra chores. For every day that goes by without a confession, you add five dollars to the total cost of the window. This could be a very expensive denial for you, young man. And in case it isn't obvious, you're done with the movie tonight. You can stay here and think about your options. Good night."

He left the room despite Jackson's protests and yelling, then walked down the hall to his own room rather than going back downstairs to finish the movie with everyone else. He wasn't in the mood anymore.

CHAPTER 16

That Friday, Faith arrived at the Youngs' house in the late afternoon so she and Griffin could stay for dinner. She still wasn't comfortable doing so, and she felt guilty because she hadn't told Aaron. She figured he didn't need to know. It was just dinner with Spencer and his parents so Mr. Young could see his grandson. Innocent enough, right?

Yet when Spencer greeted her with his signature kiss on the cheek, wearing his dark blue shirt, Faith realized he might not think it was so innocuous after all. Her heart sank, but there was no backing out now.

Spencer led her into the kitchen where Mrs. Young was hovering over Griffin in his booster chair, attempting to decipher what the toddler was trying to tell her. Griffin was clearly exasperated with Spencer's mom, and his shouts of, "No!" were becoming increasingly agitated.

"Oh, darling, thank *heavens*!" exclaimed Mrs. Young. "I haven't the faintest idea what he wants. Can you figure it out?"

"Hi, buddy!" Faith greeted her son as she gave him a small hug. "What do you need?"

"No! No!" he shrieked, pointing to the counter.

Glancing behind her, Faith chuckled. "He wants an orange," she informed them, walking over to grab a clementine from the fruit bowl.

She peeled it and gave a slice to Griffin, who stuffed it into his mouth, juice dribbling down his chin. "No!" he yelled with a full mouth, reaching out for more.

"How do you get 'orange' from 'no'?" asked Spencer.

Faith shrugged. "Best I can figure is that we say, 'an orange.' Maybe he thinks we say, 'a norange.'"

Spencer shook his head in amazement, while Vivian took her place by the stove, stirring something in a pot now that Griffin had been pacified. "Darling, I'm so glad you can join us for dinner tonight. Help yourself to some snacks over there." She waved her manicured hand in the direction of the kitchen island, where a tray of cut vegetables sat next to a bowl of pita chips. Faith piled a plate with chips, baby carrots, celery, grape tomatoes, and broccoli before taking her place by Griffin again.

Sliding into the chair next to her, Spencer covertly handed her three Oreos with a sly smile and a finger over his lips. She stifled a giggle and popped one into her mouth with a thumbs up.

As Vivian chatted about the events of the day, Faith heard the door open, and shortly thereafter Mr. Leonard Young walked in. He set his briefcase down by the built-in desk and walked over to his wife as they greeted each other with an air kiss to each cheek. Faith raised an eyebrow at Spencer, who shrugged and rolled his eyes.

"They're weird," he whispered. "I seriously have *no* idea how I ever came into existence."

Faith giggled as Mr. Young turned to walk to the table. He extended his hand cordially to her and said, "Ms. Williams, a pleasure to see you again."

Even though she and Spencer had dated for four months in high school, Faith had only met Mr. Young a handful of times. He was the vice president of his company and spent a lot of time in the office or on business trips, often overseas. Honestly, the man intimidated Faith, and she rather suspected he didn't think very highly of her for keeping a baby that reflected badly on his teenage son, and therefore, on him.

Next, Mr. Young turned to Griffin. "My goodness," he said. "He's the spitting image of Spencer at that age, isn't he, dear? It's like going back twenty-five years."

"Uh, Dad, I'm nineteen. Callan's twenty-five," Spencer reminded him.

"Yes, of course, son." Leonard turned to the mini bar along the side wall and poured himself a scotch while Faith exchanged a look with Spencer. There was an awkward pause until Vivian spoke up brightly, trying to smooth over her husband's faux pas.

"Griffin does favor Spencer, doesn't he? And, darling, he's such an amicable little fellow. Follows me around the house, babbling happily. So sweet. Makes me miss those days with our boys."

"What was Spencer like as a child?" Faith asked with a sideways grin at him.

"Oh, darling, he was every bit as charming then as he is now," gushed Vivian. "Just look at his beautiful blue eyes! Why, he could get me to do just about anything."

"Probably why he was so spoiled," inserted Leonard. "He was a mama's boy, that's for sure."

Spencer looked embarrassed by his father's observation, and Vivian swooped in to rescue her son. "All boys are mama's boys when they're little," she scolded. "Parker and Callan were the same way. And they've all turned out just fine."

Leonard looked pointedly at Faith over the top of his half glasses as he took his place at the table, and she felt herself redden. It would appear that because of *her*, Mr. Young had his doubts that Spencer had, indeed, "turned out just fine."

"Dinner is ready!" Vivian continued cheerily. "Let's eat!"

Faith noted with surprise that Mrs. Young had prepared pork chops with apples and butternut squash. She'd been expecting something with tofu or quinoa or some other ingredient she'd never tasted. There was a side of steamed cauliflower and a spinach and strawberry salad. Everything looked delicious.

After a few minutes of silence as everyone concentrated on helping themselves to the food, Mr. Young addressed Faith to ask, "So why did you pick the name Griffin?"

"It means 'strong in faith,'" she answered. "I thought it was the perfect meaning."

"Huh," he responded, clearly unimpressed. "I guess that's the kind of name I'd expect from a teenager."

"Dad!" Spencer chastised as heat rose to Faith's cheeks again. "It *is* the perfect name for him. I couldn't have picked a better name myself."

"And I couldn't imagine any other name for him either," Vivian pronounced loyally, then swiftly changed the subject. "So, dear, is there any news on your latest deal?" she prompted her husband.

His eyes lit up. "Actually, yes! Our Hong Kong venue is a go! I'll be flying over there next week to start the process on their end."

"Leonard! That's wonderful!" gasped Vivian. "Oh, darling, congratulations!"

He smiled proudly as he turned to Faith. "We're opening up

some plants in Hong Kong," he explained. "It was my idea, but it was a hard sell. It'll be a lot of work, but I think in the end it will be well worth our while."

"Wow! That's exciting!" Faith said. "Have you been there before, or will this be your first trip?"

"Oh, yes, dozens of times," Leonard assured her with a wave of his hand. "It's a wonderful, vibrant city. It'll be a pleasure to go back. But this also means I'll need you at the office, son." He turned to Spencer and fixed him with a hard stare. "I don't want you distracted by girls or babies."

Spencer and Faith both reddened at his blunt statement, and Faith wondered why she had bothered to accept the dinner invitation in the first place. Leonard obviously cared very little one way or the other if he ever saw his poorly-named grandchild. He seemed not to care much even about his own son's feelings, a fact which both saddened and angered Faith. Before she could stop herself, she spoke out boldly.

"Spencer has been a huge help with Griffin since he came home from college. I know you need him at the office, and I can work around that with Griffin this week, but he's really been great with his son, and I think you should be proud of him."

All three of the Youngs looked at her in astonishment as she finished, and she held Mr. Young's gaze stubbornly, her chin jutted out, almost challenging him to defy her statement. She honestly didn't care what he thought of her anymore, but she didn't want him belittling his own son in her presence.

Leonard cleared his throat, but Vivian spoke up before her husband could reply. "Yes, Spencer *has* been good with Griffin, and I think Griffin adores him. It's sweet to see them interact. But if your father needs you at the office, Spencer, I can watch Griffin next Friday."

Faith could tell Spencer was still chagrined by his father's tactlessness, but his mother deftly changed the subject yet again. "So! Faith, dearest, why don't you tell us about your siblings, hmm? Your household is much more exciting than our own! I can't even keep track of everyone. Do tell us about your family, won't you?"

Faith followed her lead to safer ground. Mrs. Young knew all about her siblings, despite what she said. She was doing this for her husband's sake, probably to keep him from saying anything else for the time being. The majority of the remaining conversation was carried along by Faith, with Vivian inserting questions to encourage her. Spencer contributed a few comments, but Mr. Young sat in silence the rest of the meal, occasionally checking his phone. Faith doubted he was even listening.

After she helped clear the table, Mrs. Young shooed Faith out of the kitchen. "It's getting toward Griffin's bedtime, I imagine, darling. Spencer will walk you out. Thank you for coming. It's always so good to see you."

"Yes, I probably should be getting back," agreed Faith. "Thank you so much for having me. The food was delicious. Mr. Young, good to see you again."

He nodded curtly to her, then turned his eyes back to his phone. Faith took Griffin by the hand and started to leave. Spencer followed. When she had gotten Griffin strapped into his seat, she turned to Spencer. "Thanks for inviting me over."

Spencer kicked at a pebble on the driveway. "Yeah, well… I… It's not…" He sighed and tried again. "Thanks for sticking up for me earlier. I don't know if you really meant what you said, but it was good to hear it anyhow. My dad…" He trailed off and looked into the distance. "He's not the most affectionate guy in the world, and he can come across as rude.

He's a great businessman, but social graces aren't high on his list of talents. That's what my mom is for." Spencer attempted a chuckle. "He... I..."

"Hey," Faith interrupted. "I *did* mean what I said. You've been wonderful with Griffin since you came back, and I'm glad you're making the effort to be part of his life now. You're a good guy, Spencer, and I hope your dad sees that too."

"Thanks, Faith," he said quietly.

In response, she patted him on the cheek before climbing into the driver's seat. "Don't worry about next week. Go work with your dad on the Hong Kong deal. Just let me know when you want to take Griffin again."

"I'm telling you, I'm not looking forward to this week at all. My dad makes me do this internship thing for him in the summers, but I don't like it. Office work isn't my thing. I've half a mind to stay at U of M next summer and take classes to avoid this."

"You'll do fine," she assured him with a smile. She waved at him as she backed out and drove away, her mind still on the interaction between Spencer and his father. For both their sakes she hoped their relationship wasn't always so strained. She didn't have a great rapport with her birth father, but her stepfather was a decent guy, and she'd always sort of taken that for granted. But now, as she drove back to her own house, she had the overwhelming urge to go home and give David a big hug.

CHAPTER 17

By the weekend, Jackson was stubbornly holding out on his confession. David had called earlier in the week to inquire about their homeowner's policy and was happy to find that they would cover the cost. Still, it gnawed at him that Jackson refused to own up to his actions, even after nearly a week. Grace had tried talking to him about it as well, and he still insisted he hadn't thrown the ball through the window.

On Saturday afternoon, David was pulling the lawn mower out of the garage when Ken pulled into his driveway next door. He got out of his car and waved to David as he approached. David suppressed a groan.

"Howdy, neighbor!" Ken greeted him jovially. It seemed that in his mind the recent window episode had launched their relationship to a new level of camaraderie.

"Hey, Ken. How's it going?"

"I'm fine. You?"

"Not bad, thanks. But I'm still after Jackson to tell the truth about your window. I didn't think he'd deny it outright, especially after you saw him throwing the ball in the yard."

"He's just scared, I'm sure," said Ken, waving it off. "I mean, he's what? Ten, maybe?"

David chuckled. "He may act like he's ten, but Jackson is fourteen."

"Wait—Jackson is the older one?" Ken asked, his brow creased in a slight frown.

"Yes. Freddie is nine."

"Ohh," Ken groaned, realization dawning on his face. "David, it was Freddie, then. Jackson is telling the truth. It was the younger boy I saw throwing the ball."

David's heart nearly stopped. "Are you sure?" he asked. "Freddie doesn't even play baseball. Jackson is the one who loves sports."

"It was definitely the younger one. I'm sorry for the confusion. I hope it didn't cause a family rift or anything."

David didn't dare admit that it had done just that. Jackson had barely said a word to anyone all week. Poor Jackson. He had to go talk to him immediately.

"Ken, I'm glad we got this straightened out," he said hastily. "I need to go talk to the boys again. Excuse me."

Moments later, he ran up the stairs two at a time to knock on Jackson's door. When Jackson answered, he glared at his stepfather and said sarcastically, "No, I'm not ready to *confess* yet, because I didn't throw the stupid ball through that stupid window! No one in this house ever believes me! I'm guilty of every single thing that ever goes wrong around here! I—"

"I know, Jackson. You're right," interrupted David. "And I'm sorry."

Jackson looked at him in surprise and with a fair degree of suspicion. David continued. "I just talked to Mr. Morello, and he said it wasn't you throwing the ball. It was Freddie. He got your names mixed up. I didn't think to ask him about it, because Freddie doesn't even play baseball. You were the logical candidate. But I was wrong to assume you were guilty despite your protests. You were telling the truth all along, and I should have believed you. I'm very sorry. Will you forgive me?"

Now Jackson looked uncomfortable. He wasn't usually on this end of an apology. "Yeah, whatever," he mumbled. "It's fine."

"No, it's not. I assumed you were guilty without listening to your side of the story. And I was fully prepared to dole out the consequences regardless of whether or not you ever confessed. I'm sorry I put you in that position, and I'm sorry I didn't trust you. I don't want you to think that I always assume you're the one to cause trouble."

"Usually I am," Jackson pointed out. "When was the last time Freddie got into trouble?"

"Now."

Jackson actually laughed at that. "But before this. He's usually really good. Me, though—I don't know. I can't help myself. I don't *try* to get in trouble. It just happens."

"I know how you feel," David said. "I got into trouble a lot as a kid myself. Remember when I told you I took a Walkman from Radio Shack in junior high?"

"Yeah, even though I don't know what a Walkman is."

"No, I guess you wouldn't," he chuckled. "Before iPods and MP3 players, they had portable CD players. Before *that*, they had portable cassette players called Walkmans."

Jackson shrugged, still uncomprehending, but David continued anyhow. "At any rate, I tried to steal one. And that's not the only thing I did. My mother could tell you all sorts of stories. I set fire to the carpet, I scraped our neighbor's car with my bike—on purpose, mind you—I threw a frisbee in the house and broke our expensive cuckoo clock, and I even clogged our drain-out pipe for the water line by stuffing rocks down it. They had to dig the pipes out with a backhoe because it was winter, and the ground was frozen. My mother was *not* pleased, I assure you." As an adult now, he had a new appreciation for the expense that had been for his parents.

"I was every bit as active and energetic as you," he continued. "And that's not necessarily a bad thing. It's good to be curious and excited about the world around you. Besides, active kids have better stories to tell when they're adults. I bet my childhood stories are *way* more interesting than your mom's." He winked at Jackson, who chuckled again.

"That's true," said Jackson. "Aunt Livy has some decent stories, but not Mom."

"Let's not hold it against her, though," David teased. "Despite it all, she turned out to be pretty cool. But, Jackson," he said, turning serious again, "I hope you won't hold this window fiasco against me, either. I was wrong to blame you. And in the future, I'll try very hard to truly listen to you. Will you forgive me? No hard feelings?"

"No hard feelings," Jackson assured him.

"Thank you. It takes a lot of character to forgive someone when you've been unjustly accused. Many people carry grudges afterward. You're a fine young man, Jackson. I'm proud of you. And I love you."

He scarcely dared to breath after his last comment. He'd never told Jackson that before in so many words, and he wasn't at all sure how this tough fourteen-year-old would handle the sentiment.

Jackson turned bright red and mumbled, "Yeah, well, don't get all sappy on me. You're okay too. Most of the time."

David grinned like a fool. Coming from Jackson, that was high praise indeed. He reached out and tousled his stepson's hair and hightailed it out of the room before Jackson could ruin the moment. He wasn't about to push his luck.

Taking a deep breath, David stepped out into the backyard where Freddie was playing with Pluto. He honestly had no idea how to proceed. He'd never had to discipline Freddie beyond a warning voice.

"Hey, Freddie? Can I talk to you for a sec?" he called.

Freddie trotted over. "What's up?"

"What can you tell me about the Morellos' broken window?"

Freddie turned white. "What about it?" he whispered.

"Was it you who threw the ball through it?"

Freddie looked down for a long moment. "Yes," he confessed, so quietly David could barely hear him.

"Freddie, why didn't you tell us? You should have come in and said something after it happened so we could have dealt with it right away. But even so, you *still* didn't say anything after Jackson got in trouble for it. You let him take your punishment. That's not fair, and you know it. I'm very disappointed that you made such a choice."

"I know," admitted Freddie, still staring at his shoes. "But I was afraid you'd be mad at me if I said anything. I figured you'd yell at Jackson and that would be the end of it. I didn't think it would turn into something bigger."

"What do you think I should do now, Freddie? What punishment should you get?"

"I don't know. I don't usually get punished."

That was a fact. "First of all, you owe Jackson an apology," David began. "And you owe the Morellos an apology as well. The window itself isn't a big deal in the grand scheme of things. But you need to tell him the truth. He's honestly not mad about the window. Accidents happen. But that being said, you *do* need to take some responsibility. You can do chores for me to help pay for the replacement. Instead of getting an allowance, your earnings will go toward a new window."

David paused. That was a good start, but he still had to address the deeper issue. "What concerns me most of all, Freddie," he continued, "is the fact that you tried to cover this up. You deliberately chose not to tell the truth, which is the same thing as lying. Since your lying affected Jackson this entire week, you may take his after-dinner chores all of next week, in addition to your own. You will sweep *and* do dishes each night. Understood?"

Freddie nodded meekly. "I'm really sorry, Dad. I should have told you and Mom when it happened. Then we wouldn't have had all this mess."

"I forgive you, Freddie. Thank you for the apology." David reached out to give him a hug, but his curiosity got the better of him. "Just one question, though. Why were you playing baseball in the first place? You don't even like the sport."

"Matt told me I throw like a girl. I was practicing so I could prove him wrong. But I don't think it helped much."

David hid a smile at the admission. "Then let me suggest one thing more. When you apologize to Jackson, why don't you ask him to give you some pointers? At least enough to help you show Matt you can throw."

"Do you think he'd do it?" Freddie asked, his forehead creased as he looked at David. "He's probably mad at me."

"I think Jackson would do anything that helps him show off his athletic skills." The two exchanged a smile, then David reached for Freddie's hand. "Come on," he invited. "Let's go talk to your brother together."

CHAPTER 18

As another Sunday movie night drew to a close, Faith grinned at Aaron. They'd watched *Tangled*, a favorite for both Faith and Katie. Despite her brothers' protests that it was a girl's movie, they'd watched and enjoyed it too. Now as Grace and David sent Katie and Freddie off to bed, Faith walked Aaron out to the front porch.

The two sat together on the porch swing, Aaron's arm around Faith. She put her head on his shoulder, and they sat in companionable silence for a few moments until he spoke. "Want to come for dinner on Friday? The summer is more than half over already. I can't believe I have to start thinking about packing for college. We need to make the most of the time we have left. You free?"

"Sure, that'll work," Faith said. "Griffin and I will go to your place after I get him from Spencer's. And it'll give me a good excuse in case he asks me to stay for dinner again." Too late, she realized what she'd just admitted.

She felt Aaron tense next to her. "So now you're having family dinners together?" he asked with an edge to his voice.

"And you didn't tell me?"

"It's nothing, Aaron," she protested, sitting up and turning so she could face him. "He asked me one time. That's it. His dad was home and Spencer thought he'd like to see Griffin."

"When was this?"

"I don't know…" she faltered. "Two weeks ago, maybe?"

"And you're just now telling me this?"

"Am I supposed to report to you every little thing I do?" she asked defensively. This balancing act between Aaron and Spencer was getting rather old. "I don't need your permission to eat dinner with a friend!"

"I'm not asking you to get my permission," he insisted tersely. "But Spencer isn't just any old friend. He happens to be the father of your child! It's a bit different."

"It was just dinner with his parents! Honestly, I wish I hadn't stayed. I don't think his dad likes me, and he certainly didn't make a fuss over Griffin. He's kind of a jerk. Made me feel sorry for Spencer. His dad isn't like your dad or David at all."

"You're getting off subject. Look, I don't care all that much if you had dinner with the Youngs. They *are* Griffin's grandparents, so I guess if they want to see him, they probably should. What bugs me is that you never told me about it in the first place. It's like you're trying to hide something from me, and I don't like that. It makes me uneasy."

"It's not that I didn't *want* to tell you," she said, although that wasn't completely true. "But I wasn't sure how to tell you. I knew you wouldn't be happy about it, so I figured… I don't know. I figured it was better in the long run if you didn't know so you didn't worry about it. But I'm sorry. I should have told you."

Aaron ran a hand across his face. "This whole reappearance

of Spencer creeps me out, Faith. He comes back and tries to 'help,' when, quite frankly, things were fine without him. Now everything is just too… *complicated*."

It was a good assessment. "That's true," she said. "But when he leaves for college again, hopefully things will settle down. He hardly came home at all last year, to my knowledge. Maybe he'll stay away this time too."

"He'd better," muttered Aaron darkly.

She laughed and scooted closer to him. "So, can I still come for dinner on Friday?" she asked sweetly.

"Of course!"

"Good! Maybe we can have a rematch of Scattergories. I had an off night last time."

Aaron chuckled as she'd hoped he would. She was terrible at Scattergories and had yet to win a round. "Deal," he said, pulling her into a one-armed hug. She smiled and gave him a kiss, after which he rose to leave. His curfew was quickly approaching.

As she watched him drive away, Faith couldn't push away an uneasy sense of foreboding. Things were changing between the two of them, and she was pretty sure Aaron felt it too. There was an almost-constant tension lying just beneath the surface of their conversations now, and they'd had more than one argument in the past few weeks. While it was easy to blame that on Spencer, Faith had to admit the uncomfortable fact that she shared in the blame as well. Twice now, she hadn't been completely truthful with Aaron about Spencer. Aaron had accused her of hiding something from him, and he wasn't completely wrong.

Sighing, she turned to walk back inside, but the nagging thought that she was contributing to the strain in their relationship stayed with her the rest of the night.

CHAPTER 19

Faith gritted her teeth as she rang the doorbell again. Usually Spencer answered right away, but after the third ring she still hadn't heard anything from inside the massive house. Now she was getting mad. Where was he, anyhow?

"Do you think he took Griffin to the park or something? Or maybe just in the backyard?" Aaron asked next to her. Faith knew he was still disgruntled that Spencer was spending time with Griffin, even if it was mid-August and he'd had plenty of time to get used to the idea.

"Maybe," she answered doubtfully. Their landscaped backyard was hardly a suitable place for a toddler to play. "Let's go around back and check."

As they passed the three-car garage, she tried to see if his Mustang was there, but there were no windows. When they reached the backyard, a high fence with a locked gate barred the way. Faith sighed, but there was no noise coming from the yard, either, which meant Spencer wasn't there with Griffin.

Pulling out her phone, she called Spencer only to get his voicemail. Then she texted him. *Where are you?* Long seconds ticked by as her question went unanswered, and for the first time she started to panic. Glancing at Aaron, she could see by his expression that he was concerned as well.

"What should we do?" she asked. "I have no idea where they are, and he isn't answering his phone or texts. I'm getting worried."

"I am too," Aaron confessed. "You don't think he just… took off with Griffin, do you?"

"You mean, like, kidnapped him?" Her voice rose an octave. *Spencer wouldn't do that… would he?*

"Well… I don't know… I mean, no, probably not," said Aaron, somewhat unconvincingly. "Did you try Mrs. Young? Maybe she knows something."

"Good idea. Hang on." Quickly, Faith pulled up Vivian Young's number and called. "Hi, Mrs. Young. It's Faith… Yes, I'm fine, thanks, but do you have any idea where Spencer is?… Yes, I thought so too… No, he didn't answer the doorbell… Oh, would you? That would be wonderful. I'm just worried about Griffin… Okay, thanks… Yes, I'll wait for your call. Bye!"

She hung up and turned to Aaron. "She's going to check with their vehicle GPS tracking system to see where his car is."

"He probably just took Griffin out for a treat to impress you and lost track of time. I'm sure it's fine."

"I hope you're right. It's just really unusual. I'm trying not to panic, but…" She trailed off, leaving the sentiment unfinished. They lapsed into silence, waiting for Vivian to call back.

The sudden ringing of Faith's phone made them both jump, and she answered quickly. "Yes?… *Where?*… You didn't know about this?… Okay. I'm on my way. Thank you so much… Yes, I'll have him call you… Bye."

She hung up and turned to Aaron, fighting tears. "The car

is at the hospital."

Aaron's eyes widened. Then he grabbed the keys from her hand and led her back to the car. "I'm driving," he stated flatly.

By the time they reached the hospital, Faith was nearly hysterical. Aaron found Spencer's Mustang in the emergency lot, a fact that did little to assuage her fears. Faith fairly bolted from the car, but Aaron was equally fast and grabbed her by both arms to stop her.

"Whoa, whoa, whoa," he said. "You can't go in there guns blazing. If Griffin is hurt and you barge in there, they might think you're unstable and refuse to let you see him. We have no idea what's going on yet. You have every right to be concerned, but take a few deep breaths with me now. Then we'll walk in there together and find out what happened."

She was irritated with Aaron and tried to shake free of his grip, but he didn't let go. "Dang it, Aaron, we're wasting time!" she objected, glaring at him.

"The sooner you calm down the sooner we can go in there," he replied stubbornly.

With a deep sigh and an eye roll to let him know how annoyed she was, she allowed him to coach her through a couple deep breaths. He nodded. "Much better. Let's go." He took her hand and walked in with her to the desk.

"Can I help you?" the receptionist asked politely.

"Yes, I... My son is here somewhere. His name is Griffin Williams. He's only one year old. He would be here with Spencer Young. Spencer was watching him for me, and he's not answering his phone. Could you check to see where they are?"

"Your name, *miss*?" The lady looked at Faith over the glasses perched on the edge of her nose.

"Faith Williams."

The lady nodded briskly. "Let me go see what I can find out for you. One moment, please."

After an interminable two minutes, the receptionist reappeared and motioned for Faith to follow her. Aaron started to come as well, but the lady stopped him. "And you are…?"

"He's with me," Faith said. "I want him to come back as well."

The receptionist pressed her lips into a thin line, obviously displeased, but if the mother granted permission, there was little she could do about it. Aaron and Faith both followed her until they came to the correct room. It had glass windows all along the side, but a curtain was pulled to ensure privacy. The receptionist knocked, and the door flew open to reveal Spencer standing there looking anguished.

"Faith!" he exclaimed. "Thank goodness you're here!"

She and Aaron followed him into the little room, where Griffin was lying on the hospital bed, a large bandage over his chin. He looked rather small and pitiful indeed.

"Oh, honey!" Faith cried, springing over to her son. Scooping him into a hug, she let herself cry as she glowered at Spencer. "What in the world happened?" she demanded. "And *why* didn't you call or text or anything? Do you have any idea how frantic I've been? What's wrong with his chin?"

"Settle down, Faith—"

"Don't tell me to settle down!" she shrieked. "I was freaking out, Spencer! The least you could have done was call!"

"Listen! I left my phone at home in the chaos of the last hour. I don't know your number by heart, so I couldn't use a phone here. We were playing with a little beach ball at my house, and I'd roll it to him, and he'd try to kick it back. But then he kicked it in the opposite direction, and when he ran over to get it, he tripped and fell right into the brick fireplace. There was nothing I could do. I wasn't anywhere near him to catch him when he fell."

Faith winced, and Aaron spoke up coldly. "Oh, really? You were 'playing' together, huh? Or were you just letting him run around on his own while you were on your phone or playing video games? Were you even in the room with him?"

Spencer's eyes widened. "No, man, it's not like that!" he protested. Aaron's expression remained hard, so Spencer turned to Faith. "Seriously, Faith! I was watching him, I swear! He just kicked the ball the wrong way and lost his balance when he toddled over there. It was a complete accident. And I promise, I'll pay the medical costs out of pocket."

"How nice of you," Aaron sneered. "It's the *least* you could do after neglecting the poor kid."

"Aaron, stop!" Faith spoke up sharply, seeing the crestfallen expression on Spencer's face. "Toddlers are clumsy and unsteady on their feet. Don't you think he's ever fallen while I've been with him? It happens! Leave Spencer alone!"

At that, Aaron turned on her. "So you're siding with *him*?" he asked scornfully. "How do you know what really happened? Look at Griffin's face! There's blood seeping through the bandage even now!"

Her eyes clouded with tears. "Aaron, you're scaring him," she warned in a low voice, pulling Griffin's little head to her chest in a vain effort to cover his ears.

"Look, I'm not his father, but I think—"

"That's right, you're not!" she interrupted. "And I think there are too many people in this little room right now. When the doctor comes in he'll need some space."

There was an uncomfortable silence following her statement. Faith knew she'd hurt Aaron by her words.

Although he wasn't Griffin's birth father, he'd been there for her even before Griffin was born. Other than David, Aaron was the closest thing Griffin had to a father figure. Now Aaron stared at her in disbelief at the suggestion that he leave. But she stubbornly held her ground and glared back at him. Finally, he turned on his heel and shoved the door open, stalking down the hall without a word.

Faith turned away from Spencer so he wouldn't see her cry. He spoke quietly. "Faith—"

"Don't!" she stopped him. "Just don't say anything right now. I can't handle it."

They sat in silence until the doctor came in to stitch Griffin's chin, talking soothingly to the frightened toddler as he worked. Faith held Griffin's hands and tried to maintain eye contact with her son, which was difficult, given the location of the injury. The doctor was practically in front of Griffin's face to see what he was doing.

When it was over, the doctor gave her discharge instructions and shook her hand, wishing her well. Only then did Faith really look at Spencer. He looked awful. His hair that was usually perfectly styled was disheveled from running his hands through it so often, his forehead was creased with worry, and his lips were chapped from licking them. She walked over and gave him a hug.

"Don't worry," she assured him. "I know it wasn't your fault. Aaron's just worried. Griffin will be fine. A little sore for a few days, but his chin will heal."

"Thanks, Faith," he whispered hoarsely, then cleared his throat. "Let's get outta here, yeah?"

She picked up Griffin to follow Spencer out of the hospital. Once in the parking lot, she had a sinking realization. Aaron had actually left. With her car. She was stranded with no other option but Spencer.

Sighing, she asked, "So, um... Can we have a ride?"

Gesturing to his Mustang, Spencer led her to the car and helped strap Griffin in. As they started the drive home, Faith realized something else.

"Oh! Spencer! I told your mom we'd call to let her know why you were at the hospital!"

She grabbed her phone and saw there were four missed calls from Mrs. Young and three from her own mom, in addition to a number of texts from her mom asking where she was. She groaned and called Mrs. Young back first, handing the phone to Spencer to explain the details. Then she called her own mother to give a quick summary of the events and assure her she and Griffin were on their way home.

When they pulled up in front of Faith's house, she saw her car in its usual spot on the road. Aaron must have dropped it off and had his dad take him back to his own house. Faith thanked Spencer for the ride and carried Griffin into the house, where another round of questions awaited her.

Later that evening, when the excitement had finally calmed down and Griffin was in bed, Faith checked her phone for the hundredth time since leaving the hospital. Still nothing from Aaron. She tried to form a coherent thought in her mind to text him but came up blank. She hadn't the first clue what to say. Blinking back tears, she tossed the phone next to her on the bed and waited for a text that never came.

CHAPTER 20

The next morning, Faith was on the Sullivans' doorstep, still with no word from Aaron. She figured the best thing to do was show up in person and force a real conversation, rather than trying to negotiate a truce via text.

When Aaron answered the door, his eyes were cold as he asked, "How's Griffin?"

"He's fine," Faith answered. "He got six stitches, but he'll heal."

"Good."

There was an awkward pause until Faith asked, "Can I at least come in?"

Aaron stiffly motioned her inside. "I'm glad you and Griffin's *father* got everything taken care of," he said as they sat down in the living room, he in the armchair and her on the couch. Apparently he didn't even want to sit next to her.

Heat flooded Faith's cheeks at his comment, and she bit back an equally snarky retort. She'd come to make things better, not cause another fight.

"Aaron, I'm sorry. That was a mean and spiteful thing to

say, and I know it hurt your feelings. I shouldn't have said it, especially in front of Spencer."

"Got that right."

She glared at him. "I'm trying to apologize here!"

"He's trying to steal you away from me, you know."

"What, with a trip to the ER?" she scoffed.

"You don't see it, Faith, but I do. I've seen it all along, from the day he showed up at church. He's trying to worm his way back into your life by proving how great he is with Griffin. He doesn't care about Griffin. He cares about *you*. Griffin is a means to an end."

"I didn't realize you could read minds," Faith shot back sarcastically. "Glad to know what Spencer's *really* thinking. While you're at it, what am *I* thinking? No, wait. Let me try first. I'll tell you what you're thinking. You're jealous of Spencer."

"Do I have a reason to be jealous of him?" Aaron demanded with a pointed look at her.

Faith stared at him a long moment, her jaw clenched. She couldn't believe he'd make such an insinuation. Without another word, she stood and walked to the door. Aaron jumped up and ran to block her way.

"That was mean," he admitted. "I'm sorry. I'm just... I guess I am jealous of Spencer. I mean, the guy has everything. He's rich, popular, studying to be a doctor, and on top of all that has the added bonus of a great physique and incredibly good looks. Spencer turns girls' heads wherever he goes. I can't compete with that. I don't want him to take away the one thing I care about most."

Faith sighed and reached for his hand. She was quickly tiring of making the same reassurances. "That's why you need to trust me. If I say I'm with you, you've got to believe me! I can't have you second guessing *my* feelings if *you're* insecure."

"You're right," he said. "I'm sorry. I know I overreacted yesterday at the hospital. I was a jerk, and I don't want Griffin to see me like that. Nor do I want to fight with you anymore. Truce?"

"Truce," she agreed, giving his hand one last squeeze. "You need to get to work, though. Don't want them to fire you." He chuckled. It was his last week anyhow since he would leave for college in five days.

"Thanks for coming over," he told her.

"You're welcome," she said, giving him a quick peck on the cheek. "See you later?"

"Yeah, I'll see you later."

She walked back to her car and waved as she pulled away. They had "made up," but it was an uneasy truce, and she was pretty sure Aaron knew it too. Faith felt only slightly better when she left, and Aaron's imminent departure did little to set her mind at ease. She'd been so sure of their relationship a few months ago, positive it could easily survive the long-distance separation, but suddenly she was very uncertain. Something had shifted subtly over the past weeks, and she wasn't sure she wanted to find out what that meant.

Four days later, Faith and Aaron said a tearful goodbye at her house. Faith hugged his neck almost desperately, her tears falling freely. She still didn't have a good feeling about this.

"Text me when you get there," she reminded him. "And call me later after your parents are gone and things have settled down, okay?" He nodded and tightened his arms around her waist. "And let me know your schedule," she continued. "That way I feel like you're not so far away."

"I will," he promised.

"Are you nervous?" she asked.

"Terrified. You?"

"Ditto. College is intimidating."

"You'll do great. And at least you get to stay with your aunt and uncle. I've talked to my roommate on the phone, but I have no idea if we'll even get along in person."

"You will," she assured him. "You're a likable guy."

"I'm not worried about me, I'm worried about *him*!"

Faith laughed and looked into Aaron's face. His eyes were troubled despite his light words, and she knew it wasn't just nerves. She really wished they had at least another week together to sort things out before he had to leave. It was unsettling for him to have to go before they'd really gotten over their hospital argument.

"Aaron, I—" She stopped abruptly, feeling self-conscious.

"What?" he prompted.

"I... I'll miss you," she finished lamely. It wasn't what she'd wanted to say, not what *needed* to be said, and his face fell a little at her answer.

"I'll miss you too," he whispered, tucking a strand of hair behind her ear.

There was another uneasy silence, and Aaron took a deep breath, signaling that he was getting ready to leave. He leaned over to give Faith one last hug and a gentle kiss before turning to go. "Love you," he said simply.

"I love you too," she replied, her words falling flat even to her own ears. They were both being so careful, so overly polite. She felt rooted to the spot as she watched Aaron climb into his car and drive away. Part of her wanted to run after him and throw herself into his arms, assuring him that she was over that stupid fight last week, telling him she loved him, giving him a real kiss instead of the perfunctory one they'd just exchanged.

This was all wrong, him leaving this way. It was like they were siblings saying goodbye.

With a frustrated grunt, Faith turned back to go into the house, tears blurring her vision. She went straight downstairs and got ready for bed in the dark so as not to wake Griffin. As she lay in bed, she stared into the darkness, her mind swirling with thousands of things she'd left unsaid.

CHAPTER 21

The ringing of his office phone startled David from his paperwork. Glancing up, he saw the secretary was ringing his line.

"Yes, Mrs. Daily?" he answered.

"Mr. Neunaber, there's a mother on the line who's looking to enroll her son this year. They just moved to the area. Her name is Monica Fischer."

"Okay. Put her on the line, please."

The secretary complied, and David greeted the mother. "This is David Neunaber, the principal here at St. John. How can I help you, Mrs. Fischer?"

"Yes, hello," came the reply. The lady on the other end sounded tentative. "Um, I'm looking to transfer my son, Brayden. He… um, he's in fourth grade. We just moved from out of town."

"Alright, I'd be happy to discuss that with you. Are you aware that our school year has already started? Even though the public schools don't start until next week, we're already in full session."

"I don't think he'd have a problem catching up with the class work, especially since it's still so early in the year."

"That's true. You said Brayden is in fourth grade?"

"Yes."

"That would be Mr. Lattimer's class. We have combined classrooms. Mr. Lattimer has third and fourth grade. Are you looking to join the church?"

"Oh, no, nothing like that. We aren't even Christian. I just… He… I think it might be good for him to be part of a smaller school. I like the class size."

"Ah." David had the feeling there was something she wasn't telling him. "Have you checked our website? There's a link for registration papers and tuition figures. If you aren't a church member, the tuition is considerably higher."

"That's not an issue."

"Would you like to come over to tour the school before making a commitment? Perhaps have Brayden come to meet his teacher and some classmates?"

"Well… I… I'm not sure…" She trailed off and sighed. "Let me be honest with you. Brayden's father and I are separating. I moved back here to live with my mother. Brayden is… challenging. He has ADHD and is disruptive in class. He got into a few fights at his former school." She gave a nervous chuckle. "I'm hoping maybe a smaller class size will help calm him down. Maybe if he has more one-on-one attention, he won't act out as much."

David felt bad for the mother, but their school wasn't staffed to provide extra help to "problem" students, nor did they dare to claim they could solve behavioral issues. This was more than a new student joining a few days late.

"Mrs. Fischer, thank you for your honesty. Let me speak with Mr. Lattimer about this. He's an excellent teacher and has been here twenty-four years. He's dealt with his share of strong-willed students." David thought it best he not mention the fact that the fourth-grade class already had one rambunctious student.

"In the meantime, could you and Brayden meet me here tomorrow morning?" he continued. "Perhaps ten o'clock? I can show you around, and Mr. Lattimer might be able to join us for a few minutes before you make any final decisions. Would that work?"

"That would be great."

David reached for his pen and wrote a reminder on his calendar as he spoke. "I'll schedule you in. I also want to tell you that since we are a Lutheran school, religion is a daily subject. Brayden would be taught about Jesus, and he would have memory work that includes Bible verses. There is also chapel once a week, and he would be expected to attend and participate, regardless of personal or family beliefs. You mentioned that your family isn't Christian, so I want to be clear on our policy right away."

"I don't have a problem with that. I suppose it would be good for him to be exposed to that whole religion thing."

David didn't know how to respond, so instead he wrapped up the conversation. "Okay. I'll see you in the morning at ten."

"We'll be there. Thanks for your time. Goodbye."

As he hung up the phone, David pursed his lips thoughtfully. He had no doubt Bill Lattimer could handle another rowdy student. Bill was one of the best teachers he'd ever known, and he ran a tight ship in his classroom. But this Brayden kid was an unknown. His own mother claimed he was a challenge. Then again, Jackson was a challenge. Grace compared raising Jackson to taming a wild mustang. And who knew? Maybe Brayden was being sent there to experience the love of Jesus. From the sounds of it, he and his family could certainly use it.

A week later, David met with Bill Lattimer in his office after school, discussing the new student.

"Brayden is just as his mother described him," Bill said. "He likes to make jokes so the other kids will laugh, and it's true that he has difficulties sitting down. He completely changes the dynamic of the classroom. Logan acts up even more with Brayden there to egg him on.

"But that's not the worst of it," he continued, lowering his voice. "David, I don't think he can read. I think that's why he acts out and goofs off. He's trying to deflect attention away from that fact so the other kids won't make fun of him when they find out. He bounces around in his seat and fidgets so he can copy off other kids. I've never had a student this old who can't read."

David blew out a long breath and tapped his pen on his desk in frustration. This changed things considerably. A fourth grader who was unable to read required far more attention than they were capable of giving him with their limited staff and resources. And Mr. Lattimer's class was already bigger than all others besides the preschool class. He couldn't afford to spend extra time with one student at the expense of the others.

"What should we do?" he asked, deferring to the judgment of a more experienced teacher.

"We could offer private tutoring sessions after school to help him catch up, or we could try to squeeze in some one-on-one during the school day. I usually have the fourth graders working independently on an assignment while I'm working with the third graders for a subject or two each afternoon. He could use that time for tutoring. Maybe one of the library volunteers would agree to come a few extra hours a week?"

"You don't think he's dyslexic, do you?" asked David with some trepidation. That would be even more difficult.

Bill took a moment to consider that before responding slowly. "I don't *think* so, although I'm no expert on that. I suppose it's possible, but I just think he hasn't been held accountable in the past. Sort of slid through the cracks as each teacher passed along the trouble to his next teacher. I can't in good conscience ignore the fact that he can't read. It's a lifelong skill he needs to acquire."

"Agreed. So of the options you suggest, which are you most comfortable with?"

"I'd maybe go for in-school tutoring, provided we can find someone reliable."

David pondered this a moment before inspiration struck. "You know, Ann Lixon is a library volunteer."

Bill met his eyes and smiled slowly. "Yes, she is. And she used to be a teacher. Special Education, at that. Just in case there is something like dyslexia…"

The two men considered the option until David spoke again. "Do you think she'd…"

"Only one way to find out." Bill grinned. "But I think it's a great idea. Let me know what she says." He shook David's hand and left the office.

David sat there for a few minutes, working up his courage to call the pastor's wife. He knew he was asking a lot, but Brayden needed the help. With a silent prayer, he picked up the phone.

Fifteen minutes later, he delivered the good news to Bill Lattimer that Mrs. Lixon had agreed to be Brayden Fischer's new reading tutor.

CHAPTER 22

Faith heard the doorbell ring while she was changing Griffin. She was in the room that had been Claire's but was now her own while she lived with the McNeals during college. Quickly, Faith finished with Griffin, knowing her aunt and uncle were both gone.

"Coming!" she yelled down the stairs. When she reached the bottom, she set Griffin down in the entryway and opened the door to find Spencer standing on the porch.

"Spencer!" she exclaimed, aghast that her heart skipped a beat to see him. "What a pleasant surprise! I thought you were at college!" Classes had only begun a few weeks ago.

He laughed and pulled her into an easy hug. "I decided to come home for the weekend. I wanted to see everyone here. Especially Griffin. And you." By golly, her heart skipped another beat. Feeling herself turn red, she motioned him inside.

"Hiya, bud!" Spencer exclaimed when he saw Griffin toddle toward him. "How ya doin'? How's that chin?" He bent to examine the scar before lifting Griffin up into a hug.

"His chin is healing just fine," she assured him. "It'll hardly be noticeable when he gets older. Just a battle wound to brag about."

"That's great. Faith, honestly, it just happened. There's nothing I could have done about it."

"I know. Accidents happen all the time. It's amazing they don't happen more often with active little kids. Toddlers fall. It's part of life."

He looked relieved. "I just don't want you to think I was neglecting our son."

Our son. Technically, he was right, but it still sounded so… *personal* to say it that way. Faith looked away from his intense eyes. He was giving her his *look* again. "I… um… oh! I have to wash my hands," she quickly stated. "I was changing him when you rang the bell. I'll be right back." She needed to get away from him so she could think clearly.

Faith hurried to the upstairs bathroom, taking a bit longer than necessary as she brushed through her hair and checked her reflection in the mirror, wondering why she cared so much about her appearance at the moment. She thought she heard a knock while she was freshening up, but she didn't hear voices, so she shrugged it off. Griffin had probably tossed a block on the wood floor or something.

Emerging at last, she bounced back down the stairs into the living room, asking, "Was it just me or did you hear a…" The blood drained from her face as she saw Aaron standing there with Spencer. Both had their jaws clenched, and Faith could feel the tension radiating from both of them. *Oh, this is bad,* she thought with dismay. She hadn't expected either of them to come home this weekend, but Aaron probably thought she'd invited Spencer over behind his back. The fact that Spencer held Griffin in his arms possessively did not help the situation.

"Aaron! I… I didn't… You're home!" she stammered.

"I wanted to surprise you," he said flatly. "But I see *I'm* the one who gets the surprise."

He turned and stalked out, and Faith hurried after him. "Aaron, wait!" He didn't even pause but kept walking purposefully toward his car.

"Aaron! Please!" She was running now.

He reached the car and turned on her. "So this is how it is, huh? While the cat's away, the mice will play."

"Aaron!" She was shocked by his rudeness. How dare he make such an accusation!

"I wanted to surprise you and take you out for a date, only to find you've already made plans with Spencer. Nice, Faith. Really classy."

Do you really think I'd do that, Aaron? Don't you trust me at all? she thought indignantly. "I'm as surprised to see him as I am to see you!" she insisted. "He just stopped by to see Griffin and check on his chin."

"Mm-hmm." Aaron's eyes narrowed. "From Ann Arbor? A three-hour drive to 'stop by.' Sure. Look, this isn't working. We were naïve to think a long-distance relationship ever would. It's not fair to either of us. If you want to be with Spencer, fine. At least have the decency to tell me. But don't keep stringing me along as a fail-safe in case things don't work out with him. We're done."

"Aaron, please! Just listen!" She grabbed his arm, but he shook her off, almost roughly. The hurt in his eyes was too much for Faith to bear, and she took a step backward, her breath catching in her throat.

Aaron got into his car and drove away without another word, leaving her alone in the driveway with tears streaming down her cheeks.

Gulping down a sob, she turned at last and headed back to the house slowly, numb from the shock. The timing of the past ten minutes couldn't have been worse. *Ten minutes?* Had it really only been that long? In ten short minutes her world had been turned upside down?

Spencer met her at the door, shamefaced. "I'm sorry," he said quietly. "I didn't mean to cause a fight between you two. I wouldn't have come if I'd known he was going to show up."

"He… He broke up with me," she said, her voice cracking.

A strange mix of emotions crossed Spencer's face at this bit of news, and he blew out a breath. "Wow. I didn't mean… This wasn't my intention. I know it looks bad, me being here and all, but go talk to him later. Let him cool down and look at things from a more neutral perspective. It's always worse in the heat of the moment. Aaron's a good guy. He won't let you slip away like I did."

The emotion in his eyes was sincere, and Faith realized with some alarm that Spencer really did have strong feelings for her. No wonder Aaron was upset. He'd picked up on that well before she had. But if she was honest with herself, she had to admit it wasn't a complete surprise. There had been warning signs all along, and she'd been too blind to see them. Or, worse, she'd seen them and pretended not to simply because it gave her ego a huge boost to have two guys vying for her affections. Poor Aaron. He was right. It *wasn't* fair to him.

Spencer handed Griffin to Faith and gave her a quick kiss on the cheek. Then he let himself out of the house as she clung to Griffin and cried.

Faith knocked on the Sullivans' door the next morning, her heart pounding so hard she could feel it in her ears. Mrs. Sullivan answered, her brow creased in concern. Aaron must have told her about the previous afternoon. "I assume you want to talk to Aaron?" she asked. Mutely, Faith nodded. Mrs. Sullivan ushered her into the front hall and went to fetch him.

When he came out a minute later, Faith did a double take at his appearance. It was plain he hadn't slept well the previous night. He had dark bags under his puffy eyes and looked suspiciously like he'd been crying. The thought caused a stab of pain in her chest.

"Aaron, please, can we talk?" she begged, not caring that his mother was right there to witness her grovelling. "I just... I really need to explain everything."

Stiffly, he motioned with his hand for her to follow him. He led her through the living room where Faith had spent many an evening watching movies or playing Scattergories with his family. She wondered if she would ever do that again. Aaron led her into his dad's study and shut the door behind them. Turning to her, he crossed his arms, and said, "Well?"

He certainly wasn't making this easy for her. "Aaron, please believe me. There is nothing going on between me and Spencer. *Nothing*. You and I have been dating more than a year. You know I wouldn't cheat on you! He stopped over yesterday because he came home for the weekend and wanted to check on Griffin's chin. He'd been there a grand total of four minutes when you came. That's it. I don't know what his hopes were, but you can rest assured that I was *not* intending to go out with him, whether you showed up or not! I'm not in love with Spencer. I'm in love with you!"

Her statement made him close his eyes, as if he was mentally bracing himself for the rest of the conversation. "I know you weren't cheating on me. But I also see the way Spencer looks at you. And he's very charming and persuasive when he wants to be."

"Aaron—"

"We're only eighteen," he interrupted. "I don't want either of us to feel pressured into a permanent relationship now only to grow to resent it—or each other—later, wondering what could have happened or who else we could have ended up with if we hadn't stayed together out of duty. You're the only girl I've ever dated. Maybe we both need to date other people first before we go rushing into a commitment we'll later regret. You know that saying—'If you love something, let it go…' I guess that's what I'm doing now. If we're meant to be together in the end, we will be. But I don't want it to be because either of us feels guilted into it."

Her heart had all but stopped as she realized how serious he was. "So you're breaking up with me for real?" she asked in a near whisper, tears blurring her vision.

Aaron didn't even make eye contact. Instead, he stared at her feet a few long seconds before he said, "I guess I am, yes."

Faith stood still for a moment, hoping he'd change his mind or retract his statement, but the silence grew oppressive. Having nothing further to say, she turned on her heel and walked blindly out of the house, not bothering to acknowledge Mrs. Sullivan as she passed by. It felt like her heart had just shattered into a million pieces, and she didn't know if she'd be able to put them all back together again.

CHAPTER 23

"Mr. Neunaber? Do you have a moment?"

David glanced up from his desk to see Mike Krause at his door. His heart sank. Mike did not look happy. It had to be about Logan, his fourth-grade son.

"Of course, Mike! Come in. What can I do for you?"

Mike shut the door behind him and took a seat. "I just wanted to know when we started taking in rabble-rousers off the street to interfere with our own children's education."

David felt the heat creep up his neck and into his face. He knew Mike was talking about Brayden Fischer, but he didn't want to dignify the insinuation with a response. He wanted to hear it from Mike.

"To whom, exactly, do you refer, Mike?"

"You know darn well I'm talking about that Fischer kid. He's been nothing but trouble in class. Now, I know my Logan's a handful himself, but he's tame compared to Brayden. I can't see how Bill Lattimer gets any teaching done at all. He's gotta spend all his time keeping Brayden in check. It ain't fair to the other students in the class, many who are actually church *members*, I might remind you. Are we so desperate for money that we're taking in problem kids like this?"

David sucked in a deep, slow breath, trying to lower his blood pressure. This guy had a lot of gall to come to his office and complain about "problem kids" when his own son was one of the ringleaders.

"As a matter of fact, Mike, I think Brayden is adjusting well to a new school. And quite frankly, part of the mission of our school is to reach out to others with the message of the Gospel. This family is unchurched. They need to hear about Jesus. Brayden's not a problem child; he's a mission opportunity."

Mike scoffed. "I know we're supposed to reach out, but it rubs me the wrong way when we're doing so at the expense of our kids' education."

"Mr. Lattimer is handling both Brayden *and* Logan well," David said pointedly. "He's not robbing the other students of a good education. I think he's doing a fine job."

"Maybe *he's* handling Brayden okay," allowed Mike reluctantly, "but just you wait until next year. Do you really think Mr. Barber will be able to deal with him? He'll be in Freddie's classroom next year, and it will get your attention when it's your own kid in the same room."

Bill Lattimer had long been the third- and fourth-grade teacher, but the fifth- and sixth-grade classroom had a new teacher just a year out of college. Freddie really liked Mr. Barber's easygoing style, but David knew it was true that he probably couldn't handle the likes of Logan Krause and Brayden Fischer in the same room.

"We'll cross that bridge when we come to it," David said. "As of this year, I think it's working out beautifully to have him in Mr. Lattimer's class. If you feel like Logan is getting shortchanged on his schoolwork, perhaps you'd like to speak with Mr. Lattimer yourself? I'm sure he could assign extra work to be sure Logan isn't falling behind or being distracted."

His visitor reddened at the suggestion. "I just want to make sure our students are getting the best education they can."

"And I appreciate your concern for *all* students, Mike. That would include Brayden."

"I suppose," Mike muttered. He cleared his throat and stood. "Thank you for your time, Mr. Neunaber. I do hope you keep my concerns in mind. I'm certainly not the only parent who's worried about this. I should know. It's a regular topic of conversation. I'm just the only one who has the guts to say anything about it. Good day."

He made a quick exit, leaving David alone in the office again. He sighed wearily and took off his glasses to pinch the bridge of his nose as he thought. It was true that Brayden was a distraction in class. He'd already been sent to David's office five times in the four weeks he'd been there. Then again, Logan had been there twice himself in that time period. And according to Bill, Brayden was making remarkable progress with his reading skills, which gave him more confidence in class. Despite what other parents may think of Brayden, David could see progress and was proud of the kid.

And no matter what anyone else said, it was David's firm belief that it was never a mistake to reach out to a child with the love of Jesus. Never.

CHAPTER 24

Are you free tonight?

Faith stared at her phone, trying to decide how to respond to Spencer's text. She wasn't sure what he had in mind, and fervently hoped he wasn't going to suggest they go to the Homecoming game. The absolute last thing she wanted to do was go to such a public event with Spencer. *That* would get the gossip mill running for sure. Last year she and Aaron had gone to the game and Homecoming dance together.

An ache in her heart accompanied the memory of Aaron. Although it had been a month since their breakup, she was still smarting from it. But at the same time, she was tired of moping around feeling sorry for herself. She could use a distraction.

Cautiously, she texted back: *Why?*

I'm in town. Wanna go bowling?

She mulled that over in her mind. Bowling wasn't romantic. And even though she was an awful bowler, it was a lot of fun to try. Actually, an evening of bowling sounded pretty tempting, so long as she could arrange something for Griffin.

Sure, she typed back before she could overthink the invitation and talk herself out of it.

Great! Pick you up at 6?

Make it 7. Mom's house. I'll put G down first.

Perfect. We'll grab a burger there. See you!

Faith breathed a sigh of relief. At least he didn't intend to take her out to eat first. This sounded very... *safe*. Like something friends would do. She could handle this.

At seven o'clock sharp, Spencer arrived at the Neunabers' house, and Faith scooted out before he even opened the car door. She didn't want her family to see who she was meeting. She'd told them she was going bowling with a friend and left it at that. But when she hopped into the passenger side, she couldn't miss Spencer's wide grin. He must think she was overly eager to see him again. *Great*, she thought in dismay. *So much for not encouraging him...*

He leaned over to kiss her cheek in greeting, then backed out, still grinning away. They kept their conversation on neutral subjects like classes and professors as he drove, and when they got to the bowling alley, they went straight for the snack bar to order hamburgers and cheese fries. The food was exactly what one would expect from a grease pit, but Faith enjoyed it nonetheless.

"My mom would totally freak out if she knew I was eating this stuff," Spencer grinned at Faith as they finished. She laughed, and he popped his last fry into his mouth with a smug smile. "Are you ready to get beat?" he teased.

She rolled her eyes at his arrogance. "Who says I'm going to lose?" She'd been bowling a grand total of perhaps six times in her life, though she couldn't imagine he had any more experience than she. Bowling seemed to be an activity beneath the Youngs.

"Should we request bumpers?" he asked.

Faith raised one eyebrow. "Sure, if you need them."

Chuckling, Spencer shook his head. "Just you wait," he told her, "I'm a pro."

She snorted. "I bet."

Rather than answer, Spencer gave her a mysterious grin as he led the way to the desk to arrange everything. Ten minutes later, they were both wearing the ubiquitous blue, red, and tan bowling shoes, each had chosen a ball, and Spencer had entered their names on the electronic screen.

"Ladies first," he said, a wicked gleam in his eye.

She ignored him as she picked up her ball. Taking a few clumsy steps, she heaved the ball down the lane. It went into the gutter before it even made it halfway down.

Spencer laughed behind her and said, "Maybe those bumpers aren't such a bad idea after all!"

"Humph," she protested, tossing her hair over her shoulder. "Just had to get a bad throw out of the way."

But her second one turned out to be a gutter ball as well. Spencer, still chuckling, took his ball and lined up. Then he glided toward the lane and released the ball in one smooth action. The ball looked like it was heading for the gutter, but Faith watched in astonishment as it curved and headed toward the head pin, hitting it slightly off center. All ten pins crashed down. Her jaw dropped. Okay, so bowling wasn't beneath him after all.

Spencer grinned as he returned to the seating area, shrugging in mock humility. "Not bad."

"That was amazing! How do you get your ball to do that?"

"I was on a league for a few summers," he explained. "I learned a lot."

"Obviously!"

"Can I at least show you how to line up? You're taking your steps all wrong and then you end up throwing the ball with your leg in the way. You need to end with your other leg out. Here, watch."

He spent a few minutes showing her the basics and made her do a few dry runs without the ball before he nodded. "Good. At least you have the right form. Now you need to aim. Forget about curving the ball. Just try to throw straight. You're turning your wrist like this." He demonstrated with his own arm before continuing. "Try to keep it straight until you've thrown the ball. And don't look at the pins when you throw. Look at these arrows on the lane itself. They're closer and easier to visualize. Don't aim directly at the head pin. If you hit it dead on, you'll get a split. Try to get between the first and second arrow, there." He pointed, and she nodded to indicate she understood, not that it would make a difference. Her head was swimming with all the information.

"Okay, crash course over. Now, go!" he commanded.

Faith lined up and tried to remember everything he'd said. She took her steps slowly and aimed for the arrows like he'd showed her. She was still clumsy, but at least she had some guidance this time. As the ball left her hand, she watched as it sailed down the lane. It was drifting toward the gutter, but ever so slowly. It was getting closer to the pins. She just might hit one…

"Yes!" she yelled in victory as the ball grazed the very corner pin and knocked it over. "I got one!"

Spencer clasped his hands behind his head and grinned broadly. "Hey, that's the hardest one to get! Now go get the other nine!"

Her next throw was slightly better, and she knocked down two more, earning her a high five from Spencer, who promptly knocked down nine pins for his turn. His second throw missed the last pin by inches, and he groaned, but Faith was frowning about something else.

"How come you have nineteen in your first box up there?" she asked. "There are only ten pins. You have twenty-eight already, and I only have *three*?"

Spencer explained the scoring rules, and she shook her head in disgust. "I'll never get this silly game," she complained.

"At the rate you're going, you'll never have to worry about scoring a strike or spare," he ribbed.

"Oh, yeah? Game on, baby. Game on. Watch and learn," she said, striding forward to bowl a gutter ball.

"Okay, *this* time," she insisted as Spencer chortled. She lined up and frowned in concentration, then sent a ball right down the middle. "See?" she yelled. "I'm gonna get a strike!"

"You mean a spare."

"Whatever! Just watch!"

The ball wobbled up and hit the head pin, knocking over five pins total. Faith was crushed. "Why didn't I get them all? I hit it where you told me to!"

"But it was too slow," Spencer pointed out. "You remind me of a kid I had on my bowling league one summer. He got his ball stuck in the gutter halfway down, so our coach told him to fire another ball down the gutter and knock them both the rest of the way. So he walked up, carefully set the ball in the gutter, and barely tapped the thing. When it finally got to the other ball, it hit it and bounced back a few inches."

"It did not! And I am so not that slow!"

"True story. And no, you're not that bad, but you do want to put more power behind your throws once you get the motion down. Maybe even get a heavier ball. You're only using a ten-pounder. You may want to try twelve next time."

Throughout the remainder of the game, Spencer gave Faith tips, and by the end she was starting to get the hang of it. She ended up with a whopping score of thirty-nine, while Spencer had 137.

"Okay, so you didn't quite beat me by a hundred. Let's try again. I'm finally starting to get this!" she urged.

Spencer needed no encouragement, and happily started another game. By the time they were ready to leave, they'd played four games total, Spencer scoring at least 130 each time. Faith, on the other hand, never broke one hundred, but she got a spare in the third game and a strike in the fourth. Her best score was seventy-three, and she was ecstatic about it. She finally understood why people liked to bowl.

The two drove home, bragging and teasing each other about the games. When they pulled up to the house, he walked her to the front porch to see her safely in. She turned to him to say, "Thanks, Spencer. I had a blast. This was just what I needed this weekend."

He grinned back at her. "I had fun too. Maybe we can do it again sometime?"

She shrugged amicably, and he leaned over to kiss her cheek before turning to go. Faith entered the house praying that no one had been peeking out the front window. She'd never hear the end of it if so. But she couldn't help the goofy smile that spread across her face. That was the best evening she'd had in quite a while.

CHAPTER 25

Faith's ears perked up as she heard a church member ask Mrs. Sullivan, "So, how's Aaron?"

They were in the narthex after church, and Mrs. Sullivan was facing away from Faith. Discreetly, she led Griffin over to the usher's table and picked up the weekly announcements, pretending to read them as she listened to Mrs. Sullivan's reply.

"Oh, he's doing very well, thank you! We went to Concordia last week to hear him sing for a student recital. Afterward, he introduced us to a nice young lady, so we'll see where that goes."

Faith's heart nearly stopped, and her cheeks flushed as she picked Griffin up and hastened away, the unread announcements still in hand. Aaron really was putting her behind him.

And I'll bet that *girl didn't have a baby in high school,* a little voice in her head mocked. *He's with someone who actually deserves him.*

She rushed out into the cool fall air, a stab of pain in her heart. She hadn't thought Aaron would actually pursue another relationship, and she certainly hadn't thought it would affect her so much to find out he *had*. Even though they weren't dating anymore, she was jealous of this mysterious young lady to whom Mrs. Sullivan had referred. She was also inexplicably mad at the unnamed female, and Faith resented the fact that she had stolen Aaron from her. Now she knew how Aaron must have felt when Spencer showed up again. Faith closed her eyes.

How long had they been dating? Did she know his favorite dessert was cherry pie? Or that he preferred Bach to Mozart? Did she know how cute he looked trying to play bocce ball? How good he was with babies? Did they sing together? Did they hold hands? Had he kissed her yet? Did he... *love* her?

Choking back a sob, Faith strapped Griffin into the car and climbed in the driver's seat. Suddenly she felt very, very lonely.

Dinner tonight?

Faith glanced dully at her phone as it chimed. Spencer, naturally. She let out a low moan. Griffin was down for a nap, and she was throwing herself a whopper of a pity party at Olivia's house. She'd barely touched lunch, claiming she had a headache, and holed herself up in her room for the afternoon under the pretense of a nap while Griffin slept. The last thing she wanted to do was go to dinner with Spencer.

Not in the mood. I'm a grouch, she wrote back.

Then you need to get out. I'll get you at 6.

Faith sighed. Spencer could not take no for an answer. She tossed the phone down despondently and considered begging her way out of it. But in the end she figured she could use a night out, if only to get away from Olivia's incessant questions. Her aunt knew something more than a headache was bothering her, and Faith wasn't ready to share the reason.

When Spencer came for her, he ushered her into the car and started driving without a word. She didn't even pay much attention to where they were going until Spencer turned onto a familiar street.

"Spencer! Are you taking me back to your place?" she asked accusingly.

"Of course! I'm not about to drag you into a restaurant with that expression on your face. If I'm gonna be seen with a girl, I don't want people to think I'm the last person she wants to be with."

Despite her rotten mood, Faith half-smiled at his assessment. "Are your parents here?"

"Nah. They've got some company dinner thing tonight. Speeches and all that jazz. Sounds horribly boring to me. But I didn't feel like eating alone. Thanks for joining me, however reluctantly."

They were at his house now, and he led her inside, where she found the table already set and something keeping warm in the oven.

"It smells wonderful!" she exclaimed, surprised. "Since when do you know how to cook?"

"I've been cooking for years," he sniffed haughtily.

She arched an eyebrow at him, and he laughed. "It's a Campbell's Skillet Sauce," he confessed. "Just pour the pouch over the chicken and ta-da! You've got yourself a meal! It's a step up from the Ramen noodles I make at college when I don't feel like going to the cafeteria."

Faith managed a giggle as she settled herself down at the table. She realized she was actually hungry. Her skimpy lunch was catching up to her. Spencer opened the oven door and pulled out a tray of rolls. At the look of amazement on her face, he chuckled.

"Frozen dinner rolls," he admitted. "Best I can do."

He dished out a plate for each of them, complete with a side of bagged salad, and set one down in front of her before taking his place on the opposite side of the table. There was an awkward pause until Spencer mumbled, "I guess I'll pray." They bowed their heads as he began. "Lord God, we ask Your blessing on this food and this evening. Help us to glorify You in everything. Amen."

"Amen," Faith echoed.

The first few minutes were silent as each of them started eating. It was surprisingly good, and if Spencer hadn't given away his secret about the sauce, Faith never would have suspected it had come out of a pouch. After another minute or two, she spoke. "This is delicious, Spencer. Thanks for inviting me. And for putting up with my lousy mood."

"Want to talk about it?" he prompted gently. "Are you okay?"

At his question, tears welled up in Faith's eyes again, and she looked down at her plate. She was embarrassed to tell Spencer the real reason, but she had to tell someone. At last, she whispered, "Aaron's going out with someone else." Saying the words out loud made it seem so final, and her tears spilled down her cheeks.

Spencer remained silent, and Faith glanced at him from the corner of her eye. He was staring intently at his plate, absently swirling a piece of chicken through the sauce. She had no idea what he was thinking. Eventually, he set his fork down on the side of his plate and met Faith's eyes.

"I'm sorry," he said simply, his eyes unreadable.

"Me too," she confessed with a wobbly smile. "When he broke up with me, I guess… I guess I thought it was just like, a knee-jerk reaction, you know? But now… now he really is moving on. He's really over me." She impatiently wiped the tears from her face.

Spencer rose and walked over to her. He pulled her up into a hug and let her cry, still saying nothing. It was almost unnerving for Faith. It was impossible to tell what was going on inside his head. When she pulled away, she grabbed a napkin and blew her nose. Leaving their dinner plates on the table, Spencer led her into the living room and motioned for her to sit down.

"It's my fault," he said quietly. "I'm sorry. I shouldn't have interfered. You were right. Things were fine the way they were. You guys had it all worked out, and I came in and messed everything up."

He wasn't wrong in his assessment. In a way, it *was* because of his reappearance that things went south with Aaron. But Faith didn't want to rub it in, so she protested, "It's not your fault, Spencer."

"Yes it is, and we both know it. The thing is..." He stopped and looked at the wall. "The thing is, I thought I'd be happy when you guys broke up. But I didn't think it would be like this. I—"

"So you came home to steal me back?" Faith could feel her blood pressure rise. "Doggone it, Spencer, I *defended* you! When Aaron accused you of having ulterior motives, I stuck up for you. My mom and David didn't trust you either, but I insisted you had changed. I fell for your charade. But now I'm not all that sure. *Have* you changed? Was your apology to me sincere? Or did you just view me as a challenge to see if you could get the girl again?" Faith furiously blinked back tears. She didn't want to cry in front of him anymore. "Playing with someone's heart is a *very* dangerous game, Spencer, and you've done it to me twice now!"

"I'm not playing with your heart! And that's not why I came back. Believe me, Faith. I came back to apologize. That much was sincere."

She rose in frustration and turned away from him. "I don't know *what* to believe! That's the trouble! How am I supposed to believe anything you say anymore? Just when you had earned back my trust, you throw this at me, and now I'm questioning everything you've said and done over the past number of months!" She turned back to glare at him, her hands on her hips.

"Faith, seriously, I didn't come back to get between you and Aaron. That wasn't even on my radar. But something changed that day at the hospital when you stuck up for me in front of Aaron. I think we all felt it. Things were never right between you and Aaron after that, and in the meantime, I was starting to like you again myself. I kind of hoped, you know, that maybe you guys weren't all that serious anyhow, and that it wouldn't be a big deal if you broke up. But seeing you now… I didn't count on this breaking your heart. I should never have come back at all. I… I'm sorry."

Abruptly, Spencer stood, running a hand through his dark blond hair. "Let me take you home," he said. "I shouldn't have invited you tonight. I shouldn't have told you all that, either. I'm sure you hate me now."

Faith thought about that. *Did* she hate him? She was upset right now, but hatred took way too much effort. "I… don't hate you," she said slowly. "I'm just trying to process everything you said. I'm not sure what to think right now."

"I get it. You need some space."

"Yeah."

"Then I'll give it to you. C'mon, I'll take you back."

They made the trip in complete silence, without even the

radio on. Spencer did accompany her to the front door, but for the first time in ages, he didn't kiss her cheek in parting. Instead, he gave her an apologetic smile and squeezed her hand gently before slipping away.

Faith dragged herself upstairs to her room, her emotions jumbled. She didn't know what to think about Spencer's explanation. But she also couldn't deny that something had shifted at the hospital when Griffin needed stitches. Truthfully, things had been changing even before then. Faith hadn't been upfront with Aaron, which was a surefire way to erode the trust between the two of them.

Thinking back to that day at the hospital, Faith knew with absolute clarity that *she* was the one to blame for the tension, turning on Aaron and sticking up for Spencer. What would have happened if she'd responded differently? Would she still be with Aaron now? The thought was unsettling, and Faith didn't have the mental energy to deal with it at this moment. Determinedly, she pushed all thoughts of Aaron and Spencer out of her head for the night. They would have to wait until morning.

CHAPTER 26

David heard the yelling well before anyone reached his office door. He braced himself for what was sure to be an unpleasant encounter. Shortly, Bill Lattimer appeared at his door with Logan Krause and Brayden Fischer in tow, both boys still shouting and fighting.

He stood and yelled over their noise, "E-*nough*!"

The boys stopped their quarreling and looked at their principal, startled. Pressing his advantage and the lull in the decibel level, David asked. "What happened, Mr. Lattimer?"

The boys started shouting their version of the story, competing to be heard. David whistled through his fingers to quiet them down again. "I asked Mr. Lattimer," he said firmly. "Logan, sit in this chair. Brayden, sit here." The boys sullenly did as he asked, glaring at each other the whole time. David turned again to Bill to ask, "So, Mr. Lattimer, what happened?"

"We had a rather unpleasant confrontation in the classroom, I'm afraid. These two were egging each other on, and Brayden bit Logan. Broke the skin, I fear. When Logan shoved him away, Brayden grabbed his scissors from his desk and lunged at him. I jumped in between them in time to grab Brayden's arms to restrain him, but when he jerked away from me, he fell backward and hit his head on a desk. He's got quite a welt forming, I hate to say."

David's heart had all but stopped as the details emerged. This was bad. Very bad. Both families were sure to make a stink out of the situation.

"He shoved me!" Brayden accused, glaring now at Mr. Lattimer. "He pushed me down and I fell!"

"No, he didn't!" Logan shot back. "It was your fault! All of this is your fault! Look, Mr. Neunaber! Look what he did to me!" Logan insistently held out his arm for David to inspect. He'd had a paper towel over it, but now David could clearly see the bite marks, some of which had indeed broken the skin. Mike Krause would have a field day with this one.

"Okay, Logan, I need you to go to Mrs. Daily and ask her to get some hydrogen peroxide and a bandage on that for you. When you're done, you may wait in her office until I send for you to tell your side of the story. In the meantime, Mr. Lattimer needs to get back to the classroom. Brayden and I are going to have a little chat."

Logan left, sticking his tongue out at Brayden for effect, and David walked Mr. Lattimer to the door. Speaking in low tones, he stepped just outside the office to say, "I'll need to get your side of the story too. This may go badly if any of the parents press the issue. I need to write out a report right away. Check if the librarian can sit with the class for awhile, even just while they do a worksheet. I'll get Brayden's story in the meantime, but come back as soon as you can, okay?"

Grimly, Bill nodded and replied in equally hushed tones. "Logan did antagonize Brayden. I was explaining something to another student, and Logan got up to sharpen his pencil. I don't know what he said to Brayden, but that's what started it. Before then, Brayden was doing fine."

David nodded, mulling this bit of information over in his mind. Bill set off down the hall, while David turned back to his office and set his shoulders resolutely. This was not going to be pleasant. At. All.

The November school board meeting that night was pure chaos. News of the classroom brawl spread quickly, and rumors were floating around on social media already. After getting the details from Brayden, Logan, and Bill Lattimer, David had the unpleasant task of calling the parents of each boy to explain the situation. Monica Fischer was alarmed, mortified, and upset all at once. Mike Krause was just plain mad. So mad, in fact, that he decided to show up to the school board meeting that evening.

Once Clay Henderson called the meeting to order, everyone started talking and shouting at the same time. The secretary, who was always a stickler for following Robert's Rules of Order, was clearly beside herself as the room erupted in accusations and gossip about the situation earlier in the day. They weren't even trying to follow protocol in waiting to discuss new items on the agenda.

"I told you something like this would happen!" Mike Krause shouted, pointing at David. "That kid was a ticking time bomb just waiting to explode! And now look what he's done! You should see Logan's arm! It looks like a dog bit him! And *then* the kid came at him with scissors! You've gotta be kidding me! What if Mr. Lattimer hadn't been so close? Who knows what could have happened to Logan?"

"What even *happened* in there today?" a board member interrupted. "I've heard rumors, but we need facts here. I'm not interested in speculation. Let's give David a chance to talk so we're all on the same page."

All eyes turned to David, who shot the older member a grateful look. He was right—they all needed to have the same details. He recounted the reports he'd pieced together from Logan, Brayden, and Bill, cutting off Mike Krause's attempts to insert his own comments.

"I heard that Mr. Lattimer shoved Brayden," said the secretary uncomfortably. "Not that I believe it, but that's floating around out there too…"

"Yes, unfortunately, that's Brayden's take on it," affirmed David, massaging his temples. "But Logan and the rest of the kids in the class witnessed the whole thing and none of them say Bill pushed him. You guys know Bill. He's been here for years. Has he ever harmed a student? He barely has to raise his voice in the classroom. He's one of the best disciplinarians I've ever known. There's no way he pushed Brayden."

"Just another reason we shouldn't have kids like that in this school," Mike Krause insisted. "Look what a mess we're in now. He comes in here and tries to tarnish a good teacher's reputation. That's it. I've had it. If you don't get rid of Brayden, we're pulling our kids. "

Everyone spoke at once after Mike's comment, and David exchanged a look with Pastor Lixon. Both of them dreaded school board meetings, and tonight's was particularly bad. But it was about to get worse.

Holding up his hands until everyone grew silent, David said quietly, "That's certainly a consideration, Mike. But there's one more thing you all need to know. Brayden's family is going to press charges."

***

When David finally walked in the door at nine fifty-eight that evening, Grace was there to greet him with a hug. He hadn't been home since that morning. The fight took up his entire afternoon as he dealt with angry and confused parents. The school board meeting had been a disaster. After his announcement about the Fischers pressing charges, nothing had been accomplished, unless one counted a lot of yelling and finger pointing. It had been ugly.

"Oh, honey, I'm so sorry," she said. David had given her the CliffsNotes version of things when he'd called to tell her he wouldn't be making it home, and undoubtedly Freddie and Katie had told her what they'd heard about it, but she didn't know the whole story. David didn't have the strength to retell the details yet again, but he knew Grace ought to hear the story from him. At least she wasn't going to explode at him.

Seeming to sense his reluctance to talk right away, she took his hand and led him to the kitchen. "You can tell me details later, but you need to eat first. You must be famished."

She pulled a plate out of the fridge and reheated it in the microwave for him, then set it down on the table. "Wine?" she asked. "Or maybe something stronger?"

He chuckled. They didn't have anything stronger than boxed wine. "I could use a glass of wine, sure."

She poured two glasses of House White and sat down next to him, sipping her wine and patiently waiting as he ate.

"This is really good, honey," he said between bites of lasagna and garlic bread. "I'm sorry I missed dinner. This is one of my favorites."

"I know," she said. "We missed you here, but I was more worried for you than anything. I don't envy you having to deal with a situation like this."

"Oh, I assure you, it's a mess," he said. By now, he was mostly finished with his dinner, so he pushed the plate away and told Grace the whole sordid fiasco. He concluded, "I knew Mike Krause would be mad. His kid *did* get bitten, even if he was the one who antagonized Brayden in the first place. But Mike has complained about Brayden before. This is the last straw. He's threatening to take all three of their kids out of St. John unless Brayden leaves."

"David!"

"It gets better. I half expected that kind of reaction from him. What I *didn't* see coming was Brayden's dad suddenly showing up on the scene. I haven't even met the guy before. He and Brayden's mom are separating, and I've only ever dealt with her. Nice lady. So apparently she told her… husband? Ex? Whatever he is now. So he called in a huff, telling me he's going to press charges. File a suit for harassment."

"What?" Grace's eyes widened. "You've got to be kidding me! Why?"

"Because according to Brayden, Mr. Lattimer pushed him and he fell, thus causing the welt on his head."

"No one will believe that! The entire class saw the whole thing, right? Did anyone else think he pushed him?"

"No. But that's hardly the point. Even a *suggestion* of child abuse is a serious allegation, and no one wants to be the one to ignore a student's claim. It's almost like Bill is guilty no matter what. And according to Brayden's father, he shouldn't have touched him at all."

"But, David, he was going at another student with *scissors*! What else was Bill supposed to do? He can't very well just let that happen!"

"I know," David agreed. "Bill did the right thing, and now he might get nailed because of it." He took off his glasses and put his head in his hands. "This is such a mess. I don't even know how to proceed from here."

Grace put her arms around his waist and rested her head against his shoulder. "I wish I knew what to tell you," she murmured. "I never would have thought something like this would happen at St. John."

"Nor I. This is the sort of wacky thing I hear about in teachers' conferences. I've heard stories about false accusations for inappropriate touching, damaging rumors started to destroy a teacher's reputation, parents banding together to get a teacher fired because they don't like that teacher's style—all kinds of stuff that has no place in a Christian school. Yet these things happen. And whenever I hear stuff like that I shudder and think, 'Thank goodness that's not me!' Now it is. And I have no idea what to do."

"I bet right about now you're wishing you took that call to Missouri after all, huh?" Grace asked sympathetically.

He breathed out a mirthless laugh. "The thought has crossed my mind…"

She stood and gave his shoulder a gentle squeeze. "Let's get upstairs. I'm sure tomorrow will be just as eventful as today, so you need your sleep. But you also need to pray for wisdom and guidance. We can pray together before we go to bed."

David pulled Grace into a hug as he stood next to her. "You're exactly right, sweetheart," he said gratefully. "And I'm glad to have a wife who knows the value of prayer and isn't afraid to remind me. You're amazing, Grace."

They grinned together at the reference to a line he'd pulled when they were dating, before she even knew the hymn "Amazing Grace." She raised herself up on her toes to kiss him lightly, then took his hand as they headed for their room. His wife was right. This situation needed all the prayer it could get.

CHAPTER 27

Faith glanced at her phone as it beeped. There was a new text from Spencer.

I'm home for the weekend. Want to get together...?

She wavered. True to his word, he'd given her space. He hadn't contacted her at all since that night they'd had dinner at his house a few weeks ago. She'd done a lot of thinking in that time and come to the conclusion that Spencer's explanation of things rang true. What had happened with Aaron couldn't be undone, and the truth was that all three of them could have done things differently. Regardless, she could at least have fun getting together with a friend. There was no harm in that.

Sure, she wrote back.

His response was immediate. *11:00? I'll buy lunch.*

That works. Pick me up at Mom's. The guys were gone for their annual University of Michigan football game, and Olivia had come over to spend time with Grace. Her mom and aunt could watch Griffin for her. He'd be napping in the afternoon anyhow.

When he arrived, he didn't back the car out right away.

Instead, he asked, "I take it you aren't mad at me anymore since you agreed to see me today?"

"I'm not mad at you," she said. "Things *did* change after Griffin's accident, and it was as much my fault as anyone's. I can't blame you for Aaron and me breaking up. And I can't blame you for starting to like me again. It's only natural, I guess."

"Ah, but is the feeling mutual…?" he asked with a sly grin.

"Don't push your luck." She didn't even want to venture into such a discussion. She was still trying to figure out her own feelings. "So what's the plan?"

"I'm thinking Krazy Katz."

"Seriously?"

"Oh, yeah! That place is awesome! We can do laser tag, mini golf, maybe even some bowling." He smiled mischievously at her, and she laughed.

"So we'll eat there?"

"May as well. They make the best mozzarella sticks I've ever had. I have to fill up on those before I go home for a dinner of tofu stir fry." Faith wrinkled her nose and he laughed. "It's not as bad as it sounds. Wanna come give it a try?"

"I think I'll pass, thank you very much. Mom and Aunt Livy are making chicken pot pie tonight. I'd much rather have that."

"Ooh, that does sound good. Maybe I can eat at your place?" he asked, raising his eyebrows hopefully.

She giggled again. "Your mom would be disappointed, and you know it. She's lonely with you out of the house."

"She is. And Dad's in Hong Kong again for the week."

"You should have asked her to join us for laser tag and mozzarella sticks," joked Faith. "I bet she'd love it!" They laughed together at the thought of Vivian Young sneaking around a laser tag course.

When they arrived at Krazy Katz, they decided to do a round of mini golf before lunch. Neither one of them was any good, but it was fun. Faith beat Spencer by two strokes.

"You really need to work on your golf game if you're gonna be a doctor someday," she teased him. "Don't all doctors and lawyers spend their weekends on the golf course?"

"Real golf is completely different," Spencer protested with a haughty sniff. "I highly doubt many real courses have windmills in front of the hole."

"Then next time you'll have to take me golfing for real to prove you know how," she said. He grinned broadly, and she felt her cheeks redden. Had she really just said that? *Next time?* Good grief, how could Spencer *not* get the impression that she liked him with statements like that?

He led the way to the snack bar and bought loaded nachos and a double order of mozzarella sticks, as well as two large soft drinks. After they ate, he asked, "What are you up for next? Laser tag? Bowling?"

"Let's do laser tag," she suggested. "And then maybe we can bowl a few games. I had a good coach last time we went. Maybe this time I can break a hundred!" She smiled brightly at him.

"Don't get your hopes up," he taunted with a wicked grin.

"Spencer Young!" she gasped, feigning offense. "Is that any way to treat a lady?" She elbowed him in the ribs, then giggled as he grabbed her arm and tried to tickle her. She wriggled free and scooted away, flashing him a teasing grin over her shoulder as she did so. They were unabashedly flirting in front of everyone, and Faith was well aware of that fact, but at this point, she didn't even care. It felt good to be silly again.

Between laser tag and bowling, the afternoon passed too

quickly for Faith's liking. They bowled two games, and even Spencer conceded that she was improving, although she didn't reach triple digits. But on their second game, she scored eighty-three, her personal best. It didn't bother her that Spencer got almost double that. She was too excited about her own high score.

When they left Krazy Katz at four forty-five, Spencer drove her back to Grace and David's house. As they pulled into the driveway, he asked, "So are you still depressed about Aaron?"

She eyed him suspiciously. "Why?"

"You were pretty broken up about it a few weeks ago. Does it still bother you as much?"

"Not as much, no. I mean, we *did* break up two months ago. It's not like it's a huge shock that he'd start dating someone else."

"But that doesn't mean it's easy."

"Where are you going with this?"

Spencer shifted in his seat and avoided looking at her. "I thought maybe… if you're, like… moving on, I wondered if you'd go out with me." Faith could only stare at him wide-eyed. He glanced at her out of the corner of his eye and hastened on. "I'm good with our friendship as it is, but I… I like spending time with you, and I wish we were more than friends."

Faith had known this was coming but didn't have an answer. While she was honest enough to admit she enjoyed being with Spencer too, she wasn't about to commit to another dating relationship.

"I'm not ready to jump into a boyfriend-girlfriend relationship right now," she replied. "But how about you take me on a few real dates—like more than Krazy Katz—before we talk about *dating* dating?"

Spencer grinned from ear to ear. "Next weekend? Dinner?"

"Not that you're eager or anything."

"Okay, then. Tomorrow?"

She giggled. "Next weekend is fine. You need to spend tomorrow with your poor mother. Take her to church with you or something."

"Oh, sure. Could you imagine my mom in a praise service? She'd probably fit in better at your church."

"Then bring her to my church!"

"Tempting. If it means I'd see you there…"

Faith rolled her eyes. "I'd be more than happy for both of you to come to St. John, but *not* just so you can see me. Come try our service. Maybe you'd like it!"

"I already did, remember? Now it's your turn to come with me." He cocked an eyebrow at her smugly. "You might like it more than you think you will."

She pondered that. He *had* been to her church, that was true. And she was a bit curious about what his church was like. Shrugging carelessly, she answered, "Sure, I'll go to church with you tomorrow."

"For real?"

"For real."

"I'll pick you up at eight forty-five, then. It's a nine o'clock service."

"Sounds good. Griffin and I will be ready."

"How about I take you out to brunch afterward and save dinnertime for my mom?"

"It's a date," she affirmed.

He looked inordinately pleased with himself as he leaned over to kiss her cheek. "Now you're talking. I can't wait."

Faith grinned back at him and stepped out of the car. As surprising as it was, she couldn't wait either.

CHAPTER 28

As Faith walked into Spencer's church the next morning, she was slightly apprehensive, having no idea what to expect. The large building looked more like a sports complex from the outside, and the parking lot was full. A crowd of people milled around in the foyer, many wearing jeans. She felt a little ridiculous in a skirt.

Faith glanced at Spencer beside her, who was wearing his dark blue shirt and khakis, a good choice for dressy casual. He must have sensed her discomfort, because he gave her an encouraging smile over Griffin's head. If he was at all nervous about other members seeing him with a woman and child, he didn't show it. He still exuded his usual air of confidence.

A man with jeans and a button-down shirt that was open at the top and cuffed at the sleeves saw the three of them and gave a short wave. He finished his conversation and walked over to greet them. "Spencer! Glad to see you this weekend. Back from college again?" The two shook hands as he spoke. "Is this young lady part of the reason for your frequent visits?"

Her cheeks warmed under his knowing gaze as Spencer

laughed. "Part of the reason," he admitted. "This is Faith. Faith, this is Pastor Chris."

This was the *pastor*? Faith was astonished. He didn't look a thing like her own pastor. He was young, probably only in his mid-twenties, and his hair was spiked with gel. He looked more like he was on his way to play guitar at a coffee shop than about to lead a worship service.

"Faith. What a beautiful name. 'Now faith is the assurance of things hoped for, the conviction of things not seen,'" he quoted. "That's Hebrews 11:1, the start of the great 'faith' chapter. Excellent Scripture selection. Good summary of a number of Old Testament accounts. And your name is a fitting reminder of the hope we have in Christ."

Faith made a mental note to re-read the chapter he'd mentioned to refresh her memory. Pastor Chris turned next to Griffin to ask, "And who's this?"

"This is Griffin," answered Spencer, shifting the toddler in his arms to better face the pastor.

"Ah, yes. Your son." He said this warmly, without a trace of condemnation. He patted Griffin on the head and said, "So glad to have you here to learn about Jesus. Your parents are doing the best thing they can do for you—teaching you about your Savior." He placed a hand on Spencer's shoulder in an encouraging sort of way, then turned to address a family that had just walked in the door. Faith looked at Spencer in astonishment.

"What?" he laughed.

"He knows about Griffin?"

"You're not the only one who talks to your pastor." He winked at her and led the way into the auditorium.

Faith's eyes widened in mortification at the thought of Spencer telling his pastor about getting her pregnant. So Pastor

Chris knew all about her. Yet he hadn't mentioned it or shown even a hint of disapproval. It was a welcoming, accepting feeling to have someone know the sordid events of her past, yet not to remind her of them. *That's how God sees you,* a little voice in her head told her. She recalled the Bible verse that said, "As far as the east is from the west, so far has He removed your transgressions from you." A relieved, peaceful smile replaced the look on her face as she followed Spencer's lead.

The service was nothing like Faith was used to. Instead of pews and a sanctuary, there were rows of padded chairs forming a semicircle around a stage. A large cross stood where the altar would have been at Faith's church, and a praise band was set up on the left side of the stage, practicing rather loudly already. Rather than hymnals or bulletins, there were large screens at the front so members could follow the words of the Bible readings and songs.

The songs themselves were new to Faith as well. At her church, the music was all written out for the congregation in the hymnals, and by the second or third verse most people got the hang of it. Here she didn't know melodies or rhythms, and it made her feel uncomfortable. Then again, it didn't really matter if she messed up while singing. The band was loud enough to make her ears ring, and she couldn't hear herself over their noise anyhow. She wasn't sure if that was good or bad.

Pastor Chris led the service in his normal clothes, which also threw her for a loop. Pastor Lixon always wore a robe and a colored stole. He'd once explained that he wore the white robe, or alb, as a visual reminder that he was standing in Christ's stead, speaking Christ's words, which covered his own sinfulness. The focus wasn't on the man but on the Word he spoke.

There was no formal liturgy like there was at St. John, but they followed a similar format, with songs, Bible readings, prayers, and a sermon. For the sermon, Pastor Chris pulled over a tall stool to sit on as he flipped open a Bible. "I had a different message planned for this morning, but the Lord placed something else upon my heart today." He paused and looked around the crowded auditorium. "In speaking to a visitor earlier, I was reminded of the great faith chapter, Hebrews 11."

Again he paused, and Faith tried to make herself as small as possible in the chair. *Please don't single me out,* she pleaded silently. *Please, please, please.* She was grateful Spencer had taken Griffin to the nursery earlier in the service so he wouldn't let out a tell-tale squeal. Thankfully, Pastor Chris didn't press the issue. If he had been looking for her, the spotlights were probably too bright in his eyes for him to see anyone in the crowd anyway. Faith breathed a sigh of relief as he continued with the message.

Pastor Chris led the congregation through the entire chapter, flipping back and forth easily in his Bible to refer to the accounts mentioned in Hebrews. Some were familiar to Faith, like the stories of Cain and Abel, Noah and the ark, and Abraham offering Isaac. But others were completely new to her. She'd never heard of Enoch, Barak, and Jephthah, and it was interesting to learn about them. She marvelled at the fact that Pastor Chris was preaching without notes, using only the Bible chapter as his outline.

After the service, everyone filed out and shook the pastor's hand, as they did at Faith's church. When she and Spencer reached Pastor Chris, he said, "There you are! I wanted to thank you for inspiring that message today. The one I'd planned felt a little flat, but I didn't know what else to do until

I spoke with you this morning. Thanks. I do hope you'll come back to worship with us again soon."

"Maybe I will," she replied. "It was neat to learn about all those people in the Bible. I hadn't heard of some of them before."

"And that's the beautiful thing. So many people are unknown to the world at large, but God knows each of His children by name."

"Thanks for that reminder." She gave him a parting smile and followed Spencer to the nursery to sign Griffin out.

Once they emerged into the fall air, Spencer teased, "So was it as bad as you thought it would be?"

She laughed, amused that he'd been astute enough to pick up on her initial hesitation. "Just different, is all."

"Any style of worship takes some getting used to," he said, opening the car door for her.

"That's true," she conceded. But as she bent to strap Griffin into his car seat, she hid a smile. Next time they worshipped together would be Spencer's turn to come to her church. Then she shook her head in amazement. It wasn't even a question of *if* they'd worship together again. It was only a matter of *when*.

CHAPTER 29

A knock on his door made David look up warily. These days, a visitor was seldom there to say hi or give some encouragement. More likely, this was just another parent or school board member coming to complain or give unsolicited advice. When he saw Monica Fischer there, his heart plunged.

"Ah, Mrs. Fischer. Please come in," he said, trying to be cordial. The last thing he needed was to give her any reason to get more upset with the school.

Monica entered, looking embarrassed to be there. She perched nervously on the edge of a chair and clutched her purse in both hands, as if ready to bolt at any moment.

"Um... I... This..." She took a deep breath, straightening her shoulders as if to give herself more confidence before starting again. "Brayden is attending the public school now," she stated. David nodded. This was common knowledge. "He's actually doing well, for his standards," she continued. "He's meeting with the counselor there a few times a week, and that seems to be helping him control his emotions. In terms of schoolwork, he's doing a lot better now that he can actually read. If it hadn't been for St. John, I don't know that he would be able to do that."

She sounded almost… *grateful*. Now she looked at him, apparently waiting for a response. He cleared his throat and said, "I'm glad Mr. Lattimer took the initiative to change that. He's a fine teacher." His heart hammered loudly in his chest. He could hardly believe he'd made such a bold statement, considering the person to whom he was speaking.

Monica had the grace to blush at his comment as she averted her eyes. "Yes, he is," she agreed, shocking David. She looked at him then, finally meeting his eye. "We aren't going to press charges."

David's heart skipped a beat. He hardly dared to believe the good news. "Oh?" he prompted.

"My husband was the one who insisted upon it in the first place. He always tries to take the responsibility off Brayden. It's worked in the past, but it isn't helping. He's just learning he can lie and cheat to get out of trouble. The world doesn't work that way. My husband isn't helping him; he's crippling him. That's why we separated. Brayden can't grow up like that."

David's eyebrows rose. He hadn't thought much about the circumstances surrounding their separation before since it was none of his concern. But if he'd had to guess, he would have thought Monica would be the one to go easy on her son, leaving Brayden's dad to be the tough guy. It surprised him to find it was the other way around and that Monica had the gumption to do something so drastic to change the situation.

Monica spoke again. "I told him I'd side with the school if he pressed charges. He hasn't even been around this school year, so he doesn't know what's really been happening. I know Brayden is a handful, but believe it or not, he sort of liked it here. He'd never admit that, but I could tell. If it hadn't been for that blow up with the Krause boy, I wonder…" She looked away almost wistfully, then came to herself and carried on.

"But it's just as well he's in the public school now. As I mentioned, they have a counselor. He has a lot to talk through, especially now with the divorce procedure starting. I'm glad they have that service available. And I know Brayden isn't the type of kid who normally goes to school here. His classroom is probably better off without his influence."

A wave of sadness washed over David at her words. Was that what she thought? That Brayden didn't meet their standards? He hoped they hadn't given her that impression. Then again, how could they not have given off that vibe? The complaints of other parents hadn't exactly been discreet.

"The only type of children who go to school here are *kids*, Mrs. Fischer," he answered. "Some are more active than others, some are from church families, and some aren't. But every child has one thing in common—they need to hear about the love and forgiveness Jesus offers. We strive to make sure each student here knows that Jesus died for everyone. Me, you, Brayden—everyone. I'm sorry things didn't work out differently for Brayden to stay on here as a student, but you and he are always more than welcome to attend church here anytime."

"Yes, well, I thank you for the offer," Monica said, fumbling with the zipper on her purse. "I'm not at all sure other members would be as welcoming, though." David felt his face warm. Obviously she was referring to the Krause family, and unfortunately, she had a point. Nor were the Krauses the only ones who felt that way.

She stood then, and David rose with her and shook her outstretched hand. "Thank you for coming in, Monica," he said. "You're doing a good job with Brayden. Teaching responsibility is a difficult thing. Keep at it. And God be with you."

"Thank you," she said, and then she was gone.

Slowly, David sank back into his chair. He should be ecstatic right now with the news that Brayden's family wasn't going to press charges. The school board would be thrilled to find out, and poor Bill Lattimer would have a huge weight lifted off his shoulders. But David didn't feel happy at all. Instead, he felt exceedingly sad.

Monica and Brayden both needed so much to heard the Good News of Jesus. And Brayden *had* heard the Gospel message during his two months at St. John, no doubt about that. But would he remember any of it? Would he even care? It seemed unlikely that a couple months of religion classes would make any difference to a kid in such circumstances.

And what kind of witness had their church and school given Monica Fischer? David knew that before Grace became a Christian, she was terribly sensitive to how Christians treated her. She'd thought they were all judgmental and self-righteous. Was that how Monica saw the members there? A bunch of people who thought their kids were better than her kid; people who wanted him out of their school?

David grunted in frustration. He'd had such high hopes when Brayden started attending school there, praying that he and his family would eventually come to the faith. And even though a lawsuit had been avoided, David couldn't help but feel a keen sense of failure over the way things had turned out.

CHAPTER 30

"So is Faith Spencer's girlfriend again?"

Grace looked uncertainly at David as Freddie posed the question over dinner. The issue was burning in the back of her mind, though Faith had evaded the question when Grace had posed it. She had gone so far as to ask Olivia, who had no qualms about snooping into Faith's personal life. Even Olivia didn't know.

"I'm not sure," Grace admitted. "I don't *think* so, but then again, he's coming home more weekends than not, and he and Faith usually go out when he's here."

"They could have done me a favor and figured it out sooner," Jackson complained. "I could've used some tips from him for football. It's too late now. The season's over."

"You were still one of the best players on JV," Katie pointed out.

"But not *the* best," lamented Jackson. "Cole Patterson was better. Besides, I want to make varsity next year. Spencer could've helped a lot."

"You'll only be a sophomore next year," said Freddie. "And Cole will be on varsity. You can be the best receiver on JV or an average one on varsity."

"I just want to make varsity as a sophomore," Jackson insisted stubbornly, ignoring his younger brother's solid logic.

Freddie rolled his eyes and returned to the subject at hand. "Anyway, I liked Aaron more than Spencer. He was better for her."

Grace agreed with Freddie's assessment. But from the details she'd squeezed out of Olivia, Aaron had been the one to break up with Faith, a wrinkle no one had seen coming. And from Olivia's intel, Faith had been pretty upset about the break up. It seemed unlikely she would jump so soon into a relationship with Spencer, two months after she and Aaron broke up. Then again, maybe she was on the rebound and naturally drifted toward Spencer. It was obvious the guy liked her.

"Aaron's okay," Jackson conceded, "but I think Spencer's really trying to be, like, trustworthy. And he's been good with Griffin lately too."

"I still like Aaron," Freddie insisted.

"Me too," Katie chimed in. "He goes to our church."

Jackson heaved a sigh, clearly exasperated by the hopeless piousness of his siblings. "There's more to life than what church you go to."

"Like football?" asked Katie.

"Exactly!"

Grace and David chuckled at his candid answer, and Freddie and Katie joined in as well. Even Jackson had to laugh. But Grace felt uneasy. Like Freddie, she much preferred the way things used to be.

***

That night, Grace snuggled up to David in bed, laying her head on his chest. It was one of her favorite positions. Hearing his strong and steady heartbeat soothed her anxious thoughts, filling her with a sense of constancy.

David put his arm around her and rested his chin on her head. "What's on your mind?" he asked.

She sighed. "Oh, David, I don't know what to think of all this."

"Faith and Spencer?"

"I'm conflicted. On the one hand, it would be great for Griffin if Faith ended up with his birth father. It ties everything up in a neat little package. No joint custody battles or weekend visits. It's so… tidy. But by golly, I still like Aaron! Why did he ever break up with her in the first place?"

"Because of Spencer."

She knew that much, but it wasn't a satisfactory answer. "But why? Faith wasn't indicating any interest in Spencer, was she? Why would Aaron just… give up like that? I really thought they loved each other."

"Maybe he wasn't so sure once Spencer came back. You heard what Liv said—he didn't want either of them to stay together out of guilt. Besides, he probably felt inferior to Spencer."

"In terms of looks? How shallow is that? Come on. Seriously, he's been there for Faith from the very start. He's the absolute sweetest guy I know. Besides you, of course, darling," she assured hastily.

"Nice save." Grace could tell from his voice that he was smiling in the dark. "But it's more than looks. I should know. Remember when we met Bob at Michelle's wedding?"

She grimaced. How could she forget?

"I felt like a bumbling idiot around him," continued David. "As petty as it sounds, yes, looks *do* make a big difference. At least in my perception they did. I felt old, weak, balding, and inept next to him. He's younger, stronger, has a full head of hair, and can be very suave. But it's also deeper than that. No matter the circumstances, he *is* the father of four of your children. Not all your memories together are bad. I rather imagine Aaron feels the same way about Spencer."

"That's true," she murmured. "I hadn't really thought of it like that before. But what does Aaron hope to gain here?"

"I guess if Faith ends up choosing him over Spencer, there'll never be a doubt in his mind that she really loves him."

"And if she doesn't?"

"Then I guess it's not meant to be."

There was a moment of silence before Grace confessed, "You know, I tend to think she's older than she really is. She's raising a baby, and that makes a person grow up and mature pretty fast. And Aaron's so… comfortable. I almost think of him and Faith as practically married already. But for crying out loud, David, they're not even twenty yet!"

"I know. I feel the same way. I assumed they'd be together forever. I don't know what to think of this latest development."

Neither did Grace. After all Spencer had put Faith through in high school, it seemed improbable that she'd so easily settle back into a relationship with him. "What do you think of Spencer?" asked Grace. "Do you think he's changed? Or is he just putting on a show to impress her?"

"I wonder that too. I was very wary of him and his intentions when he showed up at Confirmation. But I think he really is trying to change. He hasn't done anything inappropriate with Faith, as far as I can tell. And he's been helpful with Griffin and a supportive friend to Faith. I suppose

I'm tentatively optimistic about him. I still wish Faith and Aaron were together, but I guess if she's happy with Spencer…" David left the thought unfinished.

Grace knew what he meant. If Faith ended up with Spencer, he would be supportive of her choice. But Grace could also read between the lines enough to know that her husband wouldn't be overly excited about it. She felt exactly the same way.

CHAPTER 31

Faith smiled as Katie chattered away in the back seat about her friends at school. Her little sister was the social butterfly of the family, and Faith knew Katie considered everyone in her second-grade class to be a friend.

The two had braved Black Friday crowds to go to the mall and get a jump on Christmas shopping. They hadn't accomplished much, but they'd had fun together, even splurging at the coffee shop for a special treat. Katie acted quite grown up when Faith let her order a steamer, not realizing her beverage had no coffee in it whatsoever. Katie and Faith didn't spend a lot of time together, just the two of them, but Faith figured if her mom and Olivia could be best friends with an eight-year age difference, she and Katie could be close even with a ten-year gap.

"So then Alyssa told me we should start a club, so we're gonna invite everyone in our class to join. It'll be the Friendship Club!" Katie said excitedly.

Faith bit back a smile. It was hardly a "club" if the entire class joined, but that wasn't the point. Leave it to Katie to include everyone.

As Katie continued her narrative, Faith's attention was distracted by the chiming of her phone on the passenger seat. She grabbed the phone and saw she had a new text from Spencer. Was something wrong with Griffin? Glancing at the road ahead to make sure the coast was clear, she turned her eyes back to the phone and swiped the screen to open her new message. Spencer had sent a picture of Griffin in a pile of leaves in the Youngs' backyard. He was laughing and tossing a handful of leaves toward the camera. He looked adorable. Faith's face lit up in a smile, and she quickly typed with her thumb, "Cute!" Before she could hit the send button, Katie shrieked, "Faith!"

She jerked her head back up and saw a deer directly in the path of the car. Faith screamed, dropped her phone, slammed on the brakes, and yanked the wheel simultaneously. But it was too late.

As she hit the back end of the deer, the car careened off the road. They slammed into a tree, crunching in the front passenger side. Faith's face was cushioned by the airbag, but when she jerked back from the momentum, her head cracked against the window with a sickening thud. She felt blood gush down the left side of her face, but she was more worried about something else.

"Katie? *Katie!*" she shrieked, trying to turn back to see her younger sister. "Are you okay? Katie!"

There was no answer. Although her head was throbbing and she was getting lightheaded, she forced herself to twist enough to see Katie behind her. The last thing Faith saw before passing out was her little sister covered in blood, her arm pinned in the tangled metal of the door. She was completely still.

***

"Mom, I swear, I didn't mean for it to happen," Faith sobbed.

The last few hours had been a blur. She vaguely recalled waking up in the ambulance to ask about Katie and to request that the attendants call her parents. Grace and David arrived at the hospital not long ago, while Faith was getting stitches and being monitored for signs of a more serious head injury. "The deer appeared out of nowhere," she continued, ignoring the twinge of guilt at the little white lie.

Grace had her arms around her daughter. "I know, sweetie. Practically everyone in Michigan has had a run-in with a deer at some point. It's okay," she soothed. "I'm just glad the guy behind you stopped and called 911 and waited until they came."

"But what about Katie?" Faith asked, frantic to know her little sister's condition. "Is she okay? I have to see her!"

"Shh, honey. Don't get yourself worked up. She's in the operating room. David's waiting over there. They're working on her now."

"*Operating* room? What's wrong?" Faith was fighting waves of panic. *What did I do to her?*

"Her right arm was pinned in the accident," explained Grace, her voice wavering. "They're going to have to reset the bones in her forearm. They were broken in multiple places. And a few of her fingers were basically crushed. They might have to amputate them."

"*What?*" Faith felt sick to her stomach. This was far more serious than she'd thought possible. "But will she be okay?" Her voice was nearly hysterical. "I have to know!"

Just then a doctor appeared at the door and beckoned for Grace. She gave Faith one more hug and said, "I'm going to check on her right now. I'll let you know. Don't fret, sweetie. Just pray for her." Grace had tears in her own eyes, which did little to calm Faith's nerves. She clutched frantically at her mother's hand, but Grace kissed her on the cheek, gave her hand a squeeze, and released it, following the doctor.

Faith hugged her knees to her chest and rested her forehead on her knees, moaning through her tears. This was all her fault. She shouldn't have taken Katie with her. She should have gone a different way. She shouldn't have checked her phone. Dang it, she *knew* better than to text while driving. *She* should be the one in the operating room, taking the brunt of the injuries. It was so unfair. Why sweet little Katie?

She felt a light touch on her back and shot into an upright position, causing a burst of pain to explode in her head. It was Spencer, his eyes reflecting a look that was a mixture of concern and relief. Before Faith knew what she was doing, she threw herself into his arms and allowed herself to cry into his chest, heaving great sobs. Her body was finally processing the trauma and emotional impact of the accident, and she started shaking uncontrollably, almost as if she were having a seizure.

Spencer held her tightly, and although she could feel his heart racing, he took slow, deliberate breaths. It was as if he was willing her to relax as well. He didn't say anything, but simply held her in his arms until her shaking began to subside.

"We have to stop meeting in hospitals like this," he quipped in a thick voice. "This time you were the one who nearly scared me to death. When you were an hour late to get Griffin and weren't answering your phone or responding to texts, I was about beside myself with worry. Then when I called your parents and heard what had happened, I was frantic. It's such a relief to know you're alright."

She looked up into his face then, and he noticed the gauze

on the side of her forehead, covering the ugly red gash that had been stitched. Gently he placed his fingers near the wound. "How many stitches?" he asked.

"Nine," she reported. "My whole head is pounding. But probably as much from my crying as anything else. Katie... I don't know if Katie will be okay. No one will even tell me anything, and it's all my fault!" She could feel herself getting worked up again.

Spencer placed his thumb on her lips as his fingers cradled her jaw. "Shh," he calmed her. "It's *not* your fault. Accidents happen."

"Mom said they might have to amputate some fingers, Spencer! Oh, Katie..." she moaned. "What have I done?"

"Calm down," he insisted. "Let's wait until the doctors tell us what's going on. We can't change anything by panicking. I don't know what's going to happen to her hand, but she isn't going to die. That much I can tell you. I saw your stepdad out there, and he told me she's stabilized."

Faith knew he was trying to make her feel better, but all she felt was an overwhelming sense of guilt knowing that her carelessness may have cost Katie part of her hand. That would be an awful burden to carry the rest of her life.

Spencer sat next to her on the hospital cot and pulled her into a side hug, his arms wrapped tightly around her. They waited an interminable amount of time, and Faith found herself starting to nod off with her head against his chest. The hushed sounds of the hospital outside the door lulled her into a trance with the help of the painkillers they'd given her. And as embarrassing as it was to confess, having Spencer's strong arms around her was a very comforting feeling. She didn't fight the sleepiness and was nearly dozing when a brisk knock sounded on the door.

She startled and sat straight up, her heart pounding. It was a policeman. Faith's blood ran cold.

"Faith Williams?" he asked. She could only nod. "I'm Officer Bush. I need to ask you a few questions to make a police report for the accident you were involved in." Again, her only response was to nod mutely.

Beside her, Spencer stood. "I guess you don't need me around for this," he said. "Let me go check with the nurse to see if they'll discharge you when you're done here. Maybe you can go wait with your parents then, yeah?"

Another nod.

Spencer left, and Officer Bush closed the door most of the way to allow for privacy. "So, Ms. Williams, please tell me what happened this afternoon." His voice was kind, but his smile didn't reach his eyes. Faith's head started pounding anew, and she had to swallow before she could speak.

"Um, we were driving home from the mall," she began. Her voice came out more as a croak. Her mouth was as dry as cotton. She tried in vain to clear her throat before continuing. "Actually, I was driving to a friend's house to pick up my son." Officer Bush opened his notebook and jotted something down as she went on. "Um, the friend who was in here... uh, Spencer... He's the one who was watching Griffin today. My son. Griffin. I was driving to his house—Spencer's house. With Katie. Katie and I were together. In the car." This was not going well. Her story was all jumbled up.

"Katie being your younger sister?" Office Bush interjected.

"Yes, my younger sister."

"And you were going how fast?"

"Fifty-five."

"You're sure about that?"

"Yes." Faith was relieved to be answering questions rather

than recounting the incident on her own. It was far easier this way.

"Mm." He wrote something in his notebook. "Go on."

Rats, back to telling the story in her own words. "So... um, suddenly this deer appeared, and I slammed on the brakes and tried to swerve, but I hit it anyhow. It felt like we spun around, and I know we hit a tree."

"The airbag deployed?"

"Yes, sir. The airbag protected my face, but I hit my head against the side window when I bounced back."

"And what do you remember after that?"

"Not much. I felt blood on the side of my face, and I was starting to get light-headed. I know I looked back to check on Katie, but she wasn't answering me, and she had a lot of blood on her too. I guess I fainted then, because I don't remember anything else."

"You don't recall the gentleman behind you stopping or talking to you?"

"No, sir."

"Okay. So let's get back to this deer." Faith's stomach knotted further. Officer Bush flipped to a previous page in his notebook. "According to the other witness—the driver who was behind you—this deer was taking his time. He didn't just dart onto the road or appear from behind a bush. The other witness said the deer was standing on the road quite visibly. He could see it well in advance."

He stopped and gave Faith a look that seemed to indicate he knew something she wasn't telling him. "Hmm. That's odd," she said. "I honestly didn't see it until right before I hit it. Maybe he had a better perspective than I did."

"Maybe." He didn't seem convinced. "Or maybe you were too distracted to notice?" The blood drained from Faith's face as he pulled her phone out of his pocket. "Do you recognize this?"

"Uh, yes. Yes, sir. That's… um, that's my phone."

"Mind if we check a few things on it?" It wasn't actually a question, and she knew it. Faith felt trapped as he handed it to her. "Why don't you open it and check your texts?" Mutely, she obeyed. The screen for Spencer's texts was still open from earlier. "Hmm," he mused beside her, reading over her shoulder. "Spencer. He's the one who was just in here, right? The one who was watching your son? Let's see what he texted you today." There was a slew of messages since the picture he'd sent, asking her if she was okay and where she was, but Officer Bush didn't give her time to read them. "Scroll up a bit, please." She did so until she came to the picture of Griffin. "Huh. That one," he said. "What's the time stamp on that picture?"

Faith knew she was cornered. She slid the picture over slightly to reveal the time Spencer had sent the picture. "Four forty-six, is that right? Ah. Interesting coincidence. The 911 call about the accident came at four forty-seven. And I see there's a response on your end that hasn't been sent. It says, 'Cute!' I can only assume that's talking about the picture, and not his inquiries into your well-being."

Officer Bush looked at her sternly. "Ms. Williams, you were on your phone at the time of the accident, weren't you? That's why you didn't see the deer in time."

Faith couldn't lie. He already knew the truth. Her cheeks aflame, she stared at the incriminating phone and whispered, "Yes."

There was a moment of silence before Officer Bush responded. "Do you realize how many accidents and fatalities occur every year because of texting and driving? It's an alarming number, and the tragedy is that these accidents could be avoided. You're lucky you didn't hit any other cars in the process, or you could be looking at a lawsuit. As it stands, your little sister is seriously hurt by your oversight. This will have to be included in my police report. This is no joking matter."

"I know," Faith squeaked out in a tiny voice. "I'm sorry."

Officer Bush snapped his notebook shut. "I'm not the one you need to apologize to," he told her. "I'll be in touch if there's anything else. Thank you for your time." With that, he walked out of the room, and Faith buried her face in her hands and cried.

A minute later, a quiet knock sounded on the door, and Spencer's voice asked, "Hey, are you okay?"

Faith wiped her tears away with the back of her sleeve and looked into his concerned face. "No, I'm not okay. This is all wrong. All of this. I need to get out of this room and see Katie. I have to know she'll be okay."

"I have good news for you, then. The nurse is getting your discharge papers ready. We can go find your parents when she comes."

As if on cue, the nurse bustled into the room and gave Faith two prescriptions, instructions for discharge, and warning signs for which to watch. Then Faith and Spencer made their way to the waiting room. Spencer held her hand, and she didn't protest. She could use his support right now.

David jumped to his feet when the two entered and crossed the distance quickly to engulf Faith in a hug. "Oh, sweetheart," he whispered hoarsely, "thank goodness you're okay." Faith burrowed her face into his chest, swallowing over the lump in her throat. It overwhelmed her to see how much David cared for her.

"Katie?" she asked in a quavering voice, looking into David's face to search his expression. His face was grave, his eyes troubled, which alarmed Faith. He was usually so stoic.

"Nothing to do now but wait and pray," he said quietly. "Some of her bones were basically crushed. They set the bones in her arm, but her fingers... They can't make any guarantees. They're prepping her now to transfer to the children's hospital in Grand Rapids. They have a team of pediatric surgeons who are better equipped for this."

Her stomach twisted with guilt, and she knew she had to tell David the truth before he or her mom got a look at the police report. "David—" she started, then stopped.

"What is it, sweetie?"

"I... I'm sorry. I—"

"Honey, it's okay," he interrupted. His voice was so kind it brought tears to her eyes. "Don't worry. We'll get through this. The important thing is that you're both okay. Even if Katie loses a few fingers, she's alive, and so are you. That's what matters." He gave her another hug, and her resolve melted away. She couldn't spill the beans now. It wasn't the right time. Instead, she accepted his hug, grateful for the comfort of his embrace.

As the evening wore on, David kept his arm around Grace as they awaited word on Katie. Faith, on the other hand, chose to pass the time walking around, a fact that irritated David. He could tell Grace was annoyed as well. Faith was a ball of nerves, and her incessant pacing was putting everyone else on edge. She needed to leave before she drove everyone crazy. The problem was, her car was totaled, and he wasn't about to leave his wife there alone when Katie was soon to be transferred. There was only one other option, and he wasn't thrilled with it. Spencer would have to take her.

Resignedly, David motioned to Spencer, who followed him a few paces out of the waiting room. "Faith needs to get out of here," he said quietly. "It'll do her good to get back and see Griffin. Would you mind…?"

"No problem at all, Mr. Neunaber," assured Spencer. "Don't worry about a thing. I'll take care of her."

That was precisely what David was worried about—Spencer taking care of Faith. He still harbored the secret wish that Faith and Aaron would get back together again, but Spencer was the one there at the moment. If nothing else, it was convenient.

"Thank you, Spencer. I appreciate it. We'll be in touch." David shook his hand and walked back to the waiting room.

"Faith, Spencer is going to take you home," David told her. "We'll keep you posted. We love you, and we're glad you're okay." David hugged her and planted a kiss on her head before turning her over to Spencer.

Taking Faith by the hand, Spencer led her away, speaking softly as if he were talking to a child. "Come on, Faith. They'll call you with any updates. Griffin needs you now. He misses you and doesn't understand what's going on. Let's go see him, okay?"

David watched them go, feeling a sense of relief that Faith would be out of their hair, but he also had a premonition that he'd just paved the way for a deeper relationship between the two.

Spencer held Faith's hand the entire way back to his house, rubbing her thumb gently with his own. He could only imagine how she was feeling now, physically and emotionally. It had to be weighing heavily upon her mind that Katie might lose some of her fingers. When they reached his house, he ushered her inside and found his mother waiting with Griffin, who was whining and pushing her hands away, squirming to get down.

"Darling, I'm so glad to see you," gushed Vivian when she saw Faith. "So glad you're okay. Griffin's tired and upset. It's past his bedtime, and he only wants his mama."

Griffin lunged for Faith, and she engulfed him in a huge hug, her tears starting anew. Spencer took her by the shoulders and escorted her up the elegant staircase, down the hall, and into the guest suite.

"You need to rest," he said firmly. "You and Griffin both. Just lie down and relax. You've been through a lot today."

Faith nodded and carried Griffin over to the bed. She lay on her side with the toddler in her arms, and Spencer covered them both with the quilt on the bottom of the bed. He bent over to kiss the top of Faith's head and brush her hair out of her face. She grabbed his hand desperately and searched his face.

"Will you tell me as soon as you find out anything about Katie?" she asked, her eyes pleading.

"Absolutely," he assured her.

She breathed out a sigh and murmured, "Thanks, Spencer." She finally seemed to allow herself to relax as she closed her eyes and cuddled with Griffin on the soft mattress. "I'll just take a little rest."

Spencer sat down on the bed next to her and stroked her hair. "Take as much time as you need," he whispered. "I'll only stay until you fall asleep. I promise."

Faith nodded groggily and started to drift off. Spencer watched as Griffin snuggled into his mother's arms and rubbed his eyes, giving into sleep himself. A warm feeling spread over Spencer as he watched the two of them sleeping, and he felt completely content to be there with them.

Faith's breathing was even, and despite the large gauze bandage on her head, she looked beautiful. Spencer could watch her sleep for hours. But he had promised he'd only stay until she was sleeping, so he ran his fingers through her hair one last time and leaned over to kiss her cheek before slipping out the door.

CHAPTER 32

When Faith opened her eyes, she was disoriented and alarmed. Her foggy mind tried to make sense of where she was and what had happened. As her eyes blinked to adjust to a room bathed in sunlight, her heart nearly stopped. She'd been at Spencer's house all night. *Great. How am I ever going to explain this one?*

She sat up abruptly, the blood rushing to her head and causing her to double over in pain. The injury she'd sustained on her forehead throbbed, and her head ached as it never had before. She groaned in pain and wondered how she'd ever make it through the day like this. Glancing at Griffin, she was amazed to find him still asleep. The poor kid must have really been worn out.

Gingerly, Faith edged her way toward the side of the bed, swinging her feet over and testing her legs before standing. She leaned over to grab the dresser for support and noticed a crystal vase with a dozen long-stemmed red roses inside. Spencer must have put them there. Beside it was a medicine bottle with a note attached. She picked it up and sank back onto the bed to read it.

Good morning, beautiful! I got your pain prescription filled last night for you. I figured you'd need it this morning. Thankfully, I know a good pharmacist who was willing to stay a bit late for your sake. (BTW, he sends his regards.) Hopefully you had a good night's sleep and feel better today. I let your mom know you were here, and she wants you to know that Katie is at the children's hospital recovering from her surgery. I can take you down there later. Take your time, but when you're ready you can come down for a fancy breakfast of soy sausages and scrambled Eggbeaters. What can I say? My mom is in a festive mood. We're all glad you're okay.
Yours,
Spencer

Faith sat quietly, digesting everything for a while. What did Uncle Andy think when Spencer picked up her prescription for her? What would her family think when they found out she'd spent the night here? Her cheeks burned at the thought, even though nothing whatsoever had happened.

But then she realized they already knew that. She hadn't been home or at the McNeals' house, and apparently Spencer had been in contact with her mother. How embarrassing to have him acting as her mediator, relaying messages to and from her parents.

With a groan, Faith stood and grabbed the medicine bottle, walking to the attached bathroom for a glass of water to wash down the pills. She figured she may as well take a shower while Griffin slept, and as she stood under the hot water, she thought back over the note again.

Good morning, beautiful!

Aaron had texted her the same thing the morning after

Griffin was born. And when he'd visited her in the hospital later that day, he'd brought her flowers as well. Pretty, cheerful yellow sunflowers.

Aaron. Faith was surprised to find she could think of him now without that familiar ache—the sense of longing for the way things used to be. When had that happened, exactly? She couldn't say, but she hadn't thought of Aaron for some time now.

Her thoughts turned to Katie. Spencer's note hadn't given her much information. All she knew was that she was recovering from surgery at the children's hospital. What had they done in the surgery? Faith felt a desperate urge to get to the hospital and see Katie herself. She knew she wouldn't be able to relax until she knew what was going on. But in the meantime, she was here with the Youngs, and she would try to make the best of it. After all, she had soy sausages and Eggbeaters to look forward to. She only hoped Mr. Young wasn't here. Facing him was the last thing she wanted to do.

Twenty minutes later, feeling slightly refreshed from the shower and medicine, she and Griffin made their entrance into the Youngs' spacious kitchen. Spencer jumped up from the table, where he'd been texting, and walked over to greet her with a hug.

"Oh, darling, there you are," said Vivian in her breathy voice. "I'm so glad you slept well. You needed the rest. Sit down there with Spencer. I'll get your plates."

Faith obeyed as Spencer lifted Griffin into his booster seat. She realized that to an outsider, they very much looked the part of a young family visiting the in-laws for Thanksgiving. The thought made her cheeks warm.

When Vivian put her plate in front of her, Spencer grabbed Faith's hands in his own and said, "I'll pray." She bowed her head as he began. "Father God, we thank You for this food, and we thank You for protecting Faith and Katie in their accident yesterday. Please be with them both as they recover, especially Katie as she deals with her injuries, whatever they may be. Heal her quickly, Lord. Amen."

"Amen," Faith echoed, squeezing his hands before releasing them to eat. Despite the fact that she'd never eaten a soy sausage in her life, the food tasted good, and she realized she hadn't even eaten dinner the night before. She finished the Eggbeaters and sausages and polished off the cantaloupe before Spencer even finished half of his food.

Vivian laughed and swooped up her plate. "Someone was certainly hungry! I take that as a great compliment, darling. Here, let me get you some more."

Faith gratefully accepted the offer while Spencer grinned at her. "She'll make you into a health nut yet. Just be careful," he teased in a low voice as he winked at her.

"Now, Spencer dearest, you leave that poor girl alone," Vivian commanded from across the kitchen, apparently believing he'd been teasing Faith. "She didn't eat last night like you did. You even had thirds! You'll eat me out of house and home yet, just you watch!"

"That's because her meals have about fifty calories each. I have to have thirds or I'll starve," he said quietly to Faith. She laughed with him as they ate their food.

When they were finished, Spencer said, "I'm sure you're anxious to get to the hospital and check on Katie, but first, let me take a look at that wound. I also filled a prescription for medicated ointment to fight infection, and I bought some gauze at the drugstore while I was there. I'll clean you up and apply new gauze. Let's go to the bathroom to do this. I'm sure Mom doesn't want to see it."

"Heavens, no, dearie!" his mother answered. "I can't imagine why anyone would want to be a doctor and deal with all that blood. It makes me shudder to think of it! But I'm glad you can help Faith. Shoo, you two. I'll wipe Griffin's face and hands."

Faith followed Spencer to the bathroom where he washed his hands before he gently pulled off the gauze. Frowning slightly in concentration, he took a warm washcloth and wiped the area carefully. Faith held her breath as she watched him. He was good at this. His hands were steady and gentle, and his eyes were calm and assuring. She was seeing a glimpse of who he would be as a doctor someday, and she was impressed.

When he had washed the area, applied the ointment, and put clean gauze on, he leaned over to kiss the bandage. "I don't do that for just anyone, you know," he told her. "You must be special."

She smiled faintly, but his words struck a chord deep inside her that surfaced the feelings of guilt she'd been trying to push aside since the accident. "I… I'm not special, Spencer," she insisted, her eyes downcast. "The accident—it was my fault."

"No, it's not," he argued. "Deer are all over the place around here. You can't blame yourself."

"No, you don't understand," she argued back, gathering the courage to look up at his face. "It *is* my fault. I… I was…" She faltered, not wanting to admit she'd been texting *him*. That would make him feel guilty too, and it wasn't his fault in the least. The blame was hers alone. "I was texting when I hit the deer," she confessed. "I would have seen it if I hadn't been on my phone."

Understanding dawned on Spencer's face as he realized the import of her words. "Ohh," he groaned. "Shoot. I…" He blew out a short, frustrated breath.

"Pretty much." She averted her eyes to look at the floor once again, and the two lapsed into silence.

At last, Spencer asked, "Do your parents know?"

"Not yet. I didn't know how to tell them. It didn't seem like the right time yesterday."

"Yeah."

More silence. Faith wished Spencer would say something—*anything*—about her admission. She'd even take him yelling at her. She knew she deserved it. Somehow, his silence was so much worse.

When it was apparent Spencer wasn't going to say more, Faith sighed and said, "Look, I really want to get down to the hospital to see Katie. And yes, I need to tell Mom and David the truth before they find out another way. But I'm wearing the same clothes I had on yesterday. Could we swing by Liv and Andy's house first to pick up some clean stuff? I assume Aunt Livy is at our place watching the kids for Mom while she's with Katie. I guess we could bring Griffin with us, but if your mom is willing, it would be a lot easier to keep him here with her. If he gets too fussy, she can drop him off at my place for Livy to watch him with the other kids. Jackson and Freddie are good with him."

"I'm sure Mom won't mind watching him today," Spencer said absently. "And I don't have anything on my schedule. I'm completely at your disposal."

Mumbling a thank-you, Faith slid around him and exited the bathroom to ask Mrs. Young about watching Griffin. She agreed, so Faith and Spencer left, stopping by the McNeals' house first. Faith changed into clean clothes, then hesitated in her room. On a whim, she threw a handful of outfits and some toiletries into an overnight bag. She thought maybe she'd need them if she decided to stay overnight in Grand Rapids while

Katie was recovering.

The hour-long ride to the hospital was mostly silent, which unnerved Faith. It wasn't a comfortable silence, and her confession still hung over them. Good grief, if Spencer was taking it this hard, how on earth would her mother react?

Finally, Faith couldn't stand it anymore and demanded, "If you're mad at me, just yell at me already, will you?"

Spencer glanced sideways at her with a slight frown. "What are you talking about?"

"I know it was a stupid thing to do, texting while I was driving. And you've been giving me the silent treatment ever since I told you. So I'd rather you just scold me about it instead of ignoring me."

"Is that what you think I'm doing? Giving you the silent treatment?"

"What else would it be?"

"Don't you think I've ever texted while I was driving before? Everyone does it! I'm not mad at you. I'm realizing that could just as easily have been *me* getting into an accident! I feel more guilty than anything."

"I really try hard not to text in the car, that's the thing," Faith said. "But there was no traffic, and when I saw it was from you, I was afraid—" Too late, she realized her slip.

Spencer groaned and ran a hand across his face. "So it *was* my fault! I was afraid of that! Oh, man…"

"No, Spencer, it's *not* your fault. It's mine. You didn't know I was driving, and you couldn't know I'd be stupid enough to check your text while I was on the road. Please don't feel guilty. I'm the only one to blame."

By now they had reached the hospital, and Spencer pulled into a parking spot and turned off the car. He gave the steering wheel a little punch and swore under his breath before getting out.

Faith hopped out of the passenger side and ran around to him. Taking his hand, she insisted, "It is *not* your fault, Spencer. Don't carry guilt that isn't yours, please?"

Rather than respond, he surprised her by kissing her. It wasn't a normal kiss. It was desperate, almost harsh. Faith drew back with a small gasp and was alarmed to see tears in Spencer's eyes.

"Don't you get it?" he asked huskily. "To think that I was part of the reason..." He swallowed hard. "I could have lost you, Faith, and I don't know what I would have done without you." He kissed her again, but this time was completely different. It was sweet and tender, and a chill ran up and down her spine, both from the kiss and from his words. When he drew back, she was breathless and unable to think of a suitable response, but he spoke first anyhow.

"Come," he said. "Let's go see your family." He took her hand, and she allowed him to lead her into the hospital and ask about Katie at the information desk. The receptionist kindly gave them the room number and directed them how to get there, and the two found the room without much trouble. Before going in, Faith grabbed Spencer's arm. "Wait!" she hissed.

"What's wrong?" He looked at her in concern.

"I... I can't do this, Spencer. I just... I can't. I have to know what happened to her, but I don't want to know, you know?" She knew she sounded ridiculous, but her heart was pounding so hard she could feel it pulsing in her head. It was difficult to even breathe, and she could only take in shallow gasps of air. She'd never experienced a panic attack before, but she thought this might be her first.

Spencer led her down the hallway a few paces to a more

discreet spot. "You can do this," he said firmly. "You *have* to do it."

"My mom is going to *freak out*, Spencer! She'll kill me when she finds out I was texting!"

"No, she won't," he argued back. "She's your mother! She loves you no matter what. She might be mad at you, but she'll get over it and forgive you and move on. Isn't that what we've talked about before—forgiveness?"

"But this isn't just any old thing! I hurt my little sister because I was doing something I shouldn't do!"

"So you're putting limits on forgiveness now?" he challenged her. "You can only forgive someone if it's something small?"

"This is something that could impact Katie the rest of her life! What if they did have to amputate her fingers? Or her whole hand? Or an arm? She might have to live with this forever, and every single time anyone looks at her, they'll remember that *I'm* the one who caused it!"

"That's not the same thing as forgiveness. We have consequences for our actions, yes. Some that are pretty serious, maybe even life-changing. But *remembering* isn't the same thing as not forgiving."

She shook her head and looked off into the distance. "I hope you're right. But I'm seriously terrified right now, Spencer. I haven't been this scared since—" She pinched her lips together and closed her eyes. The last thing she wanted was to get into how she'd felt when she realized she was pregnant.

Spencer took her hand in his own. "And despite how scared you were at first, look how well everything turned out with Griffin." She opened one eye to peek at him. Apparently he was better at reading her than she'd realized.

"I have no idea how your mom's gonna react," he continued.

"For all I know, she could cuss you out and disown you. I highly doubt it, but hey, it's possible. Your mom's only human. But no matter what happens in there today, I'm pretty sure that over time, she'll forgive you. Go in and see your family, Faith. You need to, for your sake and for theirs. I'll wait out here by the nurse's station. But I'll be here for you when you need me."

"I know. Thanks, Spencer."

He gave her an encouraging hug, then released her. She took a deep breath, set her shoulders, and walked to the door. She glanced back to see Spencer give her a thumbs-up, then knocked lightly and pushed the door open a crack.

"Mom?" she called softly.

"Faith?" Her mom's voice sounded incredulous. "What are you doing here?"

Cautiously, Faith tiptoed into the room. Her mom and David must have been sitting on the chairs near the hospital bed, but they both stood as she entered. Her eyes, however, were drawn to Katie's small and vulnerable form on the bed, a large bandage on her head and her entire right arm wrapped up. It was impossible to tell what lay underneath all the gauze and bandaging. Her little sister managed a weak smile when she saw her.

Grace walked over to greet her and engulf her in a hug. "I didn't expect to see you here," she said. "How are you feeling?"

"I'm okay," she lied. Physically, she felt like she'd been in a boxing match against a pro, but her injuries were nothing compared to Katie's. And her emotional distress was far worse than physical pain anyhow. "How's Katie?"

Stepping out of the hug, Grace walked over to Katie's bedside. "She made it through surgery!" she said in a falsely cheerful voice, clearly for Katie's sake. "Didn't you, sweetie?"

She hadn't answered the question. "So what happened?"

Faith pressed.

Grace gently rubbed Katie's left arm as she answered softly. "Both bones in her forearm were broken, so they reset those. They'll heal."

Faith sensed there was more her mom wasn't telling her. "And...?"

Her mother shook her head sadly. "And they had to amputate her pinky and fourth finger." Her voice was strained. It seemed as if she was holding her true emotions in check so as not to upset Katie. Faith felt the blood drain from her face. She felt so lightheaded she was afraid she might faint. Her worst fear had come true.

"The doctor said partial-hand is the most common type of amputation resulting from a car accident. It'll take some getting used to, won't it, Katie?" Grace was using that fake optimistic tone again. "But they said you'll still be able to do just about anything you could before."

"Except play the flute," Katie said in a sleepy voice. "I wanted to play flute in band when I get older."

The simple statement cut straight to Faith's heart more than the news of her sister losing two fingers. "Oh, Katie," she whimpered, tears streaming down her face, "I'm so sorry." She walked over to stand next to her mom, taking Katie's small hand in her own. "I'm so, so sorry. This is all my fault."

"It's not your fault," Grace insisted. "You can't blame yourself, sweet—"

"It *is* my fault!" Faith exploded, stomping her foot on the ground like a petulant little child. "Everyone needs to stop telling me it's not! It's my fault because I was texting when I hit the deer!"

Complete silence met her confession, and Faith looked first at her mother and then at David. It wasn't exactly the way she'd planned to reveal the news to them, but it was out there now. The statement hung heavily in the air.

"You... you were texting?" her mom repeated weakly.

"Yes. You know, on my phone." Her words held an edge of sarcasm, and her mother reacted in kind.

"Don't use that tone with me, young lady!" she snapped. "You just admitted that you were texting while you were behind the wheel of the car, and *look* what happened to your sister as a result!"

"Grace..." David's voice held a note of warning, but Grace paid him no heed.

"What if Griffin had been the one in the backseat?" Grace demanded, her cheeks turning a splotchy red. "Would you have been texting then? If it was your own child?"

"Grace!" David's voice was sharper now.

"You could have *killed* her, Faith!" Grace went on as if he hadn't even spoken. "Or what if you'd hit another car instead of a deer? What if you'd killed someone else? Was that text really worth that much?"

"Don't you think I know that, Mom? Do you think I don't feel guilty enough already?"

"Good! You *should* feel guilty! What if *you'd* been the one to sustain serious injuries? What if you were the one to lose some fingers?"

"I bet you'd like that, wouldn't you?" Faith retorted.

Grace slapped her across the face, hard. Her action caused every person in the room to gasp. Grace clapped her hand over her own mouth and turned white, while Katie burst into tears. Faith staggered backward and placed a cool hand on her burning cheek, tears blurring her vision. Without a word, she spun around and left the room.

"Faith!" her mother's voice called after her, sounding both

apologetic and desperate.

Faith ignored her and ran to the nurse's station where Spencer waited. She grabbed his hand and practically yanked him down the hall. Afraid her mom or David would follow her, she didn't bother to wait for the elevator, but went straight to the staircase and pulled Spencer down the few flights with her, moving as fast as she could. She just had to get away.

Once in the parking lot, she turned to face Spencer, revealing the red imprint on her cheek from where her mother had slapped her. "So much for understanding and forgiveness," she said bitterly. "Let's go. Get me out of here."

Spencer's eyes were sad, and he looked like he wanted to say something but wisely held his tongue. In her pocket, her phone was already ringing. Faith knew it was her mom, and therefore ignored it. She whirled around and headed for Spencer's car, walking so quickly he practically had to jog to keep up. She didn't even wait for him to open the passenger door for her, but jumped in and slammed the door.

As Spencer wordlessly backed out of the parking spot and headed for the exit, Faith's phone started ringing again. When she failed to answer, she heard the chiming of a new text coming through. She breathed a mirthless laugh at the irony of the situation.

"I don't think so, Mom," she said harshly. "I've learned my lesson about texting in the car." With that, she pulled her phone out of her pocket, turned it off completely, and hurled it into the backseat.

The rest of the ride was completely silent.

CHAPTER 33

It was a good thing Faith had packed a few extra outfits, because the only place she felt welcome anymore was Spencer's house. She didn't want to go home and face her nosy aunt and meddling brothers, all of whom would undoubtedly heap more guilt on her.

She spent Saturday afternoon sequestered in the guest suite at the Young household, curled up in fetal position with Griffin in her arms as they both napped. When Griffin woke up, Faith let him explore in the room, opening the dresser drawers, hiding in the closet, and squeezing underneath the bed. She didn't have the energy to play with him, so she left him to his own devices, feeling sorry for herself.

Around dinnertime, a soft knock brought her back to reality, and she called halfheartedly, "Come in."

Spencer entered with a tray of food and set it down on the dresser. "Hey, G, let's go down for some supper," he said. "I've got chicken strips and mashed potatoes for you. Are you hungry?"

"No!" Griffin shrieked.

Spencer laughed. "Yeah, buddy, I think we have some oranges too. Let's go check." He picked Griffin up and carried him out of the room as Faith smiled faintly. Spencer was learning how to translate Griffin's toddler talk, and it was cute to see him taking care of his son.

A few minutes later, Spencer returned to the guest suite and sat down next to her on the bed. "How's it going?" he asked.

"Not great."

"I figured."

Faith uttered a groan as she pushed herself to a sitting position. "I've made such a mess of my life already. *Such* a mess. It would serve me right if my mom really does disown me. I got pregnant in high school, and two years later I cost my little sister two fingers and her dream of playing the flute because I was texting. That's quite a resume for someone who isn't even twenty yet!"

Spencer gave a sad smile as he ran his fingers through his dark blond hair. "Mine isn't a whole lot better," he sympathized. "I got a girl pregnant in high school, caused her boyfriend to break up with her, and sent her a text that caused an accident. So all the things on your resume are caused by me."

"Not true."

"I pressured you to sleep with me."

"But you didn't force me. We both share in the blame. And my texting isn't your fault. No matter who the text was from, I shouldn't have checked it while I was driving."

"Mmm." He still didn't seem convinced.

"But doesn't all this just seem so unfair?" Faith knew she was whining, but she was in a pouty mood and didn't care. "I mean, we slept together *twice*, and I got pregnant. You know how many other kids are sleeping around practically every weekend and never get pregnant? And I've only ever checked my phone a handful of times while I'm driving, and yet I get into an accident that makes Katie lose two fingers! Just look around you on the road on any given day and every other person is looking at their phone! Why am I the one to get all the bad breaks?"

"I know what you mean. I was thinking the same thing."

The two lapsed into a contemplative silence until Spencer turned to fully face her. "Okay, but look. Here's the thing. Maybe it's not so much that you're getting the bad breaks or being punished. Maybe it's actually a gift. Like, this is God's way of teaching you."

"Ugh. Spencer, don't get into deep theology on me. It's totally not your strong suit."

The jab didn't seem to phase him, because he pressed on. "No, I'm serious. Both you getting pregnant and this accident seem like pretty bad things, right? But look how much you grew through the process of becoming a mother already. And even though it wasn't the right way to go about it, Griffin wouldn't be here if we *hadn't* slept together. I wouldn't call him a punishment. He's a blessing to so many people already. And who knows what plans God has for him in the future?"

"Yeah, okay," she conceded.

"And answer this: will you ever text and drive again?"

"Of course not. At this point, I'm scared to death just to get behind the wheel of a car again."

"So you've learned your lesson—yes, the hard way, but it could have been so much worse. Losing two fingers is awful for sure, but Katie will adapt. She could have lost an entire arm, or a leg, or gotten major head trauma, or you could have hit another car. You could have killed someone. For that matter, *you* could have died. You were on a back road and only hit a deer and a tree. And someone even called it in immediately. Those people you see on the highway on their phones, what happens if they get into an accident, speeding along at seventy-five miles an hour? Maybe this is, I don't know, like God letting you off with a warning instead of a ticket?"

"Maybe."

"And honestly, maybe this isn't even about you after all."

"Nice, Spencer." She flopped back down on the bed, rolling her eyes. "My life isn't about me. That's a good one."

"I mean, maybe God is using your experiences to teach someone else. To change someone else's life."

"Oh, sure. Like who?"

"Me."

She met his eyes to see if he was mocking her, but he held her gaze, practically mesmerizing her with the intensity she saw in those dark blue eyes.

"You getting pregnant was as much a lesson for me as it was for you," he continued. "You've probably figured by now that our families have different morals." He offered a half smile. "The closest thing to an abstinence talk my dad ever gave me was to tell me to use a condom. When I broke up with you because you wouldn't sleep with me anymore, I figured I'd just go find another girl who *would*. As much of a jerk as that makes me, that was my mentality."

Faith couldn't maintain eye contact anymore. Spencer certainly had a knack for bringing up awkward topics.

"But then you told me you were pregnant," he went on, oblivious to her reticence to continue the conversation. "I hadn't planned on that, but an abortion could solve the problem, right? Only you didn't go for it. You were different from most other girls our age. Different in a good way. Even back then, I realized you had better principles than I did.

You're part of the reason I ended up going to church with my roommate last year. I knew you went to church, and I sort of wanted to see what the draw was for you. I thought maybe it would make me into a better person too. So despite the drama and scandal of a teenage pregnancy, God used that to change me."

She felt the tension of a few moments ago slip away. Spencer was sincere, and by golly, when had he become so open about sharing his emotions? "I... I didn't know any of that, Spencer," she said softly, sitting up once again. "Thanks for telling me. It's kind of humbling to hear how God can work despite the mistakes we make. Sometimes He even works *through* those mistakes. It's pretty cool."

"And I can't tell you how, but I bet God will work something amazing as a result of this accident too."

"My mom sure doesn't see it that way," she said glumly.

Spencer pulled something out of his back pocket and handed it to her. It was her phone. Faith shut her eyes. "Spencer, no. I don't even want to look at that thing right now."

"Your mom has sent countless texts and made several calls since this morning," he told her. "She's even called and texted *me*. She acted on impulse this morning, and she's been sorry ever since. She loves you, Faith."

"I could have killed her *daughter*, Spencer," she said through gritted teeth.

"You're her daughter too," he reminded her.

"But it was my actions that caused the accident! Katie is completely innocent in all this, and she's the one to take the worst of the injuries. It's not fair."

"You're right, it's not," he said bluntly. "And I know you're feeling guilty about this, but God has already forgiven you.

Your mom will too, if she hasn't already. God will help her get over her anger and cope with the situation. After all, He knows how it feels to have an innocent Child suffer for the actions of His other children."

"Spencer…" Tears flooded Faith's eyes and she blindly reached out to hug him, her cheek on his shoulder as she breathed in his familiar scent. Maybe Spencer really did get it after all.

He put his arm around her and rested his cheek on her head. "Your mom's forgiveness, like anyone else's, is imperfect. But God will help her—and you—to restore your relationship. Maybe even make it stronger."

Faith wasn't nearly as optimistic as was Spencer, but his confidence was reassuring nonetheless.

"Not to completely change the subject," he began a few moments later, "but we've got a few logistical issues to deal with. You're more than welcome to crash here tonight—as long as you need to, really—but I do have to get back to school on Monday. If you want to stay here with my mom while I'm gone, that's fine. She can drive you where you need to go. But you'd probably rather be with your aunt and uncle. When you're up to going to class again, they can help you get around until you figure out what to do about a car."

"I was thinking about that," Faith said, her shoulders slumping. "I'm so not ready to go back to classes. And I don't even want to *think* about driving right now. It terrifies me."

"I believe it," said Spencer sympathetically. "And you don't need to worry about it this second. Just something to keep in mind. Also, tomorrow is Sunday. Are you up to coming to church with me? Or I could take you to St. John if you want."

Faith closed her eyes at the thought of facing her family at her own church. "Let's go to your church," she said. "Eight forty-five?"

"Mm-hmm. I'll check on you and Griffin in the morning to make sure you're up and feeling okay."

"Sounds good. Thanks."

"No problem." Spencer stood and said, "I'll go help Mom with Griffin. I brought food for you, although it's probably cold by now. Eat something, don't forget to take your prescription, and I'll bring Griffin up in a while for his bath. I'm not going to guilt you into responding to your mom, but I'll leave your phone here in case you decide to." He kissed her head, set the phone on the dresser, and left the room.

Faith managed to get down a few bites of the wild rice chicken salad, but she wasn't hungry. Her phone seemed to be taunting her as it sat there. Finally, she couldn't stand it anymore. She tossed it into the top drawer and shut it. She'd deal with her mother later.

"Later" turned out to be much sooner than Faith had hoped. Within half an hour, there was another knock at her door. When Spencer failed to enter at her invitation, Faith rolled her eyes and pushed herself off the bed to open the door herself. She found not only Spencer, but her mother on the other side. Promptly, Faith slammed and locked the door.

"Faith, please let me in," Grace called, her voice cracking.

Good, thought Faith resentfully. *Let her cry.* She ignored the plea and flopped down on the bed again, pulling a pillow over her head. A scraping noise at the doorknob made her sit straight up again, her heart pounding. Spencer was unlocking the door. In two seconds flat, Faith was off the bed and at the door, placing her foot at the bottom to brace it and prevent him from entering. Unfortunately, Spencer was far stronger than she. After a small struggle, he overpowered her and forced his way into the room. She locked the door behind him again so her mom couldn't enter likewise, then turned to glare at him.

"What do you think you're doing?" she hissed. She could feel the heat rising to her cheeks and knew she had a red splotch on each one, just like her mother. The reminder made her even more upset. "Dang it, Spencer, get *out*!" she insisted, shoving him toward the door. He grabbed her wrists and held them tightly, which infuriated her. Struggling to get out of his grasp, she ordered, "Let go of me!"

"No, you listen to me, Faith," he said, his voice low and almost menacing. "Your mom drove all the way back from Grand Rapids to apologize to you in person. The least you can do is hear her out. Act like you believe all that stuff about forgiveness."

"How *dare* you interfere with my life! You don't understand—"

"No, *you* don't understand," he interrupted coldly. "You carry grudges like a pro. Once someone gets on your bad side, it's all they can do to get back in your good graces. I should know."

"Oh, please, don't even give me that!" she snapped, still trying in vain to escape from his vise-like grip.

"Your family has something a lot of families don't," he pressed on. "Yes, you guys get mad at each other. You fight. You aren't perfect. No family is. But you guys forgive each other and move on and keep loving each other. In my entire life, my dad has never *once* apologized to me for anything; do you know that? We don't do that sort of thing. If someone offends someone else, we just ignore it and pretend it didn't happen, and eventually we get over our hard feelings. Do you have any idea how blessed you are to have a family that asks for forgiveness? It's a gift. Don't throw that away."

His lecture served only to make her more angry, and she kicked him in the shin as hard as she could. With a little cry of surprise and pain, he released her wrists and bent to rub his leg where she had kicked him.

"Oh, sure," he said sarcastically, glaring up at her. "You can kick me and expect me to be okay with it, but you can't forgive your mom for slapping you earlier. Nice, Faith." He let himself out of the room.

Faith could hear him speaking in low tones to her mom, but couldn't make out the words. She did, however, hear their voices moving away from her and down the hallway. Apparently Spencer had convinced her to leave.

Her cheeks burned as she tried to imagine what that conversation had looked like. She knew she'd acted like a child, and she knew Spencer was right. Good grief, would she ever learn? She was making a mess of every single relationship in her life right now.

CHAPTER 34

Faith slept restlessly that night and woke up an hour and a half before her alarm. The lack of sleep, compounded with the wound on her forehead and the rest of her aching body, did not bode well for the day to come. Already she was grumpy, and no one else was even out of bed yet.

She tried to formulate a plan for the morning. She didn't want to skip church, but neither did she want to go with Spencer when they were still mad at one another. The previous evening he'd brought Griffin up and dropped him off without a word to Faith.

What a difference a day made. Just yesterday morning she'd woken up to a dozen roses and a sweet note from Spencer. Now they weren't even on speaking terms. So much had happened in the past twenty-four hours that they seemed like an eternity.

Griffin woke up shortly after seven, so Faith got him dressed and took him downstairs to get breakfast. Since Mrs. Young wasn't in the kitchen, Faith rummaged through the cupboards until she found the cereal. She poured some into a bowl for Griffin, peeled an orange, and poured fresh milk into a sippy cup. That would keep him occupied for a while.

That being done, she set off to find Spencer. It was not quite seven thirty, and she wasn't sure he was awake yet, but if he was, she wanted to clear the air and start the day off right.

She went upstairs and tiptoed to his room, hoping not to attract the attention of his mother. She knocked on his door lightly and heard no sound. Opening the door a crack, she whispered, "Spencer?" Still nothing.

She dared to open the door wider in order to peek in. His room was dark enough that she couldn't tell whether he was there or not, so she crept inside. "Spencer?" she asked again, a bit louder. She groped her way to his walk-in closet and reached inside to flip on the light. With the illumination from the closet, she could see that his bed was rumpled but empty.

Faith sighed and turned the light back off, then stumbled to the door and slipped out into the hallway, where she bumped directly into Mr. Young. Both gave a small gasp of surprise, and heat flooded Faith's face. *Drat! What's he doing home, anyhow?* She hadn't realized he was here, and now he had caught her sneaking out of his son's room early in the morning, wearing pajamas. Naturally he would think she'd spent the night there.

"Mr. Young! I didn't know you were home!"

"Clearly." His tone of voice was not amused.

"I... Uh, do you know where Spencer is? I need to talk to him."

"Snuck out on you, did he? I imagine he's working out upstairs."

Faith decided it wasn't worth arguing her innocence. She could totally see Mr. Young coming back with the line, *Methinks thou dost protest too much*. Besides, the less time she spent talking with Spencer's dad, the better. She never felt comfortable around him in the least.

"I'll check," she said. "Griffin is eating breakfast downstairs. Can you go sit with him? I'll be down soon."

Her request must have shocked him. She'd never once asked him to do anything with Griffin. Mrs. Young was the one who took care of that, but she was nowhere to be seen. Mr. Young would have to do.

"I suppose I can," he answered warily. "But don't be long."

She was already halfway down the hall toward the steps to the third story. "I won't," she called over her shoulder. Quickly, she ran up the stairs. She could hear upbeat music playing, accompanied by the sounds of Spencer grunting and hitting something in time to the beat. She emerged into a spacious workout room that was nicer than the weight room at the high school. All sorts of weight-lifting machines, plus a full rack of dumbbells and another of free weights, filled the room. The Youngs had spared no expense.

Spencer was hitting a punching bag, his back to her. She waited awkwardly a few moments as she tried to decide what to do, but she didn't have to wait long. The song ended, and Spencer tossed off his boxing gloves, hit a button on his phone to turn off the music, and grabbed a water bottle next to him to take a long drink. Then he turned to her and demanded, "What?"

He was breathing heavily, and beads of sweat stood out on his bare chest. He snagged a towel from a stack on a nearby bench to wipe off the sweat. Faith also noted with dismay that there was a nasty bruise forming on his shin where she had kicked him the evening before. She felt like a four-year-old apologizing to her older brother.

"Um… I came up here to…" She stopped, struggling to

remember. Why *had* she come up here? The sudden silence without the music was disconcerting, and she felt very exposed as Spencer continued to look at her. She was also finding it incredibly difficult to concentrate with Spencer standing right in front of her shirtless. "To apologize," she said at last. "I'm sorry for kicking you yesterday. That was mean and stupid. And you... you were right about me. I did a lot of thinking last night, and even though it hurts to admit it, you're right. I do carry grudges. I'm not very good at forgiving. It's... it's hard for me."

Spencer wiped his face again before answering. "Faith, I love you, but I swear, sometimes you drive me crazy."

His answer wasn't what she had expected. "You... you *love* me?" she asked incredulously.

"Yes, I love you!" He threw up his hands in exasperation. "What, this comes as a surprise?"

"Well... no. No, I guess not."

"But you always seem to be in crisis mode," he continued. "You make things so much harder than they need to be. I don't know, maybe it's because I didn't have sisters so I'm not used to girls and their moods, but I can't handle all this drama."

"In a way, I *am* kind of always in crisis mode," she reminded him stiffly. "Teenage pregnancy—"

"Yeah, yeah, I know! Go through your list again to remind me! I get that you've had to deal with a lot of crap already. But that's *life*! Sometimes we create our own messes, and other times things just happen for seemingly no reason at all. But we have to deal with it and go on. *Everyone* has something they're struggling with. You can't play the victim card forever."

A sharp retort rose to her lips as she prepared to defend herself, but Faith swallowed the harsh words. Instead, she replied meekly, "You're right."

"You always—what?"

"You're right, Spencer. I need to grow up. I need to quit feeling sorry for myself. I need to stop carrying grudges. I need to repair the relationships I've ruined. Which is why I'm up here right now. I'm sorry for the way I treated you yesterday. It was immature and completely inappropriate. I can see the bruise on your leg." She winced as she looked at it again.

"Don't worry about it," he shrugged. "It's no big deal."

His answer made her feel worse. "But it *is* a big deal, Spencer!"

"It's not!" he argued back. "That's just it. You don't need to make everything so complicated! I shouldn't have tried to force reconciliation between you and your mom. I shouldn't have grabbed your wrists the way I did. You reacted out of frustration and impulse. I know you didn't mean it. No hard feelings. I just won't wear shorts in public for a while. I don't want people to know I got a bruise like that from a girl."

Faith laughed halfheartedly. Spencer was trying to make light of the situation to make her feel better, but instead, she was ashamed. In some ways, Spencer was far more mature than she. He had already forgiven her before she asked. No guilt trip. No drama. Just understanding. That was a lesson she could stand to learn.

Hadn't her mother been acting out of frustration and impulse when she'd slapped her? Faith hadn't exactly been respectful to her before then. Her snide answers had added fuel to the fire. She and her mother were both to blame for the incident.

"So, um... I hate to ask you another favor, but..."

"But you're going to," he finished for her.

"Yeah," she laughed nervously. "I need to see my mom. She..." Her voice faltered. "I can't even imagine how she's feeling right now. I need to make things right with her too."

"You want me to take you to see her?"

"You can take me to my house, and if she's not there, I'll see if Uncle Andy can take me to Grand Rapids."

"She's back at the children's hospital. I'll take you there."

"But, Spencer," she protested. "You've already given up most of your Thanksgiving break for me. I didn't mean to monopolize your weekend. I'm sure you had other plans."

"Nothing important. I'll take you."

"You're sure?"

"Absolutely. It's worth it."

"Thanks. I appreciate it."

"What do you want to do about church in the meantime? Did you want to go, or do you want me to take you right to the hospital?"

"Let's go to church," she suggested. "Then we can get fast food for lunch on the way to the hospital. Does that work?"

"Sounds good to me." He glanced at the clock on the wall. "Is an hour long enough to get ready?"

"That's plenty of time." She turned to go downstairs, but Spencer's voice stopped her.

"Faith."

"Yes?" She turned to face him again.

"I'm proud of you. You're doing the right thing," he said, closing the distance between them with a few steps. Faith was acutely aware of the well-defined muscles on his chest and arms as he reached out to her. He was still slightly damp with sweat, but she'd take a shower shortly. She allowed him to pull her into his arms, savoring the thrill of his lips meeting hers. As she kissed him back, she felt his heart race at her response.

"A-*hem*." The sudden sound of Mr. Young clearing his throat behind them caused Faith to jump back, humiliated.

"Dad!" Spencer protested. "What are you doing?"

"Your son requires attention," Mr. Young replied curtly. "Now is not the time to be making out." He wheeled around and stomped down the stairs.

Spencer groaned. "Back to reality."

"I didn't even know your dad was here this weekend," Faith commented.

"He got back last evening, shortly after I brought Griffin up to you."

"Oh. Well, I already ran into him this morning. Like, literally. I went to check if you were in your room, and I had to go all the way in to see if you were in your bed. I bumped into him when I was sneaking out of your room. You can just imagine what he thought I was doing in there."

Spencer laughed. "That must have been an awkward encounter."

"You have no idea. I don't think he likes me."

"Ah, give him time. He'll warm up to you."

"Maybe." If he hadn't warmed up to her already, Faith very much doubted he would anytime soon. "We'd better go get Griffin before he comes up here again."

"You mean *our son*?" Spencer said this in a mock low voice, one eyebrow raised as he imitated his dad's stiffness.

Faith giggled at the impression. "Has he ever called Griffin by his name?"

"Not to my knowledge."

She giggled again. Mr. Young was certainly one of the strangest people she'd ever met.

"I'll get Griffin," Spencer offered. "You can take a shower first."

"Good plan. And, Spencer, thanks. For everything." It was an inadequate way to express what she was feeling, but Spencer seemed to understand the underlying meaning.

"You're welcome," he said, giving her another quick kiss before he grabbed a T-shirt off a nearby rack and pulled it on as he jogged down the stairs.

As she watched him go, Faith realized with a jolt that she was falling for Spencer Young all over again.

CHAPTER

35

Pastor Chris was greeting other members in the foyer when Faith, Spencer, and Griffin entered church later that morning. "Faith! Great to have you back with us again!" he enthused. Noticing the bandage on her head, he frowned. "What happened?"

"I was in a car accident a few days ago. I had to get nine stitches."

Pastor Chris placed a hand over the gauze bandage and closed his eyes as he launched into a prayer. "Lord God, we thank You for bringing Faith safely through her accident without further harm. Now we ask You to heal her quickly. You cleansed lepers, made lame men walk, and even raised the dead. We know You have the power to do all things. Use that power now, O Lord, to heal Your daughter. Amen."

"Amen," Faith echoed, thinking his prayer had been applicable to Katie's situation as well. She felt slightly self-conscious having Pastor Chris pray over her right there with everyone else milling around, but no one else seemed to think it was unusual. His impromptu prayer had been completely natural and sincere. She had the feeling he prayed like that with his parishioners often. She liked that.

Pastor Chris shook Spencer's hand and placed his other hand on Griffin's head. "And may the Lord continue to bless and keep you too, Griffin, as you grow in the faith."

Griffin swatted at the pastor's hand, wrinkling his nose in displeasure. Pastor chuckled and backed away with his hands up in surrender pose. "I get it. I won't mess up your hair anymore."

The service went well enough, all things considered. Griffin got restless early on, and the Cheerios in the diaper bag only went so far. Finally, Spencer gave up and took him back to the nursery halfway through the service. Someday he'd be able to sit through and participate in an entire service, but today was not that day.

Once church was over, they grabbed an early lunch at Burger King. As they were waiting for Griffin to finish picking at his nuggets, Spencer pushed aside the tray and leaned his elbows against the table. "So have you thought anymore about my question?" he asked.

"What question?"

"About going out with me. You know how I feel about you, and if you're ready, I'd really like to make it official that we're dating again. Everyone else already thinks we are anyhow."

Faith couldn't deny that. It was sort of assumed around her household and his alike that they were boyfriend and girlfriend. His dad apparently even assumed they were sleeping together. And while that wasn't true, Faith *had* managed to develop feelings for Spencer again. He'd probably picked up on that vibe as well. After all, she'd willingly kissed him back just this morning. Why make him wait any longer?

"Okay. I'm ready."

"So you'll be my girlfriend?" Faith wasn't sure if it was appropriate to say that a guy's eyes were "sparkling," but there was no other way to describe Spencer's eager expression.

"Yes. I'll be your girlfriend."

He broke into a huge grin. "Awesome."

Griffin chose that moment to throw a half-eaten nugget out of his hand. His aim was either so good or so bad that the nugget hit Spencer on the side of the head. He looked at Griffin, who grinned proudly, a Burger King crown perched haphazardly on his head. "Man, this kid has an arm already!" he exclaimed in surprise. "I sense a future QB here! Atta boy!"

Faith laughed and grabbed the last couple nuggets off the tray before Griffin could show off his arm anymore. "C'mon," she said. "Let's get to the hospital."

After wiping down Griffin's face and hands, they walked to Spencer's car. Faith pushed the passenger seat forward and squeezed into the back to strap Griffin into his car seat, thinking to herself that a Mustang was highly impractical for anyone with small children. When she squeezed her way back out, Spencer pushed the passenger seat into position, but before she could sit down, he hopped in himself.

"What are you doing?" she frowned. "That's my spot."

"Not today, it's not. You're driving." He held the keys out to her.

"Ha, ha. Very funny. Get out."

"Nope. I'm serious. I've done all the driving lately. You need to do this." He strapped in.

Faith started to panic. "Spencer, I can't drive! I'm not ready! Just two days ago—"

"Exactly. And the longer you go, the scareder you'll be."

"That's not even a word."

"Who cares? My point is that you need to do this sooner

than later. It'll only get harder with each passing day. Like hopping right back onto the horse that threw you. Or getting back on a bike after you fall off."

"You seriously think I'm ready to drive a *Mustang*?"

"I trust you. You're a fine driver."

Faith's mind raced to find another objection. "But what if there's ice?"

"C'mon, Faith. It's almost fifty degrees out. Quit making excuses. Just get in the car, will you?"

Since she still hadn't taken the keys, he leaned over and put them in the ignition himself, then gently nudged her aside and shut his door.

Faith stood there a long moment, fighting the anxiety welling up inside her. She wasn't ready for this. She'd never driven Spencer's car before, and a Mustang wasn't what she wanted to use to start driving again. What if she got into another accident? What if she hurt him or Griffin?

Shutting her eyes tightly, Faith thought about Pastor Chris and the natural way he slipped into prayer mode, almost as if he had a continual conversation with God throughout the day. Now was as good a time as any to start such a habit.

Lord, she prayed, *You know I'm terrified to drive again. I don't want to do this. But I need to start driving again eventually, so it might as well be now. Please give me Your peace and protection.* Then, as an afterthought, she added, *And please be with Katie in her recovery. Amen.*

Nothing dramatic happened when she opened her eyes. Spencer was still in the car, waiting on her. She didn't get a warm feeling of peace. No faint whisper encouraged her in the back of her mind. She was still scared. But she knew God had heard her prayer and was with her. There were no guarantees of anything in life. God didn't promise nothing bad would ever happen to her again. But He *did* promise He'd walk through it with her—the easy, happy parts and the scary or painful parts alike.

Moving stiffly to the other side of the car, Faith forced herself to get in behind the wheel, ignoring Spencer's smug grin.

"I'm mad at you, you know," she told him coldly as she adjusted the seat and mirrors. "This is a mean thing to do."

"Ah, you'll get over it," he dismissed. "You can't stay mad at me for long." He flashed her a charming smile to prove his point.

It irked her that he was right. "This is a ridiculous car anyhow," she groused. "It's so low I feel like I'm practically sitting on the ground. How can anyone drive like this?" Spencer didn't even try to hide his silly grin. She turned to him. "Do you really want me to do this? With your car?"

"You bet. Go ahead."

She gripped the steering wheel and took a deep breath, then turned the key to start the car. At Spencer's encouraging nod, she slowly backed out of the parking spot and drove to the exit. "Which way?" she asked. Spencer pointed to the right, and she waited until the coast was completely clear before turning out. She felt like she was in driver's ed all over again, overly cautious and scared to make a mistake. Her heart raced, and she kept glancing nervously into the mirrors and to the sides to make sure there were no other cars nearby, or, even worse, a deer.

"Spencer! There's a car coming the other direction! What do I do?" She nearly pulled off the road to allow the other driver ample space to pass, but Spencer's voice stopped her.

"Just keep driving! Stay in your lane and keep going."

Her heart pounding in her ears, Faith hugged the right side of the road so much she was driving on the rumble strip, but the other car whizzed by and was gone before she knew it.

"See? You've got this," he encouraged. "You just passed the first test. It'll only get easier from here."

She was driving twenty miles under the speed limit, but Spencer chose not to point that out. She was grateful for that. If he'd been critical or made fun of her, it just might have put her over the edge. But he allowed her the time and space she needed to do this her own way.

A few miles down the road, she relaxed her grip on the steering wheel enough so her knuckles weren't white anymore. She found that her heart wasn't pounding as it had at first. She dared to speed up a bit more until she was only ten miles below the speed limit. They were on a state highway, but it wasn't terribly busy at this time, and other cars that came from behind were able to pass her without a lot of oncoming traffic.

Throughout the drive, Faith slowly regained her confidence behind the wheel. Spencer had the directions pulled up on his phone, and acted as the navigator to tell her where to turn. As they neared Grand Rapids, he said, "Congrats! You're driving the speed limit again! I knew you could do this!" She allowed a small smile, and he continued. "So we're almost to Grand Rapids, and the traffic is picking up. Do you want to keep going, or would you rather pull over so I can drive the rest of the way? If you aren't comfortable with it, I'm not gonna force you."

"You don't trust me with your precious Mustang after all?" she teased.

"Hey, I let you drive this far, didn't I?"

"More like you *made* me drive this far." He laughed, and she continued. "But I'd rather not fight traffic in an unfamiliar city. If you can drive the rest of the way, I'd appreciate it."

"No problem. Pull off at the gas station up there, and we'll switch."

She did as he'd suggested, and once she was back in the passenger seat, she breathed a sigh of relief. She'd done it. Spencer leaned over and kissed her before pulling back onto the road. "That's my girl," he said fondly.

A warm feeling spread over Faith as she realized that's exactly what she wanted to be. Spencer's girl.

CHAPTER 36

When they reached the hospital, Faith's apprehension returned. What if her mom was mad that she'd refused to see her the previous evening? What if she didn't want to see Faith today after all? Had this whole trip been a waste of time?

"Why don't you go up by yourself?" suggested Spencer. "G's still sleeping back there. I'll drive around with him for a while, and if he wakes up I'll take him for a walk. Just call or text when you're done."

He pulled up to the entrance to let her out and gave her hand a squeeze before she left. Retracing the steps she'd taken the previous day, she could only pray that this visit would be better than that one had been. It could hardly be worse.

She felt a strange sense of disconnectedness as she walked. Her legs moved automatically, carrying her along, but she almost felt as if she were watching herself from afar. It was a strange sensation.

Too soon, she found herself outside Katie's door. She stood there a long moment, fighting the uncertainty that paralyzed her. In a way, this was no different from Spencer making her drive again. She had the irrational fear that yesterday's events would repeat themselves. But her mom had driven all the way back to Mapleport yesterday to apologize, hadn't she? She wasn't looking to heap more guilt on Faith. Buoyed by this thought, Faith knocked on the door before she could lose her nerve.

"Mom?" she called softly.

"Faith?" Her mom's voice sounded incredulous. "What are you doing here?"

It was a *déjà vu* moment if ever there was one as Faith stepped into the semi-darkened room, seeing Katie still lying in the hospital bed. Grace stood upon her entrance, though David was nowhere to be seen.

"Mom, I—" Her voice cracked and she couldn't go on, but she didn't need to. Grace closed the distance between them and threw her arms around her daughter. Both women had tears streaming down their cheeks.

"Oh, sweetie, I'm so sorry," Grace whispered, stroking Faith's long hair.

"I'm sorry too."

They stood there a long while, each basking in the comfort of a relationship restored. Faith heard the soft swoosh of the door behind her, and shortly felt David's arms encircle both her mother and herself. Fresh tears pricked her eyelids. Forgiveness was such a humbling, beautiful thing. So why was it so hard for her to put into practice?

When her mother pulled away, she grabbed a box of tissues from the table by Katie's bedside and handed one to Faith. Both wiped their red eyes and laughed shakily. Then Grace suggested, "How about we go for a little walk? I could use some fresh air."

"Sure."

Grace linked arms with her, and the two walked downstairs and out of the hospital, leaving David with Katie. They found a little walking path and took it until they came to a bench. Grace sat down and patted the seat next to her. Faith obliged and sat down as well.

"How are you feeling?" Grace asked.

"Physically or emotionally?"

"Both."

"I'm a mess."

They chuckled softly, and Grace shifted to face her. "Honey, I'm so sorry about yesterday," she said. "I was stressed out and running on just a couple hours of sleep and—" She cut herself off and shook her head. "No. That's no excuse. The bottom line is that I never should have slapped you. That was quite possibly my lowest point as a mom. I'm sorry I reacted the way I did, and I hope you'll forgive me."

"I do forgive you, Mom. It's not a big deal."

"But it *is* a big deal, Faith!"

"No, it's not," she insisted, again feeling that sense of *déjà vu*. "I was being sarcastic, you were already frazzled, and you'd just learned that I'd been texting and driving. You were frustrated. It was a reflexive reaction. I know you didn't mean it. You've never slapped any of us before. It's not like you're an abusive mother. I forgive you. We don't need to make it more complicated than it is." Silently, she thanked Spencer for the script. It was a good one.

"Oh, sweetie…" Grace trailed off and sat quietly. Finally she said, "Thank you."

"Of course. But I need to ask your forgiveness too, Mom. And this *is* a big deal, because it was my texting that caused the accident, and now Katie…" She trailed off and looked away. "I mean, Mom, I'll do anything to help. *Anything*. If you want me to pay for part of the hospital bill, you can have whatever's in my savings account. If you need—"

Her mom placed a restraining hand on her arm. "It's okay, Faith. Really. We can't change what happened. But it could have been so much worse. I could have lost both of you." Tears pooled in her eyes. "My daughters are both alive and healthy. Two fingers is a small price to pay overall. Katie is young and determined. She'll adapt. It wouldn't even surprise me if she finds a way to play the flute after all."

They shared a small smile. Katie *was* strong-willed. If she put her mind to it, she could probably become a world-class flautist, surpassing other players who possessed all ten digits.

"But this is gonna be expensive, isn't it?" Faith asked in a small voice. "All the hospital bills, and the car insurance is gonna go up, and I'll have to find a new car…"

"Sweetie, don't worry," Grace assured her. "God has always provided for us before. Our insurance will cover a lot of the medical costs. Yes, car insurance will go up, but we can handle it. And for now, you can use David's car to get around. We don't need to rush out and buy a brand-new car today. Although maybe if you hint, Spencer would get you one. Maybe even a Mustang…" She gave Faith a conspiratorial smile to let her know she was teasing, but Faith felt herself redden. Her mom must have guessed there was more going on than just a casual friendship with Spencer.

"Where is he, by the way?" Grace asked. "Spencer, I mean. I assume he drove you here?"

"He did. Well, kinda. He actually made me drive most of the way."

"Did he? Good for him." Faith didn't like the look of her mother's smile. It was as if she knew something Faith didn't.

"I didn't want to. I was scared to drive again."

"That's natural. But you'd need to do it sooner or later anyhow. Might as well be sooner."

"That's what he said."

"So what's going on with you two?"

Faith's cheeks warmed more. "We're dating now." She bit her lip and peeked at her mom out of the corner of her eye, uncertain of how Grace would respond. She knew her parents didn't completely trust Spencer yet.

"Huh. The rest of us were wondering."

"We weren't dating until recently. Like, today recently."

"Ah. I see." She couldn't read her mother's tone. It was hard to tell if she approved or not. "So you still haven't answered my question. Where is he? Did he go back to Mapleport so you'd have no choice but to stay here with us?"

"No, he's driving around with Griffin. He fell asleep in the car. Griffin did, not Spencer."

Grace smiled. "I figured as much. So what's the plan for the day?"

"There isn't one. How much longer will Katie have to stay here?"

"They should be releasing her tomorrow. The doctors want to make sure there's no infection where they had to amputate. They also want us to meet with the counselor and have Katie talk to a few other kids who have had amputations in the past. Show her that there are other kids out there with similar situations."

"That's a good idea. So tomorrow morning you'll go home?"

"Hopefully. David really needs to get back to school."

"Do you want Spencer to give him a ride back? He has to take me back anyhow, and I figured it would be easier all around if I go back home rather than spend the night with him again." The blood drained from her face, and she hastened to clarify. "I mean, at his house. Not, like, *with* him. Griffin and I were in the guest suite the last two nights. I don't want you to think we're, you know…"

Grace laughed softly. "I know what you meant."

"But if David needs a ride back, he can come with us."

"That's okay, honey. He's already notified the teachers that he won't be in until the afternoon. They all know the situation, so they understand."

Faith wondered how much of the situation they really knew. She hesitated a moment before daring to voice the question that had been burning in her mind. "So does everyone know I was texting and driving?" she asked timidly.

"I haven't told anyone," Grace said. "And that's how it's going to stay. David and I talked about it and decided no one else needs to know. I don't want to cause any more family drama than necessary."

"Thanks, Mom." Faith blinked back tears. If that wasn't assurance of complete forgiveness, she didn't know what was. "That means a lot to me. I *was* kind of afraid of how Jackson would react when he found out."

"He was most of the reason we decided it would be best not to say anything." They chuckled together, and Faith glanced up to see Spencer heading their way, holding Griffin's hand as he toddled along next to him. Her heart skipped a beat at the sight. Spencer was so cute with Griffin. He was almost like… well, like a *father*.

Griffin squealed when he saw his mother and pulled Spencer forward as fast as his chubby little legs could carry him. Faith grabbed him into a hug until he lunged for his grandma. Grace laughed and took him into her own arms. "Hi, buddy! I've missed you these past few days!"

Spencer gave Faith's shoulder a squeeze, and she smiled up

at him. He could obviously tell she and her mom had patched things up. "How's Katie?" he inquired.

"She's okay," Grace answered, filling him in on the details she'd already shared with Faith. "She's going to be released tomorrow if all goes well," she concluded.

"That's great! It'll be so nice to have her home again!"

Grace beamed. "It will be nice to have *both* of my daughters home again." She and Faith exchanged a smile.

Things were going to be okay.

CHAPTER 37

"Hey, want to go for a walk with me to see the Christmas lights?" Spencer asked. "Every house on my street is lit up. It's really pretty."

"Sounds great," she agreed, relaxing into the heated seat of his Mustang, glad they didn't have to end their evening together just yet. Faith couldn't believe tomorrow was Christmas Eve already. The last few weeks of classes had been a struggle to get through, and she'd been sick, which hadn't helped matters. But the semester was over, and Spencer was home for the break, so she was happy.

When Spencer turned into his neighborhood, Faith saw that he was right. The houses were all decked out, as if everyone were competing for the highest electric bill. He parked his car on the street in front of his house and walked around to help her out.

The two walked hand in hand, their breath coming out in frosty puffs as they talked. They oohed and aahed over the various displays, arguing good-naturedly about which one was the best.

When they had walked the length of the street, Spencer stopped and turned to Faith, taking her other hand in his own as well.

"This feels right, Faith. You and me." Her heart nearly stopped as his deep blue eyes looked into her own. "I know we've made a mess of things in the past, but we've both changed and learned a lot in the process. Let's make a new start. Marry me, Faith. You can come back to Ann Arbor with me. They have a great nursing program at U of M. We can find a little apartment off campus. We'll work our schedules around Griffin, and I'll take care of you both. We can finally be a real family. What do you say?"

Faith couldn't say anything, so Spencer took a step closer and ran his fingers slowly through her long hair, which made shivers run up and down her spine. Then he took her face gently in his hands, his voice lowered to a near whisper. "Please, Faith? I love you. Will you marry me?"

She felt tears brimming in her eyes, which he must have taken as an affirmative answer. Bending down, he kissed her with more desire than made her comfortable. Her heart pounding, she pushed away. "Spencer—"

"Come on, Faith. I know you feel it too."

He bent as if to kiss her again, but Faith stopped him with a hand on his chest, taking an involuntary step backward. She couldn't deal with the electricity of another kiss from Spencer Young. It was enough to make her head spin. He could get her to agree to just about anything when he kissed her like that.

"Spencer, this is a complete shock. We've only been dating a month. For you to just pop the question like this—I... I hardly know what to say."

"I wasn't exactly planning it, either. But we were meant to be together, Faith. I love you."

"But, Spencer, we're both so young! I'm still eighteen!"

"And we already have a son. Why wait any longer? Let him grow up with two parents in the home who love him and each other."

She closed her eyes. This wasn't at all how she'd envisioned the night playing out. "At least give me some time to think about this," she begged. "Marriage is a huge commitment, and I don't want to make a hasty decision. Let me consider it and pray about it, and I'll let you know."

"Fair enough," he said, a bit reluctantly. "I can respect that."

"Good. Then let's get back to the car," she said sweetly, taking his hand again. "My feet are freezing."

They walked back to the car, and Spencer helped her into the passenger seat, pausing to give her another kiss as he opened the door gallantly. He was certainly using all his charm.

They drove to Faith's house in thoughtful silence, and when Spencer walked her to the front door, he paused on the porch. "Just say the word and I'll buy you a ring," he promised in a whisper. "The prettiest one I can find for my girl. I'll be waiting for your answer." And then, with another kiss, he was off, leaving Faith with more questions than answers.

Faith's mind was a million miles away at breakfast the next day. Her mother made a special breakfast for Christmas Eve, but Faith barely tasted the bacon quiche or homemade cinnamon rolls, nor did she take part in the friendly family banter that morning. She couldn't get her mind off Spencer. She'd slept fitfully, her mind racing into the wee hours of the night.

After breakfast, Faith retired to her room in the basement to think and pray. She grabbed her Bible off her desk as she passed, hoping to find some guidance. Yet as she plopped down on her bed, she realized she didn't know where to begin. She didn't even know what exactly she was looking for. Thinking for a moment, she flipped to the concordance in the back to look up the word "wisdom." That was as good a place as any to start.

Faith looked up a few verses before she came to Psalm 111:10, "The fear of the Lord is the beginning of wisdom; all those who practice it have a good understanding."

She pondered that. So if the fear of the Lord was the *beginning* of wisdom, those who didn't believe in God had not yet begun to be wise. In that sense, she was already wiser than she used to be. Interesting thought, but it didn't necessarily help her in this particular situation. She kept going.

Proverbs had a lot of verses about wisdom, many extolling the benefits of wisdom and placing its value higher than that of gold or jewels. Faith was nearing the end of the list of verses when she came to James 1:5—"If any of you lacks wisdom, let him ask God, who gives generously to all without reproach, and it will be given him."

Faith leaned back against her pillows. "Okay, then, God. I'm asking," she said out loud, feeling slightly foolish. Unlike Pastor Chris, she never prayed out loud unless it was the Lord's Prayer in church. This was new to her, but she kept going nonetheless. "What am I supposed to do here? I need this wisdom You promise. Do You want me to marry Spencer? He really has changed since high school. He believes in You now, and he's matured a lot, and He's been a huge support for me. Especially over this past month, it's like our relationship is at a new level. I can totally see myself with him, but… already?" She paused, half hoping for some feeling inside her, some whisper in her head to give her an answer, but none came.

Slightly disappointed, she turned her eyes back to the page

in her Bible and checked the footnote underneath the biblical text. The note for James 1:5 said, "God gives generously to all who ask in faith, whatever their past."

Her breath caught in her throat. It was almost as if God *had* personally answered her. *Whatever their past.* She thought of her mother, who often reminded her that God loved to give second chances. Grace should know. She'd experienced that in her own life. Faith had too. And so had Spencer. They all had clean slates in God's eyes.

"Thank You, Jesus," she whispered, her eyes pooling with unspent tears.

A knock on her door brought her out of her reverie, as her mom called down the stairs, "Faith? Can I come down?"

"Sure, Mom," she called back, setting her Bible on her nightstand as her mother came downstairs.

Grace sat in the desk chair and asked directly, "What's going on? I could tell you were distracted this morning. Wanna talk about it?"

After a slight inner debate, Faith admitted, "Spencer proposed to me last night."

Grace's eyes widened and her eyebrows shot up. "He *what?*"

"He proposed. You know, asked me to marry him." Ugh! There was that sarcasm sneaking in again. She could almost hear Spencer's voice cautioning her to be polite and forget the drama. She didn't want to start a fight with her mom. Before her mother could respond, Faith amended, "Sorry, Mom. That was rude."

"It's okay, honey. I'm just… I'm… Wow. I wasn't expecting this."

"Neither was I."

"So what did you say?" Grace chewed on her bottom lip.

"I told him I needed time to think and pray about it."

Her mother breathed a sigh of relief. "That was wise. So...?"

"I don't know, Mom. If he'd asked me even a month ago, I would have told him no flat out. But... things have changed since the accident. I can't really describe it, but we're... it's... Something is *different* now than it was. Like, our relationship has changed. It's deeper."

Grace's brow furrowed in concern. "Deeper how? As in, you love him?"

Faith considered the question. "Yes, I do," she confessed. "I love him." Saying the words out loud both terrified and exhilarated her.

"But, sweetie, are you sure? Just a few months ago you claimed to love Aaron. And now you're considering marrying Spencer?"

"Are you saying I'm fickle?" Faith bristled at the insinuation.

"I'm saying you're young and have strong emotions that aren't always reliable. Trust me, I know how it is to have your heart do the thinking rather than your head. I also think you're too young to make a decision like this. A lot of people who marry so young end up separating later."

"Just because you and Dad got divorced doesn't mean I will," Faith argued. "There are also a lot of people who marry young and stay together the rest of their lives."

"Yes, that's true. But—"

"Let's say for argument's sake that Aaron had been the one to ask me," she interrupted. "Let's say Spencer had never shown up again, and you and I were having this discussion now about Aaron. Would you be objecting?"

"I... I don't know. Maybe not," her mom admitted.

"So what is it about Spencer you don't like? How he treated

me in high school? He's a different person than he was. So am I."

"What are you trying to prove here, Faith? Are you doing this to make a point?"

She stared at her mother in disbelief. "No! Why would you ask that?" Her voice came out sharper than she'd intended.

"Are you trying to prove us wrong about Spencer? An 'I told you so' thing? Or are you trying to make Aaron jealous?"

"Mother! Seriously! Do you think I'm that shallow?" She was crushed that her mother could think so little of her. "Would I honestly consider marrying someone to make another guy jealous? Can't I just be in love? Isn't that enough?"

"But you aren't *supposed* to end up with Spencer," protested Grace.

"Says who? I didn't realize there was a script for my life. Can I see it?" She was defaulting to sarcasm again. *Careful, Faith.*

"Honey, I just mean that…" Grace trailed off and closed her eyes, taking a deep breath. "From what I can observe, I think Aaron is better for you than Spencer is."

"We've been dating for a month now, and you've never mentioned any of these qualms before."

"No, but dating is one thing. Marriage is quite another."

"One does tend to follow the other." She was *still* being sarcastic. Goodness, she had a lot of work to do to break this habit.

"Yes, and we all assumed that would be true of *Aaron*, not *Spencer*."

"Mother, *he* broke up with *me*, remember? We haven't been dating for three and a half months!"

"Exactly! Three months, Faith! That's no time at all! And what will the next three months bring? Will you fall in love with Aaron again? Or someone else entirely? I'm just afraid this is more of a physical attraction to Spencer than a lasting commitment. You can't deny that he's one of the best-looking guys you've ever seen."

"He *is* cute. But that's not why I love him. He was cute in high school too, and yes, back then that's the main reason I wanted to go out with him. It was infatuation. But now… Now it's for real. He calls me out when I'm wrong, and he pushes me to do the right thing even when I don't want to, and we're… we're good for each other, Mom. We both encourage each other to do better. Plus he's been there for me when I needed him."

"Aaron was there for you when you needed him too," Grace reminded her. "With Griffin. When Spencer completely abandoned you."

"I *know*, Mom!" Faith cried. "Yes, he acted like a jerk then. But people can change! *You* did! You're the one who's always telling me that our past doesn't define us! Why should that hold true for you and me but not for Spencer?"

Grace faltered at that. "That's true. But I have a hard time trusting him after all the pain he caused you. I trust Aaron more."

Faith took a calming breath. "Would you trust me to drive the twins to Livy's house?"

"Yes."

"And yet a month ago I nearly killed Katie in a car accident. So why would you trust me to drive your other children?"

"But this is different."

"No, it's not, Mom! You're setting a double standard. You talk about new beginnings, but apparently you don't really mean it when it comes to Spencer." Her mother was silent, and Faith couldn't tell if she was offended or contemplating her words. She knew she was treading on thin ice, but she pressed on in a soft voice. "Has David ever once given you a guilt trip or reminded you of the abortion you had years ago?"

Grace's cheeks flushed deeply, and her eyes filled with tears. "Never," she whispered.

"And do you remind me every time I go on a date not to get pregnant?"

Her mom managed a tiny smile. "No."

"So why can't we show Spencer the same grace? Why can't we show him we really mean what we believe? That God's forgiveness is for *everyone*. And that His children forgive one another, even when it's hard."

Grace was silent a long moment before she spoke. "You're right, hon. I *am* being unfair to Spencer. I suppose I'm just having a hard time with this new plan. I was so relieved when you and Aaron got together, and I figured you'd get married in time. Eventually I hoped you two would work through things. I… I think you'd be happier with him in the long run."

"Why don't you let me decide that for myself?" Faith asked gently. "You can trust me, Mom."

Her mother's eyes brimmed with tears again. "I know, sweetie. It's your life. If you love Spencer and want to marry him, I'll support your decision. But I do hope you take enough time to make the right decision. If you want to talk more about it, I'm here and so is David. And if you accept Spencer's proposal, please give us a chance to get to know him better. I want to be comfortable with your decision too."

Faith pulled her mother into a hug. "Thanks, Mom." She felt a new sense of peace inside that hadn't been there before, even if God hadn't specifically answered her questions.

And yet He had.

Faith knew what her answer was going to be.

CHAPTER 38

Faith was at Spencer's door an hour later, her breath coming out in puffs in the cold winter air. She heard the chimes echo through the massive house, and soon Spencer opened the door. His eyes widened hopefully when he saw her there, and he quickly ushered her inside. "So…?" he asked, closing the door behind him as the warm air enveloped them in the foyer.

She turned to face him. "Spencer, I can't marry you right now."

His face fell. "Aaron?" he asked softly.

Faith breathed out a sob and a laugh at the same time. Did everyone think she was "settling" for Spencer because Aaron had dumped her?

"No, Spencer," she said, taking his hands in her own. She spoke gently, wanting to make sure he knew where she was coming from. "This has nothing to do with Aaron. I can't marry you *now*. Maybe in the future, but this is just too much, too soon. I want to enjoy dating you before we jump straight to marriage."

"So… you aren't saying no forever? Just not yet?" She saw the doubts in his eyes as he searched her own.

"Exactly. We have our whole lives ahead of us. There's no reason to rush into anything."

The disappointment in his eyes was replaced with a look of acceptance as he considered her words. At length, he said, "That's true. You're worth waiting for."

Warmth spread through her entire body at his words. He understood. "Thanks, Spencer." She tipped her face upward and gave him a kiss, trying to strike a proper balance of affection without too much desire. She didn't want to send mixed signals.

As she pulled away, she asked, "So what are your plans tonight?"

"We've got Dad's big company dinner as usual."

"On Christmas Eve?" Faith raised her eyebrows. Families should spend the holiday together and have the opportunity to go to church if they so chose. It seemed rather impersonal to spend Christmas Eve at a company party.

"They've done it that way as long as I can remember."

"Huh." Faith realized she had no idea how Spencer's family celebrated holidays or birthdays or… anything. "Will you be there all night? I thought maybe you could come to the late service at my church. It starts at eleven. Mom and David and I were planning to go together. Jackson will stay home with the younger kids. It makes him feel important to babysit five kids, even if they're all asleep."

Spencer laughed. "That sounds nice. I can be back by then."

"Perfect! So what will you guys do tomorrow? Is that your family Christmas?"

"Sort of. We're flying out to Aspen."

"You mean, like, Colorado?"

"Yeah, like, Colorado."

"Just a normal getaway for the Young household, huh?" she joked.

"Something like that." He attempted a chuckle as he rubbed the back of his neck.

"So this is your Christmas tradition? To fly away to some amazing destination?"

"Just every other year."

"*Just* every other year." She rolled her eyes. Sometimes Spencer was completely out of touch with reality and how "normal" people lived. "I've never even been out of state!"

"I can change that, you know," Spencer said with a sly grin. "I'll take you wherever you want to go."

Her stomach flip-flopped, but she tried to respond in kind as she gave him a flirty smile and said, "Someday I'll take you up on that."

He grinned broadly before returning to the topic at hand. "We used to stick closer to home. We usually went to Boyne when I was growing up." Faith nodded. Although she'd never been to the ski resort in northern Michigan, it was a popular vacation destination. "But once Parker and Callan moved so far away, Mom came up with this idea to do a family vacation to bring us all together again. She picks the location each time."

"Your brothers are flying out there too?" Faith had never met either of Spencer's brothers as they rarely came home for a visit. He might as well have been an only child.

"Mm-hmm. We'll spend a week together skiing and bonding and all that. At least that's Mom's hope. It never exactly happens. Christmas is the only time I ever see Parker anymore. He's my brother, but I barely know him."

He said this casually, without resentment, but the assessment made Faith sad. "What about Callan?" She knew next to nothing about Spencer's family when it really came down to it.

"We're a little closer. I mean, we text every once in a while, and he still comes home at least once a year to visit. I'm more comfortable around him than I am around Parker."

Not for the first time, she wondered what the Youngs' family dynamic was like. How did they interact with one another if they barely saw each other? Even Mr. Young was gone half the time. That had to take a toll on a family. Suddenly she perceived why Spencer used to like spending time at her house when they'd dated in high school. He'd once said her family was "alive" and that they were fun. At the time, she hadn't taken it as a compliment, but now she was extremely grateful for her family, exactly the way they were. They didn't have the money the Youngs had, but they loved one another. She couldn't imagine any of them growing up and moving away never to return home again. Even Jackson, who drove her crazy at times, was a good kid at heart. Given time, she hoped he'd mature so that they could have a closer relationship as adults.

"What about you guys?" asked Spencer. "What are your plans for Christmas?"

"Before the eleven o'clock service, we have the children's Christmas Eve program at five. Katie's an angel this year, and Freddie is a shepherd. Then tomorrow is our family Christmas. Since there are so many of us, we do just our immediate family gift opening after church, and then go to the McNeals' house for the big family gathering. It's insanely chaotic."

Spencer laughed. "That sounds wonderful."

"It is, actually." She was surprised to find that she meant it. "And David's family celebrates their Christmas the day before New Year's Eve, so they'll come out this way. We used to go to his parents' house in Detroit, but once the babies were born, we started hosting it at our place. It's so much easier than taking three babies on a trip. It doesn't compare to Aspen, but it'll be fun. Even Amber and Victoria are coming."

"Your cousins that were at your graduation party?"

"Yeah, them."

"Nice! Have a good time. But not such a good time that you forget to check your phone. I'll call you shortly before midnight Michigan time so we can ring in the New Year 'together.' Then we'll be talking to each other from different years!"

"Sounds fun," Faith giggled. "But that better not be the only time you call or text me on your exotic vacation!"

"Oh, trust me, I'll be texting you so much you'll get sick of me."

"Not possible," she said, wrapping her arms around his neck to give him a kiss. At that precise moment, the front door opened and Mr. Young entered with a large wreath. He frowned and sighed heavily when he saw the two pull apart.

"You two cannot keep your hands off each other," he said sternly, thrusting the wreath at Spencer's chest. "Here, son. Hold this to keep your hands otherwise occupied. I've got another one in the car. You can help me hang them. I thought we had enough blasted wreaths, but your mother wanted two more." He turned in a huff and banged the front door behind him as he exited.

"Seriously, does he have, like, a spy cam on us or something?" Faith asked. "Every single time he walks in on us, we're kissing or I'm sneaking out of your room! It's like he *wants* to catch us!"

Spencer rolled his eyes. "That's my dad for you. I'd better get out there and help him figure out where Mom wants these hung."

"Want me to come out there with you and hang on you while you're working?" she teased. "I'm sure your dad would *love* that!" He laughed out loud as she opened the door, allowing him to pass with his wreath. She followed him outside, and reminded him, "Don't forget about the service tonight."

"I wouldn't miss it for the world," he assured her, leaning over to give her a kiss in parting. Naturally, Mr, Young saw the gesture and snorted in displeasure.

"Merry Christmas, Spencer! Merry Christmas, Mr. Young!" Faith called, walking to David's car. She jumped into the driver's seat without giving Mr. Young a chance to respond, but as she backed out, she could almost hear him saying, *Bah! Humbug!*

CHAPTER 39

Later that night, Faith stood in the narthex waiting nervously for Spencer. Asking him to join them for church had sounded like a marvelous idea that morning, but now she wasn't so sure. The Sullivans were already in the sanctuary, and she didn't want Aaron to think she was rubbing it in by inviting Spencer. Neither was she totally sure that her mom and stepdad were in favor of the idea. Oh, they'd be polite enough to Spencer, but she also suspected they weren't thrilled that the two of them were serious enough that Spencer had proposed to her. She only hoped he wouldn't pick up on their qualms about the relationship.

When Spencer arrived, she noted with pleasure that he'd dressed accordingly. At his church, most people wore jeans, but many people at St. John dressed up, especially for a holiday like Christmas. Spencer wore a full suit, as opposed to his usual shirt and tie for dressy occasions. He looked even more handsome than usual.

"How was the company party?" she asked as he kissed her cheek in greeting. Thank goodness he knew enough not to kiss her on the lips in the narthex of church.

"Boring. But the food was amazing. Maybe next year I'll take you along."

Her cheeks warmed at his comment, and she motioned for him to follow her into the sanctuary, where Grace and David were saving a pew.

The first part of the service was refreshing to Faith as she listened to the familiar Bible readings and sang the age-old hymns. But when Mrs. Wilcox started the introduction for the hymn of the day, her throat constricted as she recognized the melody. It was "See in Yonder Manger Low." She was not prepared for the rush of emotions she experienced as she thought of Aaron stepping in to save her solo two years ago. It was their special song.

She sat through verse one, staring unseeing at the music on the page, but when the congregation started singing verse two, she couldn't bear it anymore. She choked on a sob and blindly rushed down the side aisle, feeling Spencer's concerned eyes following her as she fled. Not stopping in the narthex, she hurried straight out the doors into the cold night.

Faith stood there miserably, tears freezing on her cheeks as she gulped in lungfuls of the frosty air. She was over Aaron. She was with Spencer now. Then why should this song affect her so much? What was wrong with her?

Suddenly, she felt an arm around her shoulder and turned to find Aaron. This brought a fresh wave of tears as she burrowed her face into his shoulder. Struggling to maintain a modicum of composure, she whispered hoarsely, "That was our song, Aaron."

"I know." He gave her shoulder a little squeeze.

"I'll never be able to hear or sing it without thinking of you."

"Me neither."

His answer made her cry harder. "Aaron, I'm sorry. I'm so sorry for the way everything turned out. I didn't mean… I…"

"Hey, it's okay," he soothed, putting his other arm around her and pulling her into a full hug. "I'm the one who broke up with you, remember? You don't need to apologize for anything."

Sighing, she pulled away from him and walked to the curb, wiping her eyes with her sleeve. She sat down on the cold pavement and hugged her knees to her chest. Aaron sat next to her, their shoulders touching. They sat in silence for a while before she spoke. "I'm with Spencer now," she confessed.

"I kind of figured as much, but when I saw him sitting with you guys in church, well…"

She gave a short laugh. "That's kind of a dead giveaway, huh?"

He smiled. "Kind of, yeah." There were a few more moments of silence before he asked, "Are you happy with him?"

More tears welled up in her eyes at the question. "Yes, I am."

"That's good."

"It all happened really fast," she said. "At least on my end, it did. He's liked me for a while, but it took me a lot longer to realize I liked him too. After my accident, things shifted with us. Became more serious."

"I heard about the accident. How are you doing?" He glanced at the purple scar on her forehead that wasn't fading nearly as quickly as she would have liked.

She shrugged one shoulder. "It's been a rough month. My headaches are finally gone, but I've been really sore, especially where the seatbelt cut into me. Plus I was sick a couple weeks back, so that didn't help things either. I hope January will be better."

Aaron winced. "Sorry to hear that."

"But that's nothing compared to what happened to Katie," Faith said, feeling the familiar guilt well up inside again. "She lost two fingers."

"It could have been a lot worse, though." That seemed to be everyone's default response.

"I suppose. But Spencer was really supportive of me—of my whole family—through the ordeal. I guess that's when I knew for sure that I liked him. He really has grown up. He's not the same person he was in high school."

"I guess we've all changed," murmured Aaron.

"He proposed to me last night," she admitted after a short pause.

Faith didn't miss Aaron's quick glance at her left hand. "Already?"

"I told him no, or at least not yet. It's not the right time. We only just started dating again. I don't want to rush into anything." She shifted slightly to better face him. "But, Aaron, I swear, when we were dating—I mean when you and I were dating—I never—"

"I know," he interrupted. "I always knew you weren't sneaking around with him behind my back. You have too much character for that. But I also knew he liked you, and it was quickly turning into a love triangle. I didn't want you to stick with me because you felt like you had to."

"But... I mean, what we had... It was real, wasn't it?" She searched his face to gauge his reaction.

"It was," he agreed. "After we broke up I was pretty upset about it. I was mad at you, at Spencer, at myself... I moped around with what was probably mild depression, feeling sorry for myself for a good long while. But I worked through that and got over it. I came to realize that some things just aren't meant to be forever. Some relationships only last for a season, and that's okay. I was there for you when you needed a friend to help you through the pregnancy, and you were there for me when I needed a friend too. Dating you gave me a huge boost of confidence, and I really came out of my shell. I guess it helped me grow up in a way. Like, accept who I am but also step out of my comfort zone. I'm a lot more comfortable in my own skin now than I was, and that's been a huge help at college."

Faith considered his words. Although they'd dated over a year in high school, Aaron wasn't one to share personal feelings very often. She was surprised he'd opened up to her so freely. "I didn't know that. That's great, Aaron."

"And circumstances change too, right? We're both going different directions than we were in high school. We're experiencing different things and meeting new people. Long-distance relationships are hard to maintain. Eventually we may have grown apart anyhow. We're both changing. And that's not a bad thing. People do change over time. If Spencer has changed for the better and is ready to be there for you now, that's great. God worked good in all of our lives through everything that's happened the past couple years."

"That's a beautiful way to look at things." Faith marvelled at how objective he could be when looking back on the situation. She was grateful for that. He wasn't trying to give her a guilt trip or hint that he'd known all along she and Spencer would end up together. "Thanks, Aaron."

She hugged her knees closer to her chest and stared at the stars twinkling brightly against the dark night sky. Involuntarily, she shivered, realizing how cold it was outside.

Aaron felt her shiver and stood, offering his hand to pull her up as well. "We'd better get back in," he commented. "Probably missed half the sermon by now. And I'm sure Spencer's mighty worried, wondering what's going on out here."

Faith could feel her cheeks color and hoped he couldn't see it in the glow of the lights from the parking lot. The Sullivans were sitting closer to the front than Faith's family was, and they were on the opposite side of the church. Spencer couldn't have missed Aaron walking down the side aisle shortly after she'd rushed out. He was probably on pins and needles right about now.

Aaron escorted her to the door and opened it for her so she could enter first. Once inside, she turned to give him one last hug. "Thanks again, Aaron. For understanding. You're a great guy and a good friend. I'm glad we had this talk."

"So am I. You take care, okay? Take care of Griffin, and make sure Spencer takes care of you."

"I will," she promised. She squeezed his hand and turned to walk through the narthex and back into the sanctuary. As Aaron had predicted, they'd missed most of the sermon.

She slipped down the side aisle and into the pew next to Spencer, who was clearly a ball of nerves. His left leg was bouncing up and down, and he was rolling and unrolling his bulletin in his hands. Faith placed her hand on his knee and gave it a gentle squeeze. His leg stopped moving, and he turned to her, his eyes full of questions.

"You okay?" he whispered.

Her eyes wet with tears, she nodded.

"You sure?" he pressed.

"Yes, I'm fine. I am," she assured him.

His leg started up again. "Am *I*?" he asked. He searched her eyes, and she could see the uncertainty in his own.

She smiled tenderly. "Yes, Spencer. I promise."

The expression in her eyes must have convinced him, and he relaxed his grip on the bulletin and slowed his leg to a halt. Breathing out a sigh of relief, he laced his fingers through her own and turned back toward the pulpit. "Good," he murmured.

Faith tried to concentrate on Pastor Lixon's words, but her mind replayed the conversation she'd had with Aaron. It brought a real sense of closure to their relationship, rather than the emotional breakup they'd had a few months ago. Aaron was right—things had changed between them, and now she could confidently say that that relationship was in the past, on both of their parts.

As for her relationship with Spencer, she'd take it one day at a time and see what was in store for them. But for now, she was content. The talk with Aaron had been exactly what she'd needed—what they'd both needed. It was even worth missing a Christmas sermon.

CHAPTER 40

Faith groaned as her mom called down the stairs, waking her from a sound nap. The fact that Grace flipped on the light over the staircase didn't help either.

"What, Mom?" Her voice was more of a croak than anything.

"Honey, you've been sleeping for four hours! Spencer's here."

She bolted upright in bed. *Spencer! What is he doing here?* Still disoriented from sleep, she glanced at the clock. It was four thirty.

Struggling to piece together why she was sleeping at this time of day, she recalled coming down after lunch to put Griffin down for a nap. Yes, that was it. And she'd lay down with him for a short rest, but then... What? Griffin wasn't in his crib, which meant someone must have come to get him when he woke up. How did she not hear him? How did she not hear her mother coming down to take him upstairs?

"Uh, okay," she called back. "Send him down." She ran her fingers through her knotted hair in a vain effort to look more presentable, but she knew she looked awful. He'd have to come down here, because she couldn't summon the energy to tackle those stairs. She was just… so… tired.

A moment later, Spencer jogged lightly down the steps and appeared in her room with a big smile. "Morning, Sleeping Beauty!"

"I didn't know you were coming home this weekend."

"I wanted to see you. I miss you."

"Spencer, it's been less than a week since we saw each other," she reminded him. "Classes just started on Monday."

"That's too long," he insisted. "Besides, you've been sick. I thought maybe I could make you feel better." She smiled faintly as he flipped on the desk light and came closer. "Sheesh, you look terrible!"

Faith moaned and sank back onto the bed, pulling her pillow over her face. "Do I barge into your room after you've been sleeping and tell *you* you look terrible?" she complained, her voice muffled.

"No, I'm serious." His voice was more gentle. "Faith, let me look at you."

Stubbornly, she tightened her hold on her pillow, but he yanked it off. He flipped on the overhead light and sat down next to her. "You have huge bags under your eyes," he commented. "And your skin tone isn't normal."

"I've been sick all week. You know that. Give me a break." She swatted his arm and struggled back to a sitting position.

"Faith, this is too long to be sick."

"Like I can help it!"

"How long have you felt like this?"

"Like crap? Since the accident. I just can't shake this."

"It's been over a month! Have you seriously been sick that whole time?"

Had she? Faith struggled to remember. She was still groggy. "At first I was just sore and tired. I had a splitting headache for at least a week, and that made it really hard to sleep. The week after Thanksgiving, I crashed and slept all the time to catch up. I skipped half my classes that week."

"But you were sore too."

"Of course! Being in an accident will do that. I got a wicked bruise from the seatbelt. My abdominal area got the brunt of it."

"But that should be well past by now," Spencer frowned.

"You'd think so, but who knows?"

"You were sick back in December too, and then this week again?"

"Mm-hmm."

"And you're still tired?"

"Obviously." She was beginning to tire of this conversation and wished he'd leave her alone so she could nap again.

"You were already asleep on New Year's Eve when I called you."

"I know. I didn't even make it through the Monopoly marathon. When I put Griffin down, I fell asleep too."

"Show me where you hurt."

"What?"

"Your stomach. Show me exactly where it hurts."

Rolling her eyes, Faith put her hand on her upper abdomen. "It hurts all over but mainly here."

"Have you had any blood in your urine?"

"Spencer, stop! I'm not your patient! Quit trying to diagnose me!" She was getting exasperated with him.

"Have you?" he repeated, ignoring her protest.

"I… don't know?" It was a question rather than a statement. "It's hard to tell because… Well, you know." She could feel the blood rushing to her face.

"You know, *what*?" His brow furrowed in confusion.

Faith glared at him. Men were so obtuse sometimes. "Because I'm having my *period*, moron!"

"Oh. Gotcha." At least he had the decency to blush slightly as well. "So let me get this straight. You've been tired, nauseous, and sore for the past month?"

"Pretty nasty stomach bug, huh?"

"This isn't a stomach bug, Faith."

She widened her eyes at the tone of his voice. "What is it, then?"

"It's too much of a coincidence that this all started after the accident. I think you have internal injuries from the impact."

Faith scoffed. "Are you serious? C'mon, Spencer. If I had internal injuries, they would have shown up before now."

"Not always. Sometimes they don't show up for days or weeks. If it was a minor enough injury, it would have been undetectable at first, but if it didn't heal properly, it could be getting gradually worse until you can't ignore the symptoms anymore."

Faith sighed heavily. She just wanted this conversation to end, but she knew Spencer wouldn't let it drop. Hoping to hurry him along, she asked, "What kind of internal injuries do you think I have?"

"See, in a front-end collision, the airbag cushions the head, and the seatbelt prevents your body from flying into the windshield, but your organs are still moving forward inside you." Faith noted that he had slipped into full-on doctor mode, gesturing with his hands as he explained. "Some of those organs have ligaments that don't move while the rest of the organ pushes forward. That can cause the ligaments to slice into the organ. In severe cases, they may even cut the entire organ in half. That's not the case with you, because if an organ was cut in half, you'd be dead by now without medical attention."

"Wow, your bedside manner is so reassuring." She didn't even try to hide the sarcasm in her voice.

He ignored her. "The two most common internal injuries are the liver and the spleen. Since your pain is on the right side, I'd guess liver in this case."

"That's an awfully big assertion to make without actually giving me an exam."

Once again, he chose not to respond to her sarcastic tone. "The only way to find out for sure is to get you checked out. Let's go. Date night at the hospital."

"What are you talking about? Spencer, honestly, it's probably nothing. Just bad timing is all. I was sore after the accident from bruising, and then I caught a stomach bug. Maybe even the flu; I didn't get a flu shot this year. I seriously doubt it's been the same thing the entire time. Probably pure coincidence that one followed the other so closely."

"Maybe. And maybe not. But I'd rather be safe than sorry. Let's go. Pack your bags." He hopped up as if to motivate her to follow suit.

"Pack my bags?" Faith laughed out loud. This was completely ludicrous. "What do you see happening here? You're starting to freak me out. If you're so insistent I get checked, let's just go to the hospital in Forest Springs."

"If this is an internal injury, they won't have the staff to deal with it." He grabbed her backpack off the floor and unzipped it, emptying her folders and books onto her desk as he spoke. "We're going to Ann Arbor."

"Leave my backpack a—*what?*" She cut herself off as Spencer's words sunk in. "Spencer! I am not driving three hours to go to a hospital for a stomach ache!"

"They have all sorts of specialists, and they're highly reputable. They'll figure out what's going on right away, and they'll be able to deal with it." He handed her the empty backpack.

"This is the stupidest thing I've ever heard," Faith scoffed, tossing the backpack onto the floor. "My mom won't let me go that far away to get checked."

"I'll go talk to her." Spencer was already heading for the steps. "Pack a change of clothes and some stuff to do—books, your phone, earbuds, whatever. Let's hope you don't need them, but like I said, better safe than sorry." By the time he finished talking, he was halfway up the stairs.

Faith heaved a sigh. Spencer was totally overreacting. She wasn't about to pack her bags. Her mom would talk some sense into him.

Defiantly, she leaned over to grab her pillow off the foot of the bed, fluffed it a bit, and positioned it behind her so it was supporting her back as she leaned against the headboard. Like a child refusing to obey her parent, she crossed her arms and pouted.

A sharp cramp in her abdomen caused her to gasp, and she massaged the area until the pain lessened. Whatever was wrong with her, she sure wished it would pass sooner than later. She leaned her head back as the cramp subsided and closed her eyes just for a moment…

"Faith?" Her mom, David, and Spencer were all hovering over her bed, their faces grave. Had she just fallen asleep again? In the few minutes while Spencer was upstairs talking to them?

"See?" demanded Spencer. "She can't even keep her eyes open after sleeping all afternoon."

"Livy did say you seemed pretty sluggish this week," Grace

commented, sitting next to her on the bed. "She told me you slept a lot and missed most of your classes. Honey, why didn't you tell us any of this?"

"Mom, it's nothing. When you're sick, you're supposed to sleep a lot. That's your body's way of healing itself."

"Not if it's something that may require surgery," insisted Spencer.

"I don't need surgery! I just need sleep!" He was seriously getting on her nerves. She had half a mind to break up with him on the spot, if only she had the energy to do so.

"Look at her skin," Spencer pressed. "Doesn't she look kind of yellow-ish?"

Grace examined her closely, her eyes full of worry. "She does. How could I not have noticed this before?"

"I am not yellow! I'm *sick*! Everyone looks bad when they're sick! Once I get over this bug and get fresh air I'll be just fine."

"You've been 'sick' an awful long time," commented Grace.

"I just—" Another cramp seized her, and she doubled over in pain, letting out a long moan.

David and Grace exchanged a look before David spoke for the first time. "You're going to the hospital." He was using his principal's voice, the one that meant the discussion was over. "If Spencer thinks Ann Arbor is the best choice, then we're going to Ann Arbor. Get ready. We'll leave in fifteen minutes."

He turned and headed back up the stairs. Grace gave Faith a tearful hug and followed her husband, the two of them discussing things in hushed tones.

Spencer extended his hand to Faith. "Need me to help you up? Or do you want me to pack for you?"

She scowled at him in response. "Just go away. You're all making a big deal out of nothing."

He held up his hands in a surrender motion. "Let's hope so.

But you heard your stepdad. Fifteen minutes. If I have to, I'll carry you out to the car." He left then too, Faith glaring at his retreating figure. She had no doubt he'd do exactly that, even if she was kicking and screaming. Well, she wouldn't give him the satisfaction.

With great effort, she pulled herself out of bed and staggered into the bathroom so she could at least wash her face. When she saw her reflection, she was shocked at how bad she really did look. Her skin wasn't exactly yellow, but it wasn't a healthy pallor, either. The scar on her forehead was still bright purple, and she had dark bags underneath her eyes. If she didn't know better, she'd think she was looking at a battered woman in the mirror.

Sighing deeply, she freshened up a bit and dragged herself back to the bedroom to pack a few things. Surely this was a waste of time, but she'd humor her family and Spencer to set their minds at ease. *Not that I have a choice*, she thought resentfully.

Spencer came down almost exactly fifteen minutes after he'd left. Faith wouldn't have been surprised to learn he'd set a timer on his phone. She rolled her eyes. *That man...* He picked up her bag and offered his hand to escort her up the steps. Despite the fact that she was still upset with him, she accepted his hand because she needed the support. Stairs left her breathless lately.

Olivia and Andy were in the living room, speaking quietly to Grace and David. What on earth were they doing here, and how had they gotten here so quickly? Faith's mind struggled to make sense of everything.

The adults all looked up as Faith and Spencer entered the room. "Honey, why didn't you tell me you were feeling so awful?" Olivia fretted. "I thought it was something you ate. I should have been more nosy."

"I'm fine," Faith insisted stiffly. "This is just a silly precaution so everyone can quit worrying."

Clearly no one was convinced, but none of them argued the point.

"You two go on ahead," David said to Spencer. "We'll be on our way shortly once we get the kids settled here."

"You should call Mom and Dad to tell them what's going on too," Olivia said to Grace.

"I'll call them on the way," promised Grace. "And if you need anything, I'm sure Mom will be more than happy to help while we're gone."

"It's not gonna be that hard," Faith grumbled. "We should be back late tonight. Tomorrow morning, probably, since Spencer thinks I need to go *three hours away* to get looked at."

Spencer pulled her toward the front door as she spoke, and no one bothered to respond to her comment. The adults resumed their quiet conversation, and Faith even saw her mom wipe a tear from her eye. For heaven's sake, what a lot of hype over nothing.

When she and Spencer reached his car, he opened the door and helped her in before putting her bag in the trunk. He started the car and began driving without a word. That was fine with Faith, because she had decided she was giving him the silent treatment anyhow. The only trouble was, she didn't have much of a chance to snub him, because she was asleep ten minutes into the drive.

At precisely nine forty that night, Spencer convened in the hospital waiting room with Faith's parents, their faces pinched from the strain of the last few hours. He was sure he looked equally drawn. After arriving at the emergency room and assessing the situation, the doctor put Faith on IVs for dehydration, then called for blood work and an ultrasound of her liver. The blood test showed her blood wasn't clotting as quickly as it should be, which was another sign of liver damage.

The ultrasound was a surprise. Spencer's theory that it had been damaged by the ligament in the accident was wrong. There was no obvious laceration, but instead the ultrasound revealed much scarring of the liver tissue, as well as a significant amount of fluid in the abdomen, which they'd drained after checking her in. It was obvious this was more serious than Faith had thought.

"So, what do we do now?" David asked wearily.

"I think Spencer should stay with Faith overnight," said Grace.

His cheeks warmed. It was hardly appropriate for him to spend the night in the same room with his girlfriend, even at the suggestion of her mother. "I can't do that. I'll just go back to my dorm."

"She'll want someone here," Grace argued. "And David and I know from experience that two visitors in a hospital room overnight is not a good idea. We'll get a hotel room and come back in the morning. I know they want to run more tests, and we'll be better equipped to deal with things if we get a halfway decent night's sleep. But Faith would want you here."

"Well... okay. Sure, I can stay, then."

Faith's mother surprised him by throwing her arms around him. "You're the one who insisted she go to the hospital," she said in a thick voice. "I'm glad you didn't let her talk you out of it. The rest of us didn't realize how serious it was until you figured it out. Thank you." She patted his cheek, and Spencer's heart lurched at the familiar gesture. Faith did the same thing.

"I'm glad I decided to go back to Mapleport this weekend," he replied. "I almost didn't, because I knew Katie's birthday party was last night, and I didn't want to intrude. I just didn't anticipate it playing out like this." He smiled sadly.

"None of us did," David agreed. He shook Spencer's hand. "But now she can get the help she needs. Thank you."

He nodded in acknowledgment, and the Neunabers walked out the door, off to find a hotel for the night. Spencer turned and walked back to Faith's hospital room. He knocked softly and entered. She was nearly asleep but managed a small smile when she saw him.

"I know, I know, you can't handle all this drama," she teased him. "I'm always in crisis mode, aren't I?"

"Oh, Faith…" His voice trailed off and his throat burned. He crossed to her bedside and took her free hand, avoiding the IV tubes in the other arm. "Your hands are freezing!" he exclaimed.

"I know. I can't get warm. I'm so cold."

Spencer rubbed her hand between his own, generating friction. "Want me to lay next to you?" he asked, only half teasing. "I can warm you up."

She gave him a ghost of a smile. "I wouldn't mind," she murmured sleepily.

"But I'm pretty sure the nurses would take issue with it," he said. "Let me find you some blankets." He rummaged through the cabinets and found an extra one. He arranged it carefully over Faith, tucking it in around her to keep in as much body heat as possible.

"Thanks, hon," she said. "That helps. And thanks for dragging me here after all. Now that they know what's wrong, they can fix it."

Spencer didn't voice his biggest fear—that it was already too late to do anything about it. He knew the liver could regenerate itself; it was the one organ that could do so. But scarred and damaged tissue could not reproduce healthy tissue. And unlike kidney failure, liver failure had no real cure. There were things doctors could do to treat the symptoms and slow the progress, but knowing the only option might be a transplant made his heart pound.

Trying to speak cheerfully for Faith's sake, he said, "Exactly. Never question someone studying to be a doctor. Now, you need to get your rest. Who knows what tomorrow will bring?" He kissed her goodnight, noting that she was already drifting off again, then walked over to the plastic couch and pulled it out into a bed, if one could really call it that. He'd given Faith the extra blanket, so he curled up underneath his coat on the uncomfortable plastic bed that was far too small for someone his height.

Although he was emotionally exhausted, Spencer barely slept that night, and not because of the unsatisfactory sleeping conditions. He was afraid that the future he'd envisioned with Faith was slipping away right before his eyes, and there was absolutely nothing he could do about it.

CHAPTER 41

The next few days passed in a blur. Faith's head was swimming with the information, trying to absorb everything. The doctors' diagnosis was non-alcoholic idiopathic cirrhosis of the liver, which meant her liver had suffered irreversible damage and scarring with no known cause. She was evaluated for a transplant and released from the hospital early in the week with a list of symptoms to watch for, all of which would require a trip back to the hospital.

One of the main concerns was ascites, the accumulation of fluid in the body core. Since they'd already drained fluid from her abdomen once, it was clear her liver wasn't adequately filtering her bodily fluids and blood. She had to return to the hospital twice a week to undergo paracentesis, the procedure to remove fluid by a vacuum process.

Shuttling back and forth between Mapleport and Ann Arbor was tedious at best, and everyone was on edge, hoping and praying with each appointment that things would be improving. Unfortunately, the opposite proved to be true. About a month into the process, Faith's sharp abdominal pains returned, this time accompanied with swelling and an ugly purple bruise. She was dismayed when the doctors identified the symptoms as internal bleeding and admitted her again to the hospital.

In order to cauterize the leaking blood vessels and stop the bleeding, they had to insert an endoscope down her throat, a procedure she'd rather not have to repeat again. As if that wasn't bad enough, she also needed two units of blood to replace what she'd lost. The doctors warned that her kidneys may fail as well, requiring her to start dialysis.

Although her family remained as optimistic as possible, Faith knew her situation was critical. No one else would voice it, but the dark thought haunted Faith continually that her body was shutting down.

Since the liver could regenerate itself, a living donor was a possibility for transplantation. Grace and David, Andy and Olivia, her grandparents, and Spencer had been evaluated as potential donors, but all came back with disappointing results. Faith had O negative blood and could only accept blood and organs from other O negative donors. None of her family matched this criteria, which worried the doctors. Most patients were on the donor list for four to six months, and Faith might not have that time.

Spencer was a rock through it all, and Faith now found his medical knowledge helpful rather than irritating. He knew what questions to ask the doctors, and he was able to translate some of the medical lingo into layperson terms Faith and her family could understand. Faith noted that even her parents deferred to him when the doctors came in to talk.

Life fell into an irregular routine. Faith was seldom lacking for company, and she lost all track of time. When she checked the calendar one day, she was shocked to find it was already

March. With this sobering realization came guilt. Her parents had been at the hospital every weekend since she'd been admitted, and she knew her siblings needed a "normal" weekend again.

Grace's birthday had passed unceremoniously, and even though no one felt like celebrating it, Faith insisted. "You need to be home, Mom. You and David have been here every spare moment, and the kids at home need you. Have a belated birthday party for their sake. Spencer will be here, and he'll call you guys if anything happens." Her mother agreed, though reluctantly, and Faith found herself alone with Spencer in the hospital room with the whole weekend stretching ahead of them.

Spencer perched next to her on the hospital bed and took her hand, absently rubbing her knuckles with his thumb, looking more contemplative than usual. His expression was a stark reminder of the gravity of her situation, and the thoughts she'd tried to keep to herself finally bubbled to the surface.

"My life is out of control," she said. Spencer smiled wryly, and she continued. "No, seriously. Who gets liver damage at eighteen? Non-alcoholic idio-something-or-other cirrhosis? What is *that*? It's totally a freak thing."

"If there's one thing I've learned so far, it's that there are very few, if any, hard and fast rules about health," replied Spencer. "You hear of all sorts of things that aren't 'supposed' to happen. The non-smoker who dies of lung cancer. The marathon runner in excellent health who collapses with a fatal heart attack. The twenty-year-old who dies from a blood clot in the brain. Some people in seemingly perfect condition get terrible diseases while others who lead sedentary and completely unhealthy lifestyles live to be a hundred. There's no rhyme or reason sometimes."

"But no one in my family has liver problems! I mean, high blood pressure or high cholesterol, okay. I could see that. But my *liver?*"

He shrugged. "I don't have any answers."

"And how unfair is it that my blood type can give to anyone else, but I can only accept a transplant from other O negative people? Not to mention only eight percent of the population has O neg to begin with. I know I'm complaining, and you don't like me playing the 'victim card—'" she did air quotes with her fingers—"but this is *so* unbelievably unfair," she finished with a pout.

"No, you're right. It is unfair. I don't think you're playing the victim card. You're in crisis mode for real. We've even discussed your case file in one of my classes."

"But I don't *want* to be a case file! I want to be back home, going to class, taking care of Griffin, doing *normal* things again!"

"I wish that too. We don't appreciate normalcy until we don't have it. But there are some good thing about all this."

Faith snorted. "Like what?"

"Um, like… Okay, we're in the same city now! We can see each other more often."

She rolled her eyes. "Hardly under ideal circumstances."

"No, but still. And you don't have to worry about cooking or cleaning or laundry."

"You're really digging deep."

"Hey, work with me here, will ya? Besides, I saved the best for last. I can kiss you whenever I want without the chance that my dad will walk in on us." He smiled deviously, and Faith had to chuckle.

"How you managed to make me laugh on a day like today is beyond me," she told him, shaking her head.

"What can I say? I bring out the best in you," he teased.

"You do. For real. I love you, Spencer."

He inhaled sharply and held his breath. "That's the first time you've told me that."

"Is it?" Faith's eyebrows shot up.

"Trust me, I'd remember if you'd said it. I've been wanting to hear those words from you for weeks."

"I guess I was waiting for a more romantic setting than a hospital room, but…"

"I'll take it. This is perfect." He scooted closer to her and lowered his voice. "Say it again."

She smiled shyly as she peeked at him through her eyelashes. "I love you, Spencer Young."

"And I love you, Faith Williams," he declared. He leaned over to give her a tender kiss, and the hospital room became the absolute perfect setting after all.

CHAPTER 42

"Faith?"

She glanced at the doorway, surprised to see Pastor and Ann Lixon there. A six-hour round trip for a hospital call was nothing to sneeze at, and the fact that Mrs. Lixon had come with her husband made the gesture all the more touching. It was the end of March and the Wednesday of Holy Week, one of the busiest times of the year for pastors.

Grace took one look at the two of them and burst into tears. Without a word, Ann swooped over and hugged her fiercely, allowing Grace to weep on her shoulder.

Pastor crossed the distance between the door and Faith's hospital bed to shake her hand, then reached across the bed to shake hands with David as well. He spoke quietly. "We thought if you couldn't make it to Easter services this year, we'd bring Easter here to you."

Tears welled up in Faith's eyes, and Pastor continued. "I wish there was some miracle cure I could give you, something to heal you physically. But what I *can* assure you of is your spiritual healing, which already happened two thousand years ago by our Great Physician. And even though you're in the hospital surrounded by sickness and gloom, the Easter message shines all the more brightly. May I lead you in a short service?"

Grace and David both nodded their assent, but Spencer stood from his spot at the desk. "I shouldn't be here," he said. "You need to be alone as a family. I'll go to the waiting room." The room was already crowded as it was.

"You will do no such thing," Grace objected, grabbing his hand. "You *are* family. You stay." She pulled him back down into his chair, and Faith silently thanked her mother for the response. She could tell it meant a lot to Spencer.

Pastor pulled his maroon *Pastoral Care Companion* out of his pocket and flipped it open. He led the small band of believers in the invocation, the confession and absolution, prayers, and Scripture readings, using those appointed for the Easter Sunrise service, which fit perfectly with the current situation in which Faith's family found themselves. The Old Testament reading from Job contained the well-known proclamation, "For I know that my Redeemer lives, and at the last he will stand upon the earth. And after my skin has been thus destroyed, yet in my flesh I shall see God…"

I Corinthians 15:51-57 was the Epistle, and Faith swallowed over the lump in her throat at the concluding verses: "O death, where is your victory? O death, where is your sting? The sting of death is sin, and the power of sin is the law. But thanks be to God, who gives us the victory through our Lord Jesus Christ."

After the resurrection account from the Gospel of John, Pastor paused before proceeding to the homily. "I know it may be awkward in this setting, but shall we sing a hymn? I brought a few extra hymnals."

No one objected, so they raised their voices in song to their risen Savior in the words of "He's Risen, He's Risen," the words of verse four echoing the words of the Epistle Pastor had read earlier.

When the hymn was over, Pastor began his message. "It wasn't at all how they'd envisioned things turning out. Jesus' followers and disciples had such high hopes. The Messiah was supposed to come in power, defeating the Roman tyranny that held them in bondage for so long. He was to free them and lead them to political victory over their enemies. Just think of how excited the disciples must have been when they entered Jerusalem on Palm Sunday to see such a show of support for their Teacher. Everything was finally culminating. Jesus was going to make His move and take His rightful position as their Messiah. He was going to save them."

Pastor glanced at Faith before continuing, and she had the distinct impression that he'd written this message specifically for her.

"But in the span of six short days their hopes seemed to crumble away. How surprised they must have been when the days after Palm Sunday dragged by and He refused to make a move. Rather than gathering a show of force and an army to battle the Romans, He chose to teach in the temple courts. And then while they were celebrating their most beloved religious holiday, the Passover, He was betrayed and arrested. The Sanhedrin hurried through a sham trial and delivered Jesus to Pilate to make the final condemnation. And suddenly, just like that, their Messiah was dead, hung on a cruel Roman cross. He was buried, and His disciples went into hiding, confused and scared. Their Messiah had failed.

"But He hadn't." Pastor's voice was firm as he looked at her again, as if reassuring her that the words held true for her as well. "Imagine their shock when Mary Magdalene came to them that Sunday morning to tell them Jesus wasn't in the tomb anymore. Peter and John went to the tomb to see for themselves, but still didn't get it. Jesus appeared to Mary Magdalene first, and then to His disciples, still in hiding. And finally, *finally*, they began to understand why He had come. Jesus hadn't come to bring relief from political oppression. He had a much greater goal in mind. He came to set them free from far more deadly enemies—sin, Satan, and death. He offered Himself as the once-for-all sacrifice for the sins of all people of all time, and His resurrection was the receipt that the Father accepted the payment. The disciples' sins were paid in full. *Your* sins are paid in full."

Pastor paused, and Faith recognized it as his way of shifting perspective before he continued. "This isn't at all how you envisioned things turning out, either. Faith, you had such high hopes for the next few years—college, perhaps marriage, starting out in your chosen profession. But in the time span of less than three months, those hopes have seemed to crumble away. It wasn't supposed to be like this. You may be sad, confused, scared, even angry at God. You might be tempted to think He has failed you."

She swallowed with difficulty. She had indeed felt all those emotions and harbored secret thoughts that God was failing her.

"But He hasn't," continued Pastor. "I can't answer why this is happening to you. Nor can I promise you will get better. Certainly, it is our heartfelt prayer for a miracle. We pray that God would orchestrate a successful transplant and that you will make a full recovery. Maybe that will still happen. But maybe it won't. And that's a hard truth for anyone to swallow, but remember this—even death does not have the final say for a Christian. Remember, Jesus bought you on that cross. You belong to Him. In life or in death, you are His. Cling to that hope, that promise. Jesus has earned for us an eternal glory. Thanks be to God. Amen."

The tiny congregation confessed the Apostles' Creed together, and Pastor Lixon led them in prayer before they turned once again to their hymnals to sing select verses of "I Know That My Redeemer Lives," an apt reminder of the Old Testament reading from Job. With confidence, they sang the familiar words.

> *He lives and grants me daily breath;*
> *He lives, and I shall conquer death;*
> *He lives my mansion to prepare;*
> *He lives to bring me safely there.*

The hospital walls and doors were hardly soundproof, and Pastor had left the door slightly ajar. Faith knew their voices could easily be heard in the hallway and perhaps in other patient rooms nearby, and she prayed that someone there would hear the words and find in them the only true Source of comfort and hope.

CHAPTER 43

"Spencer, come here," Faith invited, patting a spot on the hospital bed. Carefully, he perched next to her, taking her frail hand in his own strong one. Her parents had opted to stay home for a few days, so the two were alone in the bleak hospital room that had come to feel like a prison to Faith. Easter passed just two days ago, much the same as every other day in the hospital, with little to distinguish it from an ordinary day. Pastor's visit had been aptly timed, a much-needed reminder that no matter the circumstances, Jesus was still the Victor over sin and death.

"I want you to make me a promise," she said.

"Anything at all, Faith. Just say the word."

"I want you to see that Griffin is taken care of."

He was shaking his head before she even finished speaking. "No, you can't ask me that. I know what you're implying."

"I know you don't want to think about it, but there's a very good chance I won't be around much longer," she said. He started to protest, but she squeezed his hand to silence him. "We both know it's true. And while I'm still lucid I need to know Griffin will be okay. I'm not asking you to take him, but make sure Mom has enough money for his expenses. When you graduate, if you want to adopt him, you can. I'll let you guys figure that out. But make sure he gets a good education and can go to a good college. I need to know that he's gonna be alright. Promise me, Spencer."

He seemed to be fighting an internal battle for a few moments until he whispered hoarsely, "I promise."

Her shoulders relaxed a little at his answer, and she continued. "No matter what happens to me, you'll still have a little piece of me with you whenever you look at him. He's the best thing that could have happened to us, because while my getting pregnant initially made us break up, Griffin was also your excuse for getting involved in my life again. You're a good daddy for him."

A lone tear trickled down Spencer's cheek. "And I will continue to be," he vowed. "I won't let you down."

"I know you won't. I was hoping we'd be able to raise him together someday. If I had another chance, I'd say yes if you asked me to marry you." Spencer's eyes widened, and she managed a weak smile. "What, this comes as a surprise to you?" She was teasing him, quoting the line he'd given her the weekend of the accident.

"But life here is fleeting," she continued after a deep breath. "I don't want to die this young. I don't want to leave you already." Her voice cracked. "But I want you to be strong. You have a lot of life left to live. And I know right now you think you'll never get over this, but eventually you will. And when you do, don't feel guilty about finding someone else to share your life with. I want you to be happy. Besides, we both know we'll see each other again someday."

Spencer's face was pinched in grief. "Don't talk like this,

Faith!" he pleaded. "You sound like you've lost hope!"

"On the contrary, my dear. Hope is the only thing I have left." He looked at her questioningly, pain still etched into his handsome features. "Remember the verse Pastor Chris quoted when he met me? 'Now faith is the assurance of things *hoped* for, the conviction of things not seen.' Or that one verse from Paul somewhere—how he tells his readers not to grieve as those who have no hope. Spencer, I have that hope. I know where I'm going. Jesus already has a place prepared for me."

A long, low moan escaped from his lips, and Faith pulled him down next to her, his head resting on her shoulder as she rubbed his back with her free hand. Both of them were physically and emotionally exhausted, and after a few minutes Faith realized Spencer had fallen asleep. She didn't mind. It was comforting to have him next to her, and she snuggled a little closer to him and drifted off to sleep herself.

A light knock on the door startled Faith, and she poked Spencer in confusion, trying to remember why he was next to her in the first place. The clock on the wall showed it was one thirty in the afternoon. Shoot, Spencer had missed a class.

At her side, Spencer groaned and mumbled, "Okay, I was wrong. That awful plastic couch isn't the worst way to sleep after all. I have a terrible crick in my back from falling asleep in that contorted position." He grimaced and stood slowly as he called, "Come in." He turned away from her to unzip his pants so he could tuck his shirt in properly.

The door pushed open and in walked Pastor Chris. "Am I interrupting anything?"

"Not at all," Spencer assured him. He finished tucking in his shirt and zipped his pants back up. "We were just sleeping together."

Blood rushed to her face as she stared at him in dismay. The timing of his statement couldn't have been worse. Spencer, likewise, turned dark red and hastened to cover his blunder. "No, I mean... not like, you know, *sleeping* together. Not that we could here anyhow." Faith closed her eyes, humiliated, and willed him to stop talking. Sometimes Spencer said the most wildly inappropriate things. What on earth would his pastor think of them?

Pastor Chris chuckled. "Relax, man. I know what you mean. Sorry to interrupt your nap."

"That's okay," Faith assured him, speaking before Spencer could dig himself deeper. "We didn't mean to fall asleep. We're just exhausted from everything lately."

"I don't doubt it."

"But we were actually talking about you earlier," she said.

"Is that right?" he laughed. "What a coincidence."

"I remembered when you first met me, how you quoted Hebrews 11," Faith explained.

"Ah, yes. That also inspired my sermon that day," he replied. He smiled briefly but became serious as he continued. "I hope you don't mind my asking, but what is your situation now?"

Faith gave him the condensed version and concluded, "The doctors think our best bet would be an organ from a recently deceased donor. But I feel guilty praying for that, you know? Like praying for someone to die so I can live. It just seems wrong."

"Then let's not pray that someone will die. Let's pray that God will provide a living donor or will work a miracle and heal you without a transplant. I'm a strong believer in the power of prayer. It's such an untapped resource for far too many Christians. May I pray with you?"

"Of course," Faith replied. "Please do."

"I want you to know we have a team of prayer warriors praying for you every hour too," he informed her. "They have a rotation set up so someone is praying every hour throughout the day. After all, Scripture does tell us to 'pray continually.'"

Faith was touched that they would do that for her, given the fact that she'd only been to their church a few times.

"Let's hold hands, shall we?" Pastor Chris invited, and the three of them formed a small circle. What followed was a prayer experience like nothing Faith had ever known. Pastor prayed for a long time, quoting Scripture verses off the top of his head as he went along and calling to mind many recorded instances of healing throughout the Bible, both Old and New Testaments. After some time, Pastor Chris pulled his hands away and placed them on Faith's head, praying more fervently for her healing. Then he even held his hands over her abdomen, praying for a full and miraculous recovery of her diseased liver. By the time he said "Amen," a full half hour had passed.

"Wow," she breathed in awe. "I didn't know prayer could be like *that*."

Pastor Chris laughed. "Prayer can be as long or short as you want it to be," he said. "Sometimes I get carried away. I can't do that on a Sunday in church, or people would get impatient. But in cases like this, I like to get into it a little more. Quote a few Bible verses and remind God of His promises, you know?"

"It's a beautiful way to pray," Faith answered. "I wish I knew the Bible well enough to quote verses for memory."

"It'll come," he assured. "The best way to learn is to be in the Word daily. Do you have a Bible here? What better way to spend your time than reading the Scriptures?"

Faith was ashamed to admit she hadn't been reading the

Bible during her stay at the hospital. She had no excuse, and it *was* the perfect way to pass the days. It sure beat the TV and wasting time on her phone, but she hadn't even thought to bring one. Before she could answer, Pastor Chris spoke again. "Here, take mine," he offered, holding out a worn black leather Bible. "I have extras."

"I can't take your Bible," she protested.

"You aren't taking it. You're just borrowing it. Look through it and pay special attention to the verses I've highlighted. Those are some of the key points—the verses you'd do well to memorize. Read my notes in the margins and see if they help you understand better. I want you to use it."

The idea did sound fascinating to Faith. "Well… okay. Thank you. I appreciate it."

"My pleasure," he said. "God be with you both." He shook Spencer's hand in parting, and before he was even out of the room, Faith already had the Bible open. After an experience like that, she couldn't wait to begin.

CHAPTER 44

The rest of that day was a quiet one in Faith's hospital room. She spent the time flipping through Pastor Chris' Bible, reading highlighted verses, and keeping a list of some she'd heard before. They seemed like good references to keep in mind.

Spencer had an afternoon class, and when he came back, he spent a few hours at the desk in the room, a couple books spread out in front of him, presumably working on homework as he often did.

The atmosphere in the room was pleasant as Faith continued to leaf through different portions of Scripture. She spent a significant amount of time in the book of Psalms, a book she'd never much explored. It surprised her to find such a wide range of emotions. She'd thought the psalms were mainly songs of praise, but there were a number pleading with God for mercy and relief. Psalm 41:3 was especially poignant to her as she read, "The Lord sustains them on their sickbed and restores them from their bed of illness." *Please do that for me, Lord,* she prayed.

When she reached Psalm 46, she recognized it. It was a popular one she'd heard a number of times in church. "God is our refuge and strength, an ever-present help in trouble…" she read. When she got to verse ten, she stopped. "'Be still, and know that I am God,'" it said.

The thought made her catch her breath. She'd never dwelt on the verse before, but now it struck her. Here, in this hospital room, it was never truly *still*. There was always noise from the hallways outside, there were monitors beeping and machines swooshing, TVs blaring… Faith couldn't remember the last time she'd been in absolute silence.

And yet, at this moment, she understood what it meant to be still. She could still hear all those noises around her, but it wasn't a physical stillness God was talking about. It was a spiritual one. She hadn't turned on her TV all day, nor had she checked her phone once. Not that those things were bad in and of themselves, but they were often distractions. Today she'd done what she should have been doing all along—silencing her own distractions and turning to God's Word. *He* was God. Her life was in His hands. What a comforting, beautiful thought.

With a smile, Faith closed the Bible and clutched it to her chest. She'd ask her mom to bring her own Bible next time she visited so she could highlight verses as Pastor Chris had done.

At the desk, Spencer stretched and stood. He turned to her and grinned. "You okay?" he asked.

"Mm-hmm," she nodded. "This has been a wonderful day. I'm so glad Pastor Chris came."

"So am I. It was good timing for both of us." He walked over and handed her an envelope.

"What's this?"

"Your birthday present."

"My birthday is still a few days away."

"That's okay. I was having trouble figuring out what to get you. I mean, what does someone confined to a hospital bed really need, right? But you gave me an idea earlier, and Pastor Chris helped it along."

Now Faith was curious. "Want me to open it now?"

"Yes, but I'll let you have your space. I don't want you to think I'm breathing over your shoulder. I'll head down to the cafeteria and grab something to eat. Need anything before I go?"

"No thanks. I'm fine."

"You'll be okay here?"

"I'm not going anywhere. You know where to find me," she joked.

Laughing at the feeble and somewhat morbid hospital humor, he kissed her and said, "Okay, then. I'll be back. Love you."

"Love you too," she responded, watching him close the door quietly behind him as he left. Turning to the envelope in her hand, she opened it and pulled out three sheets of paper.

Dearest Faith,

I hope you know how much I love you and how much you mean to me. Back when we first started dating in high school, neither of us could have foreseen where that path would lead us. It hasn't always been easy, and we've been through more than most couples twice our age, but I'll tell you this—there's no one I'd rather be with than you. God has used you to change me in so many ways, and I'm forever grateful for that.

As you reminded me, in these days of uncertainty, we do have one certainty: the hope of heaven. That hope isn't just a wish, like the way I hope you'll find a donor. The hope God has promised is a guarantee. You WILL be in heaven someday because of Jesus. I was

surprised to see how often the Bible talks about our hope in the Lord, and I've written out a list of Bible verses to encourage you in that hope. I'm still praying for a miracle. But in the meantime, let's both cling to the hope God has given us.
   All my love,
   Spencer

Faith was crying by the time she finished his letter, and she was grateful that he'd allowed her some privacy. She loved Spencer so very much, and more than anything she wanted the chance to marry him and spend their lives together.

She could see just by a glance that both remaining sheets of paper were filled with Bible verses, front and back. He had used his best handwriting too, which meant it must have taken him considerably longer. His normal handwriting was practically illegible. Instead of doing his homework earlier, he'd been looking up Bible verses to encourage *her*. What a beautiful expression of his love. She turned her eyes to the verses and read them, some familiar and some new, her heart taking in the healing balm of God's Word.

I wait for the Lord, my soul waits, and in his word I put my hope. Psalm 130:5
   ...Those who hope in the Lord will renew their strength. They will soar on wings like eagles; they will run and not grow weary, they will walk and not be faint. Isaiah 40:31
   For I know the plans I have for you," declares the Lord, "plans to prosper you and not to harm you, plans to give you hope and a future. Jeremiah 29:11
   Let us hold unswervingly to the hope we profess, for he who promised is faithful. Hebrews 10:23
   In his great mercy he has given us new birth into a living hope

through the resurrection of Jesus Christ from the dead.1 Peter 1:3

There were many more verses, and when she finished, she sat in the quiet hospital room, clutching the papers to her chest, tears streaming down her face. They weren't tears of desperation or fear, but rather, tears of thankfulness to her Lord. Her heart felt completely at peace. Spencer had given her the best gift possible.

When he returned to the room shortly thereafter, Faith opened her arms and welcomed him into a warm embrace. She couldn't speak over the lump in her throat, but she didn't need to. She knew he understood.

CHAPTER 45

The nurse starting the morning shift had just finished her check-in with Faith when Spencer slid off the plastic couch with a groan.

"I'm gonna need a chiropractor after all these uncomfortable nights," he groused. "Whoever designed these things should find a new profession."

"You don't have to sleep here every night, you know," Faith pointed out. "I'm perfectly capable of spending the night alone."

"Ah, it's not every night," Spencer said, trying to make the best of it as he twisted from side to side to crack his back. "When your mom or grandma stays, I'm back at the dorm. And I know you're fine on your own, but I want someone here with you just in case... um... you need anything," he finished lamely.

Faith knew that wasn't what he'd meant. He wanted to be there in case her health took a turn for the worst. He didn't want her to die alone.

"You could sleep next to me," she suggested in a flirty voice.

He chuckled. "Like the other day, when I took a nap by you and woke up with a sore back? No thanks. I'm surprised I was able to walk after that, I was so sore."

"Oh, come on. It's not that bad. And it's not my fault you were lying in that awful position. Who's the one playing the victim card now?"

Again, Spencer laughed. "Touché. I've gotta get ready for class. I've got two this morning. I'll go back to the dorm to shower and get ready, and I'll be back around lunchtime. You okay until then?"

"I'm fine."

A knock made Faith turn toward the door. Mornings were like Grand Central Station around here, with nurses making their rounds as shifts changed and doctors raced to do visits before their office hours began. "Come in," she called.

The door opened, and there stood her father. "Hey, baby girl," he said softly.

"Daddy…" Faith didn't even feel the tears well up. They came so quickly they were running down her cheeks before she could fully process everything.

Bob came to her bedside and pulled her into a hug. She cried into his chest as he rested his chin on the top of her head, rocking her gently back and forth. In that instant, she was a little girl again, feeling the strong arms of her daddy around her, knowing somehow that everything would be alright.

Spencer softly cleared his throat, and Faith pulled out of her father's arms, grabbed a tissue off the rolling bedside table, and wiped her face. "Daddy, this is Spencer."

Bob held out his hand and Spencer shook it. "You're the one who's been taking care of my little girl," he said. "Thank you. I'm Bob Coleman."

"Nice to meet you. It's been my pleasure to be here for

Faith."

Faith could sense a weird tension radiating from Spencer, so she spoke quickly before her dad picked up on that. "Spencer has to get to class, but he'll be back later, won't you, babe?"

"Yes, that's right. I have class. I'll leave you two to catch up. Faith, see you around noon." His voice sounded slightly robotic, and Faith wondered what on earth was wrong with him. He leaned over to kiss her goodbye before leaving.

Bob pulled over the desk chair to sit next to Faith as she adjusted the bed to a more upright position. "So that's the 'hunk' your mom was telling me about? The one you're dating? Ah, he didn't look so great to me." His voice was teasing, but Faith flushed. Truly, Spencer was looking pretty haggard nowadays, the stress and strain of her illness weighing heavily upon him. His normally perfectly-styled hair was usually disheveled, and he'd gone more than a few days without shaving. His face had worry lines that hadn't been there a few months ago, and he always looked completely exhausted. Yet somehow, Faith scarcely noticed any of that. To her, he was even more handsome than ever.

"Daddy, he just woke up two minutes before you came," she protested. "He's going back to his dorm to take a shower. Besides, I don't look so great myself."

"Ah, sweetie, I'm just teasing you. And you look fabulous. How are you feeling?"

"Not very good."

"So I hear. Your mom's been keeping me posted on things."

Then why haven't you visited before? she thought. *I've certainly been here long enough.* Maybe that's why Spencer was acting strange. Perhaps he wondered the same thing.

"So it's your liver, huh?"

"Yeah."

"They're looking for a donor?"

"Mm-hmm." Suddenly this conversation had gotten very cumbersome. Gone was the initial rush of emotion she'd felt when he walked in the door. Faith felt like she was talking to a stranger, making polite small talk. Resentment welled up inside her until she couldn't contain it.

"Daddy, where *were* you?" she demanded. "I've been here three months, and you're just now visiting? If I'm really your baby girl, why didn't you come sooner?" She looked away and swiped impatiently at the tears on her face.

"Baby, I'm sorry," he said, leaning forward to put his elbows on her bed. "Listen to me, sweetheart," he implored. "It's not that I didn't want to come, but I didn't want to intrude. I knew your mom and David were here, and Liv and Andy, your grandparents… I didn't want to cause tensions by showing up like the uninvited, unwanted guest."

Faith snorted. "Given the circumstances, I'm pretty sure no one would have objected to you being here for your *daughter*!"

"I know, sweetie. I'm sorry."

"It's a little late for that now, isn't it? Daddy, I'm about to die! Where were you before? All those years after you left, why didn't you ever come back to see us? You didn't even come for birthdays or Christmas! Do you have any idea how that made me feel? Or Jackson? We had a dad one day, and then we just… didn't! You were gone, and you never said goodbye to us. What were we supposed to think?"

"Sweetie—"

"Freddie barely remembers you, and you didn't even come back to meet Katie! What kind of dad *does* that? Mom was crushed. And with all the pregnancy hormones, she was more emotional than usual as it was! How could you leave her—leave *us*—like that? None of us were the same afterward."

"Sweetheart—"

"The only time I've seen you since then was my graduation, and that was only because I invited you!" She wondered now why she'd even made the effort.

"Faith—"

"Why are you here now? To finally say goodbye?" Glaring at him, Faith tried to breathe slowly to lower her blood pressure. She's set off the monitor at this rate.

Her father took a long breath before responding. "I'm here to apologize. You're right. I have no excuse for my behavior. I was a terrible father, abandoning you all like that. If I could go back and do it all over again differently, I would."

Faith crossed her arms across her chest. "Well, you *can't*," she shot back. "You can't go back and redo anything. You'll always be the dad who left his kids never to return."

"But I'm here now."

"You wouldn't have come if I wasn't so sick."

Bob was silent a long moment. "You're right," he finally said. "And you're right that I can't redo the past. But we don't have to continue like that. Can't we make a fresh start? Rebuild a relationship?"

Faith closed her eyes and leaned back against her pillow. Her first instinct was to lash out at him, to fight back, to hurt him the way he'd hurt her mom and siblings and her. She didn't want to put an effort into rebuilding anything. But her conscience was nagging her. She recalled Spencer's accusation that she carried grudges like a pro and his insistence that she make up with her mom after the accident.

Besides, hadn't she argued that one's past didn't define a person? Her teenage pregnancy didn't define who she'd be the rest of her life. And she'd been the one to stick up for Spencer when he wanted to make a fresh start. Her own words floated through her mind in the conversation she'd once had with her mother. *Why can't you show your dad the same grace? Why can't you show him you really mean what you believe? That God's forgiveness is for everyone. And that His children forgive one another, even when it's hard.*

Tears escaped underneath her closed eyelids as she waged the inner battle between what she *wanted* to do and what she knew she needed to do. *I can't do this, Lord. It's too much to ask of me,* she prayed. *You know how much he hurt us when he left. I can't just forgive and forget. All those years thinking he didn't love me anymore, thinking he'd left because of us kids...*

Drawing a deep breath, Faith pushed thoughts of the past out of her mind. *But, God, I know You command us to forgive one another. My dad doesn't deserve forgiveness, but then again, neither do I. Yet I know You have forgiven my sins. If I refuse to forgive Dad now, I don't know that I'll ever have another chance to do so, and I don't want that to be his final memory of me. Help me do this, Lord. Give me Your strength.*

She kept her eyes shut for a few more moments, working up the courage to say the four hardest words she'd ever have to say. Swallowing hard, at last she opened her eyes and croaked out, "I forgive you, Daddy."

Tears filled his own eyes at her statement, and he rose from his chair to once more pull her into a hug. "Thank you, sweetheart," he whispered in a ragged voice. He stroked her hair as she allowed her tears to fall unchecked.

It was similar to the time she and her mom had made up after the accident. She felt that same sense of peace, the same relief of letting go of resentment and bitterness, the same sense of security in knowing a relationship had been restored. Or in this case, a relationship would start to be rebuilt. She and her dad still had a long way to go.

After a few minutes, Bob handed her a tissue and sat back in his chair. She could see from his red-rimmed eyes that he'd shed a few tears himself. "So where do we start?" he asked.

"How about I start with Mom meeting David?" she suggested. "That's when things really started to get interesting."

He nodded amicably and settled back into the chair. Faith told him how their family had become Christians over the course of Grace and David's romance. She related the saga of Griffin's birth, including how Spencer initially dumped her and Aaron stepped in, but how Spencer had come back and she'd fallen in love with him again. Faith told her dad about the accident and how she'd been at fault by texting. There was no flicker of blame or condemnation in her father's gaze at the admission, only understanding. They spoke about each of her siblings, and Faith filled her father in on their activities and personalities.

When they came to a lull in the conversation, Faith checked the clock and was shocked to see that four full hours had passed. Spencer was due back any minute.

"This has been fun, baby girl," her dad told her with a smile. "I'm glad we had this opportunity. It was a long time in coming."

"It was. Thanks for coming, Daddy. I'm glad you made the trip."

"So am I. Part of the reason I didn't come sooner is that I've been working a lot of overtime lately and earned some time off. If you don't mind, I think I'll hang around Ann Arbor for a while. Spend some time with you."

Faith wasn't at all sure how her mom or stepdad would feel about that. In fact, her mom was due to arrive in less than an hour herself. How would she react to find her ex-husband here?

Before she could formulate a reply, Bob spoke again. "Besides, I have a birthday gift for you."

She was surprised he even remembered her birthday. He'd sent cards a few times over the years, but not for the last couple. "You have a gift for me?" she repeated. "What is it?"

"It's a secret," he smiled. "Literally."

"You're gonna tell me a secret for my birthday?" It sounded ridiculous even as she said it.

"Mm-hmm." He leaned closer and lowered his voice to a dramatic whisper.

"I'm O negative."

CHAPTER 46

Faith's birthday a few days later brought a feeling of anxious anticipation. Spencer skipped his classes to sit with Faith's entire extended family in the hospital waiting room for the day. The whole lot of them joined hands and prayed together before the surgery. Now Faith's life was in the hands of a doctor they barely knew and a team of strangers they'd never met.

Although Spencer was thrilled about the transplant, he knew it wasn't an absolute guarantee. Her body could still reject the foreign organ, despite anti-rejection medications. And the surgery itself carried significant risks. Still, it was the best option. Really, it was the *only* option.

Since the surgery was a double procedure, the time frame was anywhere from six to twelve hours, a fact which made them all nervous. One team of surgeons would remove a portion of Bob's liver. Another would remove Faith's diseased liver to make way for the new one. With all the ducts and vessels that had to be disconnected and reconnected, it wasn't something to be done quickly or sloppily.

Partway through the morning, Spencer heard someone

enter the waiting room and turned to look at the newcomer. It was his mother. He crossed to welcome her in a crushing hug, tears blurring his vision. She'd cared enough to drive over for the day, and her gesture meant more to Spencer than she could know. His mom was not overly demonstrative, and he knew she didn't know Faith's family well enough to be at ease around them, but she was here. *This is her way of showing she's accepted Faith as part of the family,* he thought with a tightness in his throat.

Time passed tediously, everyone making nervous small talk, praying quietly, checking phones, and pacing. Occasionally, someone would offer to go to the cafeteria, but no one was particularly hungry.

The day dragged on until mid-afternoon, when an exhausted but happy surgeon came out to talk to them. "It's done!" he greeted them. "And everything went like clockwork. I wish all surgeries were that easy."

"Easy!" laughed Grace in astonishment. "You were doing major surgery for eight hours, saving my daughter's life, and you call that *easy!*"

"All in a day's work," he replied with a grin. "She's in recovery right now coming out of anesthesia. A nurse will get you when she's alert enough to see you." With that, he shook everyone's hand and made his exit.

The entire waiting room cheered, even those who weren't part of the family. Good news was always welcome at a hospital.

Since Faith was in the ICU, the medical team tried to limit the number of visitors, so her family decided Grace and David should be the first to visit her, followed by Spencer. The rest of them could wait a day or two.

Once her parents had made their visit, Spencer walked into

Faith's new hospital room, stopping to use hand sanitizer as the nurse instructed. She had to be careful about germs now to avoid infection.

"Happy birthday!" he announced grandly, holding a teddy bear he'd gotten at the gift shop. "It's not everyone who gets a new liver for their birthday, so you must be pretty special."

She laughed sleepily. "I can honestly say that's a birthday gift I'd never considered before in my life, but this year it's exactly what I wanted."

He placed the teddy bear on the nightstand and bent to kiss her forehead. "This bear wasn't my first choice," he told her, "but they don't allow flowers for post-transplant patients. Otherwise I would have gotten you a dozen roses."

"It's okay," she said. "The bear will last longer."

"How are you feeling?"

"Dopey. I don't know if I'm making sense when I talk. I could be saying anything at all."

"Are you sore?"

"Kind of. But I'm under so much medication and so tired that it's pretty dull. I just feel… weird. I don't know how to explain it."

"It's okay. I'm just glad the surgery went well. I was praying for you almost the entire time."

She smiled. "Remember back to that day you dragged me here? Back in January? Did you ever imagine it would turn into such an ordeal?"

"Never."

"I thought it was just a stomach virus."

"I wish it had been."

"I haven't seen Griffin in weeks, Spencer." Although her mom had brought him a few times to see her, they'd quickly decided that wasn't the best arrangement. He only wanted to climb into her lap, and with everything she was hooked up to, that was not ideal. "I wonder if he'll even remember me."

"Of course he will," Spencer assured her. "He might be a little hesitant at first, but he'll warm up to you again. You're his mommy."

"He hasn't seen much of his daddy lately, either. You'll have to come back and spend some time with him too."

"I will," he promised. "I'll come back every weekend to see you both. I'm gonna miss you. I've been able to see you every day for the last three months, and now you'll be gone and leave me here all by my lonesome."

"It's only a few more weeks until the semester's done," she reminded him. "And I'll be recovering anyhow. I'll be lousy company."

"You've been lying in a hospital bed for the past couple months. How much lousier company can you be?" His devious smile belied his mean words.

"Spencer Young!" she gasped. "You're shameless!" She started to giggle, but shook her head. "Don't," she begged. "Don't make me laugh. I can't… It hurts to laugh."

"Sorry," he apologized. "How about a kiss instead?"

"I'd much rather have a kiss." Her eyes sparkled as he bent to give her a kiss, grateful that God had orchestrated everything exactly the way He had.

The next week was tentatively optimistic as Faith was closely monitored to make sure her body wouldn't reject the new liver. She spent two days in the ICU before she was transferred to the post-transplant floor. She attended a class with other transplant patients to learn about ways to expedite recovery and encourage longevity, and she was released just four days after her surgery.

After being in the hospital for so long, it felt strange to rejoin real life so quickly. She still needed to have regular checkups—two a week for the first month, and if all looked well at that point, the frequency would taper off. She also had to take anti-rejection medication for the rest of her life, but she could at long last go home to Mapleport.

Faith had a hard time adjusting to the restrictions of her new condition. Since the anti-rejection medication was immunosuppressant, she had to be extra careful not to expose herself to germs. She was supposed to wear a mask in public and even around her family if any of them weren't feeling well. At the suggestion of one of the nurses, she started carrying hand sanitizer with her everywhere. There were certain foods she couldn't eat, and she wasn't allowed to change diapers anymore unless she was wearing a full hazmat suit. Thankfully, her family was understanding of her limitations and worked together to accommodate her.

But the thing that surprised Faith the most was how much better she felt. Almost immediately after her surgery, she felt better than she had in ages. Yes, she was sore in her abdominal area, but she had so much more energy now than she had. She hadn't realized how sick she was until she knew how it felt to be well. Looking back, she supposed she had reasoned away her tiredness for so long it just became normal to her. She'd thought it was because of Griffin and her demanding college schedule that she'd always been tired. But now that she was well, she knew how serious her illness had been. It was amazing she was still alive.

When Faith walked into church with Spencer and her family shortly after she returned home, every head in the sanctuary turned as excited whispers spread the news. Pastor began the service with announcements, as usual, and when he welcomed her home, the entire congregation burst into spontaneous applause. It may have been just her imagination, but Faith thought the singing that day was particularly boisterous.

The following Sunday, Faith went to Spencer's church with him, and Pastor Chris met them excitedly at the door. "Thank You, Lord," he prayed out loud, greeting Faith with a hug. "Thank You for healing Your daughter."

"And I have to thank you as well," Faith told him as she handed back his Bible. "Thank you for letting me use this. I'm sorry I kept it so long, but I used it to highlight verses and write down some notes in my own Bible."

"Wonderful! Then you did exactly what I hoped you'd do. I'm glad it was helpful to you."

"It was. And the timing was perfect. My dad—" She cut herself off, embarrassed. Did she really want to get into this right now? Surely Pastor Chris had other people to visit or final preparations to make before the service.

"Your dad…?" he prompted.

Faith looked to Spencer, who gave her an encouraging nod. "My dad came to visit me the day after you came. I… He left when I was younger, and I didn't see him much after that. Like, at all. So it was weird and awkward to see him again. He asked if we could have a fresh start, and I… I couldn't have done it if I hadn't spent so much time reading the Bible the day before. God was using His Word to work on my heart."

"So you experienced more than physical healing," Pastor Chris said. "That's wonderful. What a beautiful gift, to reconcile with your father after all these years. Praise the Lord. Only He could turn a seemingly awful situation into a blessing. As St. Paul says, 'We know that in all things God works for the good of those who love him, who have been called according to his purpose.'"

"That's Romans 8:28!" Faith exclaimed, delighted that she had remembered the reference. It had been one of the verses she'd highlighted in her own Bible, because it seemed pertinent to her hospital situation.

"Hey, hey! Look at you, quoting the reference! Before long, you'll be quoting Scripture left and right!"

"I have a long way to go before I can do that," she objected. "I'll never be anywhere near your level of knowledge."

"But you gotta start somewhere, right? The beautiful thing about the Word is that it's a lifelong learning process. You might think I know the Bible really well, and in one sense that might be true. But there's also so much I have yet to learn. Like I said, it's a lifelong endeavor. Keep at it. It's totally worth it."

He shook her hand, slapped Spencer on the back, and went off to greet some other newcomers. Faith thought to herself as he walked away that he was exactly right. Getting to know the Bible better was worth every minute.

CHAPTER 47

Once Spencer's finals were over, Faith's mom planned a celebratory dinner. She had been steadily improving and was nearly back to normal now. Her appetite had returned, and she was able to enjoy normal food again, so Grace decided the time was right for her "homecoming" dinner. She invited Bob to attend as well, seeing as how he'd been the donor.

Faith was fascinated by the interplay between her father and her mom's family. She knew David was still uncomfortable around him, although he was genuinely grateful that Bob had donated part of his liver. But Bob was clearly at ease around Olivia and Andy, and the three of them reminisced and shared private jokes as if they were old friends. It was strange to think that years ago, he *had* been part of the family. He shared memories with them that Faith didn't even know about. Her grandparents, Carol and Walt, were more reserved than Andy and Olivia, but as the meal went on, they gradually relaxed and opened up more to Bob. Faith felt like she was glimpsing a secret part of her mom's past; one she'd never considered before. It was strange.

When dinner was nearly over, Spencer stood and held his glass up as he said, "I'd like to propose a toast to this beautiful woman, whom we're all very happy is able to be here to celebrate at home with us."

She flushed as a murmur of agreement passed around the table, but Spencer wasn't finished. "And I'd also like to include her donor, who helped make this possible." He turned to Bob, who was attempting—but failing—to look modest. "Thank you for giving her back her future." He paused and turned back to Faith again. "*Our* future."

Faith's mouth ran dry, and her palms started to sweat. Was he seriously doing this here? Now? In front of her entire family?

In one fluid motion, Spencer set his glass on the table, got down on one knee, and pulled a box out of his pocket, opening it to reveal a beautiful diamond solitaire. Good gracious, yes, he *was* doing this in front of everyone. "You once told me we were too young," he began. "I don't know about you, but I'd much rather be two *Youngs* the rest of our lives. Will you marry me?"

Through tear-filled eyes, Faith reached out to place her hand on his cheek. "You know my answer," she said. "Of course I'll marry you."

Cheers rose from her family as Spencer slid the ring onto her finger and kissed her, and Andy shouted, "To Faith and Spencer!"

"Hear, hear!" everyone chorused. Charlotte squealed and clapped her hands at the sound of the glasses clinking together, while Griffin took the opportunity to throw his sippy cup to the ground.

As Faith bent down to retrieve Griffin's cup, she caught a glimpse of Olivia covertly aiming her phone toward Spencer and her.

"Are you *videoing* this?" she asked incredulously. Olivia tried unsuccessfully to hide a smile as she nodded smugly. Faith looked around the table in disbelief. "So you guys *knew* he was gonna propose tonight?"

"He asked David and me for our blessing," Grace informed her. "There was no way I could keep that a secret, so I told Livy."

"And there was no way *I* could keep it a secret, so I told Andy. And Mom. And Dad," announced Olivia cheerfully. Everyone laughed.

"You're a better man than I, Spencer," Andy stated. "I never asked Walt for his permission or blessing before I proposed to Olivia. Just asked her point blank."

"With the way you proposed, it's amazing I said yes!" Olivia pouted.

"How did Andy propose?" asked David as Grace and Bob both doubled over in laughter.

"Don't you dare!" Andy warned.

"If I don't tell them, Grace will when we leave!" Olivia said with a gleam in her eye. "You may as well be here to defend yourself!" Andy sighed dramatically as his wife continued the story. "So he came over to my dorm room one evening and got mad at me, and—"

"That is *so* not true!" interrupted Andy. "Must you always make me look like the bad guy? Yes, we got into a fight, but *you* were the one who started it!"

"Who cares who started it? The fact was, we were both mad at each other, so you asked me, 'Do you know why I came over here this evening?'"

"And you said, 'You always come over on Tuesdays.'"

"So then *you* said, 'I came over here to ask you to marry me,'" continued Olivia.

"And you yelled, 'Fine!'"

"So you *threw* the ring at me! How's *that* for a romantic proposal?"

Laughter echoed throughout the entire house at the ridiculous story, even Olivia and Andy joining in.

"That's lame, Uncle Andy!" Jackson chastised. "Even I could do better than that!"

Olivia snorted a laugh, and David addressed Andy. "And you're trying to give *me* advice about women?"

More hooting followed his remark, but Andy was unfazed. "It's all in how you play your cards," he said with a grin. "Starting off with such low expectations, I could only improve upon that. No worries. I've charmed her ever since, haven't I, Liv?" He winked at his wife.

"Absolutely! And I personally think it's the best engagement story ever. I wouldn't have had it any other way. It's so… *us*."

"It is," Grace agreed. "Sadly."

When the laughter died down after her statement, Andy asked, "So when's the big date, guys?"

Faith looked at Spencer uncertainly. They were both still in college, and traditional mentality dictated they get married after graduation. Then again, they did have a son already, and she knew Spencer didn't wish to wait years until they were out of college any more than she did. Yet her family might not feel the same way.

"Go for Christmas," suggested Jackson, grabbing the last dinner roll from the basket. "The church will already be decorated. Less work for you guys. And the Barlowes will be in Michigan then anyhow."

"You mean *this* Christmas?" asked Faith in disbelief.

Jackson shrugged. "That gives you enough time to plan and send invitations. Transfer to U of M for spring semester next year. You guys are practically married as it is. You spent, like, three months living in a hospital room together. Why wait any longer?"

Spencer and Faith looked at one another, and he said, "Well, it *is* the year for Parker and Callan to come back to Michigan for Christmas."

The adults exchanged glances amongst themselves, and Grace raised her eyebrows at David, who pursed his lips thoughtfully before responding. "You know, I'd kind of like a son-in-law for a Christmas gift."

The dining room erupted into squeals and excited chatter as Olivia and Grace started brainstorming, already planning for the big event. The food was forgotten as people stood to congratulate the newly engaged couple. The women liberally gave out hugs and inspected Faith's ring, while the men shook Spencer's hand or thumped him on the back. Everyone was talking at once, and the decibel level increased drastically. Faith caught sight of the huge smile on Spencer's face, and she could almost hear him thinking the words he'd spoken back when they'd dated in high school. *I love coming over here… It's fun with this many people in the house.*

So much had happened since their high school days it was hard to comprehend. She and Spencer had come a long way from that shallow, immature couple. They'd been through a lot already. Undoubtedly, there would be a lot more to face in the future as well. But one thing was for certain. As long as she was with Spencer, Faith was ready to face anything that came their way.

CHAPTER 48

When Spencer ushered her into his house an hour later, Faith steeled herself for a much different reaction to their news than they'd received from her family. Her mother had toyed with the idea of inviting the Youngs to the family dinner, but Faith had talked her out of it. Callan was due to arrive that day, and it would have been awkward to invite him to a dinner with all those people he didn't know. She was relieved Grace hadn't pressed the issue, especially since Spencer had proposed in front of everyone. She couldn't even imagine how his dad would have responded.

She and Spencer entered the living room hand in hand, where Mr. and Mrs. Young were seated with a man who bore a striking resemblance to Spencer, only twenty pounds heavier and with darker hair.

"Callan! Good to see you!" Spencer said. He released Faith's hand and strode over to his older brother, who had stood upon their entrance. Faith watched as the two gave each other one of those manly half hugs. "How's it going?"

"Good. Glad to be back, although the three-hour time

change is messing with my system. It should be dinnertime, but it's already dark out! I won't be able to get to sleep until two in the morning."

"But then you get to sleep in tomorrow!" Faith said cheerily.

Callan looked at her curiously as Spencer made the introduction. "Callan, this is Faith. Faith, Callan. My older brother."

"Oh, this is the chick you got pregnant, huh?" Callan gave her the once-over with his eyes, and Faith felt heat rise to her cheeks. Was that all Spencer's family could see in her? The girl who got pregnant in high school? Apparently that trumped even the recent hospital drama. And was that all they could see in *Spencer*? The irresponsible little brother who got a girl pregnant?

"Yes, we have a son," Spencer answered. "Griffin. We'll bring him by to meet you sometime. But I didn't get the chance to make a full introduction. Faith is my fiancée."

Dead silence met his words as all three other Youngs stared at them. It was obvious that while Spencer had informed her family of his intentions, he'd failed to mention them to his own.

"Show them the ring," Spencer encouraged her. It was as if they had to prove to his family that he was telling the truth. Faith held out her hand, displaying the glittering solitaire on her fourth finger.

Mr. Young rose from his chair to walk to the mini bar, apparently uninterested in the diamond on her finger. Pouring himself a drink, he asked candidly, "Are you pregnant again?"

"Dad!" Spencer and Callan spoke in unison as Vivian gasped, "Leonard!"

He took a swallow of the liquor and shrugged. "It's a sensible question. Are you?" He peered over his half glasses at

Faith.

Even Mr. Young's rudeness couldn't touch her mood today. Faith had expected as much, and so she replied in kind. "Not yet, but if you're that anxious for another grandchild, Spencer and I would be happy to comply." She arched an eyebrow at Mr. Young. Spencer wasn't the only one who could make wildly inappropriate statements.

Everyone now gaped at her, and Spencer's face was beet red as he hastened to add, "After the wedding, of course. She means once we're married."

Callan guffawed and slapped Spencer on the back. "I like her, Spence," he said. "She'll keep you on your toes, that's for sure." He chuckled again and shook his head, walking over to the bar to join his father for a drink.

Vivian spoke before her husband could say anything else. "Oh, darling, that's wonderful! Just wonderful!" she enthused. She walked to Faith to examine the ring with a practiced eye. "Excellent choice, Spencer. This is a high quality diamond. Oh, congratulations, my dears! I'm so glad to see my baby this happy." She squeezed Spencer's hand affectionately before giving Faith a hug. That shocked Faith more than Mr. Young's blunt comment. Vivian had never once hugged her before. "Leave the decorating to me," she continued. "You'll want to rent out the country club for the wedding, I imagine."

"Not for the wedding," Spencer said. "We'll get married at Faith's church. Sometime around Christmas. But we could rent the club for the reception." He looked to Faith for her reaction, and she nodded her agreement.

"Oh, a Christmas wedding will be *lovely!*" gushed Vivian. "You can go with traditional red and green, although red and gold might be prettier. Oh! But blue and silver would be perfect with the Christmas decorations. Very elegant. When you decide on the colors, leave the rest to me. I'm a pro at decorating."

"She is," Leonard agreed as he settled back into his chair, smoothing his tie over his paunchy stomach. "I've told her for years she should make a career out of it. She'd make an excellent interior designer." He took another swallow of his drink as his wife beamed at him.

Faith was surprised to see that Mr. Young had a soft side, or at least a *softer* side. She was happy to be proven wrong in thinking he was always gruff. It made him seem less intimidating. She had a lot to learn about her future in-laws. Suddenly a giddy laugh bubbled up in her throat, and Faith impulsively hugged Mrs. Young again.

"I'd love to have you decorate," she said. "I wouldn't even know where to begin. Thank you for the offer."

"And I'll write you a prenup," offered Callan, who had followed his father's lead in making himself more comfortable. "No charge. Consider it my wedding gift." He grinned and crossed an ankle over the opposite knee.

"We don't need a prenup," Spencer said, sitting on the loveseat and patting the cushion next to him for Faith.

"That's what all newlyweds say," chuckled his brother. "But you can bet Parker was glad he did a prenup. Otherwise his ex would have cleaned him out. She was pretty ambitious, as I recall."

"We don't need a prenup," repeated Spencer, a bit more forcefully this time.

Callan frowned slightly. "Spence, man, you've got a lot of money to your name. You've got to protect your assets."

"We're not going to get a divorce," Faith said. "And good grief, I'm not marrying Spencer for his money. I'd marry him if he was poor as dirt. No prenup. We're in this for life." She found it ridiculous that they were having this debate. This was one topic her family would never even think to broach.

Callan and his father looked at one another a long moment until Mr. Young shrugged. "I told you she's not what you'd expect." It wasn't exactly an insult, but neither did Faith take it as a compliment. She felt her face warm.

"She's *better*," declared Mrs. Young decisively, smiling at Faith.

"She is," agreed Mr. Young, taking another swig of his drink. Faith nearly fell off the loveseat. Was he actually saying something… *nice* about her? "You did well, son," he addressed Spencer. "Your mother and I approve."

It was all Faith could do to remain poised. His kindness flustered her more than his rudeness. She didn't even know how to respond. Spencer took her hand, a pleased smile playing across his lips. Heaven knew he didn't get a ton of positive reinforcement from his dad.

As the conversation moved on to different topics, Faith pondered how very different her family was from Spencer's. But soon enough, Spencer's family *would* be her family. She squeezed his hand happily. She wouldn't have it any other way.

EPILOGUE

Two Years Later

Spencer entered the darkened room quietly, swallowing hard over the lump in his throat as he saw his wife's sleeping form on the bed, a white mask covering her nose and mouth. She'd been through so much in the last few years. He'd hoped never to see her in the hospital again, but some things couldn't be helped. Leaning over, he kissed her gently on the forehead. Faith stirred, and her eyelids fluttered open.

"How are you feeling?" he asked, tucking an errant lock of hair behind her ear.

"Tired and sore."

"I'm sure. Sorry to wake you, but your parents are here. Are you up for some visitors?"

"Of course," she assured him, struggling to adjust the bed to a more upright position. "Is Griffin with them?"

"Yes. He's already pestering me to see you. He misses you and doesn't understand why you haven't been home lately."

Her eyes crinkled above the mask, indicating a smile underneath. "I miss him too. Send them in."

Spencer peeked out into the hallway and motioned to Faith's parents to enter. Grace was the first one in, and she rushed over to Faith to give her a hug. David followed, holding

Griffin's hand. When the almost-four-year-old saw his mother in the hospital bed, he yanked out of David's grasp and ran to the side of the bed, crying, "Mommy!"

With a chuckle, Spencer lifted his son and deposited him carefully next to Faith on the bed. "Be gentle with Mommy," he cautioned. "Her tummy is sore. Just sit next to her, okay, G?"

Griffin nodded as Faith pulled him into a one-armed hug. "Hi, sweetie. I'm glad to see you again! Did you behave for Grandma and Grandpa while you were staying with them?"

"Mm-hmm." He nodded solemnly. "I did, but the twins weren't being have." Griffin's eyes were wide as he tattled on the girls. "Evelyn said the 'S' word."

Faith's eyes widened as well. "She did? What did she say?"

Griffin swept her hair away from her face and leaned in close to say in a stage whisper, "'Stupid.'"

Spencer bit his lip to keep from smiling as Faith acted appropriately horrified for Griffin's sake. "Oh, no. That wasn't very nice of her, was it?" She snuck a glance in his direction and winked at him, her eyes dancing with amusement. Spencer's heart did a little flip-flop. Even in a hospital bed she was cute.

"How are you feeling?" Grace asked Faith, concerned. "Is everything okay?"

Faith didn't have a chance to answer, because the door opened and a nurse entered, pushing a cart. The lusty cry of an infant met Spencer's ears, and Grace and David both crowded around to get a glimpse of their newest grandchild.

"Someone's fussy," said the nurse. "We're done with the shots, so now it's cuddle time."

Spencer walked to the bassinet to lift their newborn daughter out, being careful to support her head like they'd shown him. He cradled her carefully in his arms and kissed her forehead, marvelling at her tiny features. As he walked over to the hospital bed, he rocked her and shushed her cries.

"Griffin, meet your baby sister," he said, sitting next to Griffin on the bed so the child could get a close-up look at the newest member of the family. "Grace and David, meet your granddaughter." He paused and looked at Faith, and they made the introduction together.

"This is Hope."

ACKNOWLEDGMENTS

Whoever described writing as a lonely endeavor clearly did not understand how many people contribute to the publication of a single book. I could never do this on my own, and I am blessed to have a wonderful group of people who help and support me along the way.

To my husband Jonathan and children Benjamin, Timothy, Miriam, Sarah, and Samuel, thank you for encouraging me in my writing and allowing me to talk about fictional characters and plot twists so often. You have each contributed to this story in one way or another!

Thank you to my parents, William and Janis Hessler, for bringing me up in the fear and knowledge of the Lord, and to my brothers Marty and Anthony for all the support. Anthony, thank you especially for the website design and for your feedback on the rough draft, even if your innocent and sensible suggestion caused a chain of events that required me to rewrite a third of the book. It's all the stronger for it.

As always, my editor, Abi, is the one who made this manuscript shine. Thank you, Abi, for your hard work and excellent suggestions. I continue to learn from you how to better hone my writing skills, and I am ever so grateful.

To Suzie at Sunset Rose Books, thank you for another amazing cover design and for your kindness and help even in ways unrelated to book covers.

Thank you, Kellyn, for your help with formatting, and for the comments you make in the manuscript. Those make my day!

Melissa, thank you so much for sharing your experiences to make Faith's story in the latter part of the book come alive. You have been more helpful than you realize, and I appreciate your encouragement and your enthusiasm for this manuscript.

David, thank you for reading and offering suggestions on the police scene to make sure everything was plausible.

To all my friends who encouraged me and volunteered to read the manuscript, thank you. Thanks especially to Jenny, Michelle, Sandy, Kristen, Kathleen, Sarah, Carla, and Maggie.

No book would be complete with one major component: readers! Dear friend, thank you for taking the time to read this book and for becoming invested in my characters. Your feedback makes the writing process so worthwhile.

Above all, I thank my Lord and Savior Jesus for the certain hope I have through faith in Him. I pray that my writing points always and only to Him.

Coming September 23rd

Grace Neunaber has entered a new phase of life. With two grandchildren and her second child college-bound, she's rethinking what to do with her quiet days while the kids are at school. But she's not the only one with decisions to make.

Thanks to a football injury, Jackson Williams' college plans have been turned upside down. His confidence and ego have been shattered along with his dream of a football scholarship. Yet he's challenged to grow both by his accident and by his best friend, Sam.

With so many uncertainties for the whole family, Grace will have to muster her self-confidence in the face of change. And Jackson will have to choose what kind of person he wants to become—a man who shirks responsibility and caves to circumstance or a man who stands up for what's right when life knocks him down. Even when it means standing alone.

Kindle version available for pre-order on Amazon

CONNECT WITH RUTH

WEBSITES
www.ruthmeyerbooks.com
www.truthnotespress.com

BLOG
www.TruthNotes.net

FACEBOOK
www.facebook.com/TruthNotes

AMAZON AUTHOR PAGE
www.amazon.com/Ruth-Meyer/e/B00E6QC2RI

CPSIA information can be obtained
at www.ICGtesting.com
Printed in the USA
FSHW011723010719
59616FS